TAKEN BY THE HIGHLANDER

With Meriel's wrist still in Craig's grasp, he pulled her roughly to him. His arms tightened, threatening to crush her body against his hard strength. His blue eyes were intensely bright, and danger radiated from him like an aura. Meriel was far from afraid. She wanted this. She needed this.

"Let go of me," she whispered.

"Why? Isn't this what you have been wanting? So much that you are willing to torment another man to provoke me into action?"

"I don't know what you are talking about."

"Stop, Meriel. It's time for the truth." But before she could answer, with his free hand Craig buried his fingers in her hair, pulled her mouth to his, and kissed her. . . .

Books by Michele Sinclair

THE HIGHLANDER'S BRIDE

TO WED A HIGHLANDER

DESIRING THE HIGHLANDER

THE CHRISTMAS KNIGHT

TEMPTING THE HIGHLANDER

A WOMAN MADE FOR PLEASURE

SEDUCING THE HIGHLANDER

HIGHLAND HUNGER
(with Hannah Howell and Jackie Ivie)

Published by Kensington Publishing Corporation

Seducing *The* Highlander

❧ THE McTIERNAYS ❧

Michele Sinclair

ZEBRA BOOKS
KENSINGTON PUBLISHING CORP.
http://www.kensingtonbooks.com

ZEBRA BOOKS are published by

Kensington Publishing Corp.
119 West 40th Street
New York, NY 10018

All Kensington titles, imprints, and distributed lines are available at special quantity discounts for bulk purchases for sales promotion, premiums, fund-raising, educational, or institutional use.

Special book excerpts or customized printings can also be created to fit specific needs. For details, write or phone the office of the Kensington Special Sales Manager: Attn. Special Sales Department. Kensington Publishing Corp., 119 West 40th Street, New York, NY 10018. Phone: 1-800-221-2647.

Zebra and the Z logo Reg. U.S. Pat. & TM Off.

ISBN-13: 978-1-4201-2651-8
ISBN-10: 1-4201-2651-2

First Printing: June 2013

eISBN-13: 978-1-4201-2652-5
eISBN-10: 1-4201-2652-0

First Electronic Edition: June 2013

10 9 8 7 6 5 4 3 2 1

Printed in the United States of America

To all the women who have
endured the hardest loss of them all—
that of a child.
I am truly sorry.
No one should ever have to endure such pain.

Chapter 1

Caireoch Castle, 1316

He was definitely caught. And unfortunately not in just any trap.

This fiendish one held no escape.

That he had not seen the blatant plot as it gradually ensnared him was humiliating enough, but that he was a *McTiernay* caught by a *Schellden* was a derision he would suffer for several years—if not decades.

Craig's heated blue gaze darted to the curvaceous figure across from him. Far from apologetic, two large hazel eyes glared at him, finding no joy in the situation. Instead, the dark green depths flickered with accusations as the melted gold specks shimmered with fury. And who could blame her? Meriel correctly believed herself to be just as caught as he.

Looking at her loosely clasped hands and slightly arched eyebrow, she appeared to be in a moderately composed state. Most of the crowd surrounding them no doubt believed Meriel indifferent to their situation, for Laird Schellden's daughter had always been a difficult person to read. People's attention usually focused on her twin sister—who never left a question in anyone's mind as to her emotional state. It was one of myriad characteristics that proved that while both women looked alike, in personality they certainly were not.

Meriel exhibited a limited number of emotions, but that did not mean those were the only ones she felt. She was a master at hiding her thoughts behind a facade of naïveté born from genuine sweetness and reserve, but Craig McTiernay knew exactly what angry thoughts his best friend was thinking. In her mind, *he* was the dolt behind their current predicament.

Meriel had warned him to be careful less than two days ago. She had suspected her sister would use the chaos in the household, preparing for the feast and taking care of visiting neighbors, to make one last attempt. For while most of the Schellden clan had given up trying to prove that the feelings he and Meriel had for one another went far beyond that of friendship, a select few—namely his twin brother's new wife—had not. Craig should have been more guarded, but never had he dreamed that *two* of his sisters-in-law would join forces and resort to such subterfuge to support their false beliefs!

Needing to look his accusers in the eye, Craig turned his head slightly to the left and glared at the two regal women standing at the head table near the Great Hall's large hearth. His newest sister-in-law, Raelynd, was practically beaming with satisfaction. At least his brother Crevan, who was standing next to her, had the decency to look at least somewhat apologetic about his wife's obvious handiwork. Laurel's expression, on the other hand, was more reserved, but he knew she too was involved. Only she possessed the extraordinary level of finesse that had been required to ensnare him and Meriel so publicly.

For years, the sword dance was an event commonly held at celebrations, but the simple dance had grown into something of a unique rivalry between the Schellden and McTiernay clans. Craig remembered the night the fun pastime had evolved into a game of endurance. The music had started and several of both clans' finest soldiers pounded the floor to the quick beat of the music, deftly hopping among the quarters made by crossing two broadswords. By the end of the lively song, only one McTiernay and one Schellden remained, and both had refused to stop. After that night, the sword dance continued until someone was proclaimed the champion.

That was until Craig's eldest brother, Conor, married Laurel.

One year, Laurel decided to join the men, having failed to understand that the ritual was for men and *only* men. Conor, still not quite savvy to Laurel's ability to twist almost any situation to her design, tried to explain that women were not physically *able* to compete. That night the McTiernay men learned many things: McTiernay women were not nearly as sweet and fragile as they looked, and underestimating Laurel could be perilous to a man's pride.

Laurel had quickly challenged the men participating in the dance, stating that Highland women played the game of endurance every day by cooking, cleaning, and raising their young. And then she proved it, forcing the tradition to evolve again. Now the battle was between men and women, to prove which group had more stamina; a custom that had made its way to the Schellden clan last year, when Raelynd and Meriel spent several weeks visiting the McTiernay home.

A fact Craig deeply regretted forgetting tonight when he had entered the Schellden Great Hall after successfully winning a game of horseshoes.

Seeing the broadswords had been laid out, he had eagerly joined the growing number of people participating. Having felt the humiliation created by Laurel's first and surprisingly successful attempt at the dance, Craig had vowed never to be outlasted by a woman again. And he hadn't. When the song ended, he was always among the few men who were still on their feet.

Tonight, however, the goal had changed significantly, unbeknownst to him.

"Just do it already," Meriel hissed, recapturing his attention. She had somehow moved to stand right in front of him. She was far from short, but she still had to crane her neck to look at him when standing this close. "And make it really good so that when it doesn't work, all questions about us will be silenced, not for tonight, but forever."

Craig's eyes widened at the notion, for he had originally planned to give her only a quick brotherly peck. But Meriel's idea was a rather brilliant one. And what could it hurt? It was not as if they really *did* like each other and feared the emotional sparks a genuine kiss might cause. They were just friends! Aye, he had thought about kissing her over the past year. Slim and delicate-looking, Meriel was a beautiful woman. But he had always known that the moment their relationship became anything more, the things he cherished the most—her friendship and honesty, qualities that made her so important to him—would be in jeopardy. Besides, desire was not prompting their current situation.

So maybe he wasn't caught in a trap.

Perhaps he and Meriel had been handed an opportunity to finally lay persistent rumors to rest. Not to mention that he had heard from more than one source that Meriel, while not free with her body, was an *excellent* kisser.

As her best friend, was it not time he found out?

Meriel felt her jaw drop when she heard her sister, Raelynd, announce that the last woman and man standing would be rewarded with a kiss—*from each other*. Now that she was married, Raelynd had a penchant for seeing love everywhere. And tonight, their father, who had cosseted them as children, had indulged another of her sister's whims.

Meriel *knew* she should have deserted the dance right then, but she had still believed Craig to be in the courtyard playing horseshoes. Moreover, it had been some time since she had been kissed, and the idea of possibly meeting someone new to pass the time with was more than a little appealing. Then she saw both women and men dropping out, feigning exhaustion, at an alarming rate. The reason why dawned on her just as the second-to-last woman ended her supposed attempt. Meriel immediately halted but it was too late. She was already the last woman standing.

Her eyes scanned the few men still competing and spotted Craig near the back, grinning his irresistible smile at the crowd—completely clueless.

Mentally she implored him to look her way so that she could give him a signal to stop and prevent her sister's attempt at matchmaking. But to no avail. Nearly everyone else in the room was staring in her direction, but Craig? No. He was too busy applauding himself for his stamina. Only when the song ended and people clapped him on his back with congratulations, explaining once again the nature of the award, did his expression reflect one of true understanding.

Meriel watched as Craig briefly studied her and then shifted his gaze to the real culprit—her sister. However, Meriel suspected that Laurel might also have been involved. Raelynd was more than capable of coming up with an idea such as this, but its execution? That needed a more experienced hand. Someone who could imperceptibly move throughout tonight's crowd, influencing people without Meriel or Craig becoming wise that *something* was being planned. And only one person present had those skills— Lady Laurel McTiernay.

Meriel inwardly grimaced. Her sister and Laurel had finally succeeded, and now she was stuck, forced to do the one thing she had promised herself to *never* do—kiss her best friend. Oh, she could refuse, but if she did, in her sister's and most of the clans' minds such a reaction would only prove that Craig and she *did* feel something for each other and much more than they claimed. It would not be just difficult, but near impossible to change their minds. No, they were destined to kiss this evening, but fate in the form of her meddlesome sister had not dictated what kind. Would the crowd see a sweet, brief touch upon the lips? Or something that would shock them all?

Having decided a few years ago that while for many reasons marriage was not something she was interested in, Meriel was not about to periodically forsake the pleasant diversions men offered. She knew Craig to be of similar opinion about marriage, but being tall, dark haired, with bright blue eyes that sparkled with enormous charm, she also suspected that the rumors of his activities with the ladies were based more on fact than fiction. It was therefore not an unnatural leap to assume he was a good kisser. Had she not entered tonight's competition with a certain goal? As the winner, she was entitled to a kiss. Fortunately for her, Craig understood her cryptic message that she wanted more than just the expected peck on the lips and he seemed to agree.

She had only wanted some passion, something to remind her that she was a woman and an attractive one. However, the moment Craig's fingers buried themselves in the softness of her hair, Meriel knew that no number of encounters she had had with other men had prepared her for what was about to happen.

True to her request that he embrace her in a way that would end all rumors, Craig pulled her close and then twirled her in his arms so that she was practically lying in his hands, depending solely on his strength to keep her from falling. Determined to be just as dramatic in her pursuit to end speculation about them, Meriel let her arms steal around his neck and returned the embrace with a surge of fictitious enthusiasm.

His tongue slowly began to trace her lips and instinctively she opened her mouth to welcome him in, glad to realize she had been right—Craig *was* a good kisser. A *very* good one.

He invaded the sweet, vulnerable warmth behind her lips with an intimate aggression that seared her senses. Her fingers clenched his shoulders, and then one of them groaned. While Meriel would have sworn it was Craig, her body was starting to respond as if it had a mind of its own. She felt as if she were hot, melting clay in his hands as they massaged her spine while his mouth drank heavily from her lips.

And then, just as suddenly as the sensual onslaught began, it changed. Craig's voracious mouth became tender, inquisitive, almost reverent. One hand moved to cup her cheek as he kissed her, long and soft and deep. The gentle embrace, if possible, was even more consuming and passionate, as his teeth lightly bit at her bottom lip before capturing her tongue and drawing it into his own mouth. It wrenched her soul.

Meriel could only clutch at him, overwhelmed and aroused and unable to understand what was happening. This was *Craig*. Her friend—her *best* friend, but he was kissing her with a low, inviting passion that took her breath away. It was getting harder and harder to remember that the sparks igniting between them were part of an act to end the baseless suspicion people had of their mutual attraction.

She reminded herself that she had received many kisses, but in most of those circumstances she had been the aggressor. It had become natural, as the men too often became timid the moment they realized they were alone with Laird Schellden's daughter. But this was different. Craig was dictating the speed and intensity of their kiss and all she could do, all she *wanted* to do, was get closer to him and follow his lead.

Returning his bold strokes inside her mouth, Meriel knew she should signal him to end the embrace, but she could not muster the will to stop the passionate assault upon her senses. At least not yet. Until now, she had not known what had been missing from those kisses with other men. But this, being with Craig, touching him, kissing him—for the first time it felt *right*.

The hot, tantalizing kiss suffused her body with an aching need for more. With a soft, low groan, Craig increased the urgency, and their embrace evolved again, becoming darker, more demanding, and far more blatantly erotic. No longer could she pretend she was enjoying a pleasurable activity with a friend. Meriel was sharing a piece of herself with him, as he was with her, proved by the mutual ripple of need running through them.

Suddenly she was back on her feet and the cool air on her lips shocked her into remembering that they were not alone, but in the midst of a crowd. A crowd buzzing with half whispers.

"Now all in this room *must* agree that the kiss you just witnessed would ignite some spark of passion—*if there was one*," Craig's voice boomed, capturing everyone's attention. He stretched his arms out wide and grinned infectiously, winning over the stunned mass. Then, with a pompous show of male superiority, he threw one arm over her shoulders and pulled Meriel firmly against his side into a hug. "And that, good women and lads, should end all doubt about what Meriel and I are to each other. We are *friends* and nothing more."

Feeling physically trapped, Meriel elbowed his side and gave him a forceful, angry shove. Craig immediately let her go and playfully doubled over in an exaggerated bow. The throng of people surrounding them laughed and immediately began to dissipate, returning to whatever they had been doing before the sword dance had been called. Only then did Meriel realize Craig's overbearing actions had been purposely done to evoke such a violent response from her. *She* was the one who made his speech believable. A woman in love typically did not assault the man who had just kissed her with incredible tenderness and passion.

Unable to keep her eyes from following him, Meriel watched as Craig casually sauntered away from her, laughing and romping across the floor with his fellow soldiers as they headed toward the hall's exit. Meriel should have been filled with relief. Didn't her aggressive reaction after his hug prove that she was *not* in love with Craig? Didn't his?

"I must admit to being surprised. I really thought you two cared for each other."

Meriel glanced back briefly as her sister walked up to her side before returning her gaze to Craig. "We do care for each other."

"You know how I mean. The first time Crevan kissed me like that I wanted to tear his clothes off, and I can assure you the feeling was mutual." Raelynd waved her hand at Craig's departing figure. "That man is not acting like someone who just experienced what looked to be an incredibly sensual kiss. But then, neither are you," she finished, looking both perplexed and disappointed.

Meriel swallowed at the implication. Fact was, she was not *acting* like it, but inwardly her senses were reeling. Outwardly she forced herself to appear calm, and yet she felt as if she had been ravaged, and worse—she craved more. Maybe Craig was also hiding his reaction to what happened. His overly jocular departure *was* atypically dramatic, even for him. The more Meriel thought about it the more she was convinced. Craig McTiernay was definitely covering up some kind of emotional response to what had occurred between them. But what? Then again, what was hers?

Meriel bit the inside of her cheek and made a decision. Until she was able to comprehend her own feelings about the kiss, she was not going to tackle the onerous work of interpreting Craig's. Usually the man paraded his emotions for all to see and hear. The rare times he kept them private were when they were raw, undefined, and extremely personal. During those singular times, to keep people from detecting his true thoughts, Craig tended to become excessively cheerful, just like he had become tonight.

Raelynd grasped her arm and swung her around. "Come. Tomorrow you can admonish me severely, but tonight we are celebrating Marymass, and soon Father will be offering the first bread."

Meriel let her sister guide her around to head back to the main table. "It doesn't look like Papa is very happy."

Raelynd leaned over and whispered teasingly, "I think he was considering ways to kill Craig right before he finally let you go. But the way you and he were so indifferent afterward, it helped calm him some. Don't worry. Just think on nothing else but this year's harvest and all the good things that are to follow."

Meriel followed Raelynd, glad her sister took the route that avoided their father. As she sat down, she decided that Raelynd was right. Tonight she should enjoy the upcoming activities to honor the Assumption of the Blessed Virgin Mary.

Tomorrow, however, she would give earnest thought to what just *did* happen between her and Craig—if anything.

"Don't deny it. You were part of that display of lust we just witnessed," Conor McTiernay growled at his wife as he pointed at Meriel and his younger brother, who was quickly exiting the hall.

Laurel licked her lips, refusing to look into her husband's accusing silver eyes. "Perhaps . . . marginally."

Conor narrowed his mercurial gaze. His wife was doing it again. Purposefully flicking her pale gold hair behind her shoulder to catch his eye. Moistening her lips with her tongue. Taking a deep breath so that her chest swelled, giving him a delicious view—all in an effort to distract him from knowing her true focus. And, like always, it was working.

As the eldest McTiernay and chieftain of their clan, Conor had spent years studying the behavior of his people in an effort to become a better leader. He prided himself on being able to predict most of his people's needs, anticipate their reactions to certain events, and prevent problems before they arose. But no matter how hard he tried, he could not transfer such knowledge and power to better his understanding of his own wife. He was just glad that he was starting to be able to tell when she *was* in the middle of a plan, and carefully extricate himself from it.

He let himself enjoy the sights for a few more seconds before pushing for more information—an absolute requirement to knowing just how to avoid getting caught in whatever trap she was weaving. "And did you get the outcome you were looking for?"

Laurel was not sure how to answer as she studied the scene. Craig was cleverly making his escape while Meriel was talking to her sister instead of actually paying attention to Raelynd.

When Raelynd had revealed her plan to have the two winners of the sword dance kiss, Laurel was quick to realize that the idea, while ingenious, was highly improbable. Aye, Craig and Meriel were highly competitive and could honestly win without assistance, but not if they suspected a setup. And despite Laurel's quick intervention to persuade participating men and women to voluntarily lose, the plan had almost failed. Meriel had shrewdly grasped the situation and almost quit before the last woman could drop out. But the plan had worked, and Craig and Meriel had definitely kissed. And yet, Laurel could not discern if it had changed anything in their attitudes toward each other.

The fact that the two of them were in love was not in question. Most were not sure, but Laurel had no doubts. She just was not positive whether or not a kiss, even the very long and passionate one all had witnessed tonight, would prompt two of the most stubborn people in Scotland to admit it. Not only to their families and clansmen . . . but to themselves.

"You should feel ashamed, forcing them to prove their friendship in such a way," Conor admonished halfheartedly.

"Why? Either way, it served their purpose. If there *was* more between them, then they would have been thankful for the act of kindness. If not, then Raelynd and I gave them the opportunity to end all rumors otherwise."

"I give up." Conor sighed, grabbing a mug of ale and downing it. "Just make sure that your efforts to find and foster a love match for my brother do not affect me."

"They shouldn't," Laurel asserted and then added under her breath, "but no promises."

The kiss Craig and Meriel shared had practically heated up the room, confirming what Laurel already knew. Raelynd had believed her sister might be falling for Craig but was too afraid to admit her feelings. But Raelynd had been wrong. Meriel and Craig had fallen in love long before, almost the moment they first met. Unfortunately, both of them were so savvy to the arts of recognizing love and how to avoid it, they had instinctively improvised a way to do so with each other: just pretend they felt otherwise. Deny to everyone—especially themselves—the truth. And for the last year, Laurel had not interfered, believing their feelings would either die or force them to take action. And yet a year later, nothing had changed.

Laurel abhorred the idea of arranged marriages or forcing two people together, but what could it hurt to help Raelynd execute her plan? And yet, Conor's question troubled her. Had she secured the outcome she was looking for? With any normal couple, a kiss like that would have resulted in an immediate wedding. But getting a stubborn Schellden and an obstinate McTicrnay to admit their feelings for each other? That took something more.

It had happened once before between Meriel's and Craig's siblings, Raelynd and Crevan, but both Craig and Meriel were unbelievably strong willed and stubborn. And for some reason they each felt incredibly resolute about keeping their friendship *only* a friendship. If what transpired tonight did not convince either of them otherwise, Laurel was not sure any outside influence could. It would take far more than patience to change their minds.

It would take a miracle.

Chapter 2

Meriel lay motionless in bed and stared at the ceiling's large timber beams. The sounds outside in the bailey were growing louder and busier as the men and women who worked for the castle or within its walls prepared to address another day. She had been listening for a while, but the familiar noises provided no more peace than the silence the night had relinquished. Letting go a deep sigh, Meriel sat up and swung her legs over the side of her bed. She stared down at her dangling feet, seeking courage for what she was about to do. Each time she reviewed last night's events, her thoughts only became more tangled. And there was only one way she knew to unravel them.

A year ago, she would have sought out the comfort and advice of her sister. As identical twins, they had often used their similar features to their advantage, pretending to be the other when it suited them. But more often than not, the differences in their personalities prevented their ruses from being completely successful. But right now, it was the insight those differences provided that Meriel missed the most.

Where she tended to be reserved and even-tempered, her sister, Raelynd, was outgoing and decisive, oftentimes to the point of being officious. She also possessed an absurd desire for all things to be orderly and neat—at least in Meriel's opinion. By the time Raelynd was in her mid-teen years, she not only knew the proper way to execute practically every job around the castle, she demanded that everyone else did as well. Meriel knew her own style of open organization drove her sister close to insanity, but in Meriel's mind that was her sister's problem—not hers. Raelynd just refused to understand how being able to see everything made it so much easier to find things than if all her items were put up and out of sight. But despite these differences, the two of them had always been extremely close.

Growing up they had shared an unusually large room that allowed them enough space to enjoy their own styles of organization. Though sharing a bedchamber did create some tension when one or both of them encroached upon the other's personal sense of space, and even gave rise to some boisterous fights on occasion, it also had afforded them the chance to talk. Every night they had discussed their day, both the ups and the downs. As a result, she and Raelynd had learned to verbally work through their problems, especially emotional ones.

Then last year things changed.

Raelynd fell in love and married Crevan McTiernay, and understandably began sharing her ideas and frustrations with him. She and Meriel still spoke and exchanged their opinions and viewpoints on many topics, but no longer did they discuss their most private thoughts—the things that when revealed made one vulnerable. For Raelynd, those secrets now belonged to her husband. And though she still would have been there for her sister, Meriel could not bring herself to open up to that level of sharing since it was no longer mutual. If it had not been for Craig, Meriel knew she would not have found it so easy to welcome Crevan into their family. For Craig had truly understood. As twin brothers, he and Crevan also had a tight bond that went beyond typical sibling regard. And upon Crevan's marriage, Craig had found himself in a similar situation, where his relationship with his best friend had suddenly been redefined.

Meriel's friendship with Craig had begun without effort. Each seemed to just instinctively understand the other. With compatible personalities, they would always have found it comfortable to be in each other's company, regardless of how they met. But last year's circumstances had forged a unique and very strong connection between them. Without conscious thought, each had leaned heavily upon the other for the emotional support and friendship their siblings no longer provided.

People began to tease them as they spent more and more time together, insinuating that there was more between them than they claimed. Meriel agreed that her and Craig's friendship was deeper than most, but she had been only vaguely aware of the dependent nature of their relationship. In the beginning, they had instinctively leaned on each other. As a result, both aggressively protected their unique bond, knowing that without it they would truly be alone—something, as twins, neither had ever experienced.

In a short time, Craig had become her best friend and she had become his. And until last night, keeping their friendship free of emotional entanglements had seemed the key to its survival. But now Meriel was not so sure. When Craig had kissed her, he had done more than just arouse feelings for him she had previously refused to admit. He had brought into question some of her most fundamental beliefs.

She had always believed being unmarried equaled freedom. Keeping all men at an emotional distance had seemed like a safe, intelligent path through life. The alternative invariably led to marriage, which included rules, expectations, limitations, and an end to other possibilities; all things of which Meriel had wanted no part.

She had tried to remind herself of these beliefs throughout the night, but images of her sister's happiness with Crevan kept flashing in her mind, followed by memories of her parents' relationship when her mother was still alive. And in not one recollection could Meriel remember her mother and father having all the emotional and mental shackles she had associated with marriage. Even Raelynd was happier being married. She seemed more at peace with her life and the possibilities of her future.

The more Meriel thought about her life as an unmarried, independent woman, the less it felt like freedom. Instead, her future looked very lonely. For the first time, she wondered if falling in love and committing herself to another might be worth the risk.

Craig stopped short just outside his cottage. He *knew* he had not left the door open when he went to ensure all the soldiers had made it to morning training, whether their stomachs were ready for it or not after last night's festivities. The morning sun poured into the room. Taking a deep breath, he opened the door slightly. Items were scattered everywhere, evidence the cottage belonged to a bachelor. The level of mayhem throughout the three-room home, however, proved it belonged to a particular bachelor—him. Among the scattered items was a lithe, supple figure sitting at his table.

Oblivious to the chaos around her, it was hard to believe the angelic-looking woman before him was just as comfortable amongst clutter as he was. Her hair—neither blond nor brown, but some unusual shade in between—was down, pulled back at the sides into a single, loose braid tied with navy blue ribbons that matched her gown. Long, dark lashes remained motionless as her hazel eyes bored holes into a candle that had melted onto the table, almost capturing pieces of a bridle in its waxy pool.

Memories of how passionately Meriel had responded when he had taken her into his arms, even though she had been furious with him, flooded his mind. Part of him knew he should say something and let her know he was there, but he was drinking her in, visually feasting on her in a way he had never allowed himself before. He shook his head. He would not do this. He refused to become a simpering mess over a woman. It was a vulnerability he would not allow.

Until last night, he had always dismissed the possibility of experiencing passion with Meriel. For him, desire required an element of surprise, and too much familiarity quickly crushed the fleeting emotion. And he knew no woman as well as he did Meriel. Oh, he wanted her physically. All rational men desired beautiful women. But desires based on simple male yearnings always faded, and usually ended quite . . . badly. And it was that possibility of losing Meriel's friendship that had made it easy to suppress and ignore his physical reaction to her.

Attraction for each other—that was the one topic neither had ever broached. Oh, they had discussed their unique friendship and the benefits of it, but never if it could be, or should be, anything more. To him, what he and Meriel had was so rare, so precious, that any risk of change was never to be considered. He believed that before last night, and he still believed it—despite now knowing how incredible it might be between them. He just hoped Meriel felt the same. She used to, but seeing her at his table filled him with worry. Her coming here so soon meant this morning's visit was going to be anything but typical.

Craig took a deep breath, opened the door wider, and entered the cottage, wishing that he had more time to understand and harness the unexpected emotions the kiss had stirred up in him. Where he liked to ponder things and develop solutions to problems in private, Meriel needed to vent her troubles in order to work through them. Until now, he had not minded being the one to whom she went, but then again, he had never been the subject of her unease.

Taking a deep breath, he mustered the most sincere smile he could. "I'm surprised to find you up this early. I thought you would not rise until the morrow after all the festivities last night."

Meriel, lost in thought as she stared at the candle on the table, jumped at the sound of his voice. Suddenly she was filled with mixed feelings. Should she have come so soon? "I . . . uh . . . decided to retire early."

"Humph." The sound escaped before Craig could stop it, but he was jealous of her restful slumber. He had just assumed that she too had been plagued with thoughts of their kiss. Determined not to let her know that she was the reason behind his lack of sleep last night, and probably the next several nights, he swiped the clothes lying haphazardly on a nearby chair onto the floor and sat down. "Most of my men are wishing they had been as wise as you. I will be surprised if a few of them don't get a scrape or two for being sluggish during training today."

Meriel crinkled her brow. "You are a ruthless commander, not letting the men at least one day to recover. I'm not sure how wise it was of Papa to have put you in charge of all his soldiers."

Craig grinned, feeling some of his angst dissipate at Meriel's reference to a long-standing joke they shared. She continually claimed that he was too tall and therefore too intimidating, too bossy and obnoxious, unable to consider disagreeing opinions, or his favorite—too arrogant to recognize his numerous faults. He was always "too" something to be the Schellden commander, and she dared him to prove otherwise. One day, Meriel had even claimed he was not up to the task due to his excessive ticklishness, which, to his humiliation, she had proved.

"And *that* is why beautiful women such as yourself should not train men to wage battles," Craig replied, taking a bite from a piece of bread he had swiped from last night's feast. "And why I am such a *great* commander. Ruthlessness is an admirable leadership trait."

Meriel rolled her eyes and ignored the muffled response. "Does the baker know how many of his loaves make it back here?"

"Why do you think I chose a cottage so near the castle?" Craig replied, this time with a sincere, self-congratulatory grin.

Meriel took a deep breath, feeling herself sucked into thoughts she had never previously entertained. "I thought it was to shorten the walk foolish women had to make to be in the masterful arms of love."

Craig swallowed, hearing the words he so often used to describe himself. Fact was, Meriel was the only female who had ever set foot in his cottage, and though he never liked to examine the reason why, he could not imagine another woman being in his home. But that did not stop him from fostering his reputation for enjoying and being enjoyed by ladies. In truth, since he had agreed to permanently support Laird Schellden as his commander, not one woman had captured his interest. He had believed exhaustion and demanding responsibilities were the cause—until last night. Once again the need to kiss her, to experience again just a little of what he had discovered, was growing within him. That left him with two choices: succumb to the desire, or make her angry in order to end it. "Perhaps a woman's company is the reason behind my own weary state this morning."

Fury sparked in Meriel's eyes and Craig was both gratified and uncomfortable with her reaction. That she was upset helped a little, but he would have preferred for her to get very angry and punch him in the arm, for the sake of his physical control and mental stability.

"I can certainly empathize," Meriel said softly, suggesting that she too might have spent an enjoyable evening.

Craig's jaw tensed. "I doubt that. You just stated that you went to sleep early."

Meriel leaned back, smiled coyly, and began to nibble on her bottom lip as if she was recalling something mouth-wateringly pleasant. "I said that I *retired* early."

Gritting his teeth, Craig clenched his mouth even tighter. It was the first time Meriel had ever hinted at being in another man's company. Conversely, he had told her of his escapades with other women. Usually at night, when they were alone, and he had felt his desire for female company rise and needed her to withdraw. None of the stories had been untrue, just old; events that had taken place prior to his permanent position as the Schellden commander. But he was not sure that in the past year Meriel had been likewise unoccupied. Whispers about her pursuit of male company had not dissipated over the past year. Craig had never believed it went farther than a kiss, and he still didn't, but the idea of her being in another man's arms last night, directly after his, was more than unsettling.

"Lucky fella," Craig managed to get out. "I can now say that with confidence."

His iceberg tone made Meriel want to scream, and she could only blame herself. Instead of stating what was on her mind, she had taken the cowardly approach. When she had brought up his alleged method of seducing women, Craig was *supposed* to correct her and fess up that not only had he never brought a woman home with him, but after last night, he never would. Unless of course, the woman was her.

She stood up and clasped her hands together, determined to talk about the one subject they had circuitously agreed never to discuss. "This is ridiculous. Neither one of us was with anyone last night. And we both know why."

"Aye, so neither of us has to talk about it. We can just let it be," Craig interrupted, jumping to his feet.

"Why?" she asked, rising to stand next to him. "We have to talk about it sometime. Our feelings—"

"Haven't changed," he said emphatically, grabbing her arms. Sparks ignited between them. He stared down at her, at that tempting mouth, and every muscle in his body tensed. She could make him vulnerable in a way he never dreamed anyone could, and that was a problem. A serious one. But all problems had solutions, and he was a master at finding them. He would resolve this. He would not let their passionate kiss change anything.

He swallowed and let her go. "Aye, the kiss was enjoyable, but it was something you and I will never share again. I *know* you agree with me. We are friends. Good friends, but nothing more. You are not attracted to me and I have no interest in you physically or in any way beyond what I have for . . . your sister. I know your penchant for questioning everything you cannot explain, but do we really need to discuss our relationship at length only to conclude that *nothing* has changed about how we feel about each other?"

Meriel blinked in an effort to keep her eyes from widening in shock. She forced herself to nod. "No, Craig. We don't need to talk about how we are still only friends."

Craig visibly relaxed and let go the breath he had been holding. He raked his fingers through his dark hair, which he kept short, as tying it back gave him headaches. "Good. Very good. I was afraid that . . . seeing you here . . . and so soon . . . well . . ."

Meriel held up her hand, stopping him before he said something that would cause her to lose control and break into tears, destroying any bits of pride she still possessed. "I simply wanted to clarify our feelings now rather than avoid each other unnecessarily. That was not an ordinary kiss, and one of us could have construed things differently."

Sighing, Craig bobbed his head in agreement, faking a chuckle. "Though I doubt I have ever enjoyed a kiss more." And once again, just thinking about it made his heart race. Swallowing, he added, "And I think it worked. Not a person there or within the range of gossip will pester us again about our friendship."

"Aye," Meriel replied, suddenly anxious to escape his disturbing presence. "Even my sister has finally surrendered. And speaking of Raelynd, I need to go and see her about a few things. Talk later?"

"Absolutely!" Craig answered, walking her to the door, almost eager to see her leave.

Meriel leaned forward to receive the bear hug that he always gave her when they separated. Craig hesitated. He could not refuse, but if he held her even slightly close to him, she would know without a doubt that his claim to have no physical interest in her was a falsehood. Out of necessity, he gave her shoulders a squeeze and prayed she would not pursue the change in his behavior.

The moment she was gone, he closed the door and leaned his forehead against it, closing his eyes. His composure had been a fragile shell on the verge of breaking. So he wanted her. What sane man wouldn't? But desires could be quashed through various means, and love, like any emotion, could be controlled. Unlike his older brothers, sentiments for a woman were not going to dictate his life, let alone his future. Not even for the possibility of experiencing passion unlike anything he had ever, or would ever, know.

His feelings for Meriel would remain what they had always been—brotherly.

* * *

Meriel's heart was pounding in her chest as she left the cottage. Pride had dictated that she agree to Craig's emphatic decree that nothing had changed between them, but she knew her best friend better than anyone. She knew his looks, his mannerisms, and his reactions to uncomfortable situations. The man had very few fears. Being a disappointment was one, and emotional vulnerability was the other.

Last year, he had finally admitted to himself and to his brother that he held no desire to be a clan chieftain. Commanding soldiers, leading men into battle, these were responsibilities he could confidently and expertly execute. Craig enjoyed entertaining a crowd, but the idea of a person—man or woman—seeking him out for emotional support frightened him. And until he met Meriel, that was a secret he had been able to hide from everyone, including his twin brother. Similarly, he was one of the few who could discern her true hopes and fears.

From almost the beginning of their relationship their friendship had been an anomaly. She had never bared her thoughts and feelings with anyone as she did with Craig—not even with her sister. As a result, she had protected their friendship every bit as vigorously as Craig. But after last night, Meriel no longer felt like she was shielding a cherished relationship; now she was acting out in fear of the future.

It took her hours of pondering, examining their relationship in multiple ways, but the conclusion was always the same—she loved him and he loved her. Rather than the sudden impact of two hearts recognizing each other, resulting in torrents of passion, their love had grown with time. She trusted him with anything and everything about herself, and remembered him once confiding about the incredible peace he felt, knowing that she would never think less of him for unburdening his true thoughts to her. They were friends, and maybe they should remain just friends.

But how were they to know, if Craig refused to talk not only about their kiss, but the passion that had been between them. And last night proved beyond any doubt that between them there was not merely passion, but desire and an intense need that continued to burn inside her.

Meriel made her way through the village, becoming angrier with every step. *Friends!* Friends were honest. And she and Craig had been far from honest with each other. What they felt for each other went way beyond friendship, and this morning only confirmed he was fighting the same conclusion.

Unlike Craig, she believed preserving their friendship required them both to be candid about their feelings and decide *together* whether to act on them or not. And though a small, frightened piece of her wanted to capitulate to Craig's dictates and keep their friendship just as it was, something far more powerful had taken over her heart and she was not sure she could keep things the same. Unfortunately, knowing him as well as she did, Meriel knew only one person could change his mind: Craig. No amount of persuasion, logic, or even passionate assaults would work. *He* had to decide that what was between them was not just friendship, but something much more.

And in this case, that was highly unlikely. That left her with two options. Wait until Craig admitted his true feelings for her, or end her emotional connection with him. The first was unlikely and out of her control; the second, however, was absolutely within her power to make happen. How hard could it be? This whole revelation had come only a few hours ago. In a few days, the memory of their kiss would be forgotten and then their friendship could continue as before.

Now . . . just how did one go about forgetting a man?

* * *

Conor smiled inwardly as he watched his wife pack in preparation to leave. On the bed were the various items that Laurel insisted she bring back to McTiernay Castle—too many to keep to their agreement of only two bags. There was no possible way she was going to be able to keep that promise now.

Beside the clothes and items she had brought were a couple of tapestries and a new gown Meriel had made for her. Items Conor specifically encouraged Laurel to accept, knowing what it would mean. All week he had been look-ing forward to this moment with eager anticipation. It was not often his wife made an error in judgment—especially when it could cost her as much as this one was going to.

"Want me to pack those in my bags? I have room," he offered congenially, obviously enjoying the idea that she might have to agree.

Laurel shook her head and cringed playfully at the idea. "And have my things reek with the foul odor of your filthy clothes? I think not."

Conor shrugged, ignoring the lighthearted insult, and leaned against the stone wall near the bed. "Just remem-ber, the limit of two bags was for the *whole* trip."

Laurel flashed him a smile and carefully began to fold the first tapestry. "I know."

Conor inhaled deeply and studied the relaxed manner of his wife. After nearly ten years of being together, he still could not tell if she was expertly hiding her anxiety, truly believed that she could accomplish the impossible, or if she already had a plan to circumvent the particulars of their agreement.

He tried to hide a grin at the idea of her persuading him with kisses and lovemaking to release her from her pledge. While he would enjoy letting her try, it would not work. Today she would not escape her fate. For a whole week, she would be unable to argue, confront, disagree, or contradict him. A conciliatory Laurel on all topics. Just the thought sent a shiver through him.

"Conor, would you go and make sure everything is ready for us to leave?"

"No need. Spoke with Crevan earlier and he said that he would have the horses prepared and ready by the time you finished packing."

"Does that include Merry?" Laurel inquired. Her voice was without even a hint that there was anything unusual about the request.

"Did you say *Merry*?" Conor repeated, hoping he had misunderstood his wife but knowing he had not.

"Aye. It is the least spirited of Laird Schellden's horses."

Conor's brows furrowed. "I'm fully aware of which horse Merry is, as well as just *who* rides her."

"Oh good," Laurel said absentmindedly as she unfurled the second tapestry and tried folding it again into a tighter and smaller bundle.

"Are you attempting to tell me in a less than appealing way that Meriel is coming with us?" Conor half bellowed, trying to keep his voice down.

"Whether or not the idea appeals to you, she is coming with us," answered Laurel, this time looking him directly in the eye.

Conor blinked. Laurel was completely serious. This was not some ploy to get out of their arrangement. He only wished it was.

Conor went to the window and looked below at the courtyard. Three long curtain walls formed a large triangle, making Caireoch Castle one of the more unusual fortified homes in Scotland. And while it was a fortress with strong defense capabilities, the shape made it impossible for anything besides castle activities to be conducted within the walls. As a result, castle life had taken over the inner bailey, making it crowded, loud, and confining. And though he had enjoyed this short visit to his close ally and friend, he also could not wait to leave it all behind and return to his children and his life—which did *not* include Meriel Schellden.

He remembered the havoc she and her sister caused last year when they came to visit. Granted, it was the first time they had ever been allowed to leave the protection of Caireoch and their overindulgent father, but their short stay had been painful. And most of the pain Conor remembered enduring had been a direct result of Meriel's and his wife's brilliant idea that *Meriel* should learn about castle duties by assuming them. He was not going to go through that again. *Mo creach!* McTiernay Castle would likely be vacated within hours! Fiona, their cook, would rebel vociferously by refusing to allow any of the staff to prepare meals, and their steward, Fallon . . . his reaction was unpredictable, with the exception that it would be far from good. Did Laurel not realize that?

Conor turned around to argue when his mouth fell open. He pointed to the bags she was using to pack her things. "Those are not the bags you used coming up here."

Laurel shrugged and gave him a quizzical look before continuing to arrange things in the much larger carriers. "Well, of course not. I could never have packed all of this in the two I brought, so I asked Meriel for some larger ones and she obliged. Our agreement was the *number* of bags, love, not the bags themselves."

He watched as she shoved the last tapestry into the second leather bag and cinched it closed. The two *large* stuffed bags on the bed meant that *he* had lost their bet and not she. He should have known that just as he had been plotting a way for her to lose . . . Laurel had been doing the same.

A thought struck him. If Laurel wanted him to be agreeable, then that was exactly what she was going to get. "I think it is a *great* idea that Meriel come with us."

Laurel came to an abrupt stop. With one hand still in the second bag, she looked up. "You do?"

"Aye. After what you and Raelynd did last night, Craig could use some distance from her."

"You think *Craig* could use some distance from Meriel."

"Aye. I think he needs some time to think about what happened and determine if it meant anything."

"*Meant* anything? Of course it meant something!"

Conor came around and pulled Laurel's back against his chest to give her a big hug. "I know *you* think they love each other."

Laurel tried unsuccessfully to shrug him off. "They *do* love each other. Craig just refuses to admit his feelings."

Conor let out a long, audible breath. "Then, Laurel, my love, distance is not going to change his mind."

Laurel spun around in his arms to face him. Her brows wrinkled upon seeing that he was earnest. "How can you not want your brother to be happy?"

Conor reached around her and snatched the heavier of the two bags. "He *is* happy. They both were until last night when you and Raelynd meddled in their lives."

"I was not meddling."

"Then what do you call it?"

"What I did was called . . . assisting. At least I thought I was," Laurel said, the last words barely audible. Then suddenly her demeanor changed. "Is Hamish returning with us?"

"Why?" Conor asked skeptically, his left arm still encircling her. "I think he was considering staying a couple more days to help Craig."

"Then my question is, can he?"

Conor laughed at her eager expression. If he recognized the obvious ploy, then so would Craig. "You think you can make my brother jealous? Laurel, if anything, Craig will suspect he's being manipulated and become even more determined not to admit his feelings for Meriel—*if* he has them."

Laurel bit her bottom lip to hide her smile, but nothing could disguise the mischievous sparkle in her blue-green eyes. "Inspire jealousy? On the contrary, love. I was just thinking about you," she said, craning her head back so that her pale blond hair hung in loose waves down to the small of her back. Putting her hands on his biceps, she added, "If you can convince Hamish to leave with us as well, then you will not have to help Meriel along the journey. If I recall, she is not quite as skilled with riding horses as we are."

Conor's eyes widened. "Skilled? Ha! She can barely stay on top of one."

"So you will ask Hamish to come?"

The question seemed innocent, as well as her reasoning. But they both knew otherwise. Whatever the motivation behind her request, one thing was for certain—Laurel was in the midst of one of her plans. Conor sought only to escape its tentacles.

He narrowed his eyes. He released the bag and crossed his arms. "I do not know what is going on in that mind of yours, but just so you and I are clear, *I* will not be helping Meriel during this trip, nor will she be helping *you* with your duties after we arrive."

Laurel smiled at him. "It won't be like last time. I promise Meriel will be a guest and a guest only."

"And exactly what will she do to occupy her time then?"

Laurel went onto her tiptoes and kissed him on his stubbled chin. "Oh, I've got some ideas."

"If your ideas include Hamish, you might want to rethink them. I heard him talking last night. He is interested in someone else and he says it is serious this time."

Laurel's smile turned sour. "I am fully aware of Hamish

and Wyenda, and I would not dream of interfering with a true love match. If it is meant to be, then it will be."

Doubt crossed his face. If anything proved Laurel was not behind a match between Hamish and Wyenda, her last statement did. He knew his wife did not trust the beauty, and secretly he agreed with her. If Wyenda was showing an interest in Hamish and history was any indicator, she was doing so only until someone better came along. Still, Laurel's statement definitely held hidden meaning. "Then just what are you planning?"

Laurel leaned into him, letting her soft curves mold to the contours of his muscular body. "Nothing more than for Hamish to come along and aid Meriel. I'll admit to hoping they become friends, but truly nothing more. Maybe they will be able to help each other in ways you and I could not."

Conor pulled back slightly, but not enough to break contact. "I'm not sure I believe you."

"You didn't believe I could pack everything in two bags either, did you? When are you going to trust me?"

His mouth twisted wryly. "Craig, Meriel, Hamish—they are adults. They have to arrive at their own conclusions, Laurel."

"I absolutely agree. I also know that for them to arrive at the *right* conclusions, Hamish and Meriel need to come with us," Laurel said softly. Her voice was sweet and amenable, but her chin was set in a stubborn line. Conor knew that unless he was willing to absolutely refuse her request, talking about it further was not going to change anything.

"Fine, I'll talk to Hamish."

"And I'll go talk to Meriel."

His lips parted in surprise. "You mean she didn't ask to come?"

"Oh, she will want to."

Conor arched a single dark brow as she slid her hands up and down his crossed arms, caressing the tense muscles. "No pressure?" he asked, his doubt unmistakable. She licked her lips, intentionally drawing his eyes toward her mouth. Her perfect mouth. Her sexy mouth. *Mo creach*. He would never get enough of her.

"Do you really still doubt a woman's ability to read the needs of the other?"

"I only wish I had the gift to be able to read your mind," Conor replied huskily, giving in to his baser needs.

Laurel let her head fall back as his lips began a sensuous trail along her neck. "You are an amazingly clever man. I'm sure given enough clues that you . . ." She sighed, unable to remember the witty retort on the tip of her tongue. Conor might not always know what she was thinking, but he never failed in his ability to stop her ability to think.

Meriel's eyes followed her father as he retreated into the Great Hall. Rae Schellden, one of the strongest and more formidable clan chieftains in the Highlands, was also the most vulnerable and yielding when it came to his daughters. Last year was the first time she and her sister had ever left the protection of Caireoch, and only months after their return did she learn from the staff how tremendously hard their departure had been on him. And now she was leaving again.

Tears formed in her eyes as she remembered how close he had held her to him. "I should deny you this request, but since you were a wee thing, you have known better than anyone just how to sway my thinking. Take care, child. Go and learn how to smile again."

Meriel had never said anything about her feelings for Craig, but somehow her father had known. And though she had promised her visit would be short, in reality, she did not know just how long she would be gone.

Returning her attention to her horse, Meriel took a step closer to the animal and inhaled deeply, hoping to diminish the ripples of fear going through her. Tentatively, she stretched her arm out and barely stroked the brown hair along the horse's neck. "Remember me, Merry? We took a trip together once before and we are going to do it again. A nice, uneventful, peaceful trip."

A chuckle behind her caused her to spin around. She should have known Hamish would be coming with them. She had seen him around and remembered the Highlander well from her visit to the McTiernays last year. It was hard to forget anyone who liked himself as much as the man in front of her did, which was one of the reasons she had intentionally avoided his company during the past week's festivities.

He wore the McTiernay plaid, but he did not resemble the majority of their clan. The man was tall, but shaped more like her father, broad shouldered and muscular. Instead of being dark featured, his hair was a deep auburn and he let it hang loose just past his shoulders. But it was his eyes that were the most striking, and like so many women before her, his intense gaze had drawn her in. Meriel blinked and the magic was gone, leaving her to see that the shimmer in his eyes was caused from laughter. The hulking brute was gleaning enjoyment from her fear of riding.

Meriel turned around abruptly, hoping that he understood the hint but doubting he did. The man truly believed all females were susceptible to his charm, and after witnessing several women fall for his flirtations, it was not hard to believe the rumors of his being quite the sinner. "Beware, Merry," she whispered to her mount. "A McTiernay wolf is in our presence."

The chuckle increased in volume as two large hands gently gripped her waist and effortlessly placed her on top of the horse before she realized what was happening. "McTiernay wolf?" Hamish whispered back. "I like your pet name for me. But only in private. In public, best call me Hamish."

Meriel clutched Merry's mane in a fierce grip and narrowed her eyes in preparation to glare at him, but she decided to play along instead. This man needed to know at least one woman was immune to his charm. "*Madadh-allaidh*." She purred the word "wolf" to him, gaining enormous satisfaction when his eyes popped open wide. She was about to say more when a bellow from across the courtyard halted most conversations and all activity.

"What the hell do you think you are doing on top of that horse?" roared Craig from across the bailey.

He had waited until the last possible moment before coming inside the castle walls to say good-bye to his brother and wife before they left for home. He knew Meriel would also be there giving her farewells, and had already prepared an excuse to leave as soon as his brother departed. After his barely successful attempt to restrain himself that morning, he had decided to minimize their time together until his attraction to her was once again under his complete control. But the moment he saw Hamish's hands on her small waist, lifting her onto a horse, a wave of turbulent and indefinable emotion hit him full force.

"Just what do you think you are doing?" Craig demanded again in a steely voice as he reached her side. He issued Hamish an icy glare and immediately his friend threw his hands up and took a step backward.

Meriel, on the other hand, was not intimidated and had no inclination to retreat. "Do you really need me to answer? For I thought it was fairly obvious."

Meriel tossed her hair back so that the blond highlights in the tawny locks caught the sun. Craig knew it was a move she did to compose herself when really mad. Well, she could go ahead and be mad. He was furious too. It was *her* sister who got them into this mess and it was *her* idea to kiss like they had. *She* was the one who prematurely came to visit him when *she* should have known he was not ready to see her. And now *she* was letting *Hamish*, a known womanizer, touch her. Meriel was lucky he did not yank her off the horse and throttle her in front of everyone. "It most certainly was a real question, and I am waiting for an answer, Meriel."

His contemptuous tone only further sparked her anger. "Don't bark at me, Craig McTiernay. I am not one of your men you can order about. And as far as what I'm doing, why, I am sitting on a horse."

She did not call him a fool, but all within hearing heard the implication. "And just *where* do you plan on going?"

There was an edge to his voice, one that alarmed everyone around them but not her. With her chin, she pointed to the open portcullis. "Right out that gate, across a stretch of land and into your childhood home."

"You are not."

His voice, though quiet, had a ruthless, ominous quality, and Meriel could hear the crowd begin to whisper. She could only guess as to what they were saying. Who would have thought the most affable of the McTiernay warriors and Laird Schellden's carefree daughter could raise their voices at one another, let alone fight? Another day when she was not so emotionally frazzled, Meriel might have cared. "Be careful," she hissed, "or you will start rumors about us all over again. And I will not volunteer another chance for you to kiss me in order to quell them."

Watching the two argue, Conor was caught somewhere between shock and amusement. It was rare to see Craig emerge from his emotional shell where he protected himself with mirth and wit. Maybe Laurel was right. Maybe Craig did love Meriel. Nothing else explained his brother's violent reaction.

Laurel leaned over to him and whispered, "Is it possible we sound like that when we quarrel?"

Conor pulled back his chin in defiance of the possibility. "Nah, look around you, love. Everyone is watching them intently. Do our clansmen stare at us when we disagree?"

Laurel bit her bottom lip as she considered his argument. He was correct. Though she was honest with herself enough to know that their "disagreements" were sometimes intense enough to be called arguments, no one ever paid them any attention regardless how heated they became. Relief filled her just as Craig bellowed out another barb.

"You really expect me to believe you are actually leaving your home for any length of time?" Craig ground out as he examined Merry and the rest of the small group's horses. There were no multitude of carriers crammed with sewing threads and materials. He pointed at the two sacks on the back of her horse. "I see none of your bulging bags hanging off the hind end of every horse."

"You should feel gratified that I am finally taking your advice and becoming less attached to my things. What was it you once said? Things cannot bring you happiness—only people."

He had actually said clothes could not bring him happiness, only a woman. He had been teasing her when he turned down her offer to make him a new leine and kilt. The idea of standing around like a female while she measured, poked, and prodded him was abhorrent, and he wanted to make sure that she never made the offer again. But for her to twist the meaning and use that remark meant they were on the verge of going too far. They had argued before, but never like this. He just knew he was not happy at the idea of her leaving. He felt as if his life had been turned upside down last night, and their fighting was making it worse.

Craig gathered his composure and in a resigned yet gentle tone said, "The people you love and who love you are here. There is no need for you to leave. You need not be embarrassed."

Embarrassed? Meriel practically screamed in her head. He thought she was leaving because of embarrassment over their kiss? She had thought he felt something for her but was just unwilling to act on it. Now she was beginning to wonder if she had read him completely wrong. No man with any morsel of feelings for her could be so clueless.

Meriel knew he was waiting for her to respond, believing that he was making her rethink her decision to go. If anything, his last argument just made it absolutely clear that she not only had to leave, but immediately.

"I love my family, Craig," she began calmly, removing any bitter anger from her tone. "But if I need to kiss someone to feel excitement, then that is a sign I should seek new experiences and interact with different people. It is time I break certain habits and build new ones. Don't you ever need a change?"

He had. But not in recent memory. For the past year, he had felt more settled and relaxed than ever, which was surprising because he had moved away from McTiernay Castle, the only home he had ever known. His life was finally becoming what he always wanted. He was commander of a large and powerful army, his brother was happy . . . life was good. He wanted no changes in it, and that Meriel did, rankled.

After she left his cabin that morning, he had mentally replayed their conversation and her reaction repeatedly, and each time his conclusion remained unchanged. It was absurd to allow a single kiss to disrupt things between them when their situation was almost ideal. Meriel's claim that she felt the same as he did had provided a measure of relief but did not completely quash his fears that their friendship might have been irrevocably altered. But how were they to resume their friendship and continue as before, if she left?

"Meriel, if you really want to go visit my brothers, I will take you. Merry is gentle, but you will still need help with her if you are ever going to make it."

"I didn't ask for your assistance and I don't want it," she said. Her hazel eyes, normally warm and inviting, now regarded him coolly.

Craig shook off the inclination to shiver. "Don't be a fool," he chastised softly. "You know you need help when riding."

Meriel arched a brow, daring to look affronted by his assertion, despite its accuracy. "Maybe—but not yours."

"And just who the bloody hell is going to put up with you?" he barked, raising his voice once again.

Meriel waved her hand to her side. "Hamish is quite looking forward to the chance. Aren't you, Hamish?" she asked, flashing him one of her most irresistible smiles.

Hamish blinked. "I . . . uh . . . aye," he answered, unable to disagree with her. He shifted his gaze to his horse and patted the thick mane. It was probably the first time he had ever wanted to put distance between him and an unattached beautiful woman, but how else was he to respond? He avoided looking at Craig. He did not want to get pulled into this argument, but a part of him was somewhat shocked by Meriel's feisty demeanor. Normally she was so calm and demure that her personality bordered on dull.

Craig's eyes bounced between Hamish and Meriel. He considered the man a good friend, but Hamish was also notorious when it came to women—almost as bad as his younger brother Conan. And if Meriel had been anyone else, Craig might have felt the earnest pangs of jealousy. But she was not Hamish's type, and, moreover, she was Laird Schellden's daughter. Unless Hamish wanted to get married and be locked to the Schellden clan forever, Meriel could be with no safer guide.

"Well then, now that I know that you won't have to depend on the gruff nature of my eldest brother for support"— Craig grimaced at Conor—"I have no objection."

"Why, thank you for your permission. And here I thought I needed only my father's."

Craig shot her a twisted smile. "You'll be back in less than a fortnight."

"You think?"

"I think you will be bored within hours of your arrival. This time, you will not have me or Raelynd to entertain you."

Meriel refused to allow the fear his words gave her register on her face. Instead, she broke into a disarming smile and said, "I will miss you too." Then she gave a hard yank on the reins to get Merry to turn around. To her relief, after the third tug the horse finally obeyed and headed out the gate.

Craig was right. Based on her last experience away from Caireoch, life at McTiernay Castle would be incredibly dull, and the realization almost made her change her mind. But Craig's smug face kept her firmly on her mount. She did not know how difficult it would be, but she would find a way to be gone at least three weeks.

Craig swallowed as he watched her practically strangle Merry. Despite his attempt at teaching her, the woman's riding skills had not improved even a little bit. "Take care of her, Hamish," he said wistfully.

"I will, so don't worry about *your friend*. You know you can trust me."

The rich baritone voice carried too much amusement for Craig's comfort. He pivoted to look at Hamish to see if he was sincere or if he was mocking him, but it was too late. Hamish was already urging his mount forward to catch up with Meriel and help get her through the gatehouse and the village without mishap.

"Are you sure you do not care for my sister?"

Craig jumped. He had not seen Raelynd approach his side. "I'm positive!" he growled and stomped toward the kitchens. He was going directly to the buttery and get himself a drink. A large one.

Aye, he cared for Meriel. And why shouldn't he? They were friends. Best friends. She needed his companionship, his advice, and most of all his support. It would not be possible for her to stay away for very long.

This was her home. This was his home. And a single kiss was not going to change that.

Chapter 3

Meriel glanced sideways to confirm it was Laurel who was coming to join her by the fire. The day's journey had been exactly what Meriel had expected. Long and arduous. Merry had been inclined to follow the group and had not needed much direction or encouragement, to Meriel's relief. Most of her time had been spent trying to stay upon the horse.

Laurel sat down on the ground across from Meriel and stretched out her hands to warm them by the fire. The weather had been comfortable during the day, but both were used to being inside after the sun went down and found the night somewhat chilly. Luckily Conor and Hamish had wanted a cooked meal; otherwise it might have been difficult getting them to agree to build a fire.

Laurel picked up a stick and poked the logs to rekindle the flames, as if she was searching for the right way to start the conversation. "Conor and Hamish are out taking care of the horses. I doubt they will return until they think we are asleep. Nothing frightens a man more than two women talking."

Meriel stifled a small sigh. She wanted to talk through her problems, but not with just anyone. She trusted Laurel, but Meriel was not interested in listening to any well-meaning advice—even if she could use some.

Laurel tossed the burnt stick aside. "You look tired. I know that you are not used to riding, let alone being on horseback for most of the day."

Meriel shrugged her shoulders. "At least I knew what to expect this time. And Hamish helped some." He had actually aided her quite a lot, and surprisingly, he had done it without any condescension. "I'm not sure what to think about him." She paused and then looked at Laurel. "I'm beginning to think he flirts out of habit, not true interest. I wonder if the rumors of his exploits are simply that—rumors."

A bemused smile curved Laurel's mouth. "Not many women can recognize Hamish for what he truly is. I am glad you agreed to come."

Meriel's eyes momentarily widened at the memory. "Laird McTiernay did not seem so enthusiastic about the idea."

"Oh, Conor is just afraid that I'll put you back in charge of the castle."

Meriel sat up straight, her hazel eyes boring into Laurel. "You wouldn't." She exhaled in a panic. That idea had never occurred to her.

"No, I most certainly would not," Laurel quickly agreed and leaned back on her hands so that she could stretch out her legs. "I know some of the McTiernay staff can be a little aggravating—"

"A little?" Meriel quipped, remembering how caustic their cook, Fiona, could be—and she was nice compared to the steward.

"—but I would not exchange them for anyone else. However, I'll make sure everyone will know that you are a guest and to treat you as such. Besides, I owe you because I participated in what happened last night."

Meriel picked up a smooth rock that was next to her and twirled it in her fingers. She was not angry with Laurel. Nor was she angry with her sister. In a way, what happened was inevitable. "It would have happened even if you weren't there. Raelynd is merciless."

"Maybe, but on this I think she might leave you and Craig alone now. I'm pretty sure you and Craig convinced her that you two are just friends."

"But we didn't convince you, did we?"

Pressing her lips together, Laurel studied Meriel and thought about the question. Visiting the Schelldens for the past week, she had discerned a change in Craig. He seemed more comfortable with himself. Beyond being a warrior and entertainer, he sometimes allowed people to see his serious and thoughtful side. Maybe it was because he no longer felt like he had to protect his twin brother, but Laurel suspected his friendship with Meriel was a more likely reason behind the change.

Laurel released her gaze and turned to stare at the fire. "I think that you and Craig could be perfect for each other. That's why I helped Raelynd orchestrate her little game, but if I could do it all over again, I would not."

Meriel's gold-and-green eyes widened in shock. "Why not?"

"Two people can be perfect for each other, even love each other, but unless *they* want their relationship to be more, mean more, it will not work."

Meriel waited for Laurel to ask if she wanted her and Craig's relationship to grow into something more, but the question never came. Instead, Laurel said, "Craig is a McTiernay, Meriel. That means he is incredibly stubborn and full of pride. He is also steadfast in his beliefs and as a result, when he makes up his mind, no one—not even Conor or his own twin brother, Crevan—can change it."

Meriel cocked her head slightly in confusion. "I am very familiar with the mulish side of Craig's personality."

It was a trait they recognized in each other. Anytime she and Craig had diverging opinions, they would simply agree to disagree, knowing that neither would be able to persuade, cajole, entice, or even bribe the other to their point of view. This mutual acceptance, not having to pretend to be of the same mind on a topic in order to maintain harmony, was a revelation to them both. But on the subject of their relationship, that philosophy of agreeing to disagree would no longer work. Either she learned to ignore her feelings for Craig, or he learned to pay attention to his feelings for her.

"So you understand that the more you push Craig into doing something—even something that, deep down, he wants—"

"—the more he resists," Meriel finished. "And on this subject—the one of he and I becoming anything more than friends—he is not likely to change his mind. The man fears being in love, despite seeing the happiness it has given his elder brothers."

"Ah, love. Powerful word." Laurel paused for a long while. "And are you in love?"

Meriel looked up, tears forming. "I honestly don't know. I think I may love him and that he might love me, but he refuses to talk about it. And if I cannot talk to my best friend about our feelings for each other, what *can* I talk to him about? Suddenly I do not know how to act around him. I cannot pretend I don't feel anything, and if I had stayed at Caireoch, avoiding him would have been impossible. So in a way, I am running away, though I am also worried that I was just as much of a fool to leave. What am I going to do all day? Walk and think?" Meriel tossed the rock into the fire and watched it turn red. "Craig was right. I don't tolerate boredom well."

"Well, if it isn't too much of an imposition, you could

help me, and that would occupy your time for say . . . at least a fortnight."

Meriel frowned in acknowledgment that everyone had heard Craig's challenge. Remembering the long list of disasters resulting from the last time she had "helped" Laurel, Meriel's instinct was to decline the offer. Biting her bottom lip, she asked, "With what? I'm not like my sister, who knows everything about running a castle."

Laurel gave a small shake of her head. "I need your help with what *you* know better than most anyone. The gowns you made for me reminded me of how few can compare with your skill with a needle. When Conor's brother Cole moved north, he took with him his loyal soldiers and their wives, who included a dear friend and a most valued seamstress. Ever since, my daughters have been forced to wear what I can create. So, would you consider making them some things? I have plenty of material."

"For your children?" Meriel asked, clearly interested in the idea but also wary of offending someone. "But there must be others who can sew. . . ."

"We have some weavers and a few seamstresses, though none with your skill. Regardless, they will soon be busy preparing for winter and supporting the clan. You will not be interfering with anyone's work, and I suspect when you are done that several others will ask you to lend your skill—but only if you are willing. I am positive your days could be as full as you desire."

"Others? Can one of them be Hamish?" Meriel teased. "The man desperately needs a new leine." She was smiling. She would not go so far as to say that she was happy, but for the first time since she left Craig's cottage, she was looking forward to what the next day might bring.

Laurel laughed. "Many of the men need new clothes, but I doubt they would appreciate your ability with a needle.

And give Hamish a chance. Like Craig, very few get to know who he really is."

"You mean very few take the effort."

"I *mean* that you and he might be good for each other. He could use a female friend. I'm not sure that he's ever had one."

"Great." Meriel sighed. "Just want I always wanted to be. The *friend*."

Hamish halted both their horses at the grassy portion of the shoreline and hopped off his mount. Meriel raised her hand to shield her eyes from the late morning light to view McTiernay Castle. It lay just beyond the loch and over the hills, which she knew were much steeper than they looked. There was not a cloud in the sky and the weather was warm without being oppressive.

Walking over to Meriel's side, Hamish reached up, clasped her small waist in his hands, and helped her down. "I'm thinking we should rest here and let the horses graze for a little bit."

"How long?" Meriel asked, clearly puzzled as to why they would stop when they were so close to their destination.

"Umm, for just about the length of time it will take for the craziness to die down from Laurel and Conor's return. Both will be pummeled with hugs from their children, endless questions from their staff, and those who feel they have important news that needs to be immediately imparted. Trust me. You want to enjoy this tranquility before entering that mess."

Meriel inhaled, and with a slight smile gave a small shake of her head. "Last time I was at this very spot, the day was far from peaceful."

Hamish pulled out a piece of dried meat and offered her

a piece. She shook her head no. Chewing on the long, thin strip, he mumbled, "I remember."

Meriel stared at him incredulously. "Really? I find that hard to believe."

"Well, it is not too often that I get the opportunity to help save a beautiful woman," he answered. It was a true statement, but what he really remembered was Crevan's eyes boring into him when he had passed through the gates carrying Meriel's wounded sister, Raelynd. The man's jealousy had been practically tangible. After that, Hamish had purposely avoided both Raelynd and her sister. He had even dodged them at the Schelldens' while visiting Craig and his brother. He had been successful right up until the end. Hamish once again reminded himself of the reluctant promise he had made to Craig to look after Meriel in his absence.

Hamish glanced to his left and for a long moment studied the woman Craig held in such high regard. After traveling for two days, dirt clung to her skin; several loose, wispy strands escaped from her braided hair; and the cuffs and hem of her light blue bliaut were now brown with caked mud. And still, she could be considered quite beautiful. Meriel was not quite as tall as Lady McTiernay, but then neither was she petite. Her body was subtly provocative, with curves promising of hidden riches that did not match her personality, which was too sweet and compliant for his tastes. Still, her company had been far more tolerable than he had expected.

"Beautiful? You think Raelynd beautiful?"

Hamish nodded. "You too. It is difficult to tell the two of you apart until one of you starts to speak. Then there is no doubt." Realizing that he had spoken his thoughts aloud, he immediately stiffened and waited for her rebuke.

Meriel's eyelashes fluttered and she blinked several times. Then before she could help herself, she burst out in laughter. Such brutal honesty coming from a man who liked to beguile and flatter women with nonsense had been unexpected. Hamish was always so careful around her—about what he said and what he did—trying never to offend. It had made her just as cautious. "So I am beautiful too, am I? How about the first time you saw me?" she questioned, wondering if he recalled her first night at McTiernay Castle.

Hamish absolutely remembered. Very clearly, and by the twinkle in her eye, so did Meriel. He grinned and then struck a serious expression. "That night I think I would have used the term 'breathtaking.' Aye, that's it. You were definitely breathtaking."

Meriel reached up and tugged on Hamish's loose auburn locks. "You could be just as *breathtaking* if you let little Brenna style your hair." Her sense of humor took over and she could not stop herself from asking, "It just so happens that I remember you too. Especially the last night we were here right after my sister's wedding. You were quite the sensation among my sex. Tell me, was there a woman to whom you did *not* make an overture?"

Hamish cocked a brow but refused to deny the accusation. "One. It was you, I believe."

Ignoring the comment, Meriel continued. "I have always wondered if you ever actually succeeded in ensnaring a woman with your nonsense."

Hamish glanced down and studied the wicked grin on her lips. Mischievous was not a quality he would have attributed to either of the Schellden twins, and especially not Meriel. He was starting to get an inkling why Craig preferred the company of someone so . . . uninteresting. The woman was anything but.

Playing along, Hamish tried to appear insulted and puffed out his chest. "With this face and body? How could women resist?"

Meriel could not help herself and joined his deep, warm, rich laughter. Despite her hint otherwise, Hamish *was* good-looking *and* charming, but what he probably did not know is what really lured women to his side—the air of strength about him. She felt protected just by being next to him.

She elbowed his side with a playful jab. "Regrettably, I am sure that very few women could or do resist. But I am curious—has any woman ever succeeded in catching *your* affections?"

Hamish stared at Meriel for a long moment, assessing whether or not he should answer her honestly. He was surprised to find himself wanting to, for yesterday at this time, he would not have imagined telling her the type of food he liked, let alone the inroads to his heart. "I would really like it if a particular someone caught me now," he said truthfully.

Meriel grimaced and rolled her eyes with intentional exaggeration. "You always like someone."

"Ah, but I don't always *love* someone," he quickly rejoined. He inhaled deeply and kicked a rock, watching it splash and then sink into the loch. "And I think I may actually be falling in love with her."

Meriel could see Hamish was serious and wondered who he could mean. When she realized he had not named his *someone*, her hazel eyes widened in alarm. She had not intended to flirt with Hamish or lead him to the wrong conclusion.

Seeing her reaction, Hamish leaned down and whispered, "Not you," with a chuckle. "Her name is Wyenda."

Meriel let go the breath she had been holding. She did not care if she had almost made a fool out of herself. "Good," was all that she could say.

Hamish crossed his arms and continued looking down. His foot played with another large pebble before kicking it into the water. His expression had stilled and grown serious, as if he were contemplating revealing a secret. "It is true that I like women. I enjoy their company," he said, allowing himself a brief sideways glance to see if Meriel was paying attention. Seeing that she was listening earnestly, he continued. "I have found lately that chasing women, or my 'overtures' as I have heard some people call them, is not as much fun as it used to be."

Meriel's eyebrows rose a fraction. She understood his meaning exactly, but not the reason behind such a change of heart. "I'm not sure I understand. Do you no longer seek women's company because you have fallen in love? Or was it the monotony of the chase that compelled you to fall in love?" she asked, hoping his answer gave her some insight into her own feelings.

Hamish furrowed his brow and scratched his chin, clearly puzzled by the question. Humor, spirit, and now intellect. Meriel Schellden was not at all what he had believed her to be. And her question was a good one. "Is love inspired by one's own life or by the other person?" He paused and answered her seriously. "Why not both? Does it matter how I fell in love?"

Meriel studied Hamish for several seconds, smiled, and gave him the answer he wanted. "Not really." It really did not matter how or why Hamish loved Wyenda, but she suspected how and why someone fell in love did matter a great deal to the longevity of the relationship. But since she was far from an authority on the subject, she stayed quiet. "Does this Wyenda . . . does she also love you?"

Hamish's jaw suddenly tensed, betraying deep frustration. "I cannot tell. She seems to, most of the time, but then without warning, she will push me away, telling me that my feelings are not real. I fear my reputation is somewhat getting in the way."

Not liking to hear the sad sound in his normally jovial voice, Meriel reached up and gave his forearm an encouraging squeeze. "You can catch her, Hamish. Who could resist 'this face' and 'this body'?" she said, teasing him with his own words.

Hamish flashed her a grin, but his eyes were still solemn. "It's not so easy. Have you ever tried to catch Craig?"

She flinched and retreated a step. "Craig? No. Never. And I am very sure he never tried to catch me," she answered rapidly. "We really are just friends."

Hamish cocked his head and said with a shrug, "More than likely it is why you are *only* friends. He is certainly protective of you. I doubt he would have tolerated me coming along and helping you with Merry if I had not told him about Wyenda."

"If Craig is protective of me, it's because he sees me as a friend . . . a true friend. You see, when his brother married my sister, we both lost the one person to whom we confided everything. We kind of united out of necessity."

"And now you love him," Hamish challenged.

Meriel licked her lips and narrowed her gaze, keeping it firmly on the loch's lapping waters. "Craig and I both agree that we do not want anything to jeopardize our friendship."

"Fine, so you both love each other."

Her lips thinned with growing irritation. Meriel clasped her hands together and clarified, "That is not what I said."

Hamish produced a casual shrug. "You didn't have to. Neither did he."

Meriel ignored Hamish's implication. "The problem is that I became so used to Craig being around, giving me his opinion, just being there . . . that I forgot how to define myself without him," she said in an attempt to explain her position.

"And when you love someone, how is that a bad thing?" Seeing that Meriel was about to argue without giving his question due thought, Hamish put his hand up. "My question was a serious one. If two people love each other and are committed to one another, then why do they need to see themselves as individuals? Shouldn't you *want* to define yourself as someone's partner?"

Meriel closed her mouth and glanced back at the water. Tears burned at the back of her eyes. "Aye, that is the way it should be, but only if both people share the same sentiments. Craig does not."

Hamish chuckled. "You are completely wrong there. Craig most definitely shares the same sentiment. He just doesn't call it love."

Meriel straightened her shoulders and transferred any sorrow she was feeling to aggravation. "Aye. He calls it *friendship*." Turning to look Hamish directly in the eye, Meriel asked with deceptive calm, "If a person can fall in love so easily, shouldn't they be able to fall out of love just as easily?"

"I cannot say," he murmured in a concerned tone.

Fear for his friend enveloped him. Was *that* the reason why Meriel had come to visit the McTiernays? To get over Craig? Then again, if falling out of love was anything like falling in love, Meriel was going to be around for a long time.

"Well, I hope so," she said, sighing. "It would be nice to know that one day I could fall in love again with someone else."

"I have no doubt that you will have many chances in the future," Hamish returned with reluctant honesty, wondering if Craig realized just what he was about to lose.

Three days later, Meriel welcomed her first visitor. When she opened the door to her bedchamber, a pale blond head covered with ringlets immediately dashed inside. Laurel's eldest daughter looked like a young version of her mother, with one exception. Instead of blue-green eyes, hers were gray like her father's and their intensity changed with her mood. And today they held an impish sparkle in their silver depths.

Brenna flopped stomach-first on the bed. At eight years old, she considered herself no longer a little girl and believed she was on the cusp of adulthood. She lacked only the height and the figure, but intellectually she thought herself a match for most adults, and certainly all boys. But since she could not enjoy the benefits of being fully grown, she could not fathom why her mother insisted that she follow rules of decorum made for adults. Letting her dress fall to her knees as her ankles swung back and forth in the air, she was glad Mcricl did not care about such silly rules.

Looking behind her, Brenna smiled and waved for the wafer-thin figure to come into the room. With a small bosom and thick, umber-colored hair plaited in a long single braid, the young woman who hesitated in the doorway initially appeared somewhat plain and younger than her years until one caught her eyes. Pale blue and deep set, they reflected a power of conscious thought. When her gaze was direct and unhidden, it could unnerve one.

Maegan had been north visiting friends during the drama of Meriel's first visit, but it took less than a few minutes with the young woman for Meriel to realize that the rumors of Maegan's outspoken personality and fierce loyalty were, if anything, understated.

At seventeen, Maegan had many opinions, but lacked the experience that would allow her to see life in something other than absolutes. In many ways, Maegan reminded Meriel of herself and Raelynd not very long ago, and therefore she understood the young woman's candid comments and intentions better than many who had known her for years. But Maegan differed in one significant way.

Unlike Meriel, who in her youth had forsworn marriage and decided only to dally in innocent flirtations, Maegan believed herself to have found her one and only true love— Clyde, the youngest of the McTiernays—when she was twelve. Never having desired to learn how to flirt, charm, or be a coquette, Maegan was herself at all times, completely honest and often giving voice to things most would leave unsaid.

"Oh!" Maegan recoiled as her eyes scanned the room. She had met Meriel when she and Hamish had come through the gate; Maegan had been determined to see who would be coming to stay at the castle. As a child, Maegan had often escaped while her grandmother napped to follow the youngest of Craig's brothers Clyde everywhere. When Clyde left to the Lowlands for training, she had been thankful when Lady McTiernay offered her something positive on which to refocus her energy. After spending so much of her time helping Lady McTiernay with her children, she considered the McTiernays to be extended family and was quite protective of them. But after meeting Meriel and finding her to be both clever and unusually nice, she suspected Brenna's memory of the striking woman to be somewhat exaggerated. But, if anything, Brenna had played down Meriel's lack of orderliness.

Things were scattered everywhere, just as foretold. In less than three days, Meriel's sleeping quarters looked as if a female version of Craig had lived there for over a month. Anywhere else, Maegan might have found it less annoying, but Meriel was using *Clyde's* room . . . and worse, *she* had suggested it!

Upon hearing the idea, Meriel had been thrilled. The idea of staying in Craig's room again had not been a palatable one. Clyde's bedchamber, however, was located directly above Craig's and therefore had the same window layout that let in large amounts of sunlight.

Although Maegan was glad Meriel was enthusiastic over her proposal, the recommendation was based on a personal need. Maegan had planned to help clean the room with the goal of perusing Clyde's personal things and, if possible, taking a keepsake. Unfortunately, the area was full of odds and ends and very dusty from years of disuse. It required so many people to get it ready that if anything of interest *had* been in the room, Maegan would have had no chance of even seeing it, let alone sneaking it out.

Taking another step inside Clyde's/Meriel's room, Maegan's foot hit a large, heavy traveling bag and nearly stumbled. "Brenna, I apologize. You were not exaggerating. I just could not imagine . . ."

"That anyone could be so messy?" Meriel finished for her with a smile, indicating that she was not at all offended. Having heard it all before, she was very comfortable with her chaotic style of organization.

Maegan nodded her head as she stepped over the bag and then another. Wrinkling her nose, she said in disbelief, "You still haven't unpacked all your stuff?"

Brenna's eyes popped open with excitement, remembering the last time she had been able to help Meriel unpack. "You haven't? Can I help?"

Meriel nodded, grabbing a pillow off the bed. She placed it on the window bench and sat down, leaning back against the stone wall as she looked down at the busy courtyard below. All concerns about her being bored or missing home, which would have compelled her to expedite her return, were gone. She had not realized how many McTiernay clansmen and -women she had met and had come to know during her previous stay. What was even more surprising was that they remembered her with no ill feelings.

Fallon was still fearsome and intimidating despite his not being nearly as tall as those around him. His red hair was lighter and there was a little more gray in his beard, but he was still the same gruff and churlish steward who had chided her continuously about her lack of domestic skills. And true to form, as soon as he saw her, he gave her his standard lecture about the courtyard and its dangers. Meriel kept quiet, nodded at appropriate times, and was just promising herself to stay out of his sight when he pulled her brusquely into his arms and gave her a quick, firm squeeze. A second later she was swaying on her feet trying to maintain her balance as the burly steward turned and marched away, howling at someone for not doing something they should have, or vice versa.

Her encounter with the even crustier Fiona had been even more bewildering. The cook was known to be one of the finest in the Highlands. She was also infamous for being the most difficult. Meriel had made sure the old woman was nowhere in sight when she sneaked through the kitchens to access the scullery and the gardens. There she found the scullery maid, Myrna, one of the few who had been truly friendly and helpful during her miserable attempts to learn what it entailed to be lady of the castle.

After helping Myrna in the garden for a couple of hours and catching up on the castle gossip, Meriel forgot to be as careful on her return and bumped into the surly cook, who had been standing inside the doorway. But instead of yelling, Fiona had merely huffed and told her that she had better grab some meat, lest she become even more clumsy due to lack of food. Meriel was so shocked she nearly fell down. Fiona *never* gave her food to *anyone*. The memory of her snapping at Laird McTiernay for daring to disrupt her kitchens was something Meriel would never forget.

Then there was Laurel's best friend, Aileen, and Father Lanaghly and the other castle staff. All of whom were welcoming, cheerful, and genuinely glad to see her again. Meriel went to sleep her first night feeling quite ashamed of herself. When she thought back to her time spent at McTiernay Castle, what had come to mind was the hardship and the frustrations. She had learned several lessons in that short time, but what she had failed to realize was that she had also met many wonderful people who truly liked her, despite the mistakes she had made.

Thump, thump. Thump. Thump, thump, thump. Meriel glanced back at the bed where Brenna sat pulling shoes from one of the bags. She was tossing them against the wall so they fell next to the others. Meriel had brought too many, but she did not care. It was better than going barefoot.

"Where do you want these?" Brenna asked, waving a wad of ribbons in the air.

"Let's put them . . ." Meriel began, pondering the question as she examined the various piles on the floor. She knew others thought her mess had no reasoning behind it, but they were wrong. She just preferred to always be able to view her things. For when they were put away, she forgot that she had them. However, needing her things out where she could see them did not mean they could be just anywhere. ". . . over there. On that chest. Aye, let's remove the materials there now and spread them out on the rug, and instead, put the ribbons and thread on top so they will be out of the way."

Maegan's eyebrows rose with unconcealed amusement. "How many bags did you bring?" Maegan asked as she grabbed one of the heavier ones and swung it on the bed next to Brenna.

Meriel laughed. "Not nearly as many as I did the first time."

Maegan tilted her chin back in disbelief and then, with a shrug of acceptance, said matter-of-factly, "I think you should fall in love and marry Craig." Meriel's heart stopped as she watched the young woman open up the bag and peer inside. Had anyone said anything? Meriel thought she had been very discreet with the inner turmoil she had been experiencing. "You and he are so messy that you are the only ones who could live with each other and still be happy," Maegan finished, and Meriel felt a rush of relief.

Brenna giggled. "Meriel cannot marry Craig. He says

he is *never* going to fall in love. *I* think she should marry *Hamish*."

Comforted that neither girl had any insight as to her true reasons for visiting, Meriel regained her composure and said cheerfully, "*I* have no intention of marrying anyone! I have come to relax and visit, neither of which requires a man or being in love."

Ignoring the declaration, Maegan tapped a finger on her chin and stared at Brenna. "You know, Hamish *is* rather good-looking, and I have heard the girl he was after refused him."

"Wyenda rejected him?" Meriel asked without thinking. She was surprised anyone would give up a chance to catch Hamish. After she had finally disposed of most of her mistaken assumptions about him, she had decided that he was not only an attractive man, but he had a generous soul that could make a girl's heart melt.

Maegan's sky-blue eyes widened in shock. "*Wyenda?* Hamish was chasing after that *spùllach* Wyenda?" she repeated with outright disdain.

Meriel bit the inside of her cheek. Avaricious was not exactly a flattering description, and Meriel wondered if Maegan had spoken out of turn when Brenna said, "Men have liked her for*ever*. But she thinks she is *too* beautiful for anyone—even Hamish and my uncle Craig. She wants to marry a nobleman or someone *rich* like Iain Matheson. I heard her say so myself."

Meriel sat up. Had she misunderstood? Or at one time had Craig sought Wyenda's attention? "Is she truly that pretty?"

Maegan shrugged. "She must be. All the men follow her around."

"Hamish doesn't like her anymore," Brenna stated matter-of-factly.

"And just how do you know that?" Meriel asked, immediately wishing she could retract the question. Brenna was notorious for knowing practically everything that was happening around the castle, for she was an expert eavesdropper. She was not exactly a gossip, as she did not run around telling all that she overheard at every opportunity, but then neither did she feel the need to keep the information private if the subject came up.

"I heard Hamish telling Gilroy yesterday, by the silversmith's. He didn't make a lot of sense because he said that Wyenda didn't realize just what she was giving up. So, doesn't that mean Hamish doesn't like her anymore?"

Maegan sighed. "Not exactly. But hopefully he will soon figure out who she is and stop embarrassing himself by chasing her."

Brenna frowned. "Why doesn't Hamish chase you, Meriel? Oh . . . oh . . . oh, I know! You could go after him! And I could help you! You and he are already friends and he is *sooo* nice. He always swings me around whenever I ask."

Meriel smiled. The qualifications of love for an eight-year-old were significantly more simple. At what age did it become complicated? "I'm not sure one can change their feelings about someone that quickly."

"Why not?"

"Well, it's like this room," Meriel said, trying to think of an explanation Brenna would understand. "Even if I wanted to give up being messy and become neat and organized, I couldn't suddenly change my habits. It takes time."

"If only I could let my room look like yours. Then I would never change because I would never have to clean *any*thing!" Brenna exclaimed, tossing an undergarment into the air.

Maegan gave the little girl a disapproving look before scooping up the sheer frock and folding it. Then, looking around and realizing there was nowhere to put it, she let it drop back to the floor with a sigh. "It's fun, I guess, but I would not want to live this way."

"That's because you don't think *Clyde* wants to live this way. If he did, not a thing you owned would be where it belonged."

Maegan narrowed her gaze and then, without thought, grabbed the remaining pillow on the bed and took a threatening stance. The action only spurred Brenna to comment further, and she jumped off the bed and out of reach. "Save me, Meriel!"

"How about I show you how to braid your hair instead?"

The little girl's eyes gleamed. "Really? Like yours?" At Meriel's nod, Brenna jumped back on the bed and proudly announced to Maegan, "Meriel is going to make me a new dress."

"And I am also making your brother, Braeden, a new leine," Meriel added, beginning to brush the young girl's tresses with long strokes.

"You'll have to catch him first," Brenna said, trying not to wince as the brush became caught in one of the knots in her curly hair.

Maegan finished emptying the bag she had been working on and moved to the next one. In it she found four gowns. As she pulled them out, her eyes grew bigger as each seemed even prettier than the last. Laying the last one down, she fondled the light material. She had never seen anything so beautiful.

The bliaut was made of ivory silk that opened up at the hem to reveal an undergown of pale rose. Long fitted sleeves, puffed slightly at the shoulders, echoed the elegant high collar that came down into a low V-neckline. The edge of the neckline was embroidered in delicate pink flowers and pale green leaves that matched the design of the loose belt. Maegan could only imagine what it looked like on. "Do you think I would look pretty in something like this?"

Hearing the hesitancy in Maegan's voice, Meriel paused and studied the young woman as she held the gown against her figure. The design required more bosom than Maegan had, and the girl needed something with more color, but never would Meriel utter those words. It was the first time she had heard Maegan say anything about improving her appearance and making herself more attractive. "Would you mind if I make you a gown while I'm here? I could show you how to embroider the edges so that you could make it your own."

Maegan released the ivory bliaut and was about to shake her head, denying her ability to create such a vision, when she spied Brenna's taunting stare. Smoky eyes were daring her to reject the offer. "Thank you. I accept."

Seeing the exchange, Meriel offered, "I promise you, it will be beautiful. So much so that when Clyde does return, he will not have eyes for anyone but you."

Meriel entered the Great Hall through the large doors, eager for the evening meal. For two weeks, she had pushed thoughts of Craig aside by immersing herself in materials and patterns, creating one garment after another. Today, she had finished Braeden's leine and new kilt and even managed to get the young boy to try them on; thankfully, they fit. Maegan's idea of using one of his old shirts as the pattern for a new, slightly larger one had turned out to be brilliant.

Bonny, Laurel's youngest child, who had turned five years old during the summer, and Brenna had been eager participants and had persuaded their father to allow Meriel to use the prized material he had originally procured just for his wife. With access to a stockpile of heavenly materials, the number of garments that could be made was practically unlimited. At first, Meriel had embraced the wealth of work available, for it kept her mind off home, her family, and Craig.

She usually ate the morning and noon meals in the hall with Laurel, Bonny, Brenna, and Maegan, and oftentimes Laurel's best friend, Aileen. The nights, however, were hard. She found herself withdrawing rather than reaching out to the few friends she had made.

At home, right after the main meal, she was used to sitting quietly by the fire and talking with either her sister or Craig. To avoid memories of those treasured moments, she typically ate in her room. Then, if the weather permitted, she would venture out onto the curtain wall to look at the stars, thinking . . . and remembering. She had been gone a fortnight, and nothing had changed. Craig had not come after her and, unfortunately, she was no closer to walling off her heart. She still loved Craig, and despite her belief that he loved her as well, being apart was not going to convince him to discuss their feelings and decide together if their relationship should evolve into something more.

She needed to let him go. She just needed to know how.

If time was the answer, it was going to take more than she had. McTiernay Castle was supposed to be a temporary haven where she could sort out her emotions and move on. She had never intended to hide within its walls for more than a month, but at the rate her heart was healing, she would need to remain with the McTiernays throughout the winter and into spring—something her father would most likely protest vehemently. But until she had a plan . . . a way . . . some idea of how she was going to see, talk, and be around Craig without breaking down, she could not return.

Tonight, however, Craig would not be the first and foremost problem on her mind. His brother Conan would be.

Maegan—being Maegan—conspired with Laurel to compel Meriel to dine in the Great Hall with a small group of friends and family. In order to oblige Meriel to attend, the meal was in honor of her and the work she had done for Laird and Lady McTiernay's children. Meriel tried to have it postponed until she had finished her gowns for Laurel, Aileen, and Maegan, but the suggestion had not even been considered. Meriel was to come to dine with family and friends and that was that. Unfortunately, "family" also meant Conan McTiernay would be there as well.

Craig had six brothers. Three older and three younger, if you accepted his claim that he was the elder twin. After Crevan came Conan and Clyde. All of them, with the exception of Conor—Laird McTiernay—and Conan, were living elsewhere, either in support of a brother or chieftain of a clan.

Conan, like all the McTiernays, was a gifted strategist and a cunning fighter. He had the ability to lead, but not the personality or the patience. The man had a mind superior to all those around him and he never wasted a chance to make it known that he considered women to be inferior intellectually.

Last year, Raelynd had confronted his prejudice and quite relished getting the upper hand in the mental battle he waged when she and Meriel first arrived. Unfortunately, the encounter had not garnered Meriel his respect, only a suspension of any more of her sister's verbal attacks. The truce that had developed between him and Raelynd had not extended to Meriel. A fact which Conan had made clear soon after Meriel arrived two weeks ago.

With his study on the fourth floor, directly above the bedchamber she occupied, she could have heard his movements even if he had not intended for her to. But the inordinately loud thumping and periodic dropping of something heavy on the floor were so obvious that not even a fool could mistake the meaning.

What Conan had yet to realize was that Meriel was not her sister. And while she possessed a more even-tempered and tolerant demeanor, she was far more stubborn. Something he would discover tonight.

With its large windows and high vaulted ceiling, the

McTiernay Great Hall was one of the most majestic in the Highlands. Despite its size, it was also one of the most welcoming. Tonight was no exception. A single long table was set up near the far wall's canopied fireplace, enabling diners to converse without having to shout or strain to hear.

Meriel fought a grimace as she strolled toward the assembled group. She knew she should have arrived even earlier than she had. She was not late, but considering Lady McTiernay's affinity for beginning the evening meal exactly on time, everyone was already present, with one exception— Laird McTiernay.

Maegan was nestled next to Laurel and Laurel's friend Aileen. Across from them were Aileen's husband, Finn, the commander of the McTiernays' elite guard, and a few of his men, including Hamish. That left only one available space on the bench—right next to Conan. No doubt the ogre had arranged for her to sit by him.

Hamish's hazel eyes caught her look of dismay and he immediately stood up, ordering the other two soldiers to slide down so that he could place himself right across from Conan. Meriel issued him a warm glance of appreciation and proceeded to stand next to Conan while everyone waited for Conor to arrive.

Unable to wait even a single minute to deliver his first barb, Conan leaned over and murmured, loud enough for those nearby to hear, "Well, well, well. So the rumors are true. Lady Meriel has joined our little family once more. Are you still chasing after my brother Craig?"

Meriel gasped, her eyes widening to saucer size.

Hamish rallied to her defense. "As Craig is at Caireoch and Meriel is here by *her* choice, your question is rather a senseless one."

Conan issued a smirk accompanied by a belittling shrug of his shoulders. "I asked only because she has been going after him for nearly a year. I thought this might be another tactic of hers. You know, *maybe he'll miss me*." He squeaked at the end, feigning a woman's voice.

"Or," Hamish hissed, "Craig has been going after *her* and Meriel is escaping him."

Conan barked out a single derisive laugh at the concept. "Is that true, Lady Meriel?" he asked, turning to look directly at her. "Are you doing the running or the chasing?"

"Neither," Meriel said, proud she was able to keep her voice level and calm.

Focused on his goal of proving that she was unworthy of his brother's affections, Conan continued. "So then you are here because someone is again dictating the direction of your life. No, wait, could it be that your mind has finally developed to the point you can now make decisions for yourself?"

Meriel could feel her jaw clench. The man was not only rude beyond description, it was as if he could somehow see into her soul and announce her private fears. Life was full of nuances that Meriel had no opinion on and therefore tended to ignore, letting others have their way. But somehow Conan recognized that without any of her family around to push their will upon her, she was, for the first time, having to make decisions for herself. And it had been uncomfortable.

Thankfully, she was reprieved from coming up with a witty response when the doors opened and Conor stepped inside. He quickly joined the small group, placed a kiss upon his wife's cheek, and uttered his apologies for being late.

Hamish sat down, glaring at Conan. He respected the younger McTiernay in many ways, for the man was unbelievably brilliant—quite possibly the smartest Highlander he had ever or would ever know. But Conan was also the most maddening.

Not only had he been gifted with intelligence, he was in many ways the most handsome of the brothers. In addition to the McTiernay bright blue eyes, the man had dimples so deep that it should have been an embarrassment. And yet somehow the feminine feature only made him better looking. His thick, dark brown hair was shorter than most, and though it normally looked ruffled and unkempt, that did not deter women's advances. Too many times had Hamish heard the female sex whisper about how Conan's hair created a state of longing to run fingers through it. But it was not Conan's physical attributes that aggravated Hamish, it was how the young man used them. All too often Hamish had found his hopes and plans to woo a female dashed because he met her after she had experienced Conan's reckless and callous behavior.

"Don't mind him," Hamish said, his voice deep and stern, aimed not at Meriel but at Conan. "He's been grumpy for the past week or so, constantly complaining of a headache. *Tolla-thon.*"

Sitting down, she reached over to pick up her pewter mug. Before drinking the ale, she turned to Conan and said, "Headaches? Hmm, while I knew it would take more than a year for you to mature to a level of normal conversation, I was under the impression you were somewhat clever. Perhaps the next time you decide to torment someone, you will choose an activity that does not also inflict pain upon yourself."

"On the contrary, *Lady* Schellden," Conan countered, grinding out her title between his teeth, "my headaches, *if I have them*, are not reducing my ability to think or comprehend anything you would have to say."

"Be careful," Hamish warned. "Craig may not be here to lay you out flat, but I am."

Meriel shot Hamish an icy look that kept him in his seat and his fists to himself. Only the addition of a soft smile let him know that while she appreciated his help, she not only intended to fight her own battles, she wanted to do so.

Licking the ale from her lips, Meriel leisurely replaced the mug on the table and tore off a piece of bread. She leaned to the side to allow a servant to put a large platter of meat on the table. When the servant had moved on, Meriel bestowed her most engaging smile on Conan. "I know of one subject that has eluded you and I suspect will continue to baffle your twisted mind for some time," she said before plopping a small chunk of the warm loaf in her mouth.

"Let me guess—women," Conan growled just before ripping off a piece of meat from its bone with his teeth.

Laughter rippled through the air, catching the attention of those near. "Ah, a glimmer of your intelligence is finally emerging, Conan. You are half-correct. I know of no one who knows less about women than you. But I was referring more to gentlemanly behavior."

Hamish put down his leg of meat and crossed his arms, listening with interest. Once again, he was reminded that there was much more to sweet, docile Meriel than appeared. The woman whom he had pegged as boring and unappealing despite her physical beauty, was again turning out to be far more interesting . . . and entertaining.

Conan's focus was completely on Meriel. If he was aware that the conversations around him were dying as people began to shift their attention toward him, he gave no indication. "And yet, my supposed lack of understanding on that topic has not seemed to interfere with my . . . *social* activities."

From the head of the table, Meriel heard Laurel inhale deeply at the implication, but before she could intervene, Meriel returned the verbal sparring, blocking and attacking in turn. "You mean *limited* activities, do you not, Conan? I mean, it is a shame your knowledge of women is solely of the female anatomy. There is so much more to us. For example, when someone childishly throws things on the floor to annoy the person in the room below, women know how

to take scraps of material and use them to block the noise."
She reached into the small pocket of her bliaut and pulled
out two small pieces of cloth and began to wad them up.
After inserting them into her ears, she added, "It also helps
to prevent headaches when you are forced to sit by someone inordinately obnoxious."

Conan, however, was not remotely deterred. He refused
to concede to another Schellden *woman*. Last year, he had
been forced to compromise with her sister, but he was not
going to do so again. Yet, before he could issue his scathing
response, the one that would let him end this conversation
as the victor, Conor butted in.

"Conan, keep your mouth shut and eat. If you ruin another meal because Hamish decides to pummel you for your
lack of civility, I'm going to assume your stupidity extends
beyond your mouth to your arm, and order you to attend
training every day for a month."

Conan glared at his brother, but it did little good. Eighteen
years his senior, Conor had always been able to physically
enforce Conan's compliance. As he got older, Conan's respect for Conor grew, and his brother's opinion was one of
the few about which he actually cared. Still, Conan was no
longer willing to be lectured by Conor, and it did not matter
that he might have earned his brother's admonishment. He
would not openly defy Conor, but neither would he remain
at the table when he had practically been ordered to eat and
be quiet, as if he were a child. Conan grabbed a whole loaf
of bread, put it on his plate, picked up the plate and his mug,
and stomped out of the hall.

Along with the rest of the table, Laurel was in shock. For
years she had been hoping Conor would say as much to his
younger brother, knowing he was the only one to whom
Conan would listen. But Conor had forever refused to take
on a fatherly role. He would lead his brothers, help and
guide by example, but he was not their father and felt

pretending to be such would ruin the brotherly bond they shared. So when Conor said what he did, Laurel felt compelled to lean over and whisper, "You, my love, are going to be richly rewarded later tonight."

Meanwhile, Meriel sat and exhaled the breath she had not realized she had been holding. Ignoring the stares that had shifted from watching Conan walk out the door to her, she pasted on an unconcerned expression and began to nibble on her meat, glad when heads turned to resume their previous conversations.

Only Hamish remained quiet as they finished eating. He waited until she rose to leave, then stood up and spoke. "Lady Meriel, would you take a walk with me? I find I need company tonight and would much appreciate you lending me yours."

Meriel closed her eyes and smiled, shaking her head at the flowery invitation. Hamish could not stop himself from flirting, even with someone who held no real interest for him. "I would be delighted, but only if you give me an update on your latest pursuit."

After giving their thanks to their host and hostess, who were both embroiled in conversations that would keep them bound to the table for another half hour to an hour, Meriel followed Hamish out of the hall and into the courtyard. The night air was crisp and clear.

"You cold?" Hamish asked.

"I'm fine. This gown is much warmer than it looks."

"Then shall we dare to venture out beyond the walls toward the loch? There, away from the fires, the stars shine their brightest."

Meriel laughed and again Hamish was surprised to be enchanted by the sound. "With your charm, how every woman does not fall into your arms is a mystery."

"And yet, I do not see you even coming near to swooning."

Meriel's elbow poked his side. "Lucky for you then, that I am immune."

Hamish was not so sure about that conclusion but decided not to pursue the matter. Meriel, despite being on McTiernay land and technically being unattached, was not a free woman. His thought had been to protect her in his friend's stead. But that was no longer the only reason behind his actions. He was truly beginning to see Meriel as *his* friend as well. "I am sorry about Conan's behavior this evening."

Meriel tossed her head back and shook her hair, which she had left mostly down so that only small, intricate braids framed her face. "Oh, I knew even before I arrived that the truce he and my sister declared last year lacked the teeth of permanency."

Hamish felt his flesh tighten as the golden hues of her hair were caught in the moonlight. "Does not matter. Conan should not have gone after you like he did."

"Maybe not, but it is time that I stop leaning on others to run interference. Craig always told me I was stubborn enough to do so; I just lack the fighter instinct."

"Well, you didn't tonight! I must admit to being impressed."

"Who knows? Maybe I had the instinct all along, I just didn't need it before."

Hamish's eyes came up to study her face, to see if she was serious. "Regardless, you should not have had to defend yourself like that. Conan . . . he was . . . offensive."

"Actually he was something far worse. He was *right*," Meriel muttered with frustration. "I do avoid making decisions. It is not that I cannot make them, I just choose not to."

"There is nothing wrong with that."

Meriel shook her head in disagreement. "There is when the reason behind such a choice is laziness."

Hamish stopped and halted her beside him. "Anyone

who knows you, knows that you are *not* lazy. Just look at all you have done since you've arrived! I understand that you have been working practically nonstop. I was very close to talking to the laird about it."

Meriel stared at him, baffled. She had barely seen Hamish since they arrived. She had run into him periodically in the courtyard, but never did they talk for more than a few minutes and of nothing of any import. "To Laird McTiernay?" she asked incredulously. "But why? No one was *making* me do anything. And if I was pushing myself, it was not because I am industrious; it was for a more humiliating reason."

Hamish once again started walking toward the loch. "Which is?"

Meriel hesitated telling the truth and exposing herself, but decided that she was tired of being afraid. "Fear. I did not want to face my future. I still don't. Conan was just intuitively picking up on this."

Hamish could not help but be impressed. It was not often someone could be that honest about their faults. Those who could, possessed a rare asset. "Well, you will not have to worry about Conan much longer. He's leaving at the end of the week."

"Because of me?" Meriel asked, horrified that her attack on Conan's pride might have forced him out of his home.

"No! Not at all," Hamish argued as he pointed down to alert her to avoid a hole barely large enough to twist a foot. "Conan had already been planning to join Father Lanaghly on his trip to Lindores Abbey. Something about needing to speak to one of the master teachers about the language on one of his beloved maps. He wanted to visit and return before winter arrives in a couple of months."

Meriel rolled her eyes, clueless to Conan's fascination with his drawings. In doing so, she did not see a rock and stumbled. She would have fallen if Hamish had not caught her in time and held her upright. Startled and feeling the need to break the intimacy of their contact, Meriel brought up Wyenda. "And how about you? Will you be making special plans with a certain someone before this winter?"

Hamish let her go and shifted his gaze to the body of water that lapped against the distant shoreline. "Capturing Wyenda's heart is proving to be more difficult than I anticipated."

Meriel was not at all surprised. Since her arrival and her inadvertent mentioning of the woman to Maegan, she had learned quite a bit about Wyenda and had even chanced upon the opportunity to verify people's opinions for herself. Meriel had been on her way to the village well to get Aileen some water when she overheard Wyenda talking to another clanswoman. Wyenda freely admitted that she was toying with Hamish's affections in an effort to make Iain Matheson jealous. The woman thought only of becoming a nobleman's wife, thinking her beauty alone was enough to merit such an honor.

Before Meriel could mention what she had heard, Hamish cautioned her. "Please do not be like everyone else and tell me that she is playing with my affections until she finds a better suitor. She may say such things, but I'm not sure it is true. Wyenda grew up with no siblings, and her mother died when she was young. Her father was an important man to King Robert, and she spent a lot of time with people constantly doting on her. So she grew up without the benefit of a lot of the lessons you and I received in our youth. She has a good heart, but after her father passed, she was forced to move to the Highlands and stay with her last living relative—her maternal grandmother. Wyenda believes her beauty is the only thing she has to escape her current situation. She just needs someone to look beyond her hardened exterior."

"And you think you can do that when so many others have failed?"

"I refuse to admit defeat . . . yet," Hamish cautioned. "It

will take several attempts to prove my sincerity and win her affections."

Meriel shook her head. "You are the first McTiernay I have met who doesn't have a triple dose of pride that he is compelled to defend at all times."

"Maybe that is because I am not a true McTiernay. I'm actually from a small clan way north of here near Eilean nan Ròn."

"Then, why are you—"

"—here?" he finished. "Or why am I loyal to the Mc-Tiernays?" At her nod, he gave a shrug and said, "For many reasons, all of which are too onerous to discuss on a pretty night like this."

Meriel found it hard to bite her tongue and keep from asking probing questions, but she knew it would be pointless. She recognized determination when she saw it. And Hamish had enough to rival her own stubborn personality, at least on this topic. "And so how do you intend to win Wyenda's hand?"

"That I am unsure of. I just know that I am not ready to give up." He glanced at Meriel and seeing her expression, chuckled. "You're surprised."

Meriel nodded. He had said otherwise, but she had truly thought Hamish to be only half interested in Wyenda.

"That's the problem," he said, sighing. "I've thrown my heart out there for all to see so many times, it makes it hard for a woman to believe when I am truly interested in her."

Meriel rolled her hazel eyes, completely aware that he saw her. No longer did she try to hide her opinions in fear of offending him. She had not thought it possible to be so relaxed in any man's company other than Craig's, and yet with Hamish she was. She could not decipher the innermost secrets the Highlander held, like she could Craig's, but she did not need to, either. "I do not believe that you, handsome one, have ever exposed your heart quite as you have claimed. Feigning interest is far from making yourself vulnerable."

Hamish opened his mouth wide with artificial pain. "I have never feigned interest."

"Nor have you made yourself vulnerable. Even now you are waiting for Wyenda to fall in love before you further commit yourself emotionally."

Hamish scratched his chin and regarded Meriel in the moonlight. He was caught somewhere between wanting to pull her into his arms and kiss her and needing to walk away lest he do so and lose her friendship—and Craig's.

Meriel, unaware of the direction of Hamish's thoughts, walked over to a nearby boulder and leaned against it. "Can I ask you a question I've been musing for a while?"

Intrigued, Hamish tilted his head in a nod.

"How do you know when you are in love? For example, you claim to be in love with Wyenda. What is it about her that is so attractive?"

Hamish threw back his head and scoffed. If Meriel were a man he would have blurted out, *Have you seen her?* Instead, he tried to explain it in a way he hoped she could understand. "Wyenda is . . . *very* pretty."

"I know that. I meant attractive *besides* her obvious beauty. What's beyond that 'hardened exterior' you mentioned?"

"I guess . . . well . . . when she looks at a man, she makes him feel like he is the most special, important man in the world. Once we men feel that, we want to feel it again and again. We cannot help ourselves."

Hamish's words washed over Meriel. "You may be surprised to learn that we women are no different. We want to feel special too."

"And does Craig make you feel special?"

Meriel crossed her arms and looked out at the water rippling in the light breeze. The answer was complex. Their bond was unique and something she treasured, but Craig had not actually made her feel special. At least not until he kissed her. "Let me just say he has the ability to do so if he chooses. But not all the time, no." Then she turned her green-and-gold eyes to stare directly at him. "What about you? Have you made Wyenda feel that way?"

Hamish strolled over and leaned back against the large rock so that his hips touched hers. "I have no idea. I've tried all the typical things—flattery, gifts. I even offered to help her and her grandmother with various things around their cottage. She knows that I have enough money to offer her a good life." He paused and then asked, "Do you suppose she is cautious because most men when they get to my age are married? That perhaps there is a reason why no one else wanted me?"

"I . . . I . . . don't know," Meriel answered honestly.

Hamish sighed. "I only wondered because of you and Craig."

"What do you mean, *me and Craig*?"

Hamish shrugged. "Just that, why commit to someone who is around anyway? No need for anyone to be jealous."

Meriel wondered if Hamish was talking about himself. Had he heard the rumors about Wyenda and Iain? But then if she, a visitor, had, it only made sense that he would have, as well. "I don't know Iain Matheson, but I understand how you could be jealous of—"

"Iain Matheson!" Hamish spewed. "He would be the *last* person I would be jealous of. Have you ever seen him? If he ever tried to pick up a sword it would topple him over. The only muscles he has reside in his jaw, which never stops moving. He professes to be a descendent of the royal house of Lorne and have all the wealth that comes with such a lineage, but there is not a scrap of evidence to support such a claim. He filches off of various family members, and last

I heard he was mooching off Dougal Matheson, who lives just on the other side of the McTiernay's northwest border."

"Does Wyenda know this?"

Hamish furrowed his brow. "She has to. *Everyone* knows Iain Matheson. If she is telling people that she is interested in him, it is simply to keep them from knowing her true fondness for me."

Meriel was not convinced, but she could see that Hamish was. Nothing she could say would induce him to believe otherwise. "So what did you mean then about jealousy?"

"I *meant*, that if Wyenda thought someone else was interested in *me*, it might help. Have you ever tried to make someone jealous?"

Meriel wrinkled her nose and shook her head. "Don't ask me. I'm here to get *over* a man, not devise ways to humiliate myself."

"And how is that coming along? I mean, are you any closer to forgetting Craig?"

Meriel squinted her eyes and then gave in to the urge to shove him. It only added to her annoyance when Hamish did not move even a little bit. "It doesn't matter. I refuse to love someone who does not love me."

"I told you before that he does."

"And you also said that when a man feels a certain way about a woman, he cannot help but want to feel it again and again. Craig won't even discuss the topic."

Having now been around Meriel long enough to get to know her, he understood his friend's dilemma more and more. But while he understood Craig's reluctance to commit himself to someone who turned out to be a very spirited and challenging woman, Hamish still thought his friend a fool for not snatching Meriel up before anyone else did. "Craig loves you," Hamish repeated. "He simply refuses to admit it."

"To himself or me?"

"Himself," replied Hamish with absolute conviction.

"You see, the moment he does—and he knows this, just as every man does—that he will be truly and forever entrapped. And it scares us men. It's why so many of us marry for other reasons besides love."

Meriel felt her jaw drop in open shock. "You don't *want* to love the woman you marry?"

"We want to be *attracted* to them, aye. We want to enjoy their company and be able to have a conversation, but *besotted*? Nothing is scarier. Think about it. If something happened to Lady McTiernay, how do you think the laird would respond? I can tell you, the same way his father did when his mother died. To wrap oneself up emotionally in someone else is wrought with danger."

Meriel could not believe what she was hearing, but deep down she knew that Hamish spoke not only for himself, but many other men out there. Here all this time she had thought both sexes equally sought the love and support of a life partner, when in truth, men just wanted someone to whom they were attracted and whom they could tolerate when not physically engaged. "But do you think if Laird McTiernay could go back and avoid meeting and falling in love with Laurel, he would?"

"Nay. He would not, now that he knows the pleasure of being in love. What I am saying is some men do not seek such pleasure because they know the risks that come with it."

All the pain she had been feeling the past couple of weeks shot through Meriel and it manifested into anger. Throwing her hands in the air, she moved off the boulder. "I guess Craig does not consider loving me worth those risks."

Hamish waved his hand as if he were brushing aside the obvious. "Only because he thinks he doesn't have to risk his heart to have you. I mean, you *are* going back, are you not? And once you return, your friendship will become the way it was before, or have I misunderstood your intentions?"

Meriel swung around. She took a deep breath for control

and then let it escape slowly. Her anger with Craig—which had been swimming just below the surface—was genuine, but she now was equally furious with herself. "You make me sound pathetic and pitiable."

"Honestly? That is how I first thought of you," Hamish replied. Seeing her recoil, he knew he had hurt her with his candor, something he never intended to do. Instinctively, he got up and pulled her into his arms. "Meriel, now that I know you better, I can assure you, you are neither. But I am surprised that you, who can be incredibly stubborn when you want something, gave up so easily on winning Craig's heart. What's worse is that you already have it; you just need to claim it for your own."

Meriel felt the tears she had been fighting let loose and stream down her cheeks. She leaned against Hamish, soaking up his strength, feeling safe in the knowledge that he desired someone else. But Hamish was wrong. She could not go back and have things as they were. Feeling the way she did, she could no longer seek Craig's support without feeling the rejection from his refusal to see them as anything more than friends.

Calmer, Meriel slowly let go and stepped back. "I think I'm forced back to my first plan—to fall out of love."

"Or you could make Craig admit his feelings."

"But how? The man is beyond obstinate when he has made up his mind, and I can promise you, when it comes to me, he has definitely decided that love and marital bliss are not in our future."

Hamish's dark green eyes probed hers. "Ever try jealousy? I hate to admit it, but it usually works."

Meriel scoffed. "Craig? Jealous? Even if he were here to witness me with another man firsthand, he would never believe it. Just like I would never give any credence to a story about him becoming suddenly love-struck over some female."

Hamish reached out and clutched her arm before she could turn away. "Wait—you've *never* been jealous?"

Meriel shrugged her shoulders and shook her head.

"And he has never been even a little possessive of you?"

Meriel glanced to the side, trying to remember. "Honestly, I don't think so."

Hamish did not have to ask. He knew the truth. Since Craig and Meriel had met, neither of them had ever looked at another member of the opposite sex. They had been so wrapped up in their "friendship" that their true feelings had never been tested.

"Maybe you should try it."

Meriel favored him with a blindingly bright smile, laughing at the idea. "It just would not work."

"You'd be surprised. Men fight for those they love, if they think they are going to lose them."

"Maybe, but only if the potential loss was real. Craig would recognize the ruse for what it was—a trap. His pride alone would keep him from becoming jealous."

It was Hamish's turn to laugh. "Perhaps, but even Craig cannot fight human nature."

Meriel froze. Hamish was right. In certain situations, Craig's disposition would cause him to react a certain way. It would practically force him to. And no one knew Craig as well as she did. Craig would always go where he wanted to, but there might be a way to make him want to go in her direction.

She reached up on her tiptoes and planted a warm, soft kiss on Hamish's cheek. "You are brilliant and so am I," she said, beaming. "I think I have a way to solve both our problems—you and Wyenda and Craig and myself. But I would need your help."

Hamish's face broke into a large grin. Her eyes were sparkling and it was like looking at Rae Schellden in the midst of a grand scheme he knew was going to work. It drew one in and somehow elicited a commitment without full knowledge of what one was agreeing to. "Call me brilliant again and I might agree to anything."

"You truly are wonderful and my hero for giving me the idea!" she exclaimed. Then she bit her bottom lip. "Now to convince Laird McTiernay about our plan . . ."

Hamish stepped back and then, seeing the seriousness on her face, took another step back. "*Our* plan? Laird McTiernay? Oh no, you can call me brilliant a thousand times and I still wouldn't agree to whatever you are thinking."

Still deep in thought, Meriel bunched her brows and murmured, "Too late."

Hamish shook his head violently. "First, this is *your* plan. And second, the laird made it rather clear to me that your presence here was to have as little effect on his life as possible. And I got the distinct impression that he thought me responsible for ensuring that outcome—both during and *after* our journey here."

Meriel waved her hand, dismissing his sincerely felt anxiety. "Oh, don't fret so. It ruins your handsome face. Besides, it won't be you and I who will be talking with the laird. We will leave that up to Lady McTiernay."

Chapter 4

Conor entered his solar and paused before slowly closing the door. Laurel was sitting in the farthest of the two hearth chairs, slowly brushing out her hair. With her head tipped back, the firelight played against pale gold curls as they tumbled over her shoulders. Unable to stop himself, he walked over to fondle the soft mass, still unable to believe that he and only he was lucky enough to do so.

He watched as a soft, inviting smile graced her lips, telling him in her private, feminine way that she was completely his. Conor felt his whole body tighten with desire. "I hope you are not tired," she murmured.

Conor arched an eyebrow but continued to stroke the silky tresses, enjoying how they felt as they slipped through his rough fingers. "I don't believe I am," he replied as one curl coiled around his finger. If he didn't know better, he would say that somehow his wife had trained her hair in the art of seduction.

Laurel turned slightly and placed her hand on his arm. The feel of her skin touching his sent sparks flying through his body. "Tonight is going to have to last for a while, so do not plan on falling asleep anytime soon."

Conor swallowed, filled with a sudden need to possess

her body, her entire being, and fulfill her wish without further prelude. He pulled her up out of the chair and into his arms, burying his face in her neck and breathing in her scent. His hands slowly soothed her back in the gentlest of touches when his efforts were suddenly stalled. He pulled back just enough for him to verify that the garment she was wearing was *the* gown—the practically transparent one that played havoc with his senses. Laurel only wore it when they were about to have an argument that she suspected she might lose without the aid of some distraction.

Gray eyes met, locked, and held those the color of a stormy sea. Two souls communicating with each another, neither willing to yield.

"This," Conor began, taking a step back while waving his hand at her chemise, "is not because of dinner tonight, is it?"

Laurel licked her lips. She had actually forgotten her promise to him after his little speech to Conan. "Not *only* because of dinner," she admitted.

Conor grimaced and began to undo his belt. Letting his kilt fall to the floor, he stripped off his leine and tossed it over the chair next to hers. Naked, he went over and stoked the fire before getting into bed. He hoped he had made his point and that she would join him without any more pretense, but Laurel remained standing. And she was still wearing that damn chemise that made it near impossible to think when looking at her.

He closed his eyes. "Based on your comment, you believe one of us is going to be leaving on a trip."

Laurel nodded. "You."

Conor leaned back against the pillow and crossed his arms behind his head, letting his heated gaze drift over her, touching her breasts, her belly, down to her toes and back up. He knew what it did to her and felt a small sense of triumph when she shivered under the caress. When his eyes met hers again, her face burned with a combination of need and something else entirely. "Just where am I going?"

"To see Colin."

The answer surprised him and he dropped his arms, forgetting his plan to bother her as much as she was disturbing him. If she meant for him to visit Colin in the Lowlands, then this was no quick journey she was sending him on. This was more like a month. "I had plans for us both to visit him in the spring."

Laurel clasped her hands in front of her. "I know, but we have not heard from Clyde in awhile, and after what happened to his friend, it would be good to know how he is faring before the long stretch of winter prevents communication with your brother."

Conor was concerned about his youngest brother as well. They had heard little about Clyde and how he was doing since news arrived of the appalling death of his best friend, Kam. And while Laurel's similar concern was no doubt partly why she wanted him to go south, it was not the reason behind her sudden desire to have him gone for a significant amount of time. Obviously, she wanted him out of the way, but why? So that he couldn't interfere? Or so that he would not gripe when she put whatever plan she had into action?

Laurel leisurely strolled to the bed. Hooking a finger on one shoulder of her chemise, she said, "And since you and Conan are both going to be gone for a while, I thought it might be a good idea to invite Craig to help out until you return."

Craig and Meriel. Conor sighed inwardly. He should have known that Laurel had not given up on bringing them together. And it appeared she had decided to escalate matters. Suddenly the idea of visiting Colin was looking like a reprieve.

Conor reached over and gave a gentle tug to the other side of the undergarment, just enough so that it slid down her frame to her waist and eventually the floor. "Good idea," he whispered hoarsely, "and it just so happens that I have another one."

Lured by his touch, Laurel joined Conor on the bed and was about to give in to her need for a kiss when it occurred to her that Conor had agreed to leave, and much too quickly. Such a request should have been rejected multiple times before he succumbed to her logical and cajoling arguments.

Placing a hand on his chest, she sat up and stared at him, the tiny muscles around her eyes rigid with suspicion. "Just why are you so willing to leave?"

Conor shrugged and reached out to brush his fingertips along her face with incredible gentleness. "Does it matter?"

Laurel closed her eyes, cursing her traitorous body and the way it dissolved under his touch. "It matters," she managed to get out.

Conor pushed her hair off her shoulders and let his hand wander behind her neck. He pulled her close, reveling in how she felt, all soft and vulnerable pressed up against him. "Just be glad I'm willing to be gone, unable to stop your meddling," he murmured before he kissed the spot below her ear, sending her pulse racing. "How long will you need to"—he paused as his lips traveled lower down her neck—"prove Craig and Meriel belong with each other or"—he moved lower—"accept that they do not?"

Laurel moaned. After ten years, she was still completely and utterly lost by the potent heat of his touch. Each kiss created a fire within her that burned only for him. In moments, she would lose all ability to think and speak. "I don't know," she answered, beginning to return each of his kisses with one of her own. "Ask Meriel. It is her plan. She thought it was the best way to convince Craig to come here."

He would be well along the way to the Lowlands before he recalled that bit of information. If Laurel was serious and this whole scheme was Meriel's, then Craig was in more trouble than Conor originally believed. Despite what he told Laurel, Conor did think his brother loved Laird Schellden's daughter. And if Meriel now had it in her mind to make Craig acknowledge it as well, Craig had little chance to avoid it.

The only good news was that Conor had escaped the mayhem that was going to accompany the days preceding and following such a revelation.

That, and Laurel had indeed been serious about not letting him sleep.

Craig stepped into his cottage, and for a brief moment the moonlight illuminated the interior before his left leg kicked the door closed with significantly more force than was needed. The thunderous sound matched his mood. And it was all Meriel Schellden's fault.

"Ciùrradair," he muttered to himself, knowing deep down that he was far more responsible for his current torment than Meriel, but she was not here to defend herself. For nearly three weeks Craig had called her names that if muttered by someone else would have caused him to flee for his life. But he being her best friend, and she his, had some privileges, including calling her all types of a stubborn fool.

Craig knew if he had not pricked her pride about being unable to stay away for even a fortnight, Meriel would have been home by now. They would have practically forgotten everything, and things would have returned to normal. With any other woman that would have been the outcome. But not Meriel. No one was more stubborn than she.

Most people believed her sister, Raelynd, to be the more inflexible of Rae Schellden's daughters, but *wrong* would not be a strong enough word to describe just how mistaken they were. Unlike Meriel, Raelynd considered most things—

including trivial ones—important; therefore, Meriel often acquiesced to her sister's desires. However, when it came to matters of personal meaning and consequence, Meriel's will of iron far surpassed that of anyone he knew. And that included himself.

Oh aye, he could be stubborn. He was a McTiernay, after all. They were known to be somewhat mulish about things, but all of his brothers would agree that they only acted obstinate when they had good reason or if they knew they were right. And in this particular case, Craig had no doubts about the legitimacy of his reaction to their kiss. So if Meriel wanted to continue punishing herself by staying away from her home, friends, and family, then he would not save her from such a self-inflicted wound until she asked. Unfortunately, with Meriel, just when the pain of loneliness would surpass her obstinacy was hard to determine.

For the first few days after her departure, Craig had actually welcomed her absence. Meriel could read him too easily and she would know exactly how much he was struggling with his emotions. It was a particular ability she had demonstrated from day one of their relationship. No one else could discern what he was feeling if he did not want them to—whether it was anger, lust, panic, or even *love*. He could still remember Meriel riding—or attempting to ride—next to him last year, inquiring just why everyone acted as if he wanted to be a laird when he truly had no desire for the responsibility.

For years, his brother Crevan had functioned as his best friend, but in truth they had both kept secrets from the other. Meriel was the only person Craig had ever been completely honest with, and that was because she could see the truth anyway. Lying was not an option around her. She had been able to see what no one else had and accepted him despite that knowledge.

Most women would think less of a man who had no

desire to become laird. They would think him afraid or maybe less than capable. Not Meriel. From the beginning of their friendship, she understood and accepted him and her ability to read his thoughts had only grown in accuracy. A trait until now he had thought rather advantageous.

It was nice to be able to look across the table or room and with a single look convey a stream of thoughts, knowing they would be accurately interpreted. Too many times they had "saved" each other from an uncomfortable situation, under the guise of a chance encounter. That was before *they* became the cause of each other's discomfort.

Craig untied his belt and swung it onto the table with the sword still attached, so it landed with a loud *thud*. It hit something and clattered to the floor. He stood there in the dark and fought the compulsion to see what it was he had knocked over. Damn woman. A year ago he would not have cared. But now she practically lived in his head. He could hear her light laughter, chiding him to see what the sword had hit, to ensure nothing important was broken or ruined.

He turned and grabbed the door handle, yanking it back open. He needed to start a fire anyway, he told himself, and bent down to grab one of the logs he kept outside. Grimacing, he noticed that the pile was once again low and he would need to replenish it soon—a particular chore he loathed. Snatching up the smallest log, he marched toward the gatehouse to light it using one of the sconces.

Craig could feel the anger in him rise, and tried to shake it. Of all his brothers, he was the least easily riled. He rarely struggled with his emotions but knew from experience that until he admitted them, at least to himself, he would never be able to suppress or eradicate them.

"Fine," he grumbled to himself. "I am . . ." he began, but before he admitted to being the fool that had caused every bad decision of the night, another excuse popped into his head. "I am . . . no . . . I was just not in the mood. Aye, that's right," he said more forcefully. "Sometimes a man doesn't want a woman—any woman—and that doesn't mean anything more than that."

Convinced he was right, Craig was already feeling better. He only wished the reaffirming advice he gave himself at night provided equal relief. It all came down to feelings. Did he have them for Meriel? Aye. Deep ones. Did they go beyond that of friendship? This confession was harder to make, but, aye, his feelings did go beyond those of a traditional friend. However, he and Meriel did not have a conventional friendship. Did that mean he was in love? That was one question he refused to answer, for it would not change anything. And to prove it, Craig had made sure that his routine had remained unchanged since her departure.

He trained first thing in the morning. This was followed by discussions with Rae and Crevan concerning the clan, army needs, or whatever needed their attention. The noon meal was usually a quick event coupled with some other meeting at either the castle or someone's home during one of his rides to visit outlying clansmen and their families. Dinner remained a relatively simple affair; he ate with friends, or at the Great Hall with his brother and his wife, and Rae. Only afterward, when everyone retired, did it become difficult. Too easily had he identified a reason why: he missed Meriel's company.

Until a year ago, he and his twin brother, Crevan, had discussed the day's events before going to sleep. Then, after Crevan and Raelynd married, Meriel slipped into that role, just as he had for her. Aye, he enjoyed having her as a *friend* and a confidante; but if someone else, like Hamish, had been there instead to fill the vacuum his brother's marriage had created, it would be Hamish he was missing and not Meriel. Which was another reason he felt positive that his feelings for Meriel had nothing to do with the type of love everyone persisted in believing was between them. And earlier that evening, Craig had decided to confirm his conclusions by seeking out the affections of another woman; for what could be more definitive evidence against love than a duplicitous heart?

One of his men had been asking him to join his family for dinner for several months. The man had never said outright what his true intentions were, but it was not a secret that he was newly married and that he wanted to introduce his younger sister, who was living with him, to any and all available men. Craig had no plans to help the man out with his living situation, but he understood the sister to be pretty and coquettish. So what could it hurt to give the newlyweds a few hours of privacy?

The girl was pretty enough. Her face was a collection of well-defined, reasonably attractive features. But sitting there, eating dinner, he decided her eyes were unusually large and too dark, and her head was overly small for her long, thin neck. She reminded him of a snapping turtle. He tried not to look at her too often, but it was impossible to escape her laughter. He had heard worse, but the timing of her high-pitched giggles made it obvious that nothing he said made any sense to her. She was lucky his brother Conan was not in the vicinity, for Craig doubted his younger brother would have been able to keep himself from verbally slaying her . . . only she would never have known it.

But the goal of the night was not to become smitten but to satisfy certain male urges that he had been repressing for three weeks. Aye, this sudden onslaught of desire he was experiencing started with Meriel but was not *because* of Meriel. It was because of a *kiss*. It could have been with anyone. With moving, setting up a home, and all of his new responsibilities, he had not had time to be with a woman for over a year. So, since it was a kiss that had started this mess, a kiss was going to help end it.

The second he and the girl were alone, she became the

aggressor, grabbing his neck and pulling his lips to hers. It took everything he had not to cringe and embarrass them both. So perhaps not just *anyone* could end these lustful thoughts of Meriel he had every night. Maybe he needed to replace those images with someone he already thought was attractive and knew from experience was knowledgeable in pleasuring a man.

Craig had been arriving at these conclusions while he made his way back home through the village, when he had run into Vera, a lively, voluptuous woman whom he had met on his first stay at the Schelldens' years ago and had visited whenever he returned. Vera had scolded him about living there for nearly a year and failing to seek out her company. She had begun to think it was true that he and Meriel Schellden were in love—that is, until she heard about the kiss.

Needing no more prompting, Craig had immediately swung Vera around to the nearest secluded spot and pulled her into his arms, determined to eliminate any doubt in her or his mind that he was definitely still available.

Her arms stole around his neck and the inside of her mouth was warm and welcoming. She trembled, leaned into him, and kissed him back with growing eagerness. Too much eagerness. Too late did he realize any one of a number of men would have satisfied her at that moment. The thought had repelled him. The fact that he had also been using her made no difference. He had quickly ended the encounter and, without even attempting to make a pitiful excuse, left.

How Meriel had convinced him to kiss her, he would never know, but it had been *her* idea and not his. Damn woman! Who knew a simple, ingenuous kiss would ruin everything? Kissing was enjoyable, mostly because it was *not* emotional. It allowed one to experience the moment and move on.

The idea that his attraction to women now resided with

only one—Meriel, the one woman he refused to have—angered him. Alarmed him. Terrified him. Before three weeks ago, he had never visualized being physical with Meriel, having intentionally compartmentalized their relationship in his mind. But now that he had, his thoughts constantly seemed to drift in that direction.

Returning from the gatehouse, Craig held the burning stick away from the cottage door as he opened it. He stepped inside and aimed the light to the floor, verifying that what he had knocked over was a mug and nothing more. He took a deep breath and whispered with soft intensity, "I was simply not in the mood for *anyone* tonight, and that most especially includes a *ceannlaidir*."

"I agree," came a deep, penetrating voice from the dark. "Don't know anyone who would be in the mood for a self-willed, headstrong woman . . . except for maybe a McTiernay."

Craig swung the temporary torch around to see the large figure in the corner, sitting in a chair with his feet propped up on the chair next to him. Craig had recognized the tone immediately, but it was still several seconds before his brain accepted what his eyes and ears were telling him. That his eldest brother, Conor, was sitting in his home, waiting for him in the dark, and listening to everything he said.

Narrowing his eyes, Craig marched back and yanked the chair right out from under Conor's feet. "You best be talking about yourself and Laurel."

"Now, who else would I be talking about?" Conor deflected as he let his legs fall to the floor only to cross them at the ankles.

Craig ignored his brother and started a small fire in the hearth, glad to have something to do. Instincts and Conor's expression were clear signs that his brother's unexpected visit had not been to bring Meriel home, nor was it to impart bad news, but rather to make Craig the pawn of some plot. Question was, whose?

"Well, out with it," Craig muttered with exasperation. "By the look on your face, I'm not going to like whatever it is that drove you to my door."

Conor stretched his arms and settled them behind his head. "Neither pleasure nor discontent. I have decided not to delay my visit to the Lowlands. With Conan away at some abbey, I've come to ask Rae if he can spare his commander so that you can help Laurel with clan matters in my stead."

Craig stoked the fire and then closed his eyes. The sudden decision and need for Conor to leave his home was not just unexpected, but unorthodox this close to winter. Only a long trip would trigger a need for one of the brothers to go and stay at McTiernay Castle. That Conor had chosen *him*, at the same time Meriel was there visiting, was too much of a coincidence. "I thought you were going to wait to visit Colin in the spring—when it made more sense."

Conor ignored the barb. Craig was in an unusually foul mood, and since the man would have troubles soon enough, Conor felt no brotherly compulsion to add to them. "I was, but we have not heard about Clyde for a while now, and there is enough time for a short visit if I leave now."

Craig studied his brother. Conor's face was grim, and the lines etched along his forehead were slightly deeper. The fierce Highland laird, who used to search for excuses to be away from McTiernay Castle, now rarely ever wanted to leave his family, and he especially did not enjoy leaving his wife. "You've changed, Conor," Craig said with sad resignation.

Conor did not even try to deny the direction and accusations of Craig's thoughts. "You will too someday . . . if you are lucky."

Craig issued a small smirk. "I think I am just fine as I am."

"Makes no difference to me," Conor countered with a

small shrug of his shoulders. "But somehow it does have the women stirred up."

So it was Laurel who sent you here, Craig said to himself. She just could not accept him as a bachelor and was determined to have him be in love. *And you, older brother, are probably all too happy to avoid whatever she is planning.* And any other time, Craig would have found himself trying to do the same, rather than eagerly throwing himself into the path of danger. But this opportunity was exactly what he needed.

A break from his daily routine. A safe haven to prove he could be in Meriel's company just as before. Evidence that he was no more attracted to her than any other beautiful woman. But most of all, in the end, he would be able to *bring Meriel home*. "I take it you've spoken with Rae?"

"Aye, I have, and Rae has no qualms with you being gone for a few weeks to help ensure the safety and peace of our clan. Although I'm thinking that his daughter staying at McTiernay Castle had a little bit to do with his willingness to give you up. I do believe the man intends for you to bring his daughter home."

"When are you leaving?"

"At daybreak, which is why I saw Rae first before coming here. I was not sure where you were sleeping at night these days. Of course, that was before I realized you were seeking out the company of *ceannlaidirs*."

Craig let his brother have his little laugh. Conor might be leaving in the morning, but Craig had no intention of immediately following suit. The McTiernay clan could wait another day or two before he got there. And so could Laurel's matchmaking schemes.

He only hoped his sister-in-law was not planning to try to make him jealous. The idea of Meriel in love with another man . . . well, it just was not possible. If she was going to be with anyone, it would be him.

* * *

Craig heaved a satisfied sigh and rubbed his full stomach. Tonight's dinner had been exceptionally good and he had eaten too much. "Nothing beats Fiona's cooking."

Meriel nodded in agreement. "Just be glad you never have to deal with her. This good food comes at a serious price," she stated with a twinkle in her eye. Meriel would never forget the look in the gruff woman's dark eyes that afternoon when she showed her the gown she had made for Fiona's daughter's wedding. Fiona would deny it with her last breath, but Meriel knew she saw a tear fall in appreciation.

"I'm glad we finally had a chance to all eat together," Laurel said with a sigh as she rose from her chair. "But, I think it best if I go and say good night to my children. All of whom appeared to have an abundant amount of energy this evening."

Meriel stood up and asked, "Would you like some help?"

Laurel waved her hand dismissively. "No, no. In truth, I like to take advantage of nights like this when Conor is away. They gravitate to him because they can jump all over him and like to believe they can wrestle him down. But I am in the mood for a good tickle fight, and they need to be reminded that I am just as worthy an opponent as their father."

The remaining people in the small group rose in respect and lethargically began to follow her out of the Great Hall. Craig coughed into his hand and caught Meriel's attention. "Where are you going?" he asked, attempting to sound only mildly interested in the answer.

Flashing him a brilliant smile, Meriel put her arm in his and pointed him toward the eastern wall where several comfortable chairs were set in a semicircle around the hall's main canopied fireplace. "Right there and no farther. I knew I should not have had that last helping of mutton," she said, and let her head fall against his shoulder as they made their way across the room.

"I know!" Craig choked, hoping she did not hear the near crack in his voice. Walking arm in arm from the dinner table was far from unusual, and while he could recall her resting her head against him as she was doing now, he did not remember it disturbing him so much. But since his arrival, every time they touched he felt his pulse race. Then his skin would spark to life, and that in turn would ignite other portions of his body, making it very hard to think, let alone maneuver. But it was not the physical discomfort that truly unsettled him. It was the fact that *he alone* seemed to be bothered by their proximity. How could a few weeks apart do for her what it had not done in the least for him? It was difficult to believe. He was positive that Meriel's sudden departure from Caireoch had been because she had needed physical distance from him. Now, she treated him as if he were . . . a brother. *Well, if you can disregard the sparks I know are between us, then so can I,* he told himself.

Moving to sit in the chair next to her, he said cheerfully, "I also ate too much, but I couldn't stop myself. I think I ate that whole loaf of bread."

"*And* all the honey," Meriel chided, closing her eyes as she leaned back into the comfortable chair, listening to the bustle as servants cleaned up the dinner and disassembled the trestle tables. Only the high table at the far end of the room would remain when they were done. "So, tell me all that is going on at home. It has been awhile since we have had a chance to talk."

Awhile? Craig thought. More like forever. And the last five days had been the worst of them all. Not wanting Laurel to think that he was in any way eager to see Meriel and add fuel to her schemes to get them together, he had delayed his departure for McTiernay Castle by two days. And then after he had arrived, the warm welcome he fully expected to receive from Meriel was nonexistent. He had practically been accosted by the steward with myriad issues to be addressed and had to eat with the soldiers in the Lower Hall as everyone else already had plans with friends.

Craig suspected Meriel's absence was part of Laurel's scheme to bring them together, but that did not explain the next two days. Meals were back to being served in the Great Hall with the normal family gathering—usually Laurel, her children, and the families of one or two of her closest friends. But no Meriel. Only glimpses of her throughout the day. Not enough to convince him that she missed him as he did her, but too much to believe she might be avoiding him.

"It's been a month," he grumbled.

"That long?" Meriel sighed. "I guess you are right, but it doesn't seem like it. I have been so busy."

"I know!" Craig groused. "I'm glad to have finally made it to your select list of people to spend time with."

Meriel opened one eye and shot him a playful look. "Aye. You almost didn't as I am quite tired tonight, but Laurel said you were looking a little lost and might need some company."

Rather than feeling the urge to retaliate, Craig felt an overwhelming sense of peace invade his body. He knew she was just teasing. Whenever he tried to assume the martyr role, instead of contradicting him Meriel would pretend to agree and sometimes, like tonight, even add to his reasons for self-pity.

He stretched out his legs and interlaced his fingers behind his head, a large grin overtaking his expression. "She did, huh? And here I thought she was scheming to keep us apart in an effort to get us together."

A shadow of disbelief crossed Meriel's face before she rolled her eyes to indicate exactly how ludicrous she thought he sounded. "You are impossible. I can pretty much promise you that I have met no one here who has any interest in us as a couple and that *includes* Lady McTiernay."

He heard her mumble *"choob"* under her breath at the very end of her denial, and with a shrug of his shoulders, he settled more comfortably in his chair. He smiled inwardly. Meriel had called him an idiot. The last few days may have caused him to doubt it would be possible, but life was definitely getting back to normal. The only thing that would ease his mind more was if they were home at Caireoch Castle. Still, this was the most serene moment he had felt since Marymass. "Well, this *choob* made several brilliant decisions today." And then, as if the last month had never happened, he began to tell her of what had happened over the past few days, including the variety of questions and challenges Fallon kept bringing him.

"You seem much more comfortable with the role of temporary laird. Your voice is surprisingly relaxed. The thought of standing in for your brother used to cause you serious tension."

"You're right," he acknowledged, loving the ability to simply talk with Meriel and hear her respond. She had no idea how sensuous her voice sounded. "Laurel handles most of the basic needs of the clansmen. I just have to support Finn as the commander of the guard and help him oversee the soldiers."

"And deal with Fallon."

"Aye, the man is practically attached to my side. But it doesn't bother me now that being a chieftain is no longer my fate. Instead of thinking I'm a burden, I actually feel like I am helping my brother and my clan."

Meriel nodded her head, truly comprehending what he meant. The couple of times her sister had traveled with her husband to visit their northern clansmen, she had been left in charge of running Caireoch Castle. After Laurel's painful tutelage last year, Meriel could manage the basic responsibilities without too much anxiety, but mostly that was because she no longer feared the role would someday become hers.

"I have been doing all the talking," Craig said, fighting a yawn. "It's your turn. Tell me what you have been doing. Just where have you been the past few nights?" he asked. "I've only seen you a few times since I got here and that was briefly in passing."

"I am sorry if you felt slighted. I knew Fallon had several people he wanted you to meet with and thought you would be tired. We had thought you were to get here a couple of days earlier than you did, so I moved back my dinner plans with Maegan and her grandmother, which ended up being on that first night you arrived."

"And last night?" Craig swallowed a groan when the pathetic and needy question slipped out. But if Meriel caught any of his unease about the delay in his being able to spend time with her, she did not act like it.

"Oh, I had promised a picnic dinner by the loch with the children, and once you make such a promise to them, there is no getting out of it, short of stormy weather."

Craig remembered the last time Meriel was out at the loch with Brenna. She could have been killed. The wildcat had chased Raelynd, but Meriel had been just as much in danger of being mauled. The cat could have charged her and Brenna, and he had spared no words that night voicing his displeasure. The thought of Meriel out there again, and at night, sent a shiver up his spine.

"I hope someone was with you," he murmured, hoping not to give his thoughts away by saying too much.

"Laurel came, of course. And Hamish," she added softly, intertwining her fingers.

Hamish. Craig had been waiting all evening for the name to be said. The majority of times he had come across Meriel before this evening, she had been talking with Hamish in the courtyard. Which was a surprise considering that the man thought her to be a rather uninteresting person. Consequently, the third time he saw them together, Craig decided Hamish was being used by Laurel as a ploy. It would be very much like her to use his friend to try to make him jealous, in an effort to compel him to admit his feelings for Meriel. Now, he was not so sure.

Craig had waited throughout the entire dinner for Laurel to drop juicy tidbits about how close Meriel and Hamish had become, all in an effort to spark his anxiety, but not a word was said. In fact, Laurel was acting suspiciously indifferent to Meriel, Hamish, and even himself. It was almost too *normal*, if that was possible. Nothing his sister-in-law had done was out of character nor any different from what she would do or say when Conor was around. But Laurel acting normal made him highly suspicious. Craig began to wonder if his brother had a bet with his meddlesome wife on whether or not she could prevent herself from interfering in his life.

"Craig," Meriel began. Her voice had gone low, reflective, and Craig wondered at the reason. He hoped she would continue to unburden her thoughts to him, but instead she changed the subject. "Do you remember when I left home, and you said I would have nothing to do?"

"Aye."

"Honestly, I thought the same thing. Last year there was so little to do, I actually almost reconsidered coming here. I'm so glad I didn't. I have not been this happy in a long time. It is like you said, I feel like I am contributing here."

"By making clothes?" Craig asked incredulously.

"Do not sound so amazed. It's insulting," she chided him. "Take Fiona, for example."

"Fiona? The last time you and she were in the same room, that vicious woman was chasing you out of it, warning you of impending death should you decide to enter her kitchens again."

Meriel laughed at the memory. "She was really mad that day, wasn't she? But I discovered her soft spot."

"Ha! There is no way to get that venomous woman to retract her fangs."

Meriel issued him a disapproving look and said, "*You* may have to continue avoiding being bitten. I, on the other hand, made a gorgeous gown for her daughter when she gets married this spring."

"Fiona's daughter is getting married?" Craig asked. He vaguely remembered the girl. She had the same big-boned frame and dark eyes as her mother, but what he remembered most was that she was painfully shy.

"Aye, Fiona rarely talks about her and has made sure that she never comes near the kitchens. I don't think she wants a cook's life for her daughter. But she is a pretty thing and has fallen in love with a successful farmer." Meriel waved her finger disapprovingly at Craig. "I saw that look. She *is* pretty and will be the envy of everyone next spring in the gown that I made."

"If that is true, then I am no longer surprised Fiona is being so nice to you," Craig scoffed.

Meriel suspected he was right. "I would call it more of a truce than a friendship." She still could not venture into the kitchens without getting a scolding, but Meriel sensed that the gown meant more to the old woman than she could express. From what Meriel understood, the man Fiona's daughter was marrying was a rather prominent farmer, and Fiona did not want anyone to think her daughter was not his equal because her mother was a castle servant—though a highly thought-of castle servant. The old woman was difficult but not mean. Merely crusty around the edges.

"I guess you have been busy," Craig mumbled. He was glad Meriel was not miserable, but it sounded as if she wanted to stay. He had wanted her home. More importantly, he needed her to *want* to be home. "You know, there is no reason you could not make garments for the women at Caireoch. I am sure your father would support such an idea."

"True, and I probably will, but I still have things to do here."

"Such as?"

She hesitated. "I made some promises to myself that I need to take care of before I leave."

Once again her voice held a wistful quality that seized Craig's heart. "Such as?" he asked, nervous to hear her answer.

Meriel tucked her feet underneath her and turned to look at him with her elbows resting on one arm of the chair. "I want to go home. I love this place, but I miss my things and my sister. Yet I cannot return to the way things were."

Craig inhaled and held it in. Here it was. An ultimatum. He had thought Meriel and he were of the same mind, but maybe not. Maybe Laurel had mistakenly convinced her that their relationship could not continue as it was before. "I understand," he lied.

Meriel's lips parted in wonder but then curved into an easy smile. "It's so good to be able to talk to you again. There are things that I can tell you that I am not sure anyone else would understand. I hope we will always remain friends."

Craig let go the breath he had been holding. Whatever was behind her hesitation, he was not the target of some devious plan to entice him into throwing off his bachelor ways. "So what kinds of things need to change?"

Meriel bit her bottom lip and returned her gaze to the fire. "I am not sure. I just cannot go back to my old routine. I need it to change. For example, I'm socializing here more and I like it. With Rowena gone and Raelynd married, you have been my primary friend, and that is not fair to either one of us."

Craig frowned. Meriel and Rowena had been close, acting more like sisters than friends. When Rowena married Meriel's cousin, it had brought both happiness and sorrow, for it meant moving south and away from the Highlands.

"I cannot rely on you for everything," Meriel continued, "and I have discovered that I like making new friends and doing things with them."

Craig knew Meriel was telling him the truth, but he also had the feeling she was holding something back. What she was keeping from him did not bother him nearly as much as the fact that Meriel now *wanted* to keep a secret from him. "Something is bothering you," he finally stated, hoping to prompt her into full disclosure.

Meriel closed her eyes and gave a small shake of her head. "It's nothing. I'm just tired." Then, with a deep sigh, she got to her feet, tilted her head, and bestowed upon him a radiant smile.

He reached out to grasp her fingers. Realizing only at the last moment his unconscious desire to touch her, he swerved his hand upward to rake his fingers in his hair. Touching her had felt like a natural thing to do, but he could not recall if physical touch truly was a part of their good-night ritual.

Then before he could come to any conclusion, he was startled as Meriel ran her fingers lightly up his arm. He was debating whether it was a sign of affection when her hand stopped and firmly squeezed his shoulder. "I am going to retire to my room, but can we do this tomorrow night? I miss our conversations," she said, giving his shoulder one last unconscious pat.

Craig returned the smile and made himself nod, watching her as she gracefully left the room. She did not turn around once. *Definitely not a caress*, he told himself, trying not to feel disappointed. He should have been relieved that their nightly talks were not one of the things she wanted to change in her routine. And yet, her uncharacteristic bouts of quiet made him uneasy.

Seeing conspiracies everywhere was something his younger brother Conan did—not him. The man was too smart and thought entirely too much. Aye, when it came to Laurel, there usually was a scheme, and Craig had already confronted his sister-in-law about the sudden need for his help. But Laurel had promised that while she supported Conor's idea of leaving immediately to seek news about their younger brother, it had *not* been her idea. And he believed her. Yet, he could not shake the feeling that he was being manipulated in some way.

Laurel may not have been the instigator of his arrival, but that did not mean she was not taking advantage of it. Not once in the past four days had she referred—directly or indirectly—to the kiss he had given Meriel. That alone practically proved his sister-in-law was scheming. There was no way she would be able to say *nothing*.

Plus *everything* about tonight's dinner had been within expectations. Meriel, after nearly a month of not seeing him, was friendly and platonic, just the way she had been before the night of Marymass. This was explainable in that both of them were trying to be as normal as possible. Then afterward, when they were finally alone, they had been able to establish an easy rapport without too much effort— though he did not believe it to be completely natural . . . which was bothersome. Meriel was the master at being able to control which emotions she displayed. So with both of them trying so hard to be "normal," her bouts of introspection were baffling. The only explanation he could come up with was that they were not accidental, but intentional. Was Meriel involved in Laurel's plot? It would be most unlike her, but not beyond the realm of possibility.

Craig rubbed his face vigorously, chastising himself for

overthinking. With a deep sigh, he stood up and walked over behind the high table to look out one of the large arched windows into the well-lit courtyard. The corners of his mouth lifted but did not quite form a smile. Laurel was out there with Hamish, and not one of her children was in sight. She was enthusiastically waving at Meriel to join them. Immediately the three of them engaged in an animated conversation.

He *knew* it. Oh, they were clever in their efforts at subtlety. But did Laurel and Meriel really think that he would be jealous of *Hamish*? The man had never exhibited any constancy of affection to any woman. Rule one of any strategy: One must be able to influence if not control all the key players to achieve success.

The group was finally dispersing when Craig saw Hamish reach out, grab Meriel's hand, and hold it for a moment before letting her go. The act was friendly, and knowing Hamish, it meant nothing other than a habitual, flirtatious way to say good night. But it irked Craig to know that he had had the same instinct *and* had restrained himself. Meriel was *his* best friend. If anyone was going to shake her hand good night, it was going to be him.

Craig needed to warn her again about Hamish's less savory habits and was about to go and confront her when he caught her expression. Far from jubilant, he could see she looked like she was about to break into tears. He rubbed his eyes, wondering what could have been said to upset her. When he glanced back up, Laurel and Meriel were no longer in sight and Wyenda was nestled at Hamish's side as the two walked toward the gatehouse. The woman must have been in the shadows or had just arrived, for she had not been visible before.

Craig stared at the now empty courtyard. *What was that all about?* he wondered. *What was Hamish doing with*

Wyenda? He had warned Hamish about that girl. *And just who said what to cause Meriel to cry?*

Craig frowned. He had nothing but questions. And too many of them lacked answers.

Craig stepped out of the Lower Hall and moved out of the way to let Fallon and two feuding farmers exit. Their "discussion" had been about whose turn it was to help the other with their plowing, and it had taken far longer to resolve than it should have. As a result, Craig had missed the midday meal and was far from happy about it. He was about to go and brave the wrath of Fiona when he spied Meriel and Hamish exiting the kitchens.

Meriel's back was to him, but Craig could easily discern his friend's expression. It held genuine affection, but nothing beyond amity.

For the past four days, Craig had covertly watched Meriel and those who interacted with her, searching for anything to reveal the essence of a scheme. He had made sure Hamish attended dinner with them the past three nights, but not once did Meriel and he exchange a word or gesture to indicate anything more than friendship. They spoke and laughed with each other, but no more than they did with the others in attendance. If Laurel was attempting to make him jealous, neither Hamish nor Meriel was playing their part very well. Maybe they had realized Laurel's little gambit would never work.

Each night after dinner, Hamish would leave and Meriel stayed to chat with Craig by the hearth. They would discuss their day, funny events they had seen or heard, and anything that interested them or they thought might entertain the other. On the surface, their relationship was normal. Old habits and activities were once again being enjoyed. Neither felt the need to act as if they had to prove their friendship was more than it was, and both had intuitively avoided any unwanted stress by not bringing up the past. And yet, Craig knew things between them were far from perfect.

Meriel was keeping a secret. All too often her mind wandered to whatever it was, leaving him alone even though she was sitting right next to him. But that was not the worst of it.

The images of Meriel continued to haunt his dreams, robbing him of much-needed sleep. Previously, his dreams of her had always begun the same. Gone was the pressure of marriage. Thoughts of a shackled future were nonexistent. There was only Meriel, and she was finally in his arms. He would be balanced above her on his elbows, barely in control of his breathing, whispering intimate endearments into her ear. How soft and sweet she felt, how much he wished to satisfy her . . . all the little words he longed to say. He would take her little by little, repeating the entire erotic rhythm over and over until his heart and mind were awash with pleasure.

He had almost looked forward to lying down to sleep. But no more. For the past several nights, those fantasies had abandoned him and had been replaced with what felt more like nightmares.

Meriel hovered at the edge of his dreams like a vision of white in a dark, dangerous, all-too-intense, mist-filled scene—one in which they were far from alone. She would stand between him and another faceless figure. Smiling, she lit up all that was around her, but it was not quite bright enough to let him see who was competing for her affections. Then she chose, and began to run away. He always woke before he could see who was running with her—him or someone else.

Craig had never been one to let fate dictate his life, and he was not about to let it shape his relationship with Meriel. He had thought to wait until she was ready to bring him into her confidence, but he was beginning to wonder if she ever would. Or worse, when she did decide that she needed someone to talk to, she would seek out Hamish's counsel and not his. Craig refused to let that happen. *He* was her confidant and she was his.

If Meriel had forgotten that fact, then during their evening chat he would remind her and end these insane nightmares.

Tonight, she would choose him.

Craig watched from the high table as Meriel joined the small group preparing to leave the Great Hall. His blue eyes warmed as soon as she stopped at the hearth chairs. She hugged Aileen and Laurel and actually blushed when Hamish, in a display of bravado, bowed and kissed her hand good-bye.

He could not blame his friend for flirting with Meriel. She was looking exceptionally beautiful. Her skin was pale and impossibly smooth against her dark green bliaut. The low cowl neckline showed off her slender form, and the soft, curling lock of tawny hair that fell down her back gave her an alluring feminine quality. Craig felt a surge of pride that in a few minutes he would be the one left alone in her company. She could have continued on with any of them, but it was his company she desired.

As soon as everyone left, he sauntered over and watched with amusement as Meriel went through her nightly ritual of slipping off her shoes and adjusting her gown so that she could comfortably tuck her feet underneath her when she sat down. He was searching for a way to convince her to open up to him, when Meriel spoke first.

"Craig, I was hoping you could help me with something."

His eyes widened in surprise and then realized she was

waiting for him to speak. "I was wondering when you were going to ask." If *you were going to ask*, he added wryly to himself.

Meriel was a bundle of nerves. She bit her bottom lip and prayed that Craig thought her anxiety was caused by what she was about to ask. In truth, the next few minutes were going to affect the rest of her life. This conversation was going to dictate her future, and she was having it with the one person who could read her the best. "I *was* going to ask, a few times, but I guess I was worried how you would react." She paused. "Or that you would not take me seriously."

Craig felt his brow furrow at the accusation. "Why wouldn't I?"

"Because this is something that you . . . that I . . . that we, well, we just have never discussed."

Craig froze for the space of a heartbeat and suddenly wished for Fallon to burst into the hall with some emergency that demanded his attention. "And which topic would that be?" he asked, his voice raspy with both question and warning. The only subject he could recall their ever avoiding was that of their kiss, and he had planned to continue dodging it all the way to his grave. But it was clear that Meriel did not share his opinion.

"Love," she said simply.

Craig felt his breath catch in his throat as he fully comprehended the single word she had just said. He stood up, walked over and grabbed a pitcher of ale and filled a mug, fighting to calm his thoughts. He had considered the possibility that she might eventually push them into talking about their kiss and perhaps even the passion it had ignited between them, but *love*? He had no idea where to even begin such a discussion, let alone how to bring it to a quick and definitive end.

"Or at least what I think might be love," Meriel continued,

pretending to be unaware of the tension radiating from Craig as he sat back down. She watched him covertly through her lashes, waiting until he began to swallow his drink before continuing. "I know you have never been in love—at least you've never mentioned feeling strongly for anyone. Maybe I'm wrong. Have you ever fantasized about someone?"

Craig sputtered, nearly choking on his drink. "I'm a man, Meriel," he managed to get out, hoping that was answer enough.

Meriel rolled her eyes. "Not like that. I mean, has anyone ever broken your heart?"

Craig felt increasingly uneasy. "Uh, no."

Meriel bit her bottom lip hard to keep from smiling and forced herself to stare at her fingers, intertwined in her lap. If she looked at him directly, she would give everything away. But she was going to have to, and soon. Otherwise he would never believe her . . . never help her. "I really had hoped to deal with this all on my own, but I realized this afternoon that I am only fooling myself, and if I am to have any chance at all, I am going to need some assistance."

Craig reached up and roughly raked his scalp with his fingers, hoping that the rush of blood would help stem the headache he could feel coming. "I don't think I understand."

Meriel stood up and began to pace in front of the large hearth. "I cannot believe I am so nervous."

Craig leaned forward so that his elbows rested on his knees, rolling the mug back and forth between his hands. She was so breathtaking, he wondered for a moment if it really would be all that bad for her to be in love with him. "Meriel, you and I have never kept secrets from each other. At least that is the way I want it to be. I know I don't have any from you."

"And I have never kept any from you until now, but it occurred to me today that I am being silly. You are my friend, and of all the people here, I should be able to go to you for advice."

"I would like to think so," Craig affirmed cautiously. Suddenly, the anxiety he had been feeling about their conversation shifted, for it was not going in the direction he had originally believed.

Meriel threw her hands up in the air in resignation. "I think I have done the one thing I never thought I would do—could do. I've fallen in love! Or at the very least, I'm falling in love with him—and fast."

Craig was silent for a moment, then his eyes narrowed. It was clear she was not talking about being in love with *him*. There was only one other male he had seen her spend any amount of time with, and Craig refused to believe Meriel was so foolish. "Are you sure it's love?" he posed. "Maybe it is just the excitement of being somewhere new . . ."

Meriel shook her head and waved her hand, cutting him off. Sitting back down, she leaned toward him and said, "I told myself the same thing at first, but I feel so happy, so *alive* when I am around him." She pushed her hair back behind her shoulders and slumped against the back of the chair, twiddling her fingers. "I think it was that darn kiss between you and me that started this whole thing."

Craig could hardly breathe, his lungs were squeezed so tight. He had wanted to know what was bothering Meriel, and now that he knew, it rattled his core—more than he cared to admit. His mind refused to register the significance of her words. All this time he had thought their kiss to be the predominant thing on her mind, like it had been on his. To discover otherwise was more than a little unnerving. To learn she believed it had sparked in her feelings for *someone else* turned him cold.

He told himself he should be glad. He did not want love to confuse their relationship. Loving Meriel meant marriage and all the emotional ties and responsibilities that came with it. His brothers might be happy to compromise practically everything in their lives, but he liked being the sole ruler of his domain and had no intention of releasing his reins to anyone. Even to a person he *loved*.

"That night something woke up in me I never even realized was there," she continued. "I mean, you have to agree that the kiss you and I shared *was* incredible. I had not experienced that level of passion or desire with anyone before, and I'll admit that it confused me for a while. I even thought Raelynd had been right. That I was in love with you—madly and completely. So much so that I ran away, hoping you would feel the same way and come after me. But you knew that. You practically told me that the morning I left. Remember?"

"I remember," Craig replied, his mind spinning.

"But after I arrived here, I realized you were absolutely correct. What I had been feeling wasn't love, but the *desire* to be in love—to share *real* passion with someone."

"It seemed pretty real to you at the time. . . ." Craig challenged, unable to stop himself. True passion *had* been generated between them. Just because he had refused to be ruled by it did not negate its existence.

"Aye, but that was because it was so unexpected. If we kissed again, we would only be disappointed when the thrill we were anticipating never came," Meriel said matter-of-factly. "Like you said, no one wants to kiss a friend, especially that way."

Craig scrunched down farther in his seat. That was *not* what he said. Fact was, he didn't have any other female friends, and he was pretty sure that if he decided to kiss Meriel again, it would be far from a disappointment. And despite her claims otherwise, deep down he believed she felt the same way. It was just her way of coping with the fact that he refused to risk their friendship for a fleeting emotion known as lust.

Meriel saw every small flick of his cheek muscles but did her best to pretend otherwise. The man was struggling with his thoughts and beliefs, which was encouraging. If Craig were anyone else, he would be ripe for all types of persuasion, but not him. She had to come to her own conclusions and so would he. "And while I truly am glad to know we will always be friends," she said, resuming where she left off, "I still want something more. There are so few men I am physically attracted to, and whenever I do find one, it turns out we are not compatible enough to even have a simple conversation. So when I realized that I not only enjoy this person's company, but seek it out, *and* that I desire him as well, it . . . well . . . scared me."

"I'll bet it did," Craig said softly, unable to hide the cool tone in his voice. "So just who have you met that you are so compatible with and attracted to?" he asked, already suspecting he knew the answer.

"Who else?" Meriel asked with a shrug of her shoulders. "Hamish."

"*Hamish?*" Craig repeated, not attempting to disguise his disbelief. He thought he was ready for his friend's name to roll off her lips, but upon hearing it, his whole demeanor grew in severity. Hamish was a great Highlander, solid soldier, and an excellent friend, but suitor and, God forbid, *husband*? No. The man was incapable of being faithful. Besides, Meriel was just not his type. The women Hamish sought were brazen and open with their advances. The sassier the better. If Meriel really did care about Hamish, she was going to get hurt.

"Aye, Hamish!" Meriel said defensively. "He is . . . well, romantic. *And* good-looking. But he's also so much more. He's understanding, smart, funny . . . and, well, you know him."

Not like that, I don't. "He loves Wyenda."

Meriel's jaw clenched. "No, he does not. What he feels

for that woman is physical attraction, not love. Besides, Wyenda doesn't appreciate Hamish like she should. She has no idea how special he is."

"And you do."

"Every time we talk, I learn more and more just how wonderful a man he is. Or at least we did until *you* came and ruined everything. He used to seek me out to ensure that I was fine, but that ended the day you arrived. I have tried to think of ways to spend more time with him, but except for dinner, he is never here. That is why I need your help."

Craig exhaled, feeling the breath from his lungs burn his throat. He raked his fingers through his hair again, before turning to look at her. "The man is a rake, Meriel!"

Meriel jumped to her feet. "He is not! At least not any more than you are."

A year ago she might have been right, but Craig had practically been living the life of a monk since he had met her. "I'm a reformed rake," he argued. "Hamish, on the other hand, well, I don't think he could ever change his ways."

Meriel glared at him for several seconds, her cold gaze drilling right through him. "You are wrong," she said simply. "He is very different from what people think. He likes to flirt, so everyone—including his *friends*—believes him to be a womanizer. But I can see the person he really is—a kind, sincere, accepting, and surprisingly witty man."

It took everything Craig had not to flinch at her every word. She was talking about *Hamish*. Craig took a deep mental breath and forced calm into his thoughts. Meriel had known Hamish, what, a few weeks? He had known the man for many years. They had spent days and nights together, battled at each other's side, and once competed for the affections of the same woman. Meriel had no idea the person Hamish really was—especially his faults, of which he had many. Once Meriel witnessed even a hand-ful of them, this nonsense about her loving him would come to a quick end.

Forcing his body to appear relaxed, Craig stretched out on the chair again and laced his fingers on his chest. "So what is the problem? From what I have seen, he likes and enjoys your company as well."

Meriel fell back into the chair and threw her head in her hands, biting the inside of her cheek hard. "*That* is the problem. Am I doomed to be only friends with every man I actually enjoy spending time with? Why doesn't he find me attractive?" She looked up and shot him a penetrating stare. Her eyes were welling with tears. "What's wrong with me?"

Craig swallowed, searching for a way to answer, glad when she broke her teary gaze and returned to burying her face in her hands. He was not about to explain how he thought she was more than just attractive. She was mouth-droppingly beautiful. And if Hamish was not picking up on her interest, he was either a fool or his friend was really and truly caught in Wyenda's nasty web.

Clearing his throat, Craig said, "Nothing is wrong with you. It's just that right now Hamish has eyes for someone else."

"I know he likes Wyenda and believes that she is misunderstood, but I met her and she is *awful*," Meriel said through her fingers, muffling the sound.

"I know that," Craig groused. "I've even warned him about her, but believe me when I say Wyenda is something each man has to figure out for himself."

Meriel was thankful her face was still in her hands. She had been playing her role perfectly until a few minutes ago. There was a fine line between emotional and melodramatic, and she feared she might have gone past it. But with Craig's last comment, the distress she had been feigning now felt quite real. *Craig had once gone after Wyenda?* Meriel knew she should not be surprised after seeing firsthand the woman's stunning beauty, but to know that Craig had once been interested in the vile woman was more than a little annoying.

Meriel refocused her thoughts, reminding herself that her future was at stake and that Craig was significantly more wary of being manipulated than most. Any second, he would sense the trap she was laying and escape before she had a chance to spring it.

She took a deep breath and sat back up, hoping her expression reflected sincere concern—for she really did worry about Hamish and his affections for the *àpas*. "I thought he would have realized her insincerity by now. I have even imagined myself helping him through the recovery," she added, digging her fingernails into her palms, praying the pain would mask the lie. "Hoping that maybe if he leaned on me, Hamish would see me as more than just a 'nice, sweet' girl."

Craig choked. Meriel *nice*? *Sweet*? She was both, but the way she phrased it made her sound insipid and boring—both of which she was decidedly not. And more importantly, he knew that Meriel did not think of herself that way either. His suspicious nature once again came to life. "So since Hamish is still pining for Wyenda, I take it your plan to 'help him pick up the pieces of his heart' is not working."

"Not at all. The man is not ready to give up on her, and I fear that before he does, Papa will have demanded my return home. So I am coming to you for help."

"Help?" Craig squeaked unintentionally. "How do you expect me to help? This," he swirled his finger at her, "is Laurel's area of expertise. I hate the concept of matchmaking."

"I could ask her, but after what you and I went through this past year, I am not looking to trick Hamish into admitting something he does not feel."

"And you think Laurel would do that?"

Meriel scrunched her nose and then shook her head.

"Not intentionally, but look what happened with us. Every time someone tried to 'prove' we had feelings for each other, it only made us more resolute to stay just friends."

Craig scowled. Meriel made it sound like the reason they were friends was because of pride. Once again, the notion that she was not being fully honest with him came to mind. Every instinct he had told him that the conversation they were having had varying layers of truth. Could he have been right all along? Was this a ruse to make him jealous?

"Hamish and I initially spent quite a bit of time together," Meriel continued. "I think he thought he was protecting me in your stead. Our friendship started to grow and he was just starting to take notice of me when you arrived."

"So your lack of success with Hamish is *my* fault?" Craig barked.

Meriel twitched her lips and frowned. "I never said that."

Craig noticed how she did not refute his accusation either. "Then exactly what are you saying?"

"I only want a chance for Hamish to get to know me! Unfortunately, *with you here*, he no longer has a reason to spend time with me."

Craig sat up straight in his chair, his blue eyes radiating disbelief. "Let me make sure I understand what you are asking. *You*, want *me,* to help *you*, catch Hamish."

She nodded.

Craig felt as if he had been struck by lightning. For a few seconds he was too stunned to do anything more than stare at her as thoughts ricocheted through his stunned brain. Then almost at once they stilled.

Craig almost sighed in satisfaction and quickly suppressed the smile invading his expression. It did not matter if this was a ploy to make him jealous or an earnest effort to seek the affections of his friend. Either way, helping her worked to his advantage.

If Meriel really did like Hamish, she would get hurt

and return home to Caireoch and her life, and things would finally get back to normal. There, he could ensure she avoided ever getting emotionally mixed up with the wrong man again. And if he was right and this was nothing but a very clever ploy, then Meriel was about to learn a well-deserved lesson.

If Meriel wants my help, then she shall have it. It was time she realized why McTiernays were known as expert strategists. Rule one of any strategy may be to know all the players, but rule two was just as important—never tip your hand. "I cannot imagine anything more foolish than a man helping a woman catch the heart of another man."

"Then I will ask Laurel," Meriel replied through tight lips.

"Laurel?" Craig yelped, sitting upright. He had forgotten about his sister-in-law. Getting her involved would be a disaster. If asked, Laurel would help even if she had promised Conor not to interfere while he was away. In her opinion, it would not be meddling because she had been asked. But what really scared Craig was that Laurel was known to pull off miracles. If anyone could actually succeed in getting Meriel and Hamish together, she could. No! If anyone was going to "help" Meriel, it was going to be him. "I thought you didn't want to involve her."

"I didn't, but—"

"So what do you want me to do? Talk to Hamish about you? I could always tell him you are a good kisser."

Meriel narrowed her eyes in warning. "All I need are valid reasons for Hamish and me to spend time together."

Craig's face went grim. "Seems a little simple," he replied. In truth, it was far too simple. Such straightforward tactics would not work if she really wanted to catch Hamish, and they certainly would fail to make him jealous. But mostly, her request made it highly difficult for him to ensure Meriel would experience all of Hamish's qualities, many of which Craig knew would drive her insane.

"Should there be more?" Meriel countered. "You once said that anyone who was privileged enough to spend time in my company would desire only for more."

Craig's eyebrows furrowed and his mouth took on an annoyed twist. The woman remembered everything and could recall it whenever it was most convenient for her. He had said that early into their friendship, and he had *meant* that he was surprised that no one took the time to see the astounding person she really was. If this scheme had involved anyone but Hamish, Craig would be actively figuring out a way to end this silliness, but his friend was too set in his womanizing ways to be a real threat. Besides, as a man, Craig knew exactly what attracted his sex and just what pushed them away.

"Fine," Craig grumbled, staring at her long and hard. She had a sparkle in her hazel eyes. One suspiciously like Laurel's when she tricked Conor into doing something that he never would have agreed to if he'd known his wife's true thoughts. Craig almost hesitated, but then remembered that either way—scheme or no—helping Meriel was to his advantage. "I'll come up with something, but if Hamish still does not desire your company by the time Conor returns, will you vow to give up and come home?"

Meriel swallowed and waited for several long seconds before agreeing to the stipulation. "I promise."

Craig smiled, happy to see that twinkle significantly diminish. *Aye. It is I who have tricked you*, Craig lauded to himself. He might have chosen never to pursue Meriel in order to keep her in his life, but he was not about to let anyone else have her.

Meriel was his.

He was her confidant, her friend, and the one she went to with her problems. And when this was all over, *he* would be the one she leaned on in both good times and bad. She did not need anyone else. She would never need anyone else.

Hamish's hand snuck out and grabbed Meriel's arm just as she emerged from the Great Hall, dragging her into the shadows. More than a week had passed since Craig's arrival, and Hamish had naïvely hoped she had given up whatever plan she had been hatching. Then, right after dinner, she had winked at him just as he was leaving. His gut had been in knots ever since. In a moment of weakness, he had agreed to participate in a scheme to inspire jealousy, which would work to each other's benefit, but now he was not so sure. Craig was his close friend, and if the man wanted to screw up his life, he should be allowed to do so *without* assistance.

"Have you been waiting for me this whole time?" Meriel whispered, sending him a smile that even in the shadows glowed.

"Aye," he answered, deciding not to divulge his doubts about her plan. Meriel was looking so happy, completely trusting and believing that he was going to help her capture her true love. "But did he believe you?"

Meriel inhaled and looked up to the right. "Enough," she finally answered. And then added a confident nod.

Hamish, however, was not convinced. "What does that mean?"

"Just that he is not sure either way," she said with a mischievous grin. "But a part of him *thinks* I could be falling in love with you."

"So *a part of him* actually suspects the truth? That this is a ruse to make him jealous?" Hamish challenged, trying to keep his voice down.

"Of course," Meriel said reassuringly. "I had to build Craig's natural suspicion of being manipulated into our plan. In his mind, by helping me, he can work to dissuade me from falling for you or he can reveal the 'truth.' Either way, it is to our advantage. Remember, our goal is not to trick Craig and Wyenda into admitting they have feelings for us. It is to show them what life would be like if we actually were to find someone else. Give them a chance to think about things before it is too late."

Hamish leaned back against the stone wall, crossed his arms, and shook his head in disbelief. "You women are scary."

Meriel grinned and lightly elbowed him in the ribs. "Ah, now it's you who is being jealous. You like the idea of a woman conniving to get a man. You just wish it was Wyenda scheming to get you. But don't worry; I'm being devious enough for the both of us. This plan will work."

"And if it doesn't?"

"Then we will be able to move on without any regrets. We tried our best, but it was not meant to be."

Hamish had to admit that Meriel's confidence was infectious, and once again he was falling under her spell. He had intended to talk her out of everything, to let things be, or to at least leave him out of her plans. Instead, he found himself wanting to continue to support her crazy idea to capture the hearts of two very stubborn people. Worse, he was actually eager to get started. With Meriel, there was no telling what was about to happen.

This time, he would not be one of the ones watching the fun and excitement that seemed to gravitate to the McTiernays; he would be a participant. And maybe, just maybe, he might also triumph and actually land a lady's heart.

Chapter 5

Craig strolled out of the smithy and glanced around the busy courtyard. He was about to head toward the kitchens and risk Fiona's wrath for a midmorning snack when he spied the two people responsible for robbing him of much-needed sleep. Hamish was standing outside the Lower Hall in what looked to be a deep conversation with Seamus, one of his fellow elite guardsmen. Meriel was leaving the North Tower arm in arm with Maegan. Both women paused as if to say good-bye, but instead kept talking. Craig's eyes skimmed hungrily down Meriel's graceful figure as she lifted a hand to push an errant tendril of golden-brown hair behind her ear.

She was wearing a pale yellow ankle-length chainse with a rich, gold-colored knee-length bliaut and a matching belt that accentuated her shapely frame. A band of royal blue needlework circled the long sleeves and the gown's plunging neckline. Her thick hair hung in long graceful curves down her back, highlighting her slender white neck. She was exquisite.

Craig blinked and forced himself to look away. It was then he realized that he had not been the only one to spy her entry into the courtyard. Now that his gaze was no longer captivated by his view of Meriel, he could see that every male within eyesight was frequently glancing, if not outright staring, at Meriel, appreciating what he saw. Craig was half tempted to shout out a reminder of just who they were ogling—Laird Rae Schellden's daughter. Instead, he decided to help them remember who her protector was and began waving his hand.

After catching her attention, he motioned for her to walk over to him. Meriel quickly hugged Maegan good-bye and began to stroll through the maze of carts, animals, and items yet to be moved into storage. Her expression was one of curiosity, and Craig rubbed his chin with concern. He knew she was going to ask him why he had called her to him. He had to have an answer ready, and unfortunately, only one topic came to mind. *Ideas on how she could spend time with Hamish.*

He had avoided thinking about it, for the mental image of the two of them enjoying each other's company was more than a little unsettling. That he had agreed to aid in the creation of such a happy situation was repugnant. He did not want to help Hamish spend time with Meriel doing anything, let alone something she might like. Suddenly the corners of Craig's mouth raised a fraction of an inch. He was asking the wrong question. *What activity did Meriel enjoy doing that Hamish was sure to hate?*

"Where's Fallon?" Meriel teased as she met up with Craig outside the stables. Everyone knew how seriously the McTiernay steward took his many duties and responsibilities, but never more so than when one of Conor's brothers was left in charge. Craig was beginning to believe the man actually searched for squabbles for him to mitigate.

"Hopefully far, far away," Craig answered sardonically.

"So I see." Meriel's genial mouth curved into a luscious smile and her eyes sparkled at him, almost as if she suspected the truth, that he had no real reason for waving her over. "Normally, Fallon or Laurel has you so busy that we never get a chance to talk during the day. Why am I so lucky this morning?"

"Umm, I just wanted to let you know that I have an idea of how you can spend *valid* time with Hamish."

Meriel's eyes grew large for several seconds as she tried to discern if he was being serious. Deciding that he was, she clapped her hands together. "Truly?"

Her honest joy at the prospect of seeing Hamish momentarily rattled Craig. "Aye," he answered after a long pause. Then on a much more confident note, he inquired, "What can you do better than anyone else?"

Skepticism invaded Meriel's expression. "Make tapestries," she said slowly.

Craig closed his eyes, wondering if Meriel was intentionally working at being exasperating. "You *sew*," he groaned.

Meriel furrowed her brow and crossed her arms. "Actually there is much more than just sewing when working on a tapestry. There is knitting, felting, plaiting, lace making . . . not to mention understanding how to do the various types of weaves and stitches. There is also the design aspect to consider, having to determine the size of the piece as well as where to place—"

Craig threw up a hand to stop her from going any further. She had once lectured him on the intricacies of weaving a tapestry, and he had done his best to forget everything she had said. The one thing he could still remember on the topic was that it made his head hurt. "I'm not talking about tapestries. I'm talking about *clothes*."

"Clothes?" she repeated, her brows remaining scrunched. "A lot of women sew clothes. How is making a new dress going to help me win Hamish?"

"Not for you!" Craig yelled in frustration, catching the brief attention of those nearby. Then, bringing his voice back down, he flung his hand toward Hamish, who thankfully was still talking with Seamus outside the Lower Hall. "For him!" Craig huffed. "Remember when you offered to make me a new shirt, but I did not have the time to stand around while you did whatever you do?"

"*That's* the reason you refused?"

Craig shrugged his shoulders upon hearing the incredulity in her voice. "Why else? Anyway, Hamish could use some new clothes by the looks of it. Why not offer to make him a kilt and a leine? You've been sewing things for everyone else around here. The request should not seem out of the ordinary."

A flicker of apprehension flashed on Meriel's face and she bit her bottom lip. "What if he refuses?"

Craig rolled his eyes. "I'm not going to do everything, Meriel. You wanted help with ideas and I gave you one." He again pointed to Hamish, who had just clapped Seamus on the back, a clear sign their conversation was done. "There he is. Now go over there and convince him that getting a new outfit will be fun."

"Fun? *Now?*" she asked, clearly uncomfortable with the idea.

"Aye, now," Craig affirmed, eager to see Hamish's rejection. "Best do it when people are around. This way he'll be inclined to accept just to keep from offending you in front of everyone."

Meriel crossed her arms and narrowed her gaze in an effort to mask her true thoughts. "You really don't know Hamish very well. He is like you. If he does not want to do something, he is not going to do it, whether people can hear his rejection or not." Taking a deep, unsteady breath, she stepped back and before turning away said, "But since I asked for your advice, I will at least try."

Craig watched as Meriel ambled across the courtyard, briefly saying something to Seamus as he headed in the opposite direction. Whatever it was, it caused the seasoned soldier to break out into a lofty grin, reigniting Craig's earlier feelings of possessiveness. Then without warning something hard collided into his back.

"Mo creach!" Craig hissed as the stable master opened the door to grab some leather straps hanging on a hook outside the stables. He gave Craig a strange look and turned his head to see what was of so much interest. Craig, realizing that he had just been caught staring at Meriel, grimaced fiercely at the old man, who wisely retreated back into the stables without a word. Craig then stepped into the shadows and returned his attention to Meriel.

He felt his jaw clench. She was standing directly in front of Hamish, who was looking down at her far too attentively as she spoke. Craig waited for Hamish's reaction, knowing that the idea was going to fill his friend with the same nausea he had experienced. Too many times had Craig inadvertently witnessed women gathered together working on some garment, jabbering on as someone tried to pin a piece of fabric into place. The thought of standing there for hours as someone poked at him, draping materials over his shoulders and arms, was the least appealing way Craig could imagine for a man and woman to spend time together.

At last, Meriel stopped speaking and Hamish began to talk, no doubt trying to be kind and as charming as possible as he turned her down. But after he had spoken just a few words, Meriel started to talk again, this time more animatedly. Obviously, she had not mentioned the idea yet. Craig was beginning to wonder if she would, when he finally saw Hamish's eyes widen before looking down at his clothes.

Any moment now, Craig hummed to himself quietly. Should he go in at the first sign of horror, or wait until Hamish fully unleashed his disgust at the idea? Craig was still wrestling with whether he should help persuade his friend to accept Meriel's offer when she glanced over her shoulder and winked at him before returning her attention back to Hamish.

Craig was stunned. The small part of his brain still functioning was quite relieved that he was leaning on the stable wall, for otherwise he most likely would have fallen. Meriel had *winked* at him. What the hell did that mean? Refusing to speculate, Craig shoved himself upright and marched right over to where she and Hamish were talking.

"*Dia dhuit.*"

Hamish stopped in midsentence and grinned, unruffled by the interruption. "Hello to you."

With pursed lips, Craig turned to Meriel, who was beaming with delight. "You seem pretty excited about something," he grumbled.

Meriel nodded, but it was Hamish who responded to the implied question. "Seems our mutual friend here thinks I need some new clothes and that she should be the person to make them for me. I must admit to being surprised by the idea."

Craig scratched his chin in an effort to hide his thoughts. Perhaps Meriel needed his help after all. "You *could* use them, my friend," he said, pointing at the tattered end of one of Hamish's sleeves. "What's wrong? Scared of a woman with a needle?"

Hamish, with a significant lifting of his right brow, gave Craig a puzzled look and said, "Hardly. We were discussing when she could start."

A momentary flare of annoyance shot through Craig. No man in his right mind would agree to such a request. Hamish was many things, but he was not foolish enough to subjugate himself to a male's version of purgatory unless there was a greater purpose behind his acceptance. Only one thing made sense. Hamish had somehow been persuaded to be part of Meriel's scheme.

"You are a better man than I," Craig commented coolly. "I couldn't imagine standing there as women twittered around me, acting as if I was their new toy."

"*First of all*," Meriel snapped, "there will be no *women*; just me. And I dare you to search your memory and find a single time I have ever *twittered*."

Hamish let go a deep belly laugh that caught the attention of those walking close by. "I'd advise you to beg forgiveness now, Craig. One thing I have learned is that Meriel is one incredibly feisty lady when riled."

Meriel? Feisty? Craig repeated to himself. Hamish was right, but Craig had not thought his friend had spent enough time with Meriel to recognize that quality in her. Worse, it was a particular characteristic that Hamish happened to appreciate in women. "Believe me, I am fully aware of the more spirited side of Meriel's personality," Craig muttered, further annoyed that his tone had betrayed his emotional state. In an effort to change the subject and put Hamish on the defensive, Craig added, "I am just very surprised you so quickly agreed to participate in something so unpleasant."

Meriel shifted her stance so that her glower could be seen only by Craig. *What are you trying to do? Convince Hamish to refuse? This is your idea*, she mouthed through silent lips before returning to her previous position.

"Ahh, but that is because you were never trying to impress a lady who held very high standards," Hamish countered.

"You mean Wyenda? Because unless your new clothes come with a title, she is not going to consider you, my friend. It's a waste of time," Craig declared before he could stop himself.

This time Meriel held nothing back in her threatening glare. Unwilling to take a chance that Craig might actually convince Hamish against her making him some new clothes, she grabbed Hamish's arm and started to lead him away.

"We could begin tomorrow afternoon, if you can make yourself available."

Hamish shrugged. "Aye, that would be agreeable. And just where is all this fun going to take place?"

"Since we want to keep this a surprise from Wyenda, we best meet in secret. How about . . . the North Tower?"

Craig made a choking sound and stomped up to join them once again. "In your bedchamber?" he barked in a low, menacing tone. "I think not!"

"I am not a fool, Craig!" Meriel hissed, coming to a stop. "I was thinking of Conan's workroom. He's gone, and no one would think to look there for either of us."

Silence followed as Craig gaped at her in shock. Meriel was staring back, waiting for him to get truly riled and shout out another objection. Instead, Craig snapped his jaw shut. His lips stretched into a thin smile. Oh, the woman was fiendishly clever, but not enough to outwit him. Meriel had *known* he could still hear their conversation and had anticipated his reaction. If she thought to trick him and then claim that his anger was the display of a jealous lover, she was going to be disappointed. He refused to be manipulated by anyone—but especially her.

"As long as you are comfortable with that decision," Craig finally taunted under his breath.

"Oh, I am," Meriel replied through gritted teeth, anger snapping in her green eyes. Then she turned back to Hamish and pulled him aside to discuss what garments he needed the most.

This time Craig did not follow. Mostly because he suspected she wanted him to, but the woman was playing a game that she was going to lose. But the fact that Hamish had appeared so damned earnest about needing and wanting a new outfit rankled. Craig knew it was ridiculous. No doubt Hamish was under strict orders to willingly participate in any idea put forward. Still, the man did not need to look so happy at the prospect of being tortured.

Then again, after a few hours of being plagued by a needle, there was no way Hamish was going to retain his charming attitude. Not more than an hour would pass before he would emphatically refuse to continue being a pawn in her games. Craig almost felt sorry for Meriel, for even if by some small chance he was wrong about her inventing this whole nonsense about loving Hamish, she was going to see a side of his friend that would undoubtedly make her rethink things altogether.

Aye. By tomorrow night during their evening chat, Meriel would be telling a sad story about her misguided, broken heart. Whether it be true or the result of a failed plan, Craig intended to be ready to pick up the pieces.

For when it came to Meriel, they were *his* pieces to pick up. And no one else's.

Brenna lay stomach down on the bed with her chin propped in her hands. She considered herself a very mature eight-year-old, but she did not think she would ever understand grown-ups' affinity for talking about dull stuff. Rolling over on her back, she asked in a weary voice, "Are you almost done?"

"Almost," came Meriel's reply, muffled due to the number of pins she had between her lips.

"I hate the Warden's Tower. It's so boring and musty and—" Brenna stopped midsentence as the staircase began to howl. "And there are ghosts!"

Meriel adjusted the length of the shirt's hem and twirled her finger to signal Hamish to turn a little so that she could continue pinning. "You and I both know that sound is just the wind coming in whenever someone opens the door."

Brenna searched for another argument but could not find one. "Why do *I* have to be here?" she wailed.

Meriel weaved the last pin into place. "You know why," she finally answered, her mouth free of hardware. "Maegan was unavailable."

Brenna missed her friend. Maegan was more than twice her age, but she was still more fun than any of the other adults. It was not fair that Maegan's grandmother got sick and required her help. She needed Maegan too, especially now that Meriel had practically kidnapped her and forced her to be a chaperone. She was a kid! She did not even know how to be a chaperone, let alone why having one was so important. "No one cares about Hamish getting new clothes," Brenna groaned, sitting up to look out the window.

Meriel's mouth was full of pins once again, preventing her from arguing the point or pointing out that Brenna had been there less than half an hour. Secretly, Meriel also preferred the North Tower. The Warden's Tower's bedchambers were large, well lit and in many ways comfortable, but the tower itself was infused with a lingering smell that proved many an unbathed soldier slept in it at night. But when Hamish had come over, she could see his reluctance about meeting alone in her room. Afraid he might change his mind, she had offered to meet in the Warden's Tower instead. But after being here for an hour, she suspected Hamish would be more willing to convene in her bedchambers next time.

Brenna sighed again and Meriel was about to consider the idea of letting the child go, with the promise to keep this meeting a secret, when she jumped off the bed with an excited scream. Then, without asking for permission for fear it would not be granted, Brenna ran out of the room before Meriel could empty her mouth of pins and object to Brenna's speedy exit.

"What was that about?" Meriel gasped, spitting the pins into her palm.

Hamish gestured with his chin toward the window and the courtyard below. Meriel stood up to look for herself. Brenna's brother, Braeden, who usually tried to avoid the castle and his mother's watchful eye, was in the courtyard playing swords with his best friend, Gideon. The wooden sticks banged together and a second later a slight girl with pale blond curly hair burst onto the scene with her hands on her hips. Both boys looked indignant, but a couple of seconds later all three children began to chase each other around the enclosure.

"Now what are we supposed to do?" Meriel sighed.

Hamish shrugged. "Nothing. The door is open, and even if the servants coming in and out of the storage area downstairs knew where we were, they wouldn't venture up here. Brenna was right. No one cares about me getting a new kilt."

"Hopefully one person does," Meriel murmured as she stood, continuing to look out the window. "I was actually surprised Craig did not conjure up a more painful way for us to spend time together. Not only do you need new clothes, but now we have a reason to meet several times."

Hamish swallowed. Meriel had always been pretty, even that famous night last year when Brenna had decided to style her hair. The result had been horrifying, and yet anyone could have seen that she and her sister were attractive women. But right now, with the light shining behind her making her smooth, milky skin glow, Meriel's gentle beauty had transformed into something unexpectedly breathtaking. "Aye, certainly simplified your plan," he finally managed to say, trying to shift his thoughts to Wyenda and his supposed purpose for agreeing to Meriel's schemes. "Think Wyenda will find me irresistible when you get done?"

Unaware of Hamish's appreciative thoughts, Meriel

glanced back so that he could see the roll of her eyes. "Wasn't it you who told me that you are already irresistible?"

"I think I might have lost my ability to charm women," he replied, trying to sound woeful. "Alas, you have not fallen under my spell despite my earnest efforts."

"You truly are incorrigible," Meriel said as she swatted his arm and removed the last of the loosely pinned pieces of material from his frame. She really hated the idea that she was helping Hamish win Wyenda's heart. In reality, Meriel despised the woman. And though she knew it was unlikely Hamish would succeed where all other men had failed, there was still a chance he could. Meriel had been telling Craig the truth when she had described Hamish as a man worth pursuing. Handsome, amiable, and entertaining, it would not be beyond the realm of possibility for anyone, including Wyenda, to fall for him.

A sharp noise caught their attention. Realizing the risk they ran if anyone overheard them talking, Meriel looked at Hamish and mouthed, "Can anyone hear us?"

Hamish broke into a wide grin. "All the men are out training, and only very few guards are manning the battlements this time of day. I have been watching, and with the exception of the baker, whom you just heard drop a box onto the ground, no one besides Brenna has entered or exited the tower."

"I know you said that Craig would be gone for the afternoon, but . . ." Meriel paused, narrowing her eyes. "Well, I know this castle is littered with secret passages, including one that leads directly from the village into the North Tower. And I wouldn't put it past a certain someone to use it," she whispered, unconvinced that Craig was not lurking nearby. It did not matter that he was far more likely to barge in on them than sneak around and eavesdrop; the fact that she had seen no sign of him at all was disconcerting.

Hamish's dark green eyes locked on to Meriel. "You *know* about the passageways?"

Meriel frowned and picked up the pinned tartan material she had cut for Hamish's kilt and began folding it. "Of course I do."

Hamish pulled his chin back and gave her a jealous smirk. "Well, then you are one of the privileged few."

"You don't know where they are?"

"Ha! Like any McTiernay is going to hand over an advantage like that to anyone—even a friend. And as far as Craig goes, I made sure he would be nowhere near here for the whole day. He and Seamus are visiting some of the more distant farms and will not be back until dinner—if then," Hamish relayed proudly.

Relief filled Meriel and she waved her hand for him to sit down and relax. "We're done. You don't need to stand anymore. I have everything I need."

Hamish sauntered over to the chair and plopped down in it. "Really? That didn't take long."

Meriel chuckled. "I only needed the basic measurements. It isn't like a leine and kilt are difficult to make."

The pounding sound of a horse's hooves coming through the gatehouse caused them to look at each other, eyes wide. Hamish glanced outside and said, "Good thing you are done. Looks like our temporary chieftain has figured out a way to abandon Seamus and return early."

Meriel bit her tongue. She *knew* she had been right to believe Craig would find a way to be around. Meriel peeked down at the courtyard just in time to see Craig toss his reins to the stable master and jump down off his horse. "He doesn't look happy."

Hamish's face broke into a large smile. "At least not happy to see Brenna down there playing with the boys," he said, watching Craig approach the children, his face clearly displeased as he said something to Brenna.

Concern for the little girl flashed through Meriel but died quickly when the girl's back went rigid and her hands flew to her hips. Brenna was obviously not taking any admonishment from her uncle lightly. "I want to meet the man that little girl marries someday."

Hamish rolled his eyes. "Not me. He'll either be spineless, choosing to surrender whenever Brenna makes a demand, or a man to be feared."

Alarm was growing in Meriel. "But with Craig's untimely arrival, how are we going to make him believe that we were together in my bedchamber and not here, since Conan's study was mysteriously bolted?"

Hamish chuckled, grabbing his sword and sticking it through his belt. "I love it when I get the chance to outmaneuver a McTiernay. Leave it to me. I may not know how to sneak inside the castle from the village, but I am expert on traversing these curtain walls after spending endless hours of guard duty on them. I can get from any tower to another without being seen."

Meriel grinned. With Brenna and her penchant for relaying gossip, there was a slim chance of outwitting Craig today, but Hamish obviously relished the idea. Meriel gathered her things and followed him out the door and up the staircase. Bending below the openings in the battlements, she crept behind Hamish until they came to the North Tower. For a moment, she thought their plan was doomed. For there, perched and surveying the lands, was a guard. Hamish signaled for her to wait until he gave her a sign. He next strode onto the tower and waved hello to the guard as he yanked open the tower door. Then, as if he had changed his mind, he walked over to the younger man and pointed somewhere in the distance, allowing Meriel a chance to slip by unnoticed and down into the tower stairwell. Seconds later, Hamish met her on the third floor outside her bedchamber.

Meriel was beaming with delight. "Thanks, Hamish. For

everything. For agreeing to my plan, being agreeable about getting new clothes . . . for all of it."

Hamish gathered one her hands in his. "My lady, there really is no need to thank me. I said I would be glad to help, and I am. Besides, I actually rather enjoyed myself today. It certainly wasn't nearly as tiresome and painful as Craig made it sound."

"That man has no idea what he is talking about. I honestly wonder how he came by the clothes he is wearing."

"So what is the next step in this grand idea of yours? Need to see me tomorrow?"

Meriel bit her bottom lip. "Craig thinks you are suffering. If you consent to coming back too soon, it might counter that belief."

"What if we say that you *want* to see me again tomorrow, but I refused because I was . . . oh, too busy. The reason why I am unavailable, Craig can just assume."

Meriel clasped her hands in delight. "Perfect!"

"You know I should feel a little guilty helping you, but in all honesty, I'm enjoying myself. Craig likes to think of himself as the most amenable of his brothers, when in truth he is just as stubborn in his ways as any one of them. So consider me your humble accomplice. So, farewell, until next time." Hamish gave her a flamboyant bow and then disappeared down the spiral staircase.

Removing the smile on his face, Hamish pushed open the tower door, unsurprised to find Craig on the other side.

Craig stepped forward. "So, how did things go?"

Hamish drew his lips into a grimace and said, "Wasn't expecting this to last for days."

Craig crossed his arms and rocked onto his heels in a failed attempt to hide his pleasure. Brenna had already revealed how boring it had been with Hamish and Meriel in the Warden's Tower, but it was obvious they both wanted him to believe that they had met in her bedchamber. Seeing

Hamish's frustrated expression only added to his feeling of triumph. Just as Craig predicted, the man had been in hell. "Come drown your sorrows with a drink."

Hamish shook his head. "Next time. I've got some things to take care of."

"So I take it things were not quite as *pleasant* as you thought they'd be," Craig said with a smirk.

Hamish's jaw tightened and his mouth formed a stubborn line. He could feel beads of sweat forming across his forehead and he knew at any minute Craig would interpret his angst for what it really was. "There are many words I could use to describe today's experience."

Craig inhaled and pursed his lips, shaking his head. "I guess Meriel wasn't happy to hear you wouldn't be coming back."

Hamish started walking away, eager to end the conversation. "She wants me back tomorrow," he corrected over his shoulder. "I told her I was busy but agreed she could finish Wednesday."

Once inside the stables and out of Craig's sight, Hamish leaned against the railing in relief. Normally he would have been reluctant to deceive anyone, especially a close friend. What he had told Meriel was true—he did think Craig needed a reminder that he was not always right. But after spending an afternoon with her and seeing Craig's unconcerned response to their being alone, Hamish's reasons for helping Meriel with her plan had morphed from amusing pastime into something far more serious.

Fact was, Rae Schellden's daughter was *nothing* like Hamish had originally thought. She was funny, smart, and could dole out sarcasm as well as receive it. Combine that with a smile that could instantaneously warm a man throughout his body, she was someone men would fight body and soul to make their own. And Craig knew it; worse, he refused to accept that he wanted her for his own. But if Craig thought he could prevent anyone else from discovering just how special Meriel was, he was a fool.

Meriel had come out of her shell, and Hamish doubted she would return to it ever again. Whether Craig knew it or not, this was his last chance to claim her for his own. For if he remained steadfast to his idiotic notions of bachelorhood, Hamish knew, as someone who had once loved deeply and walked away, that Craig would forever regret it.

Two days later, Hamish rounded the corner and saw the door to Meriel's bedchamber wide open. She was sitting casually on a bench by the window with one foot tucked underneath her. Her head was bent and her focus was completely on stitching what he guessed to be part of his shirt.

He leaned against the door frame and shook his head as he looked around the room. He had heard stories of Meriel being less than tidy. Most of them had come from Craig's twin brother, Crevan, but recently Brenna had added a few. It was hard to believe, but not a single tale had been exaggerated. The place was not dirty, just very messy with piles of random items everywhere.

Hamish would not have defined himself as a person who needed things orderly, but he suspected if he did have a place to call his own, it would be far neater than Meriel's bedchamber. Then again, he did not have much to clutter a room. With the exception of his sword, his targe, and some clothes, any items of real value that belonged to him were housed far away and were irretrievable. As a result, he needed little when it came to housing. He usually slept outside, in the Warden's Tower, or in one of the larger cabins that sheltered several of the single soldiers. With his seniority and position within the elite guard, he probably could have requested a cottage, but he had refrained from doing so. His home was north and not on McTiernay land. Only when he had a wife and a family would he finally set down permanent roots—and then it would be her responsibility to keep it clean, not his.

Hamish studied the room as if it were a complex obstacle course. Only two areas remained uncluttered—the bed and a space around the hearth, which Hamish had no doubt had just been recently straightened for his benefit. Unfortunately, there was no way to get to it without stepping or rubbing against something. And in his present filthy state, doing either would certainly raise Meriel's ire, if it was not already high due to his being considerably tardy.

He had been at the training fields helping some new recruits when he remembered his promise to join her that afternoon for another "fitting." Because he was running late, he had elected to skip diving into the loch to wash off the sweat and grime. A decision he now wished he could remake. "So this time we are to meet here . . . in your bedchamber," he smirked.

Meriel looked up and her face noticeably brightened upon seeing him. Hamish had prepared himself for her anger or at least some admonishment, but if she was feeling perturbed at his tardiness, it was not evident. "As you can see."

"You, my lady, are living dangerously. I have the feeling I should be the hero, protect you from yourself, and request we meet elsewhere."

Meriel smiled wickedly. "I can assure you that we are quite safe from the blue-eyed danger you speak of, and besides, Brenna was right. The Warden's Tower is musty." Suddenly, her eyes grew large and reflected regret at possibly having offended him. "Of course if you feel uncomfortable, we could go somewhere else."

Hamish shook his head. He knew meeting in her bedchamber was far from the wisest thing he had ever done, but he also knew that neither of them was going to do anything that would cause them shame. And surprisingly, knowing that he would not even attempt—let alone succeed in—such an endeavor stirred a bit of disappointment in him.

"So where is our little chaperone?" he asked, taking a step inside.

Meriel turned a fraction and tucked her free leg underneath her. Her back was now toward the window, causing the early afternoon sunlight to pour over her shoulders and onto what she was working on. As she sat there, Hamish thought he was looking at an angel. Her loosely twisted hair gleamed like strands of lustrous glass and he found himself wishing it were hanging down loose around her shoulders and accessible to being touched.

Meriel sighed. "Maegan could not come, for she is still taking care of her grandmother. I was about to ask Brenna to join us when the intuitive little thing announced that she *had* to help her mother's friend Aileen. Though when I asked her what exactly she was to be doing, Brenna claimed she could not remember, only that it was *very* important. So it is just you and I again."

Hamish blinked. He had heard her answer the question, but his mind had been elsewhere. In an effort to disguise the lascivious nature of his thoughts, he quirked his eyebrow roguishly. "Brenna is a smart one. And unfortunately for the men in her future, she is also cunning and far too pretty."

"And why is that such a terrifying combination?" Meriel asked, pretending to be personally affronted. "Don't men want their women to be smart, beautiful, and a little spirited?"

Hamish grunted, refusing to answer. Her playful question was rhetorical, but Meriel had no idea just how accurately she had described his ideal woman. Unfortunately, the only ones he could ever find with all three characteristics were always taken—and usually by a McTiernay. "I probably should have jumped in the loch before I came. But I'm here. So where should I stand this time?" he grumbled as he unsheathed his sword and leaned it on the wall next to the door.

Meriel cocked her head. Her green-and-gold eyes searched his face. Deciding not to inquire at his unexpected change in demeanor, she pointed to the large cushioned chair by the hearth.

Hamish remained standing where he was. "I distinctly remember you saying last night at dinner that you needed to check some fittings and that it would take awhile."

"And you believed me?" Meriel giggled, lifting up his shirt, which looked close to being complete. "For such a simple garment?"

Embarrassed, Hamish snorted. "Now that I think on it, I wasn't exactly *alone* when you asked me to come, was I?"

The twinkle in Meriel's eye brightened at the memory. "Aye, you were not. Did you see Craig's look of shock when I suggested he come join us today and keep you company?"

Hamish remembered. He also remembered not being thrilled at the idea. He enjoyed talking with Meriel, and if Craig were there, he suspected his role in the love triangle would become one of silent observer.

Hamish glanced out in the hall, although he already knew Craig was not lurking somewhere within hearing. Meriel was being far too open about her plans. "Just where is the object of your affection?"

"You know, I'm not really sure," Meriel said, licking her lips, returning her focus to her stitching. She hooked the needle through the material and tied off the knot. The leine was done. All she had left to do was cut the thread. "I do remember having a conversation with Laurel though, soon after I invited Craig to join us. She might have mentioned her needing Craig's assistance *all* afternoon, especially since he had no real plans other than relaxing with us."

Hamish crossed his arms and shook his head. It was no wonder Brenna was more devious than most adults, let alone children. With Laurel as her mother and Meriel and Maegan as her two mentors, how could the little girl not be? "You are evil," he said simply.

"*I*," Meriel began, "am just much smarter about who assists me in my endeavors to keep Craig away."

"Endeavors? That's what you call it?" Hamish asked as he closed his eyes and shook his head, relieved that no woman was busy scheming to control his life unbeknownst to him. Though a small piece of him did wonder what it would be like to have someone interested enough in him to do so.

"Aye, and those endeavors will work to your advantage as well if you will sit down and listen," Meriel said, pointing to the large hearth chair once again. "Since Craig will be gone *all* afternoon, we have plenty of time to discuss this evening's meal. Tonight, there are going to be a number of people coming. Lady Laurel is requesting all of the laird's honor guard along with their wives to attend, and I told her that I would extend the invitation to you. And as you are not married, I asked Wyenda to accompany you."

Hamish perked up and started to move toward the chair. "Really?"

"Aye, and not until I mentioned you were going to escort her did Wyenda agree to come." Meriel quickly looked back down at her sewing as a feeling of guilt washed over her. She had not lied exactly. She *had* met with Wyenda and asked her to come. And the woman had promptly refused, insinuating that she was expecting an invitation to dine with far more important people that evening. Meriel had been half tempted to pivot and leave the haughty woman to her grand plans, but unfortunately, the primary goal of the dinner required Wyenda's attendance.

As long as Hamish met with the vain woman privately, he could deceive himself as to what she was. Meriel hoped that if he spent a few hours with Wyenda amongst his friends, the experience would reveal some of the woman's more unpleasant traits. So, when Wyenda had refused the invitation, Meriel had bolstered her resolve and expressed deep regret that she could not come, as tonight was not going to be just any gathering. Several visitors would be attending at Lady McTiernay's behest, including a young, single nobleman in line to becoming a laird of one of the most powerful clans in the Highlands. Unsurprisingly, Wyenda had quickly invented a reason to change her mind and agreed to come.

I pray you understand that I did it for you, Hamish. Meriel sent the mental plea. She had been a child the last time she had purposefully misled someone, and that was when she and Raelynd were taking advantage of being identical twins. But in the last month, Meriel felt like she was becoming an expert in the art. First with Craig, then Wyenda, and now Hamish. Guilt should be eating her alive, and if everything did not work out as she hoped, Meriel suspected it eventually would.

A wary but indulgent glint appeared in Hamish's eyes. "So I guess I'll sit down. Umm, what should we talk about?"

"Anything you would like."

Hamish bobbed his head and began to look around, as if something in the room would give him an interesting topic they could converse about for hours. Meriel inclined her head, and for several minutes covertly watched him shift positions in the chair, not from discomfort but from boredom. Finally, taking pity on the man, she placed the completed leine on the bench next to her. "While I may not know you very well, Hamish, I had guessed that sitting and doing nothing would entertain you for about as long as it would me. But I was wrong. You didn't even manage five minutes, and I am sure I could have lasted at least ten."

Hamish looked at her, intending to return her tease with

a withering and intimidating stare, but her infectious smile made it impossible. "My lady, relaxation for a man like myself is nothing but a slow, painful process to insanity."

"You speak of being bored, which you shall not be today," she countered and walked over to the door. She picked up his sword and carried it to him. As she placed it in his outstretched hand, her lips curved conspiratorially as she pointed to the long wooden chest next to the chair. "Open it," she instructed.

Hamish arched a single brow but did not argue as he leaned down to pull on the chest's strap. The heavy lid fell back and his dark emerald eyes grew large as he realized what was inside. Everything he needed to polish a sword.

"Relaxation *does* ease the spirit," Meriel countered. "For me it is anything to do with a needle and thread. For you, well, I'm hoping I guessed correctly. I remembered how you polished your sword at night when we traveled here, and I thought that you might like to do so today."

Hamish blinked as he studied the contents of the chest. She had acquired everything he needed. Either Meriel remembered or she had questioned the sword smith, but either way, she had thought about him and had taken the time to do something specifically for him. Outside of his mother, Hamish could not recall when anyone, let alone a woman, had done something just to make him happy. "This must have taken you some time," he said softly.

"Not time, but ingenuity," Meriel corrected him. "The wood and the cloth of course were easy enough, but Obe was more than a little curious as to why I would want a whetstone and a file. I was trying to come up with a plausible reason when he suddenly gave them to me and shooed me out of his shop."

Hamish pulled both items out of the box and nodded his head, imagining her conversation with the sword smith. Obe was incredibly shy, and the idea of a pretty woman talking to him, in his space, had to have made him extremely uncomfortable. No wonder he just gave her the items without explanation.

"So did I get everything?" she asked expectantly.

"Aye. And my sword could use a polish, especially after today's beating," Hamish answered, the tone of his voice revealing just how eager he was to get started.

Meriel returned to her bench and picked up his leine, pretending to still be sewing on the sleeve.

Hamish placed the wooden block on his lap to brace the sword as he began to use the metal file on the sword's edge. After several minutes listening to the repetitive sound, Meriel stopped pretending to work and watched him make long, even, unhurried strokes to reshape the weapon.

Tiny metal fragments flew off and scattered onto the hearth rug, but he seemed oblivious to them. She would have to remember to roll the rug up and have it beaten before she walked on it with bare feet. Before long, the silvery specks were noticeable enough that it would not be hard to remember. And yet Hamish continued with the long strokes. Meriel waited to see when he would test the edge, but he never did. "How do you know when it is sharp enough?"

"Aye, that is the challenge. Most people have the sword smith sharpen their blades because, if they do it themselves, they pay too much attention to the edge, ruining the weapon. They think sharper is better."

"But . . . isn't it?"

"Nay. The trick is to remove just enough metal so that the edge is exposed. If you make a sword too sharp, it will chip more easily during fighting and may even break."

Meriel considered what he said. "So less is more."

Hamish looked up and she could see a faint light twinkle in the depths of his green eyes. "Aye."

They locked gazes for several seconds before Meriel

made herself break away and refocus on her sewing. The rasping sound of metal rubbing metal resumed, and Hamish began to hum to the rhythm. The overall effect was strangely comforting.

After she had arranged with Laurel to have Craig disappear for the afternoon, Meriel had almost panicked. While she and Hamish got along quite well—better than she dreamed possible with someone other than Craig—the thought of keeping him entertained for an hour or more had seemed daunting. Then she remembered their recent journey to the McTiernays', when at night Hamish and she had spoke some, but mostly he had sat in silence, polishing his sword. At the time, she had the impression that he found the activity relaxing. So she had immediately gone to seek all the components she remembered him using.

After awhile, Hamish leaned over and searched the chest. He sat back up. "Do you have any oil?"

"Oil?" Meriel repeated, unable to recall him using any previously. She blinked at him for a second and then glanced around the room, though she knew she kept none. Then she remembered the flower oil Maegan had brought her soon after she arrived, to remove the musty smell from her room. "How much do you need?"

"I need only enough for a thin layer on the blade's surface."

Jumping up, Meriel went over to the small table by the side of the bed and picked up the small wooden bowl. Hamish looked at the flowered contents and sniffed the odor. "Umm, nice, but uh, why don't you hand me that candle instead?"

Meriel squinted at him mischievously. "Afraid the other soldiers might tease you?"

With an impish grin, Hamish lifted his sword and held it in front of him. "This is a *man's* sword, Meriel."

"What are you saying? That the metal might go soft if a

little lavender oil touched it?" She chuckled, replacing the bowl on the table, selecting the candle instead.

"Maybe not the sword, but I'm pretty sure I would," he mumbled, taking the offered candle. Leaning over, he stuck the wax into the hearth to light it and then quickly moved to allow some of the melted beeswax to drop onto the blade.

Meriel shook her head and sat back down. "I bet Wyenda would like her man to smell like a flower garden. Believe it or not, the odor of male sweat is not all that appealing to us female types."

Hamish arched a brow and bit back a smart comment. He replaced the wooden block with the whetstone and began to pass the blade over the stone. Again and again, while keeping the edge at an angle, he scraped the metal using a slow and uniform stroke. The sound was much different than that of the file, and though both were somewhat loud, this particular one made her grit her teeth, praying he would finish soon. "Uh, how long does that take?"

Hamish stopped suddenly, realizing the reason behind her question. "Just until I have gone over the entire surface. I'm almost done." He inspected the blade and worked an edge a handful of times until he was satisfied. Then he leaned back to open his sporran and pulled out a small piece of coarse leather similar to the one she had seen in Craig's. He carefully began to rub the metal until it shone. Now she understood why they carried around such an abrasive item.

Hamish stopped abruptly and looked up, catching her staring at him. "How are you coming on that thing?" he asked, nodding toward the finished leine in her hand.

Startled, Meriel blinked and gave a small shake of her head, embarrassed and unable to think of a plausible explanation for why she had been watching him so intently. "I, uh, I'm practically done," she lied.

"So then this is it?" Hamish asked, hoping he did not sound as disappointed as he felt. He was starting to look forward to the time he spent with her. She seemed to understand him and he felt he could be himself in ways he could with no one else.

Meriel sighed and looked out the window. It had been nice having company, especially since she had not been required to make idle conversation. That the company was Hamish had been an unexpected and nice surprise. "Umm, probably should do one last fitting. This time, a real one. I should make sure that I have the length of the sleeves and the kilt correct," she said, though she was confident they were.

With his chin, Hamish pointed at the leine in her hands. "Why not now?"

"Because I will need Craig here to witness the fitting. If he doesn't, at least once, he will believe that I coerced you into working with me in order to make him jealous."

"I doubt one meeting is going to convince him otherwise."

"Aye, but then I don't need him to be convinced one way or the other. I just need him to suspect that we were conspiring to keep him away . . . at least for now," she said, getting momentarily lost in her thoughts. "But seeing that you are done, I should probably prepare myself for dinner. Based on my encounters with Wyenda, I'm not sure she sees me as a competitor for your affections. But tonight I am determined to create some sparks of jealousy in those blue eyes of hers. As soon as you leave, I intend to put quite a bit of effort into my appearance."

Apprehension filled Hamish. He wanted to say that such effort was unnecessary, but the gleam in Meriel's eye was disconcerting. He was beginning to know her well enough to understand that those looks of hers were the precursor to an evening of mayhem. Usually he welcomed the entertainment that tended to come with chaotic events, but that was when he was not the center of attention.

Unfortunately, tonight, the focus would be on him. And Hamish was not sure he was ready for what might happen.

* * *

Laurel stepped into her place at the dining table and paused for a slight moment, looking toward the gaping hole in the middle of the line of guests to her left. She gave a polite nod to all those present and sat down. Once everyone was seated, she leaned toward Craig, who was occupying Conor's seat at her request, and whispered, "Where are our two guests?"

Craig glanced at Meriel, sitting to his right, and once again felt the jolt of irritation. She wore a gown he had not seen before, and in his mind it was altogether too revealing, as the bustline was significantly lower than he preferred. The bronze color was not one she had worn before and must have come from one of the various bolts Conor had purchased for Laurel. The dark shade of copper would not have complimented his fair-complexioned sister-in-law, but on Meriel the garment looked to be made of liquid metal as it swirled around her slender frame, gently clinging to her curves. The brilliant hue complimented her hazel eyes, enhancing the green so they looked like polished emeralds while the golden specks drew whoever gazed upon them to a place where bodies collided in rhythmic movement and passion.

"Craig," Meriel repeated for the second time; this time her hushed tone had a little more bite. "You are staring at me."

Craig's jaw clenched. "I am not. I am merely . . . um . . . waiting on an answer to my question."

"You have not said a word to me."

Craig was afraid that she might be correct, but pride forced him to flat out deny the possibility. "I did. I said that you were with Hamish all afternoon and if anyone were to know of his whereabouts, it would be you."

Meriel returned his glare with one of her own. "*That* was

not a question. That was a—" Before she could issue a scathing retort, the doors to the Great Hall swung open, snatching everyone's attention. Hamish entered and on his arm was a stunning woman wearing a blue gown that made it clear her background was far removed from a mere Highland clan. Meriel inwardly groaned. She should have known that trying to outshine anyone, let alone a famed beauty, would be a failure.

Everything about Wyenda was theoretically beautiful. She was tall and shapely, her face was a perfect oval, and her lips were full and red. Even her reddish-blond hair hung in long graceful curves over her shoulders. It was no wonder she captured the attention and hearts of men. And yet each time Meriel saw her, either in person or at a distance, the woman held no charm or appeal. If anything, Wyenda reminded her of an insect.

Perhaps it was because she had a very thin nose, or that her features were slightly too close together. Maybe it was that the bones in her shoulders protruded somewhat. But more than likely it was the void of emotion in her pale blue eyes. Not only were they slightly larger than they should have been, they constantly darted around with crisp, restless movements. Even now they shifted from person to person, as if she was inspecting everyone in the room in an effort to uncover any weaknesses.

With a rueful look, Hamish walked right up to Laurel, who stood to greet the two guests. "My apologies, my lady, for our tardiness. I'm afraid that I did not gauge my time well this evening."

Laurel was no more deceived than Meriel was. Hamish had left in plenty of time to escort Wyenda back to the castle. Rumors of her punctuality—or lack of it—had been circulating for some time. Wyenda believed that arriving late reminded those present of her former importance. Similarly, she believed that dining at the McTiernay Castle was highly overrated because she knew Laurel's penchant for enjoying the company of McTiernay clansmen and -women far beneath her station. When Meriel had asked Laurel if Wyenda could be a dinner guest, they had discussed the situation. Conan could be rude, but they knew Wyenda's tongue could be lethal.

Hoping that Meriel truly was prepared for what she was about to provoke this evening, Laurel took in a deep breath and quickly readied her own patience. She issued a small smile to the couple. "Please be at ease, Hamish. And Wyenda, I am glad you were able to attend after all. I understood that you had at first declined my offer."

Hamish stared briefly at Wyenda before his puzzled gaze moved to Meriel. But her hazel eyes had already been ensnared by Wyenda's glaring sky-blue ones. The malice the watery depths held was unhidden. "*Someone* convinced me to come, my lady," Wyenda answered, never once glancing at Laurel. "I was led to believe that *a man of importance* would be in attendance."

A sudden storm invaded Laurel's darkening blue-green eyes as she pointed at the empty seats Hamish and Wyenda were to occupy. "Are we not important?"

Refusing to move, Wyenda looked her hostess unapologetically in the eye. "I was promised *nobles* from other clans."

Laurel licked her lips in sudden understanding of how the woman had been convinced to come. Laurel glanced back at Meriel, who met her eyes with a calm look of innocence. Rae Schellden's daughter was a difficult one to read, but then everything was going according to Meriel's well-thought-out plan. Wyenda had arrived late and, as expected, she was decidedly not pleased.

Peace settled over Laurel and she reminded herself she had but a small role to play. And with that thought, she began to look forward to the rest of the night, for it was going to be far from boring. Pasting on a large grin, Laurel gracefully waved her hand toward her right. "But there *is* a noble here this evening. Laird McTiernay's younger brother Craig, who now permanently resides with another clan, is visiting us."

Wyenda, not caring how she came across, tossed her hair behind her shoulders and looked directly at the one who had tricked her into accepting the invitation. "You deceived me."

Meriel, feeling far from threatened, was having to fight the urge to smile and break out into fits of laughter. The woman was far too easily baited. Then she saw the look of mortification on Hamish's face. Wyenda was not only humiliating herself, but him. For a moment, Meriel second-guessed her decision, but just as quickly reaffirmed it. Hamish needed to know exactly who it was that he desired.

"Did I?" Meriel cooed in an almost-innocent tone. "I cannot imagine that was my intention."

Wyenda took a step back and Meriel realized that she might have tricked the woman into coming, but that did not translate into a sense of obligation to stay. Jumping to her feet, Meriel rushed around the table and placed herself between Hamish and Wyenda, hooking one of their arms into one of hers. Guiding them to their seats, Meriel addressed the entire dinner party. "I must apologize, for Wyenda is correct. Shy as she is, I knew she would never agree to come unless I pressured her to attend by suggesting that she could be of great support to Lady McTiernay with her out-of-town guest."

Placated somewhat by Meriel's explanation of her supposed deceit, Hamish sat down. Wyenda, unable to maneuver around Meriel without pushing her out of the way, followed suit.

Craig watched the whole scene in disbelief. How was

it that no one but he could see the joy Meriel was finding in Wyenda's hatred of her? When Meriel was once again sitting beside him, he leaned over and whispered into her ear, "If Hamish believed that nonsense you just spewed, he was the only one present who did."

Meriel cocked her head so that her mouth was not more than two inches from his. He waited, curious to see if she could fight the urge to kiss him. He was about to lose his own battle when she reached over and broke off a piece of bread to put on her plate. "Nonsense?"

Craig leaned back in his chair, annoyed with himself for feeling disappointed. "Aye. That story you told to Wyenda."

Meriel twitched her lips and produced a look of ingenuousness. "It was not a story. It was the truth."

"Oh, I'm sure you uttered every word, but you and I both know that Laurel needed no help with her *out-of-town guest*."

When Meriel said nothing, Craig selected a large piece of pheasant off the meat platter and pulled it apart, giving her the leg bone while keeping the breast. "I have no problem with you deceiving Wyenda," he continued in a hushed tone. "I'm merely puzzled as to *why* you would excuse her rude behavior. For the first time, Hamish had a chance to see that woman's true shrewish nature, not to mention the fact that she was on the verge of leaving, when you ran over there and brought her back. Makes me wonder. I mean, if your supposed goal is to *win* Hamish's affections, why would you jeopardize an opportunity to free him of Wyenda? Maybe your feelings for him are not quite what you said they were."

Craig sat back, crossed his arms, and gave Meriel a smug look, believing he was about to finally force her to admit the truth.

Meriel popped a small chunk of meat into her mouth and slowly licked the savory juices from each of her fingers.

"Ah, well, now I know why *your* efforts to hinder Hamish's pursuit of Wyenda have failed so miserably," she said, keeping her voice low and private. "Wyenda is angry with *me* because she believes I deceived her—which, in truth, I did. And while Hamish might be rankled by her attitude, he would ultimately blame me as the cause. I did not save Wyenda. I saved myself. And as for future opportunities with Hamish, I believe I just rescued them."

Unable to find fault with her logic, Craig hid none of his frustration as he yanked off another piece of bread and chewed it angrily. The woman was supposedly interested in a man sitting only a few seats away, so why wasn't she toying with Hamish's mind and leaving his alone? "Looks like you are wanted," he quipped, pointing to Wyenda.

Midway down the table, the gorgeous woman sat fuming. Wyenda had tried several times to get Meriel's attention and knew she was being intentionally snubbed by the lesser woman. If she thought a simple laird's daughter could outwit her, the foolish *ciùrradair* was quite mistaken. When Meriel finally looked her way, Wyenda hissed, "Should I be eternally grateful to have finally received the courtesy of your notice?"

"I apologize for not seeing your need of me," Meriel replied, completely unfazed by the attack. "What did you want to know that was of such great importance?"

Wyenda blinked and could feel her chest rise and fall rapidly to match her breathing. In truth, she did not have a question but had only intended to make the aggravating Highland woman squirm under her stare. She could feel the silent weight of everyone listening and quickly manufactured a question that she hoped would put Meriel on her guard. "Do you still need to keep Hamish away from his duties with your petty needs?"

With wide eyes filled with artificial pain, Meriel slowly

shook her head and sighed softly. "The kilt is complete, but unfortunately, I realized this afternoon that I misjudged the size of Hamish's chest and arms and therefore will need him one more time." The truth was that she had already completed the first leine and had decided to make him a second shirt to support the pretense of needing another fitting.

A cold look of skepticism invaded Wyenda's expression. "And to think that so many believe you to be a superb seamstress," she cooed.

Seeing hard resentment saturate every facet of Wyenda's expression, Craig realized, even if Meriel did not, that Wyenda's furor was growing. If someone did not redirect the conversation, an explosion was going to occur and it would not stop with a simple exchange of fists. His gaze swung over to Laurel, expecting to see his sister-in-law preparing to step in and halt the discussion. Instead, she sat focused on slurping her soup, completely oblivious to the growing tension. The thought that something else was taking place flashed through his mind, but his simultaneous need to protect Meriel was so strong, it caused him to speak when he had had no intention of doing so. "It is amazing how often mishaps happen to even the most skilled artisans."

"It *is* amazing," Meriel concurred calmly, giving him a solid kick in the shins underneath the table. The man was *not* supposed to interrupt, and if he continued, he was going to ruin everything. "Almost as amazing as *you* knowing about the frustrations a woman endures with a needle and thread."

Craig's face turned an even deeper shade of red and Meriel realized she had taken the wrong route. Quickly shifting direction, she leaned in close and in a soft voice so that only he could hear, whispered, "This is your fault. I could have made those clothes days ago, but I have been waiting for you to give me another way for Hamish and me to spend time together. I need another idea and soon."

Craig blinked as he realized just what was happening. Laurel's silence, Meriel's confidence in the shadow of Wyenda's hatred . . . this whole night was part of the elaborate game Meriel was playing. But what was her goal? Regardless of her aim, she was unwittingly on the path to getting herself hurt. She might think herself equal to Wyenda, but she was not. Meriel was incredibly clever, but she lacked the mean spirit needed to tangle with the likes of that hellcat. "Our bargain was for me to give you *a* reason, not a litany of them."

Meriel's green-and-gold eyes glittered with an unidentifiable emotion, which could have been either anger or anticipation. "Then you misunderstood," she said evenly. "Our agreement was that you would help me until Conor arrives."

A frisson of anger rippled up Craig's spine. If anyone misunderstood their agreement, it was Meriel. But before he could clarify exactly what his role would and would not be, Hamish intruded with a question. "Are you available Friday to make the corrections?"

Meriel forced her face to relax before turning to look at him. She nodded. "That should be perfect, Hamish. Thank you."

Wyenda sent Meriel a wintry smile and curled her fingers possessively around Hamish's bicep. "I do hope the items you are making him will be at least well made. I mean they *should* be flawless. One would think even an incompetent seamstress could create superb garments given all this time."

The angle of attack shocked Meriel. The quality of her work had always been praised, treasured, and in many cases, coveted. *Never* had anyone dared to insult her skill with a needle. Consequently, the idiotic barb was painless rather than wounding. Hamish was wrong. Wyenda was not misunderstood—she was shallow and heartless, and Meriel refused to let such a creature rile her.

Wyenda truly thought she would leave the Great Hall victorious. The woman had no idea that she was a pawn in a much larger scheme, executing her role perfectly. Meriel needed only to give Wyenda a final push to make the night a complete success.

A firm hand gripped Meriel's knee underneath the table, causing her to turn around and look at Craig. Meriel was momentarily stunned. He was not afraid of what she might say; he was afraid for *her*. A wave of indignation went through Meriel. Did he really believe her incapable of dealing with the antipathy of a *gleòidseach* like Wyenda? Did Craig think her so weak as to actually be affected by the insults the woman hurled at her about her sewing?

Refocusing on tonight's true goals, Meriel returned her attention to Wyenda and said with a wicked smile, "Then I am relieved, for I doubt your skills with a needle will enable you to appreciate, let alone critique, my expertise."

The whole table went quiet. Every single person dropped all pretense of being engaged in other conversations and turned to listen to how Wyenda was going to respond.

No one cared that Wyenda's mother was supposed to be from an important clan and that she had once visited with Elizabeth de Burgh, the queen consort of King Robert. Her father was a McTiernay farmer, which made her no better than anyone present. Most of those around the table had glimpsed Wyenda walking around the village and were aware of her beauty, and those who had just met Wyenda that night would freely admit that the tales concerning her comely appearance were not exaggerated. But it was the other stories about her that were of most interest, for while everyone knew of Wyenda, few had actually met her. They knew her only through rumors of how she believed herself to be above laborious chores, uncaring that her grandmother shouldered all the work in their home.

As a result, most of the dinner party had been stealthily eavesdropping on anything she had to say. And while each was interested in knowing how Wyenda was going to respond to Meriel's retort, they also knew that Lady McTiernay was more than capable of controlling Wyenda and her tongue. So they anticipated Laurel would intervene and address the offensive woman before anything more could be said. But instead, Laurel sat in silence, openly listening with wide eyes filled with intrigue.

Wyenda looked around the table at all the people studying her. Her expression grew even harder. She refused to be intimidated by them or by Meriel. "I thankfully have *no* experience as a seamstress," she said, swinging her focus back to the head of the table. "People of quality, like myself, are removed from doing such menial work. But I do have one area of expertise I would think you would covet—the ability to know how to look and be desirable."

Meriel swallowed. Her intuition suddenly flared to life, screaming that she was in serious danger. "I covet nothing of yours."

"Really? I doubt it. For I, without any effort, gained the attention of two men who only seem to desire you as a friend. I could not imagine going through life unable to inspire a man's passion, even when you try—like you obviously did with your little dress tonight."

An audible gasp came from Laurel's best friend, Aileen, who had remained silent after Laurel gave her a clear gesture to say nothing.

Meriel was vaguely aware of what was going on around her. She knew that Wyenda's venom would be painful only if her verbal strikes penetrated, and Meriel had thought herself invulnerable to anything the woman could fling at her. But she had not anticipated that Wyenda would detect and then expose her deepest, most secret fear.

Since her youth, Meriel had lured many a man to her side to dally with and share a kiss or two, but no one had ever really tried seriously to pursue her. She had assumed it was because she had made it known that any such effort would be pointless, but deep down Meriel had always wondered if that was the real reason. *Could* she inspire passion? Would any man ever find her truly desirable? Based on Craig's reaction to their kiss, the answer could possibly be no.

Wyenda's vile words hung in the air, causing Hamish to be immobile and mute for several seconds. He understood that Wyenda had felt attacked and lashed out instinctively to defend herself. She had come to dinner under false pretenses and was angry at being lied to. She did not understand that Meriel had thought only to help him, but it did not matter. Wyenda had gone too far.

Normally, Hamish found it challenging to discern what Meriel was feeling about any subject, but the pain etched into her face after Wyenda launched her last attack was one he would never forget. Meriel actually believed the nonsense Wyenda had spurted. He wanted to go over and assure Meriel otherwise, that she only had to give a man one of her warm smiles to inspire passion—but one glance at Craig held him back.

His usually bright blue eyes smoldered with murderous anger, creating an aura of danger that radiated from him. With clenched fists and his neck turning crimson, Craig looked as if he was ready to do battle. He glared at Wyenda, but it was to Hamish he spoke. "Get her out of here."

Craig said the words slowly and deliberately, but his voice was laced with dark warning. Hamish did not want to give the appearance that he supported anything Wyenda had just said; the woman needed to leave and Craig fully expected him to make it happen.

Hamish rose to his feet and touched Wyenda's shoulder. "My dear, it is time you and I leave."

Wyenda broke her cruel look of victory directed at Meriel and glanced up at Hamish. She was about to speak when Hamish coldly cut her off. "You have said enough."

Wyenda's baby-blue eyes widened as she saw the censure in Hamish's expression. She was mystified. What had she said that was untrue? He had told her himself that he was not interested in the Schellden woman. That she was too quiet and understated to be inspiring. That he preferred someone with more vitality. And yet it was obvious Hamish did like Meriel enough to be upset that she might be hurt.

Wyenda's gaze shifted from Hamish to the head of the table. Only then did she realize that she had also seriously misinterpreted the relationship between Craig McTiernay and Meriel Schellden. Wyenda suspected that if she had not been sitting so far away from Craig, she might be leaving with a red mark across her face. Craig looked as if she had insulted his beloved wife, not some woman with whom he was occasionally forced to spend time. It made no sense. He himself continually announced that he and Meriel were just friends, a term that meant little because a man and a woman could never actually be *close*.

Wyenda rose slowly to her feet, refusing to look repentant. The facts that were crystallizing into understanding only hardened her original belief. She was better than all of these crude Highlanders. She had been living in these insufferable mountains for nearly two years, with men as her one distraction from life's monotony. But she was tired of waiting for an opportunity to leave and return to Perth. It was time to take action.

She placed her hand in Hamish's and looked up at him

with tears in her eyes—another useful skill she had mastered. Leaning into his side for support, forcing him to put his arm around her, she allowed him to escort her out of the castle. Inwardly Wyenda smiled, knowing that all behind her—including Meriel that little *baobh*—were watching. Tonight, she would mollify her anger with Hamish one last time, but starting tomorrow she would focus on her real goal—to live the life she was born to have.

Iain Matheson was not the best-looking nobleman and far from the fittest, nor was he laird of a clan. But he did live in an impressive stone tower within riding distance, and had numerous servants to address his whims. But most importantly, he was wealthy. It had been awhile, but Wyenda did not doubt her abilities to charm and ensnare. And it was time she put them back to work.

Laurel closed the door to Meriel's room and leaned against the wooden planks. "I'm impressed. You accomplished everything you wanted to achieve tonight. You must get your skills to predict human behavior from your father."

Meriel shrugged despondently. "Papa would have foreseen Wyenda's viciousness with far more clarity and avoided it."

Laurel nodded. "Aye. That last remark of hers took everyone by surprise," she said quietly.

Meriel nodded solemnly and hugged her arms around her as she looked out her bedchamber window to the courtyard below. Hamish had been out there moments ago talking with Wyenda. The couple had been too far away for her to hear what they were saying as she and Laurel headed to the North Tower, and it had been impossible to tell from their behavior whether Hamish's feelings for the woman had changed.

"I hope you are not putting any credence into what that

creature said," Laurel cautioned. "Wyenda is just a bitter woman who wanted to make sure she was not alone in feeling pain."

"I know," Meriel said quietly. "But her aim was remarkably close to the truth. And if I should fail . . . then everything she said tonight would become my reality."

"Take heart. It will not be much longer before you will know for certain if your plan is going to succeed."

Meriel turned to look at Laurel. "Not my plan, *our* plan. I could not have done this without you."

Laurel waved her finger back and forth and casually walked up to Meriel, guiding her to the hearth chair to sit down. Carefully, Laurel began to take out the pins to unwind Meriel's hair and then began to unbraid the long strands. "I will admit to helping with the execution, but *you* came to *me* with this brilliant idea. And more importantly, it is working."

Meriel sat quietly and stared at the flames. "I am no longer so sure," she murmured to herself. She thought she had been prepared for this evening. Wyenda's aggressive behavior had been key to prompting the next step in her plan, so much so that Meriel had escalated the friction. And yet, despite all the thought that had gone into everything that led up to this evening, Meriel never anticipated Wyenda being able to hurt her as she had.

"I shall speak plainly, Meriel," Laurel said in a soft but firm tone. "This is not my plan, but I did agree to be a part of it . . . and I don't fail. So therefore your plan *will* work." Laurel shook out the remaining thick, intertwined strands of Meriel's hair. "Do you remember when you came to me and told me of your idea? I believed, just as you did, that you already had claimed Craig's heart, but faced the difficulty of not only getting him to admit his love for you but actually acting upon it. You asked me what was the quickest, most sure way for a man to recognize his feelings. And I told you jealousy."

"Craig certainly was not jealous tonight."

"No, he wasn't. But your plan required for him *not* to be jealous. Tonight was about removing any doubt in Craig's mind that you and I are scheming together in an effort to win him. Wyenda may have offended you, but her caustic comments will be the instrument leading to your success. Remember, if she had not insulted you, the depression you are feeling right now would still be present, but for a far different reason."

Meriel blinked at the reminder. Laurel was right. There were far more important things upon which to spend energy. Tonight had never been about Wyenda. Having Hamish see her true demeanor was a secondary goal. The success of the evening had really depended solely on Laurel's *lack of* reaction to Wyenda's attacks. "Did it work?" Meriel asked with a mixture of eagerness and fear.

"Just as you predicted," Laurel assured her. "At first Craig was upset about the insults toward you, but when Wyenda launched her last attack, he was openly assessing me, trying to understand why I did not intervene. His face practically announced his conclusion that tonight was just another piece of an elaborate plan to make him prove his love by jumping to your defense. He thinks I was staying quiet to give him the opportunity to play the hero."

Meriel nodded with satisfaction. "I told you he would not rally to my defense if he thought for one moment he was being manipulated. Whenever Craig thinks his actions are part of some master plan, he does the exact opposite of what is desired. It was his honor that forced him to order her to leave."

"Hopefully that theory of yours remains true. If it does,

then tonight proved that you have a very good, almost frightening understanding of my brother-in-law."

Meriel bit her bottom lip. "Now everything depends on this coming Friday and Saturday."

"Are you ready?" Laurel asked, moving to sit down and look Meriel in the eye.

Meriel swallowed, but her hazel eyes were clear and committed. "What you really mean to ask is, can I do it? And the answer is, I have to. I have no other choice. But it will be the hardest thing I have ever had to do."

"Controlling passion can be difficult. . . ." Laurel sighed. "Honestly? It is not something I have remotely mastered. And unfortunately Conor knows it. Luckily, he has even less ability than I to manage his desires."

"I only have to control it for a short while. And if I succeed, then I have Saturday night to . . ." Meriel paused and then looked at Laurel questioningly. "How are you going to persuade Hamish to ask me to dine with him? If he doesn't, then all this will be for—"

Laurel put up her hand, dismissing Meriel's look of concern, and smiled. "Leave that up to me."

Meriel bit her bottom lip. "Am I being fair to Hamish? I mean, not telling him everything?"

"He has become a good friend to you."

Guilt flooded Meriel as she nodded her head. "More so than I ever anticipated. He uses flirtation as a mask to hide who he really is—one of the most generous, kind men I have ever met. He cannot see his own potential and underestimates his abilities as a leader. His friendship means a lot to me and I am wondering if I am being dishonest in not sharing all aspects of what I am trying to do."

Laurel inclined her head, giving sincere thought to Meriel's misplaced concern. Laurel had watched Hamish at dinner almost as closely as she had Craig, and his facial expressions were quite mixed. The man was beginning to really care for Meriel, but it was also clear that he was fighting his feelings and did not want Meriel to know. If Hamish continued placing himself in her company, that was his choice. And if Craig wanted to risk Meriel falling for Hamish's charms, then that was another choice as well.

"No, you are not being dishonest or unfair," Laurel finally answered. "And I do not answer your question lightly. If Wyenda loved Hamish, it would matter little what you or I thought of her, but she is using him. And even though Hamish may not know all the details of what you are planning, he knows that you are trying to win Craig's heart, and he has agreed to participate in that endeavor."

Meriel stood up and hugged Laurel. "I just need a little luck."

Laurel returned the affectionate embrace and whispered into Meriel's ear, "Conor always tells me that with a good plan, you need not luck, only the ability to execute it."

Meriel exhaled. *Conor had never strategized ways to win a heart*, she thought to herself.

Chapter 6

Craig drummed his fingers on the table as he sat slumped in his chair, alone in the McTiernay Great Hall. He took a deep breath, and once again mentally reviewed the surprising news he had heard.

He had not seen Meriel since the dinner party. She had looked so forlorn that night, and yet not one time had she looked to him for comfort, support, or understanding. Right after Wyenda had launched her final assault, he had been trying to quickly devise a plan to whisk Meriel away, but before he knew it, the other guests were surrounding her, giving her the kind of support she used to seek from him. Sensing her need to flee the pitiful stares of the group, Craig was again seconds from intervening with the intention of escorting her far from the mob, when his sister-in-law announced that she was going to take Meriel back to her room. Forced to accept the delegated role of host, he could only watch as Laurel comforted Meriel in his stead.

Then he had waited.

For two full days he had been waiting, staying close to McTiernay Castle, making sure Meriel knew his whereabouts at all times. But not once did she ask for him. She had requested to see Laurel and Maegan—even Brenna—but not him, and thankfully not Hamish.

This morning, he had decided to give her one more day to sort out her thoughts and feelings only to discover how wrong he had been about her fragile emotional state. He had returned to the Lower Hall to fetch something he had left behind, when he chanced upon Fallon and the housekeeper, Glynis, discussing how one of the rooms in the Warden's Tower needed to be cleaned by midafternoon. Craig suspected he knew why, but it had still been somewhat of a jolt to learn that Meriel had scheduled a meeting with Hamish for a final fitting.

Jealousy had seized him, but only for a moment. The explosive anger had sprung upon him so quickly it had taken a few minutes to recognize the irrational response and suppress it. Being jealous was a waste of energy. Besides, had not Meriel invited him to join her and Hamish? Granted, the invitation had been issued before the disastrous dinner, but it had not been rescinded, and Craig saw no reason why he should not attend. Consequently, he had immediately sent word to Meriel that he had decided to accept.

Then he had gone to prepare himself in the Great Hall for the various means Meriel would cleverly employ to pull him away from the castle grounds once again. He waited for the emergencies, the pleas, Fallon's delivery of unexpected chieftain duties—but none came. The noon meal had been prepared, served, and removed. Still nothing. It was now afternoon and Craig was still in position to join Hamish and Meriel. It did not make sense. Previously, every attempt to make him jealous had stemmed from his wondering what was happening between her and Hamish.

Craig's drumming fingers paused in mid-tap as his last image of them together came to mind. Honest pain had been swimming in Meriel's eyes when Hamish's arm had curved around Wyenda's waist as they left the room. Was it possible Meriel had become attracted to Hamish? Her earlier claims of possibly falling in love with him had initially sounded preposterous, but suddenly Craig wondered if, in the process of trying to win *him*, she had discovered she actually liked *Hamish*. The possibility was slim, but it was also unnervingly reasonable.

Immediately, Craig rose from his chair and left the Great Hall, heading toward the Warden's Tower. It was still early, but when Hamish arrived, Craig intended to alrcady be there. The three of them would enjoy the afternoon, talk about essentially nothing, and they would part with no future meetings planned—at least not between her and Hamish.

Then tonight Craig fully intended to resume his and Meriel's nightly discussions. If she did not come to visit with him, then he would come to her. If Meriel felt he had failed her the other night, he would explain how honestly enraged and close to violence he had been. Problem solved.

Craig stepped inside the tower and began to make his way up the spiraling staircase. He had not even reached the second turn when he could hear Meriel's laughter. The infectious sound was like no other and it warmed his heart. He sent a silent thank-you to Brenna for keeping Meriel entertained.

Taking two steps at a time, he bounded up to the second floor while simultaneously coming up with two or three ideas that would induce his little niece to leave and give him some time alone with Meriel. He approached the wide-open door expecting to see a young girl with a mass of pale blond curls, but instead his eyes landed on Hamish, who stood in the middle of the room, half dressed, wearing only his kilt and pieces of an unfinished leine. Next to him was Meriel, who was looking particularly beautiful. The dark green gown she was wearing was one of his favorites, accentuating her small waist and feminine curves. She had pulled the sides of her hair into a braid, leaving the wealth of her tawny locks tumbling down her back.

Spying Craig at the door, Meriel's eyes grew large. "*Dia dhuit!* We were expecting you awhile ago."

Hamish twisted his head and grinned. "Come on in, Craig! I need someone to run for help if I begin to bleed to death from being poked with a needle."

Meriel glared up at Hamish, but anger was not what sparkled in the green and gold depths. "I *barely* pricked you *once*. But I suspect it will happen again if you don't stop moving," she said as she slowly slipped one sleeve up his arm until it met the seam of the shirt.

"Ouch!" Hamish barked. "And before you dare think to tease me," he called out to Craig, "you should know that everything I am wearing from the waist up is riddled with lethal pins."

Meriel rolled her eyes and began to slide on the second sleeve, this time not so carefully. "And I thought you soldiers were supposed to be tough. It must be awfully loud on the training field with all you men squealing every time you get nicked with a weapon."

"Highlanders do not squeal," Hamish denied. "Tell her, Craig!"

Craig stood dumbfounded. He was not sure what he thought transpired during Hamish's and Meriel's time together, but this was not what he had envisioned. Before Craig could affirm the fact that McTiernay soldiers most certainly did not squeal, Meriel tugged a piece of the partial shirt. Hamish let go a yelp and instinctively pulled back, only to be poked once more. Meriel looked up at the recoiling man before her and arched a brow. "I know one Highlander who squeals."

"Well, *men* don't pull chest hairs! Your pins do!" Hamish argued. "Go wrench one out of Craig's chest and let's see how he reacts."

Meriel's eyes flew to Craig. There was a mischievous

look in her hazel gaze, as if she was contemplating Hamish's dare, but Craig's thoughts were consumed with the realization that the type of relationship Hamish and Meriel had was eerily familiar. They enjoyed each other's company and they were obviously quite comfortable with one another. Almost too comfortable. And if Craig had not been certain that Meriel's and Hamish's friendship was about to come to an abrupt end, he might not have been able to remain calm. But any day now Conor would return home, and once Craig had divested himself of his brotherly duties, he fully intended to depart *with Meriel* for Caireoch Castle.

Forcing his mouth into a smile, Craig sauntered into the room. He was heading for a chair when he realized that his chest actually was in real danger of being plucked. Just in time, he outstretched his arm to keep Meriel at a safe distance and pointed his finger at her. "Don't you dare," he warned, and immediately sought out the nearby chair and sat down, crossing one leg so that his right ankle rested on his left knee.

He sat back to relax, and was thinking the room was much more comfortable than he remembered, when he grasped the reason why. Furrowing his brow, Craig looked down, confirming what he already knew to be true. The Great Hall's padded chairs had been commissioned by his father and were prized possessions of the McTiernay household. So valued that each of the brothers had managed to procure one or two for his room before the thievery had been put to a sudden and near violent end. "Just where did this chair come from?" Craig snapped at no one in particular.

Unaffected, Meriel focused her attention on Hamish's leine and said, "I had someone bring one up from the Great Hall. The cross-frame chairs in here were far too uncomfortable."

Craig snorted. "You're lucky I learned of this before

Conor did. You thought he was mad last year when you ordered all those rushes? He would explode upon learning this."

"Your brother gets angry at anything. I don't know why a missing chair would be any different." Meriel sighed, completely unfazed at the idea of Conor getting angry. Seeing Craig's growing distress at her lack of concern, Meriel shrugged her shoulders in defeat. "Fine. When we are finished today, you and Hamish can haul it back down to where it belongs."

Unable to do anything but agree with the suggestion, Craig leaned back in the chair, but his brow remained furrowed. He considered explaining how these chairs were luxuries most Highland clans knew nothing of, but he knew Meriel would not understand. Before she was even born, her father had sat in them and decided that his pride required that he own such grand furniture. As a result, Meriel had never known life without their comfort.

Meriel accidentally tugged on another one of Hamish's hairs, this time under his arm. Unable to stop himself, he let go another squeak, capturing Craig's attention. With both sleeves on, Meriel had shifted to work on the front of the shirt.

Another man's physique was not something Craig typically contemplated, but seeing Meriel so close to Hamish's chest, he could think of nothing else. It was bad enough that Hamish had massive shoulders and a broad, muscular torso, but it was sprinkled with just the amount of hair women preferred. In Craig's experience, his friend fit the ideal image women sought in a man. Meriel was not exactly fondling Hamish, but her fingers, pinning the material, were coming close to it.

Tension was gathering throughout Craig's body. To keep from making a fool of himself, he was about to order Meriel to stop all physical contact when she returned her attentions to the sleeve on Hamish's arm. Folding the end until it was at the correct length, she pinned it in place. Anticipating another poke, Hamish jerked. Meriel rolled her eyes and glanced behind her. "You should try plucking your enemy's hairs the next time you lead men into battle, Craig. After one encounter, your adversaries would run in fear every time they saw you."

The absurdity of the idea made Hamish chuckle, causing his body to twitch. This triggered cackles in Craig, which spawned unrestrained laughter in Meriel. Unable to stop himself, Hamish joined her, causing Craig and Meriel to laugh even harder. Fighting for air, Meriel punched Craig on the arm as if it was all his fault that she was doubled over in pain.

"Would not work," Craig finally managed to get out. "Most Highlanders are not as delicate as Hamish here."

"I may be delicate, but I am also brave," Hamish grunted, "unless, of course, you too are going to request a new kilt and leine."

Craig threw up his hands in the air and then intertwined them behind his head as he stretched out. "I would, but I doubt there will be enough time before Conor returns."

Taking a deep breath and wiping away a tear, Meriel shifted to work on Hamish's other sleeve, bringing her backside within arm's reach of Craig. She carefully folded the second sleeve as she had the other. Then she reached down toward the pin cushion on the floor, but instead of getting a pin, her hand flew to Craig's exposed calf and gave a quick yank to a couple of his hairs.

Instantly, Craig jumped out of his chair. "That hurt!" he bellowed before he could stop himself.

The smile that erupted on Meriel's face almost made the mistake worth it. "I prove my point. *All* Highlander men are delicate."

Craig's leg burned, but the pain was a balm to his soul. Suddenly all was right with his world. Meriel was teasing him as she used to and he had yet to witness any sexual tension between her and Hamish. A sense of peace enveloped him, something he had not felt in days.

"And you," Meriel said, nudging Hamish with her knuckle, "had not yet answered my question when Craig walked in."

Hamish inhaled deeply and gave Craig a look that implored him to help. Unfortunately, Craig had no idea what her question was. With a shrug of his shoulders, he sat back down.

"That is because you have not answered mine," Hamish countered.

Taking the last pin out of her mouth, she said, "I would, but I do not think Wyenda would approve." Meriel pinned the sleeve. "I'm done! All I have to do is get this thing off of you and you will be free from further torment."

Hamish gave her a wink. "Except for a few missing hairs, I shall miss these afternoons. And I am not inviting Wyenda to dinner. I am inviting *you*. She did not make me these clothes, you did. And you need to let me say thank you."

Craig blinked and forced his body to remain still as his mind whirred. Had he heard Hamish correctly?

"I already told you, Hamish," Meriel began as she slipped her hand between his skin and the material to keep it from poking him as she removed the sleeve, "it is not necessary."

"But it is. You made me not one but two kilts, and today you have cut and pieced together a second leine. That requires more than just spoken appreciation. Do you not agree, Craig?"

Craig was vaguely aware of Hamish's question. He was watching how once again Meriel was protecting his friend from any potential pricks by sliding her hand up the shirtsleeve as she removed the item. He knew that in her mind it was not a caress, but Craig was altogether aware of what any man would be thinking under the circumstances. And by Hamish's broken, raspy tone, his friend was absolutely aware of her touch.

Meriel stepped back and bent over to put the folded sleeve with the other on her sewing basket. Craig finally found his voice. "Two does seem a little excessive."

Meriel stood up and her green eyes momentarily glinted at Craig before shifting to Hamish. "Perhaps, then, since I have done an *excessive* amount of work, I should let you thank me. I accept your offer of dinner."

Hamish's eyes shined with genuine excitement. "Great! Tomorrow night?" he half asked, half proclaimed.

Meriel moved to stand in front of Hamish, leveled her gaze on Craig, and then gave a slight tug to the body of the half-finished leine, gesturing for Hamish to bend over so she could slip it off. He did so and Craig felt his insides twist in anger. Not at Hamish, but at Meriel. She was not completely unaware of what she was doing, as he had believed. Oh, she was ignorant of how her touches were affecting his friend, but Hamish was not her focus—he was.

Damn woman. She was once again trying to make him jealous and it was working. Such deviousness required him to fight with similar tactics. He sucked in a deep breath and let it out slowly. "Why don't you *make* dinner, Meriel?"

"Did you say *make* dinner?" Meriel repeated as she folded the last piece of the leine to place it on her basket. As she stood up, her hazel eyes narrowed to slits as they fell onto Craig.

"Hey! That is a great idea!" Hamish exclaimed, unaware of the cold look she was issuing Craig.

Meanwhile, Craig had to fight to keep his facial expression from giving away the triumph he felt. Meriel had a choice: refuse to go, or cook and deal with the consequences. Either way, she and Hamish would *not* be enjoying a pleasant meal together. "Aye," Craig encouraged. "You had all that practice last year. Some of the most memorable meals I ever had were from the time you worked with Fiona in the kitchens."

Cold calculation filled Meriel's eyes. "I have never made dinner by myself before, but it would be interesting to try. Hamish, I will agree to a picnic with you on one condition."

"Anything," Hamish replied with a shrug of his shoulders. The tension between Meriel and Craig was unmistakable, but Hamish no longer felt the need to end it or avoid it. He was not sure why; he only knew that he enjoyed Meriel's company and wished she had another reason to slip her hand once again along his arm.

"Let's have it by the loch—and you can show me your favorite place, the one you were telling me about."

Instead of grabbing his shirt and putting it on, Hamish crossed his arms, causing the muscles in his chest to ripple and bulge. Desire darkened his eyes, and seeing it, Craig knew that whatever game Meriel had been playing, Hamish was no longer an uninterested bystander. His friend might not yet recognize his growing feelings, but Craig had seen that look on Hamish's face multiple times. The man enjoyed the company of women and he was starting to see Meriel not just as a friend, but something potentially more.

Craig snatched Hamish's leine and threw it at him. "Now that you two have made your plans, it is time you *dressed* and left."

Meriel's head snapped around. Craig's voice had been soft, almost casual, but it held a menacing sound that sent a shiver through her. Hamish took the tossed leine and tucked it under his arm. If he had heard the warning, he was not acting like it. "I think I'll carry it since it irritates you so much."

Taking a deep breath, Meriel placed her hand on

Hamish's chest and pushed him so that he began to walk backwards. Emotions were building, which was a good thing, but the accompanying tension was growing. Any more might create a situation that could potentially ruin all her plans. "I think you better go, Hamish."

When they reached the door, he extended his hand to grab the door frame, stopping his backward movement. "Sure, but I promised you that I would help Craig with the chair."

Strong fingers gripped Meriel's wrist, removing her hand from Hamish's chest. "I think I can handle the chair by myself," growled Craig. "Meriel still needs to get her things."

Hamish gave his friend an infuriating grin. "No problem. Meriel and I have *all* of tomorrow night." Then he produced an exaggerated bow and turned to leave, pulling on his leine as he disappeared down the stairwell.

With Meriel's wrist still in Craig's grasp, he pulled her roughly to him. His arms tightened, threatening to crush her body against his hard strength. His blue eyes were intensely bright, and danger radiated from him like an aura. Meriel was far from afraid. She wanted this. She needed this. Everything depended on Craig's response.

"Let go of me," she whispered.

"Why? Isn't this what you have been wanting? So much that you are willing to torment another man just to provoke me into action?"

Meriel moistened her lips and dragged in air. "I don't know what you are talking about."

"Stop, Meriel. It's time for the truth." But before she could answer, with his free hand Craig buried his fingers in her hair, pulled her mouth to his, and kissed her. He had to kiss her; he had no other choice. Meriel was relentless, and until he yielded to what they both desired, he would have no peace.

The moment she had slipped the half-finished leine off Hamish, Craig had made up his mind. She had intentionally besieged his sanity, and now it was her turn to suffer. He could think of no better way than to give her what she wanted—a long, soft, lingering kiss that would leave her both longing and unfulfilled.

Meriel felt his lips against hers and shivers of delight ran down her spine. His closed mouth was warm and sweet and highly enjoyable, but far from satisfying. Meriel smiled inwardly. Craig thought himself to be in control, but she was far from a novice at the art of kissing, and she could feel the evidence of his desire.

Standing on tiptoe, Meriel weaved her arms around his neck, tangling her fingers in his thick dark hair. Pressing her mouth against his, she gently traced his lips with her tongue and then began to nibble on his lower lip. The heat in her veins rose and she could not restrain the tiny sound of desire coming from the back of her throat. If Craig did not respond soon, she would erupt into a blazing fire.

Need slammed into him, hard and painful, and the hair on the back of his neck stirred in primal reaction to her seduction. She was forbidden to him, not just by her father but by his own decree, and yet God knew how he wanted her. He felt on fire and overcome with need. Giving way to his baser desires, he took over and thrust his tongue inside her mouth. Then he kissed her, hard and deliberately, letting her feel the savage intensity of his desire. He half hoped it would scare her, but when she responded, eagerly tasting him in return, it only inflamed him more.

Meriel was drowning in sensation. Her blood was pounding in her head and she fought to remain alert enough to do what she must. And yet, part of her knew she was fighting a losing battle, for the more his lips moved against hers, the less will she had. Meriel felt alive and wild and thoroughly without discipline. Her mouth slanted over his, her tongue meeting each stroke.

His body was pressed against hers, and instead of pulling away, her instinct was to sink even more into his warmth. She had never known such pleasure, felt such shameless desire. With Craig, there was no fear, no inhibitions, and Meriel knew she was close to losing the one thing she could not afford—control.

Craig was a bit surprised at how quickly his own restraint had left him, but from the moment her tongue had touched his lips, the need to taste her in his mouth had been almost crippling. And his desire was only growing.

Craig's hands glided from Meriel's neck down her spine, molding her body against his so that she could not help but feel the throbbing mass of his erection. And still she did not resist. His fingers followed the smooth curve of her back and up her sides to caress her breasts as his kiss took her deeper and deeper into a place neither of them had ever gone. Her mouth—sensuous, perfect, so hot and moist— and her body, nestled into his, became his world and he wanted it all. He had started something he had promised himself he would not finish, but Craig was now unsure if he could summon the will to move away from her.

Under his touch, Meriel's breasts swelled and her nipples contracted, sending waves of desire between her legs. The sensation was new and unexpected and it momentarily jolted Meriel back to semi-awareness. Craig was stirring feelings inside her she had not thought possible. It was incredibly enticing. Only the knowledge that every dream, every hope she had for her future would be lost if she succumbed, kept her from shutting her eyes and giving in to what her body wanted.

Meriel eased her tongue out of his mouth and closed her lips. With extreme willpower, she pulled back slightly. She took in a deep breath and then let it go, before giving him one of her most brilliant smiles, hoping it looked genuine. "Fine," she said huskily. "I admit it. I did want you to kiss me again."

Craig swallowed, unable to speak. Every nerve in his body was screaming for release, while his mind was attempting to digest the idea that *Meriel*, not he, had ended their embrace.

Going back on her tiptoes, Meriel laid a hand on his chest for balance as she placed a soft, warm kiss on his temple. "Thank you," she whispered in his ear. "That was wonderful. You really are good."

Moving leisurely around him, she walked over to her sewing basket and picked it up. After making sure all the pieces she had pinned would not fall out, Meriel turned around to leave.

Craig had watched, incredulous at her relaxed demeanor while his own emotions were an insane mix of confusion, turmoil, and dazed pleasure. "That's it?" he asked. "You just wanted a kiss?"

Meriel walked up to him and reached up to quickly brush her lips with his. "Why not?" she answered. "Our friendship survived the first one, and I have complete confidence that it will survive this kiss as well. Perhaps several more if we are in the mood."

Craig stared at her. Never before had Meriel seen the amount of intensity he was channeling through his eyes. It made her heart race in both fear and anticipation. She had to leave, and based on the flurry of emotions flickering in the various muscles of Craig's face, she was not sure he was going to let her.

Licking her lips, Meriel pointed to the hearth chair with her chin. Then, in what she hoped to be a singsong voice, said, "Don't forget to bring down your brother's beloved chair," and turned to leave. She made it out the door and to the stairwell before she began to visibly shake. Taking one step at a time, Meriel told herself that it was over. She had done the impossible. She had succeeded.

Craig could no longer deny he wanted her.

Now she only needed to get him to admit that he loved her.

Chapter 7

"I must admit that you were right. This view of the water may have taken a long time to get to, but it was definitely worth it," Meriel said, sighing.

Hamish swallowed a snappy reply as he set the heavy basket of food on the ground. The reason it had taken so long was her absolute refusal to get on a horse. Nothing he promised would convince her to ride, and he finally conceded to her demands that they walk. And despite his initial trepidation, the journey had not been as onerous as he had expected. With the exception of hauling what felt like a ton of food, Hamish had actually preferred it to riding because they had been able to converse more easily.

His typical dialogue with a woman was primarily filled with flirtatious comments. The concept of expressing his opinions, likes and dislikes, hopes and dreams was inconceivable— he did not even discuss these things with his friends, let alone a woman. He pondered them often, but revealing his innermost thoughts was not something he had believed possible. And yet he had done just that. Somehow, when Meriel asked a question, he knew she truly was interested in the answer. Not in changing it or judging it, but just learning what he felt or believed. As a result, he found himself answering her questions one after the other without realizing he was doing so.

"What all did you put in this thing?" he asked, gesturing toward the basket. "I cannot believe that food for two people can weigh this much."

Meriel laughed. "I doubt the food is what is making it so heavy. I brought plates, and mugs for the ale."

Shock lit Hamish's dark green eyes. "Ale?" he breathed, and bent down to look inside. Sure enough, there was a jug. When he had thought about eating out by the loch, he was thinking that they would dine like they did on the trail. He had no idea Meriel would prepare an actual meal. He was glad, for he was ravenous after the walk and lugging the hefty basket, but unfortunately, it also meant that he would be carrying the thing back nearly as weighty as it was now.

"Next time *I'll* pack dinner," Hamish groused, closing the lid and crossing his arms. Huge, tall, and very muscular, standing with his feet shoulder-width apart, he looked quite imposing. It was not a conscious action to stand in such a way to illicit an apology, but that was what he was expecting nonetheless.

Meriel, however, just shrugged, refusing to feel guilty. "It wasn't *that* heavy," she remarked. Hamish made a low sound in his throat, but Meriel refused to offer him any of the sympathy he was indirectly demanding. "If it truly was that burdensome, then perhaps all those muscles of yours are getting soft. Maybe you should carry a heavy basket around with you more often," she suggested.

Hamish rolled his eyes, giving up. "And to think I once thought you a sweet little angel that could not speak or do anything that might offend a soul. I could not have been more wrong."

Meriel laughed out loud, kneeling down beside the basket. "You thought I was an *angel*?"

"Aye. Innocent and agreeable, always seeking to accommodate and please others," he answered, sitting down and then stretching out on his side.

Meriel opened the basket and pulled out a bag of almonds. She ate one and tossed another at Hamish's open mouth, missing her target by several inches. "Good Lord, you make me sound incredibly boring."

Hamish did not say anything and popped the wayward nut into his mouth. In truth, he had thought she was boring. Never again would he be so quick to judge a person.

"I'm actually far naughtier than my sister," Meriel continued, with an impish smile. "I was the instigator in most of our antics, and though I rarely admit it aloud, I can be the most stubborn of my family."

That fact Hamish would not argue. A few weeks ago, he might not have believed such a trait could reside in someone who came across as so nice and sweet, but he now knew differently. Never had he met anyone like Meriel and she was becoming incredibly alluring.

Meriel put the bag of almonds down, stood up, and walked to the loch's shoreline. Crouching, she selected a small round pebble. The afternoon sun was setting and Hamish wondered if the moonlight would create the same mesmerizing glow on Meriel's hair. Tied in a loose twist that hung over her shoulder, several strands had come loose and were now dancing in the light breeze coming off the loch. Her blue gown was one she had worn several times, and yet it wasn't until now that he realized how incredibly flattering it was on her.

Unaware of the direction of Hamish's thoughts, Meriel glanced back and gave him a mischievous wink. Then she fingered the rock she had picked up and slung it into the water. It sank on impact. This time she looked back and glared at him as if it were his fault.

Hamish grinned. "You cannot seriously blame me for that dismal performance."

Meriel tilted her chin at him. "I can never get one to bounce along the water like my sister, Raelynd, can. I once saw her skip a rock six times."

Hamish laughed, hauling himself back up to his feet. "*Six?* That's no accomplishment. You, my lady, are looking at one of the most skilled Highlanders in the art of stone skipping."

Meriel arched a brow and crossed her arms, not even trying to hide her doubt. "Easily said, and I quite look forward to the reason you will invent when your pebble fails to live up to your boast."

Hamish's eyes twinkled as he narrowed them in mock wounded pride. "Prepare yourself, my lady, to grovel for mercy."

Walking up to where she stood, he knelt down and selected a handful of smooth rocks. Then, palming one in his hand, he turned it over several times before giving her a speculative, sidelong glance. Then he slowly reached back and, swinging his arm low and near his hip, he let the rock fly. It bounced once, twice, and then it hit the water rapidly so many times Meriel could not count the number of skips it made before sinking. Then Hamish let another fly, and then another. Each did the impossible, skipping numerous times far out into the loch before finally disappearing.

Hamish slapped his hands against each other, wiping off the dirt. A boyish look of satisfaction beamed from both cheeks. "What say you now?"

Meriel laughed. "I would say that you had too much free time in your youth."

"Aye, perhaps I did," Hamish admitted, scuffling his feet, knowing that other women found him to be quite irresistible when he acted thus. "And yet I detect a note of jealousy in your voice."

"Maybe a little, but then I have always been slightly envious of those who could do things like that. I never can seem to get my body to do what I want it to—including throwing rocks!"

Hamish knew she was being overly dramatic, but he had also personally witnessed her lack of physical prowess. Meriel had skills with a needle, and she was creative, but she was not at all athletic. Still, just because she wasn't naturally gifted did not mean she was completely incapable. "Come here, and I'll teach you how to throw a rock."

Meriel shook her head. "There is no way that I can do what you just did."

"Of course you could if you practiced for five or so years, but with a few minor adjustments, you could beat your sister."

Meriel's hazel eyes widened, totally inspired by the idea. Raelynd had always been superior in everything they did outside—riding, swimming, running, the list was never ending. Her sister had even once ridiculed her inability to throw a simple rock. Being able to best Raelynd at skipping stones was a minor thing, but it would be incredibly cathartic.

Seeing her interest, Hamish began. "There are four things about skipping rocks you must remember—the rock, speed, spin, and release."

Meriel swallowed. Even skipping stones sounded too complicated for her uncoordinated body. "I just realized teaching me how to throw things is probably not a good idea. Trust me, after a few minutes you will be pulling out your hair and cursing at me inside your head. Let's stop while we are still friends."

"I am no coward and neither are you. Now, come here," Hamish said and squatted, pointing to a group of rocks. When Meriel finally acquiesced and came over to join him, he continued. "The pebble you chose was not only too small, it had the wrong shape. For it to bounce, it needs to be fairly flat, like this one."

Meriel inspected the palm-sized rock. It was flat, but it also looked heavy and even more inclined to fall to the loch's bottom when thrown. "What about this one?" she asked, selecting a rock similar to the one he was holding.

"Aye!" Hamish responded eagerly. "Now, find several more and I'll tell you about the next three secrets."

Meriel chuckled to herself and did as instructed. She could not believe she was searching for rocks, but Hamish was so excited at the prospect, she was beginning to feed off of his enthusiasm. Standing up, she said, "What next?"

"That would be speed, which you have. Most people think that a stone has to be moving really fast to skip along the water—"

"It doesn't?"

"Nay. It requires some, but the throw you gave a few minutes ago was more than strong enough. But instead of throwing over your shoulder, throw at your side, like this." Again Hamish whirled a rock at the water, and this time she tried hard to count the number of times it bounced before disappearing and decided it was close to two dozen.

Meriel reached back, trying to swing her arm low by her hip, and hurled the stone. It bounced twice. She spun around to face him, beaming with pride. "Did you see that? It *skipped*! I actually got it to *skip*!"

Her smile was a force Hamish was not prepared for, and it utterly disarmed him. For several seconds, he feared to move. "Aye," he managed to finally say, coughing into his hand in an effort to regain some of his composure. "Now with a little spin and just the right release, you will think yourself quite the accomplished rock thrower."

Meriel licked her lips and placed her hand, which was holding her next rock, in his. "Show me."

Hamish swallowed, taking the stone from her fingers and stepping back. Focusing on the rock, he twirled it in his palm, gripping it so that one finger was on its side. "The stone does not have to spin much, but it helps. Just hold it like this when you throw, but the real trick is the release." He held the rock parallel to the ground and then angled it slightly upward. "To get the stone to bounce, it must hit the water at an angle like this. Too flat, it immediately sinks. Slant it too high and it will skip but not far. Try it."

Meriel retrieved the rock and rolled it in her hands as she had watched Hamish do. Then with a deep breath, she pulled back her arm and let it fly. It skipped once. She bent down, got another rock, and was about to try again when Hamish walked up behind her, nestling her back against his chest. Aligning his arm along hers, he cupped her hand and guided it into several practice swings.

Meriel instantly felt smothered and fought the instinct to push him off her, knowing the moment she did, Hamish would retreat and the evening would be ruined. Keeping her mind focused on throwing the stone, she forced her body to relax and accept what Hamish was showing her.

He stepped aside. "Try it now."

Meriel pulled her arm back and, trying to keep the same arc Hamish had been showing her, released it. The stone skipped five times. Uncontainable excitement radiated from her. She spun around, jumped up, and threw her arms around his neck, giving him a quick, enthusiastic hug. "I did it!" she exclaimed and immediately crouched down to scoop up several more smooth rocks so that she could try again and again.

Hamish was glad Meriel was so engrossed. His body was betraying him and before she noticed, he had to get it back under control. Meriel was not his to desire, and yet, when he had come into contact with her backside, all he could think about was how nice she felt against him. If such an innocent touch could be so arousing, what would it be like if he turned her around and pulled her close?

Hamish shook his head and went to lie back down on the blanket, suddenly glad she had made him carry a jug of ale. He would need to down it all to redirect his thoughts.

"Eight times! Did you see that, Hamish? Me, Meriel Schellden, skipped a stone *eight times*!"

Hamish waved her over to come and eat. He had grabbed one of the plates and filled it with meat, bread, and cheese and was piling up the second one. Meriel took the offered plate and sat down on the grassy spot next to Hamish.

"This *was* a good idea," she said, and sighed. "Much better than eating in the Great Hall. I'm glad you asked to have dinner together, and I'm even more thankful that you made me accept."

"Why were you so hard to persuade?" Hamish asked, using his teeth to rip a piece of meat free from the leg bone.

"Because I should be the one thanking *you* for enduring all the unnecessary fittings. I only accepted your offer when I figured out what you were really trying to do. Genius idea, us having dinner together in order to make Craig and Wyenda jealous."

Hamish felt his lips twitch. Of course Meriel thought jealousy would be the reason for his asking her to eat with him. This entire farce had been based on his suggestion of how she should go about winning Craig's heart. Never had he anticipated that he might fall prey himself. "Genius idea, perhaps, but it was not mine. I confess I overheard Laurel talking to her friend Aileen about her doing something like this as a sign of appreciation."

Meriel masked a smile. So that was how Laurel planted the idea in Hamish's mind. "Then you still get credit. Good ideas should be stolen and replicated. Don't you think?"

Hamish put his hand beneath his head and stared up at the darkening sky, thinking about how Meriel naturally tried to make those around her feel good. "It is pretty out here."

"Quiet too," Meriel added, continuing to eat the food on her plate. She had been so busy helping Fiona get ready for the outing, she had missed the noon meal.

"This is probably my favorite spot on these lands, but not everyone can appreciate it."

"Wyenda would not like it here?"

Hamish shook his head. "I mentioned coming out here once and got a lecture on how long walks ruin gowns."

Meriel ripped a section of bread in two and offered a piece to him, choosing to remain silent.

Hamish shook his head no to the offer and then, as if he could somehow discern her critical thoughts, said, "You need to understand Wyenda. She is not like you." That caused Meriel's eyes to pop open, but Hamish, who had turned his gaze upward, was unaware. "She believes her beauty is all that makes her attractive."

Meriel disagreed. In her opinion, a hateful disposition could keep anyone—man or woman—from being appealing, regardless of how many striking features they might possess. But she kept her expression neutral and instead replied, "I guess it is a good thing she has someone who understands her so well."

Hamish took a deep breath and let it go. He had been expecting a discourse on Wyenda's distasteful qualities, all of which he knew about long before the dinner party. But what he had not expected was Wyenda's almost outright admission that she was there to meet someone else. When he had confronted Wyenda after they left, she had looked at him with shock, but not with shame. In her mind, he should have known that she only came with him in hopes of meeting someone else. With those words, he had finally understood Craig's warning from months prior. He indeed had received a nasty scar to remind him about the folly of falling for beauty alone, but at least he was now free. "I'm not sure she ever had me, or I her, but . . . we do not anymore." Then he readied himself for what was coming.

Meriel sat in shock. She knew he was waiting for her to say something but was not sure exactly how to respond. So she spoke from her heart. "I am sorry."

Hamish shifted so that he could look at Meriel. Color flooded her cheeks, for he caught her licking her fingers clean. And yet her gaze was steady and sincere. She did not like Wyenda, but she was not going to detail the reasons why. What she wanted was for him to be happy.

Hamish lay back down, suppressing a groan. He started to count the emerging stars in an unsuccessful attempt to divert his thoughts. What was wrong with Craig? Was the man impotent? Every time Hamish looked at Meriel he wanted to kiss her. And just now, when he spied her innocently— and yet very provocatively—cleaning her index finger, it had taken everything he had not to roll over and pull Meriel into his arms. Only the knowledge that Craig was probably out there, lurking somewhere, spying on them, kept him from acting on what every male gene in his body was screaming for him to do.

Meriel uncurled one of her legs and nudged his side with her foot. "You're scowling. Why?"

"Just wondering where Craig is," Hamish grunted.

Meriel brightened and looked around. "You think he is out here? Watching and listening to us?"

Hamish squeezed his eyes shut. Craig was definitely out there. Probably not close enough to hear, but Hamish had no doubt that his friend was keeping a watchful eye on the two of them. And if Meriel ever got that eager look on her face at the mention of *his* name, Hamish intended to throw his good sense away, lock her in an embrace, and give Craig something to look at.

Hamish threw an arm over his eyes, wondering how much longer he could pretend he still felt only friendship for Meriel. "So what is next in your grand scheme to win Craig?"

Meriel twitched her lips and shrugged her shoulders. "I'm not sure. This was as far as I planned."

"Well, Craig expects Conor to be back any day, so whatever you decide, it will have to be soon."

Meriel pulled her knees up and hugged them, letting her chin rest on their knobby tops. Hamish was correct. Conor would be coming back soon and she would have to make a choice. "Nothing has worked so far. And since you are no longer trying to make Wyenda jealous, it would not be fair to ask you to continue helping me."

"Don't worry about me. And jealousy always works," Hamish reassured her.

If Craig isn't jealous by now, then he redefines what a fool is, Hamish told himself. If his friend did not realize soon that others might be interested in Meriel, he deserved to lose her. *Mo creach*, Hamish swore silently. *Given the way she affects my own body, I should be the one pursuing her.* The only problem with that idea was that with Meriel, it would not be a mere dalliance. It would be serious, and marrying him would be much more than just a statement of vows. Wyenda did not have family or roots, but Meriel did. Still, there was something very appealing about the idea of confronting his past with not just a spouse at his side, but a friend.

Hamish uncovered his eyes and watched her rock slowly back and forth. "If Craig remains an idiot, do you think you will ever love someone else?" he asked, sitting up so that he was leaning on his side.

"You mean there might be someone out there who appreciates me, understands me, *and* is not afraid of being more than a friend?" she asked sardonically, intentionally avoiding answering his question.

"You forgot attraction. Man cannot live on food alone. He needs passion," Hamish returned playfully. He picked a handful of grass and threw it at her.

Meriel was stunned. Anyone who knew her would never do such a thing, for her inclination was to retaliate quite massively. Deciding to let it go, she shook her head, freeing most of the bits of grass clinging to her hair. "Women need passion just as much as men."

Hamish picked up another blade of grass, but this time began to chew on it. "And if that is true, then why have you refused to marry for so long?"

"Because," Meriel began, and then stopped. Kissing Craig had changed everything. Until then, she had never experienced real passion, but she was not about to say as much to Hamish. So she stuck with her standard reply to the frequently asked question. "I did not understand why anyone would want to go to sleep and wake up next to the same person for the rest of his life."

That Hamish understood. "But now you *want* to be married."

Meriel bit her bottom lip. "Let's just say that I am no longer against the idea. And with Craig, I would not have to make the compromises most husbands would expect."

Hamish knew exactly what she was referring to—her propensity for being very messy. But it was encouraging to hear her say that she realized if she were to marry someone other than Craig, that particular habit would have to change. "So what is it about Craig that makes you believe you love him?"

Meriel reached down and picked a dandelion. "You know how you said you understood Wyenda, accepted her as she was, even when most could not? Craig does that for me. He saw me and appreciated me when no one else did." She blew on the wildflower and watched its seeds fly away.

"He took the time to see past my ways and quirks and get to know me. He really is my best friend."

"A best friend who did not stand up for you," Hamish grumbled, unable to remain quiet. "I was not happy about how he treated you that night. Only when practically every man in the room was ready to come to your aid did he ask her to leave. By then, I realized the best way to help you was to get Wyenda out of there as quickly as possible so she could say nothing more."

Meriel arched her brows at the memory. She had been pushing Craig into action. He knew it and consequently rebelled, but she also knew that he would have eventually stopped Wyenda, even if no one else had been present. "So I have hope of inspiring a man's passions, do I?" she asked, hoping to lighten Hamish's scowl. It did not work.

"I saw the pain in your eyes. You believed Wyenda's nonsense. Don't deny it."

Hamish's gaze captured hers. There was no mistaking the dark look. He was truly angry for what had happened to her—and not just at Wyenda, but at Craig and his lack of action to protect her from being hurt. "You're right. Until the last attack, her words had no impact. But she struck true with her last blow. It was as if she knew I had spent hours getting ready for that evening, debating over my dress, my hair . . . and the effort had gone unnoticed. I could have worn my work dress and single-plaited my hair and I doubt Craig would have noticed the difference."

Hamish sat completely immobile for several seconds before erupting into laughter. At first, Meriel was taken aback. Here she had just revealed a sensitive piece of herself, and instead of being considerate, Hamish was acting the buffoon. She ordered him to stop, but he continued. Her fury took over and she grabbed the nearest thing she could throw and hurled the half loaf of bread at his head. When that had no effect, she seized his half-eaten plate of food and took great satisfaction when, upon impact, he finally stopped.

Hamish wiped away a tear and glanced at her. Her back was rigid, her arms were crossed and her fingers were digging into her so deeply that she had to be in pain. "*Mo creach*, you really are mad. But you must admit that you gave me reason to laugh."

Meriel's jaw clenched. She glanced at her plate, making it clear she was considering throttling him with it.

Hamish sat up and waited for her to look at him. "You have to know how beautiful you were that night. When we walked in and Wyenda saw you, she immediately tried to turn around and leave, but I would not let her. She does not like to compete for attention, and you, Meriel, were by far the most striking thing in that room. Couldn't you see the look of lust in most of the men's eyes? Trust me, I did, and I am certain that Craig was just as aware. Wyenda was actually voicing *her* fears. That you actually believed them . . . well, is very amusing."

"If you start howling one more time . . ."

Hamish raised his hand in surrender. "I promise. But Meriel, you are incredibly alluring to a man, even when you don't try. I'm surprised you haven't noticed how hard it has been for me to keep my distance." Hamish froze, realizing what he had just admitted.

Meriel rolled her eyes and relaxed. "You are good for the ego and are an exceptional liar. Two essential qualities in a friend."

To hide his relief, Hamish hunched forward as if she had just stabbed him in the stomach. "You wound me, my lady. My ardor is real."

Meriel giggled and got to her feet. "I would like to meet the woman who could truly snatch your heart, for I don't think it has yet been taken."

"All you have to do is find your reflection."

Meriel ignored his flirtatious comment and stared down at him, tapping her finger against her lips as if in deep thought. "She is going to be quite stubborn, I think. More wild than refined, and definitely quite beautiful. But that is not what is going to draw you to her. It is how she can and will challenge you that will keep you interested. I can just hear her now, openly defying your orders and completely unrepentant. Aye, the woman who will win your heart will be your match in all things."

Amused by her babble, Hamish turned up his smile a notch. He could not think of a description *less* likely to be his ideal woman. "I'm not sure I want a woman who can beat me in a sword fight. And I doubt Craig does either."

"Ah, but what Craig needs from a woman is far different. Being continually challenged would only turn him sour. He has enough people around him doing that all the time. What he needs most is an anchor. Someone he can rely on, knowing she will always be on his side. Someone like me," she finished with a grin and a curtsy.

Hamish narrowed his eyes and reached out to pull her down next to him. "My turn to describe *your* ideal mate. You should be with someone who makes you laugh. Someone who knows how special you are and makes you feel valued in all that you bring. Not just your skills with a needle, but your thoughts and opinions." *Someone like me*, he added to himself.

Meriel took a deep breath and let it go. "We all long for that," she whispered. Then more cheerfully said, "Who knows, maybe we will cross paths with our soul mates on our way back to the castle."

Hamish heard the hint, but he wasn't ready to leave. Not until he had secured another promise that they would get together. Craig had had his chance. And courting was

Hamish's most practiced skill set. It was time Meriel stopped seeing him as a friend, but as a man.

Sitting up on his knees, he helped her put their things back in the basket. "You know, I was thinking that I should teach you how to ride a horse."

Meriel paused just as she was about to put the jug of ale in the basket. "You are teasing me."

"I am being earnest. Spend a day or two with me and I promise you will be riding the horse rather than merely staying upon its back."

Meriel thought about it for a quick second, for the idea of being able to ride without a constant fear of falling off and being trampled was indeed quite alluring, but quickly dismissed it. "Trust me. Others have tried and failed miserably. Even Craig, and it almost ended our friendship before he finally accepted that I am hopeless when it comes to horses."

"Then I accept the challenge," Hamish announced with an enormous grin, picking up the basket to head back.

Meriel stared at him incredulously. "I offered you no such thing!"

"Ah, but you did. And I'm not going to take no for an answer. We start the day after tomorrow."

Craig stood up and stretched his limbs the second the two figures were out of sight. This was the last time he was going to put Meriel's virtue above his own personal comfort. In fact, he was done playing chaperone and matchmaker. If the silly woman wanted to have a picnic with a known rake in the middle of nowhere, then she would do so at her own peril. He was not following them on their next excursion to spend another four hours watching Hamish struggle with his desire. If she did not realize her near folly, then that was on her.

Craig had not been able to hear a word that was spoken, but he could see plenty. And none of it was good.

Hamish's demeanor was consistently anything but that of "friend." He had practically ogled her all evening, and what he was thinking even the most obtuse could discern. Near the end, when Hamish pulled her down next to him, Craig had been poised to rescue her the moment Hamish succumbed to his baser desires. But the man had only held her hand, and not even for very long. And while nothing overt was ever tried, Craig recognized a seduction scene when he saw one.

For once, Hamish was not choosing to play his typical flirtatious role when attempting to lure a woman. And why would he? After all the times Craig had spoken to Hamish about Meriel, Hamish would know that constant flattery and stolen caresses were not the way to gain her attention. No, instead Hamish taught her how to skip stones, asked her questions and actually listened to her answers. Something his friend would not have done unless he was truly interested. And he was. Meriel was unlike any woman out there. She was funny and smart and utterly sincere. Qualities that could entrap a man if he wasn't careful.

But how Meriel felt about Hamish—that remained a mystery. All women were puzzles and difficult to understand, but Meriel—she could drive a man mad.

Sitting on the ground, watching her and Hamish interact from a distance as he hid behind a bush, Craig had plenty of time to think. Everything Craig knew about Meriel, every instinct he had, told him that she had concocted the story about her being interested in Hamish just to make him jealous. Usually Laurel was the mastermind behind such plots, but Craig was certain that while his sister-in-law might be an active and no doubt willing participant, she was not the architect. Laurel just did not know him well enough. But Meriel did.

Looking back, Craig had to admire her skill in developing such an intricate plan. It was quite reminiscent of her father's style, which relied heavily on understanding human nature.

She had made sure she was not convincing in her plea for his help. If she had been, he probably would have done the exact opposite of what she asked and done everything in his power to keep her and Hamish apart. But while not convincing, she was consistent—key to making him wonder if there was some small truth to her claims of falling in love.

He had expected not to be included in her and Hamish's time together, but the one meeting he did attend, Craig was fairly certain that it too was orchestrated. Even the kiss he'd shared with Meriel that day was suspect; no woman with a pulse could be that blasé when he could barely speak afterward. It was just another way to rattle him.

Pretty much *everything* she had said and done since his arrival had been designed to create some kind of an emotional outburst from him.

Until tonight.

While Meriel's posture had mostly varied between normal, neutral, and friendly, more than once she had been all too willing to accept Hamish's obvious advances. When Hamish had offered his not-so-subtle rock-throwing instruction, Craig had waited for her to get mad or at least pull away. If *he* had been the one to give her such advice, Craig knew without a doubt that her elbow would have been planted in his gut.

And that was not the only time her reaction caught him by surprise. Throwing grass on Hamish? Starting a food fight? Nudging him with her foot? What was going on? If

Craig didn't know better, he would swear Meriel was falling for Hamish's charm.

Just the thought sent a shiver of rage down Craig's spine. All this time, Meriel and Hamish had pretended to like each other only to fall prey to their own trap.

Craig was not sure how, but he needed to end this budding relationship and soon. Conor would be back any day, and Craig was not about to leave Meriel behind to pursue a *real* relationship with anyone. Especially not Hamish.

"You cannot be serious," Craig muttered in disbelief, slumping back into the hearth chair. He had planned to use a number of ploys on Meriel to discover just what she and Hamish had discussed for four hours, but they had barely sat down for their nightly chat when she told him that Hamish wanted to see her again and why.

Meriel tucked her feet underneath her to get more comfortable. "I was just as shocked, and believe me, I tried to talk Hamish out of his offer."

"You need to try again," Craig said gruffly. "No man should suffer the wrath of your mean streak."

Meriel visibly bristled in her chair, letting Craig know that her recollection was quite different. "And I could live for a hundred more years and never encounter a bigger tyrant than you."

Craig suppressed a snarl. He was in a bad mood and had been all day. Twice he had run into Hamish, who was indeed in what several people had described as "a chipper mood." The fact that more than one person had mentioned his friend's unusual level of cheerfulness meant that Hamish's disposition was real and not for show. Now that he knew why, Craig wanted to shake his friend until his sanity returned.

Had not Craig described on more than one occasion

the fiasco that had resulted from his own attempt at the impossible? When it came to teaching Meriel how to ride, the woman had been and always would be impossible on the subject. For no one could have been more patient than he. He had given her simple instructions, one that a five-year-old could have understood, and even said as much at the time. "The man has no idea what he is in for," Craig huffed under his breath.

Meriel's hazel eyes glinted directly into Craig's blue ones. The long, deep look they exchanged infuriated her. The man honestly believed if *he* could not do something, then no one could. "You know, Hamish has taught me several things in the past few weeks. Perhaps his success is based on the outlandish concept that I am not an idiot for being ignorant."

Craig was far from convinced. "Maybe. But you and I both know that if you were truly acting like yourself during his little training sessions, Hamish would not be so eager to teach you how to do anything, let alone ride. I caution you with justification when I tell you to reject his offer. And if you do not, I have complete faith the shrewish side of your personality will reign once again. Even if I *am* watching."

Meriel's lips thinned with anger, but Craig knew she could not deny that there was an element of truth to what he said. She was not an easy pupil, and Craig was positive that the only reason she had not explained this to Hamish was that she knew Craig had been somewhere nearby. But he realized too late that to state it out loud like he had would prompt a response from her—and not the one he wanted.

"You are wrong," Meriel said crisply. "And I intend to prove it by accepting Hamish's offer."

Craig shook his head at the foolish but expected announcement. The first and only time he had tried to teach Meriel how to ride a horse had been more than just a disaster. And it was not as if he were the only one to have been scathed by the experience. Craig remembered asking her father about her riding skills and Rae Schellden had let go a streak of swear words that ended with "never again" and "death." Her sister, a superb horsewoman, had a similar reaction. Looking back, Craig should have put more stock in their experience. But he had not, thinking that he and Meriel had a unique bond that would enable him to do the impossible.

What resulted was their biggest and nastiest fight, and it had nearly destroyed their friendship. They had locked horns almost at the onset. He quickly learned that nothing could penetrate that stubborn will of hers when she was dead set against learning how to ride.

He thought she had been unwilling to listen and try; and she declared him to be a dictator, issuing not advice or help, but orders. After a week of not speaking to each other, her father had intervened, stating that he was not going to let two obstinate people and a pitiable horse ruin his clan's army and chase off all his servants. Realizing that Rae Schellden was right and that his negative attitude was affecting how he was interacting with his men, Craig agreed to leave the incident in the past and never bring up the subject of teaching Meriel how to ride a horse again. And so had Meriel. Another fact she had conveniently forgotten.

Craig considered mentioning her oversight but decided against the idea. Nothing could penetrate that stubborn will of hers, which was something Hamish was soon going to discover if she actually followed through with her threat.

Craig began to search for another tactic that might dissuade her from accepting Hamish's offer, which would result only in pain, when he mentally skidded to a halt. He could kick himself. Too quickly he had thought to interfere when he should have been eager to support such an idea.

Aye, he had thought to keep Hamish and Meriel apart. But this was an exception.

Craig's and Meriel's friendship had lasted because time had been on their side. Hamish had such no advocate. So while the man might have the seeds of desire for Meriel right now, an hour into their first riding lesson, not even feelings of friendship would remain.

Craig caught the large grin forming on his face just in time. It was quickly replaced with a grimace. How could he suddenly change his position? The answer came to him, for he did not have to. He had already goaded her into considering accepting Hamish's offer. Now, all he had to do was prick her pride just enough to ensure she actually went.

"I do not think you really will accept," Craig announced confidently. "You are saying you will, just to get a rise out of me, but it won't work. You and I both know that neither you nor Hamish will last an hour before you are yelling at each other. And an hour is being generous."

Meriel stiffened. "Sometimes, Craig, you rival your brother Conan when it comes to being an ass."

A chill hung on the edge of her words, and Craig realized his prick had been more like a stab. Even though he truly believed what he said, that a fight would ensue upon any attempt to instruct her on anything dealing with a horse, Craig had not meant to be so offensive. He was about to say as much and apologize, when Meriel once again surprised him.

"But I have to admit that I have given you—and mayhap one or two others in my family—reason to believe that I would be hostile to any attempt to teach me how to ride a horse. But I think this time it might be different. I've changed. I no longer shirk from learning new things and meeting new people. And Hamish knew just what to say to actually make me look forward to the challenge."

Her head had fallen against the back of the chair, and her eyes were staring at the arched ceiling of the Great Hall. Meriel's thoughts were obviously not with him, but somewhere else. Craig considered demanding to know just what Hamish had said to make her so willing, but long-developed survivor instinct made him bite his tongue. He was not going to encourage any ploy that she might be using to try to make him jealous.

Meriel lifted her head and smiled. "You got quiet."

Craig furrowed his brow. Outwardly he was not saying much, but silently he was devising one very long lecture that he intended to give her sometime in the near future. "Sounds like you have made up your mind."

"And you?"

"What about me?" Craig shot back.

Unfazed, Meriel answered, "We started talking about what our day would be like tomorrow. So far, all we have discussed are my plans. Do you have anything interesting scheduled? Fallon have some dastardly deed he is going to inflict upon you?"

Craig adjusted his position in his chair and tried to think about his own day tomorrow. If Fallon did need him, it had better be able to be accomplished in the morning, for in the afternoon he intended to watch the end of Hamish's and Meriel's growing friendship. But he was not about to admit that to her. "Nothing of any import," he finally replied.

Meriel sighed and rose to her feet. She walked toward the door, stopping to give his shoulder a squeeze. "Good night."

Craig instinctively lifted his hand to clasp hers, only becoming aware of what he was doing when she let go. With a sigh, he ran his fingers through his hair, hoping to hide his sexual frustration. "Where are you going?" he demanded more abruptly than intended.

Meriel ignored the gruffness of his tone and gave him an affectionate smile he had often seen her give little Brenna. "To my room, of course."

"Don't you want to talk some more?"

"What about?"

He gave her a small shrug. He had no answer to her question. They had never had to think about what they discussed. In the past, they had more to say than time available, and he could recall many a night when she or he would reluctantly call their conversation to an end. But not tonight.

Meriel laughed gently and waved good-bye before making her way across the room. Craig could only stare. It was not as if he had nothing to say. He did. More than ever before. He just didn't know how. Talking with Meriel had always been so effortless, but that was when he was not analyzing everything she and he did and did not say.

Craig was still dithering about whether or not he should call her back when Meriel stepped out of the room. Just before the doors closed, he could hear her say hello to someone. Her voice had been full of life and eagerness. And Craig could not deny what it was he was feeling—he was jealous.

He tried to convince himself that Meriel had been hailing Laurel or Maegan or one of myriad people around the castle, but despite his best efforts, an image of Hamish, smiling his obnoxiously large grin, came to mind. Craig could hear him chattering on about his day, and Meriel, who could find nothing to talk about a few minutes ago, easily conversing back.

Feeling possessive about a conversation was ridiculous, and yet Craig could not squelch the notion that her thoughts, frustrations, hopes—anything that she wanted to talk about—belonged first and foremost to him. He was her best friend, damn it. Or at least she had been. He was being replaced and he was just letting it happen.

Craig rose from his chair and left the Great Hall, fully intending to join whatever conversation Meriel was having, regardless of whom she was having it with.

But the courtyard was empty. And so were the North Tower, the kitchens, the stable, and everywhere he could think she might have gone at night before retiring.

Chapter 8

Craig awoke the next morning intending to recommence his search for Meriel but had not been able to take two steps into the courtyard before Fallon saw him and redirected him from the North Tower to the Lower Hall. In truth, he had had to handle very few crises since his brother had gone, especially for a clan the size of the McTiernays. But the few that did crop up always seemed to do so when Craig had plans to do things other than manage clan affairs.

Hoping it was a disgruntled farmer and not an irate housekeeper, upset that he had allowed too many castle servants leave from their duties, Craig was stunned to see a weeping Wyenda slumped over one of the trestle tables in the Lower Hall. Craig's face twisted into a quizzical expression that conveyed his confusion about just what the steward expected.

Fallon, shorter than most Highlanders but with a forceful presence, crossed his arms and looked up so that he could stare Craig in the eye. "The men will be arriving soon and she, well, she just cannot be here!"

"*I know that*," Craig hissed in frustration. He also knew that the soldiers were not due to arrive for the noon meal for several hours yet, so the urgency in Fallon's tone was more from frustration than immediate concern. Still, the idea of a woman choosing the Lower Hall as a place to cry was unfathomable. "Why is she here?"

Fallon threw his hands up in the air. No one ever defied him—well, practically no one. Laird and Lady McTiernay had the right, so that could be overlooked, but a simple clanswoman? It was unheard of, and Fallon's frustration at being unable to intimidate Wyenda into compliance was growing with each passing moment.

"I came in to conduct some business privately and found her as she is. This . . . this . . . *gonag* has since refused to move or respond to my inquiries!" Fallon huffed, and was only slightly mollified that his final insult had gotten a reaction. Wyenda raised her tear-streaked face and glared at the old man for calling her *miserable* before letting out a soft wail and dropping her head back into the crook of her arm to cry some more.

Craig raked his hand through his hair. Crying women! Worse, it had to be Wyenda. How was this *his* responsibility? He tried to imagine Conor dealing with such a situation and he knew immediately what his brother would do. He would quickly extricate himself from the affair and make his wife handle it. "Why didn't you seek out Laurel's assistance? *She* should have been told, not me."

"Lady McTiernay left early this morning to deal with clan issues outside of the castle walls," Fallon answered tersely, as if it should have been obvious why that option had not already been applied. Seeing Craig open his mouth to respond, the steward quickly added, "And Lady Meriel is currently engaged in her room and . . . well, she is very much unavailable."

Craig stiffened upon hearing this news. The idea that private meetings between her and Hamish had not ceased, as he had thought, but were continuing in her bedchambers sent a shiver of alarm and anger rippling up his spine. The only thing that kept him from turning abruptly and marching up to the North Tower was the steward's seeming unconcern that something improper might be taking place. Still, the words "very much unavailable" had been carefully chosen, and Craig's new and immediate priority was to pay a visit to Meriel. But he had to deal with Wyenda first.

Craig toyed with the idea of tossing the meddlesome creature over his shoulder and physically forcing her from the room, but decided to save that as a last resort. Taking a deep breath, he stepped as close as he dared to the crying *aigeantach*. "Wyenda, stop this and tell me just why you are in here . . . and so upset."

Her head snapped up. "Don't pretend to care about my sorrows."

"*Mo creach!*" Craig snapped, doing nothing to hide his exasperation. "You obviously want someone to care, otherwise you would have found a more private place to carry on."

From the corner of his eye, he could see Fallon's jaw drop in shock. Part of Craig wanted to shout at the old man that while he did not particularly enjoy playing the role of laird, he was not incapable of doing so. And when it came to Wyenda, he had learned the hard way that she did nothing—*nothing*—without a calculated reason. "So answer me. Why are you here, and just what do you want?"

Wyenda rose to her feet. "I want absolutely *nothing* from you McTiernays. I have never wanted anything. It was forced upon me as my only option, and every attempt I have ever made to remove myself from these circumstances and return to a life I deserve, is intentionally thwarted. So I ask you, if you all dislike me so much, why do you work so hard to keep me here?"

Craig had no idea what Wyenda was talking about. If she wanted to leave, he suspected more than one man—including himself—would be happy to help her depart. "Nice speech,

Wyenda, but you forget that I know you. So answer my question—*why are you here?*"

Wyenda's large blue eyes glared at Craig. Her voluminous hair fell in waves around her. She stood up straight and he could see the exquisite figure that had at one time caught his eye. Knowing the person the body housed, Craig wondered how he could ever have been attracted to such a creature. "As if you do not know that I have nowhere else to go," she wailed. "My grandmother has evicted me from her home, and the one man I intended to marry has decided against me. Seems his friend, a Dougal Matheson, was invited to that awful dinner party and relayed a twisted version of what happened that night. I tried to explain to Iain that I had been tricked, but he made it quite clear that based on what he had heard from various *McTiernays*, no man of any consequence would ever seek my hand in marriage."

Craig inhaled and crossed his arms. Wyenda had it wrong. He remembered Dougal Matheson being there that evening. Though Matheson lived just a few hours' ride on the other side of the McTiernays' northwest border, their clans were not close allies. Yet, they were friendly. Craig had spoken to Dougal only briefly before the dinner, and all of the conversation had centered on the tedious and lengthy visit of Dougal's distant relative—Iain. So if Iain was the man Wyenda had been seeking to marry, she had no idea what kind of man he was. But those facts did not change her—and his—current situation. "So you are here for . . ."

Wyenda narrowed her gaze and said through tight lips, "I need a place to stay."

Craig nearly choked. "Here? In the castle? I think not. We like our servants, and are not in the habit of making them endure self-absorbed women who enjoy hurting those around them."

Wyenda's head jerked and she was forced to take a step backward to regain her balance. She had overheard similar remarks but had attributed them to jealousy, as no one ever dared to say as much to her face. "Then where am I to go? You cannot refuse me!"

Craig shook his head. She truly did not see how she had brought the situation upon herself. How could she not see how her words and actions collectively had created her current situation? Was she truly unable to accept that her life had changed, that her continued pursuit of the past would only bring her unhappiness? Craig took a deep breath and it caught in his throat as a single thought came to his mind. *The same could be said of you.*

Craig flexed his hands, which had balled up into fists while folded across his chest. He could not find it in himself to forgive Wyenda for her treatment of people, especially Meriel, and yet he was not inclined to abandon the woman to the elements. "This situation is of your making, not mine, and therefore so shall the remedy be yours. While you may not like them, you do have choices. Return to your grandmother and grovel for forgiveness, pledging never to abuse her kindness again. And if by chance some fool is overtaken by your beauty and offers marriage, accept it and then make sure he never regrets the decision."

Craig turned to leave when Wyenda shouted back, "That is only one option! I demand to have another!"

Craig reached the Lower Hall door and paused before he opened it. Looking over his shoulder at the befuddled steward, Craig ordered, "If she has not left within the next five minutes, then forcibly remove her." Craig pushed open the heavy door and stopped once again to address the steward. "Oh, and Fallon, I do not mean depositing her outside the hall here in the bailey, but beyond the castle walls. Be sure to instruct the guards at the gatehouse as to my wishes."

The door was swinging closed when he heard her shriek something about Conor and Laurel. Craig was unfazed. He suspected that in comparison to his brother and sister-in-law, he had been overly tolerant of her tantrum and fairly compassionate. And while Craig did not have high hopes that she would ever realize the truth of her situation, he no longer was willfully ignorant of his.

The truth was that the relationship he and Meriel had was no more. Too many things had happened for it to remain unchanged. And there was Hamish.

Whether or not she had been playing a ruse at the beginning was becoming less and less relevant each time she and Hamish met. His friend liked Meriel, and his feelings for her were growing. Whether they would grow beyond his usual infatuation was hard to determine, but the man was acting disturbingly more serious and sincere. Had Meriel's feelings also changed, or did she still see Hamish as a friend? Where did the truth begin and end?

Craig clenched his jaw. If Meriel wanted to talk, then they would. And right now.

Craig pivoted and marched toward the North Tower. *Hope you are ready, Meriel*, Craig mumbled to himself. *You wanted a subject to discuss—well, I have several.*

Craig entered the castle and could hear Meriel laughing, indicating that the door was open and that someone was with her. He bounded up the staircase preparing how he was going to interrupt the lively party and evict Hamish, and not just for now, but forever. By the time he reached her room, the tension in his body had neared its breaking point, causing him to erupt at the scene in front of him. "What exactly is going on in here!"

Laughter came to an abrupt halt and two pairs of shocked eyes were leveled on him. One was hazel and belonged to Meriel. The other was silver and had just become quite icy. Craig blinked and sent a prayer to the men in Brenna's future. If at eight years of age she knew how to level a cold stare at a man, then whomever pledged himself to her for life had no hope of ever winning an argument, whether in the right or not. "Sorry, little Bren, I . . . uh . . . I thought you were someone else."

Now confused, Brenna put the brush down on the small table beside her and asked, "Meriel, I thought you said that I was the only one you allowed to play with your hair."

Meriel smoothed back the girl's playful light blond curls and said, "I did say that." And when that did not completely placate the little girl, she added in a whisper that was intentionally loud enough for Craig to hear, "Remember what I said about boys and how they think?"

Brenna's eyes grew large and she broke into a wide grin and gave Meriel a huge hug around her neck. She whispered something back, which caused Meriel to giggle and squeeze her in return. "Unfortunately, I think your uncle wants to talk to me about stuff you will find boring and silly. So we are going to have to postpone the rest of our hair-braiding lesson for another day."

Brenna nodded and gave Meriel another hug. Then she pivoted, stomped to the door, and waited for Craig to move out of her way. Once he did so, she crossed her arms demonstratively and gave him a loud "Hmph!" followed by "I'm going to Mama!" before sashaying out the door and down the stairwell.

The threat did not faze Craig. If anything, when Laurel discovered that he and Meriel were alone in her room, he suspected his sister-in-law would secretly be pleased at the idea. She had stopped meddling in his life overtly— for the moment—but that did not mean she was not still secretly hoping, if not planning, for things to go her way.

Craig sighed and stepped inside. "Just what is it you have been telling Brenna? And what is Laurel going to say when she learns . . . good God, what have you been doing to your hair?" he choked when Meriel turned so that he could see her straight on.

One side of her head—the side he could see when he had walked in—looked matted, as if she had been sleeping on it. He assumed this was the result of Brenna's handiwork.

But when Meriel turned to look him, he was able to see her other side, which was a cross between ghastly and terrifying. Last year when Brenna had done Meriel's hair, the mess on top of her head had been wild, if not humorous. This time there was nothing remotely amusing about her appearance. Braids of various sizes were sprouting from all angles, so she looked like a creature that might have been spawned from the pits of hell.

Meriel raised her chin slightly and said, "I have done nothing to my hair. Brenna, however, was learning the different techniques of braiding."

Craig took a deep breath, walked over to where she sat, and grabbed the looking glass on the table, handing it to her. Meriel furrowed her brows but took the glass. She yelped as soon as she saw her reflection and immediately sought out a brush. "I had no idea," she murmured, her embarrassment sincere.

Craig shrugged his shoulders. "Be glad it was me who walked in here and not someone else."

Meriel began undoing the braids. "Just who did you think was in here with me?" she asked with a frustrated squeal as she fought a nasty tangle.

Craig sheepishly frowned and took the brush from her hands. "Hamish," he admitted, and carefully removed the strands that had gotten trapped in the brush's bristles.

Only after he began to take pieces of her hair and slowly comb out the tangles did it occur to him that the act of brushing Meriel's hair could be considered an incredibly intimate one. One that, if he had walked in and seen Hamish performing, might have resulted in bloodshed. Craig knew he should back off, but he could not find the will to stop the small pleasure and let it continue.

It was not as if he had never touched or stroked a woman's hair before, and he remembered enjoying the sensation. Based on those experiences, he had always suspected Meriel's hair would be soft to the touch, but the silky texture as it slid across his callused hands felt almost unreal. He had never experienced anything to compare. It was all he could do not to bury his hands in the mass and slowly let it fall between his fingers.

Meriel sat still and kept her face blank. She refused to let her expression reveal what Craig was doing to her as he continued brushing her hair in long strokes. He was being so gentle, and the sensation was creating a liquid warmth that coiled inside her. So much so, she never wanted it to end, but if she revealed any hint that he was generating such desires, Meriel knew Craig would immediately stop and back away.

His arrival today had been far from planned, and for once she had no idea what to say or do. But she did know that she did not want him to leave. Not yet.

"I . . . do not expect to see Hamish before this afternoon, when we are to meet in the fields. Are you going to come watch?" she asked, though she fully expected he would spy on her.

"Not sure what my plans are."

Meriel chewed on her bottom lip. Fact was, she hoped Craig would be out there in case she needed his help. She did not know what to expect this afternoon. During the dinner picnic, Hamish had changed. Their interactions had moved beyond silly flirtations and into a true friendship. She had thought she had begun to understand the man, but now she was not so sure. Hamish had suddenly become quite charming—something completely unforeseen. Her plans had been working so well, almost flawlessly, and now, with no real explanation, things were altering course and Meriel was not sure how to react, or even if she should.

Meriel swallowed. "Fallon was looking for you earlier."

Craig nodded. "He found me. Seems that Wyenda's plans for snatching the hand of a rich Highlander have gone astray and she expected me to makes things right."

Meriel held her breath. "And did you?"

"Of course!" He chortled and then leaned down to whisper in her ear, making Meriel's chest tighten even more. "Though I doubt my suggestion that she return to her grandmother and beg for forgiveness was satisfactory. But it was either that or find another family connection to deal with her nonsense!"

Meriel's lungs began to work again. Since she had first seen Wyenda and knew of her and Craig's history, Meriel had wondered just how much of his original attraction lingered. Learning that not even a small amount remained sent a surge of relief through her. "Is it horrible of me that I feel nothing? I do not delight in Wyenda's current circumstance, but neither do I feel pity—and normally I believe I would."

"Don't ever feel *anything* for that woman," Craig spit out as he selected the last bit of hair to work out the few remaining tangles. He shook his head. "That old steward was right. The way you looked when I entered the room, you were *definitely* 'very much unavailable.'"

Meriel chuckled. "Is that what Fallon said? Well, having a glimpse of what I looked like, his choice of words was kind. You should have seen his face, though. It was something akin to terror, now that I think on it."

"I do not doubt it after seeing this," he said, waving one of the more horrifically knotted braids.

Meriel sighed. "Brenna intercepted me last night and begged me for another hair lesson. She enjoys braiding, so I thought I would teach her different ways of twisting hair, but next time I think a session in styling might be required."

Craig snorted. "I strongly suggest that you do not let there be any more next times," he replied and gave Meriel back the brush. "Or better yet, tell Brenna to practice on her own hair."

Meriel shifted in her chair to look up at Craig. "Thank you, although I am afraid helping me has detained you from your duties."

Craig took a deep breath and settled into the chair across from her. "I actually came up to talk with you, and did not want to wait for this evening. After this afternoon's lesson, you may not be up to walking, let alone sitting," he said teasingly.

Meriel narrowed her eyes, for she needed no reminding of the bad fall she had taken when he had attempted to make her into a horsewoman. With a twinkle in her eye, she raised her chin defiantly and said, "I shall be ready for your apology this evening when I not only *walk* in without injury, but with a newly acquired skill."

Rolling his eyes, Craig leaned back and crossed his ankles, hoping it made him appear untroubled and not as tense as he truly felt. "Conor is due back any day and I will want to leave very soon after. Are you ready to return home?"

Meriel sighed, put the brush on the table next to her, and eased back into the seat. "Aye, I am. I miss Papa and my sister."

Relief filled Craig, for he had begun to wonder if Meriel *did* want to go home. If it had been feasible to leave right at that moment, he would have ordered their horses to be prepared. "I too cannot wait to go back to my duties. Strange, as this"—he paused to wave a finger around in a circle—"is where I grew up and lived for most of my life. But when I think about home, my mind goes to Caireoch."

Meriel smiled and closed her eyes, resting her head on the back of the chair. "I am eager to find out how Raelynd got along without me. I do not believe she has ever appreciated my contributions."

Craig intertwined his fingers on his stomach. "I just cannot wait to get back to my daily routine. I long for normalcy."

Meriel shivered, keeping her eyes closed. "Not me. Returning home and doing what I did before . . . I don't think I can do it." She opened her eyes and, seeing that Craig was studying her intently, sat up and continued. "It's not *what* I was doing so much, but how. I think I let myself become too sequestered. Coming here has made me realize that I, in many ways, acted timid when I wasn't. I did so because it was easy and expected, but not because that was who I truly was." Meriel closed her eyes and relaxed back against the chair again. "Aye, when I return home, I am going to surprise quite a few people, for I intend to change many habits and begin to seek out new experiences."

Craig was in a state of shock. There was something in her tone that he recognized quite well. Obstinacy. Anyone else might have believed she sounded carefree and nonchalant—but Meriel was quite serious. "Just what changes are you talking about?" he blurted.

Meriel took a deep breath and stretched her shoulders before sitting up and answering. "Like, well, going riding in the mornings."

"On a horse?" Craig choked.

Meriel's brow furrowed in sincere agitation. "Of course! That's what my riding lessons with Hamish are all about!"

Craig jumped to his feet, for that was *not* what they were about. Since his arrival, nothing had been simply what it was represented to be. "Enough!" he grumbled. "Enough with the ruse."

Interested amazement sparkled in Meriel's eyes, but the rest of her demeanor remained indifferent to his outburst. "What ruse are you referring to?"

The corner of Craig's mouth twisted with exasperation. *Which one?* he thought to himself. *Mo creach!* "The one to make me jealous so that I will admit that I love you."

Unfazed by his assertion, Meriel cocked her head to one side and innocently asked, "And do you? Love me?"

With one hand, Craig raked his fingers vigorously along his scalp. Then, with a look of defeat, he shrugged his shoulders. "Honestly? I feel a lot of things right now and I'm not sure I'm ready to admit any of them."

"Me too," Meriel replied, turning her hands up in the air.

"Really?" Craig asked as he plopped down onto the chair again. His demeanor was slowly morphing from capitulation to willingness to participate in a conversation that dealt with the one subject he had been avoiding—her and him.

"All I wanted was for us to *talk* about what happened. One of the things I loved about our friendship, what I thought was so unique, was that neither of us decided anything for the other—including what we could and could not discuss."

Craig winced. He had not really thought about his reaction in those terms. Recovering, he returned to a casual sitting position and said, "Well, last night you said we ran out of things to talk about—"

"I didn't say that, I just meant—"

"Well, there is one we have yet to discuss. Our kiss."

Meriel steeled her features. She wanted to laugh. Craig had resumed what she secretly referred to as his debate posture. He thought it made him look calm and agreeable, and to those who did not know him well it probably did, but she knew otherwise. It meant Craig was preparing for verbal battle. The more relaxed, the more serious he was about winning. Lucky for her, she was not going to try to achieve any victories today.

Meriel licked her lips and asked, "Which one? We kissed twice if I recall correctly."

Craig leaned forward and said with a sly smile, "Let us discuss both."

Meriel shrugged her shoulders and linked her fingers, making a steeple. "What about them?"

Narrowing his eyes, Craig studied her for several seconds. "You really are not going to make this easy for me, are you?"

That riled Meriel. *Easy* for him? "Do you know the toll it has taken on my patience to even get you to this point?" she barked. "So, no, I have no intentions of making this even a little bit easy."

Craig took a deep breath. He realized Meriel was not going to begin the conversation, and if he did not start admitting at least part of the truth, their friendship would be exactly where it had been when he entered the room—in trouble. "The kiss. The first one. I never expected it to mean anything. I truly thought it would be like when I kissed your sister. Not unpleasant, but certainly nothing memorable, let alone life changing."

"Life changing?" Meriel echoed, clearly skeptical.

Craig ignored her. "At first it was an act—the one *you* suggested, by the way. But somewhere in the middle it became something more. I suddenly desired you—and I mean *desired* you. And when that happens, it changes everything between a man and a woman, and I was and *still am* determined to keep that from happening."

"But why do you see change, especially when it comes to us, as something to be avoided?"

A glimmer of anger hovered in his eyes. "How can you ask me that after all that has happened? You left! You've built new friendships! I . . . well . . . I feel like I have lost you."

Meriel shook her head, the look in her eyes not of kindness but of candor. "You didn't lose me, Craig. I lost you. You were the one who shut down communication. You no longer wanted a friend, but a devotee who readily agreed with your opinions and accepted your silly rules about what topics could be discussed."

Forcing his jaw to unclench, Craig said, "Well, I've realized my error and will never do that again."

"Promise?"

"Only if you will tell me what you wanted to discuss the

morning you came to visit. I knew you wanted to talk and I was afraid of what you would say. I'm no longer afraid."

"Even if I say I am madly in love with you?"

Craig swallowed. "Even if," he lied.

"Relax." Meriel sighed. "I'm not sure I can tell you what it was I wanted that morning. I was confused and needed my best friend to help me work out the turmoil I was feeling. Until we kissed, I truly did not think that it was even possible that I was in love with you. It was shocking to discover that maybe my sister was right. That maybe my feelings for you were not just those of friendship."

Craig took a deep breath and considered what she had just said. Meriel had not claimed to be *in* love with him, nor had she said she was *not* in love with him. And he was unsure if he wanted to ask for clarification. Love was a questionable emotion when it came to people like him. It meant things—things he was not willing to promise any woman. "And *if* you were in love with me," he began, giving in to his curiosity, "what would you want? Marriage? Children? I thought you were being sincere when you told me you didn't want those things."

"At the time, I *was* being sincere. But, Craig, I was speaking out of ignorance. Until you and I kissed, I never understood how one could truly desire another." Meriel leaned over and clasped his hand in hers. "You've experienced passion many times, I am sure. You know what to do with such feelings, or did you not feel any desire for me when you and I kissed?"

Craig stared at her fingers. They looked so small next to his. The memory of those fingers on his back and in his hair made his whole body tighten. "You know the answer to that," he said softly.

But what he had felt was not mere simple need and desire. She was right—those emotions he had felt many times and had acted on them. But with Meriel, it was more.

Hot, intense, sexual need that was both elemental and dangerous. For everything in his experience told him that such desire, even the damn near torturous kind he felt for Meriel, would eventually dissipate. And relationships based on desire did not survive when the desire faded away.

But that was just an excuse. He knew it now. Just as he knew that with Meriel he could experience the joy his brothers shared with their wives. But the way to possessing such happiness terrified him.

It was not marriage that scared him. It was marriage to Meriel. After their first kiss, Craig knew that he could not only desire her forever, but that it would render him defenseless. The idea of willingly becoming vulnerable—let alone *that* vulnerable—went against Craig's very nature, and from what he had seen in his elder brothers, being in love was the ultimate form of exposure. Like his own parents, if anything happened to the wives of any of his brothers, they would be forever damned.

"So," Craig began reluctantly, drawing out the word, "that is what you want. To be tied together. Forever."

Hearing him speak as if in pain, Meriel gently released his hand and waited until he locked his blue eyes onto her hazel ones. "Aye. Someday. To someone who truly loves me . . . I think I would."

She had not said her full meaning out loud, but Craig understood. Meriel wanted what her sister and his brother had. She wanted all that love had to offer her, and she deserved it all. Someone who could not just desire her, but openly love her and give her his heart and his soul. Be his very reason for living. And if he were willing, it could be him. But Craig knew he could not make himself vulnerable to anyone.

"I care for you deeply, Meriel."

Meriel leaned over and gave him a kiss on the cheek, followed by a small smile. "I know. Just as I will always care for you."

Craig gazed into her eyes, unspoken emotions swirling in the darkening blue pools. "Are we still friends?"

Meriel nodded. "The best of friends. Two people who once again can share their true, innermost thoughts." Then she sat back, kicked off her slippers, and placed both feet on his lap, pointing at them. "And if you rub, I will tell you some stories from around the castle that little Brenna has innocently divulged. They will have you both in tears from laughter and in so much shock, you will be picking up your chin from off the floor."

Suddenly feeling like his world had been righted in places he had not even known were wrong, Craig obliged. A couple of hours later, when Brenna, accompanied by her younger sister, Bonny, came to find him and bring him to their mother, he rose to leave with his spirits higher than they had been in a long time.

He and Meriel had revealed their private sentiments, sharing stories about certain clansmen and -women, knowing that their opinions would stay private between them. They had even discussed their kisses again and how both were surprised to find out that the other was as good a kisser as rumored to be.

Exiting the stairwell, Craig took a deep breath and looked across the courtyard. One of the stable boys was preparing Meriel's horse for her upcoming riding lesson. Only then did Craig realize there was one person he and Meriel had not talked about.

Hamish.

Hamish strolled away from the training grounds toward the castle. Finn, the commander of the McTiernay elite guard, had pushed the men hard today, no doubt in preparation for the anticipated return of their laird. Enough time had passed for Conor to have ridden down to the Lowlands, enjoyed a short visit, and journeyed back. So while nothing had been heard and no scouts had reported that Laird McTiernay had been sighted, it did not mean he was not close. And whether Hamish welcomed Conor's return or not changed with every hour.

A bird swooped down, nearly colliding with Hamish. Annoyed, he glared at the large black feathered animal as it glided toward the loch. Looking down, he examined his sweaty, grimy hands, knowing that the rest of him looked the same, if not worse. It was to be expected. He had been in the fields besting younger, less experienced soldiers with various weapons, which often required rolling in the dirt to avoid a clever strike. Over the past couple of weeks, he had met with Meriel while in a similar condition and she never said anything regarding his appearance. Also they were to go out riding—something he suspected neither of them would return from clean and smelling nice. Still, he did not like the idea of meeting her in such a state. It bothered him. And realizing that he truly cared about what she thought about him bothered him even more.

Hamish walked down to the shore of the loch, yanked off his clothes, and dived in, hoping the cold water would shock his senses and return some of his sanity. What was he thinking when he had suggested teaching Meriel how to ride? An ill-advised plan made impetuously, to serve what—his pride?

He took a gulp of air and went under again, swimming underneath the surface until he thought his lungs would burst. He knew exactly what he had been thinking, and if Meriel had known, she would not have been so easily persuaded to accept his offer.

His flirtatious comments had been brazen and unmistakable and yet, based on her past experiences with him—not to mention the stupid ruse in which he had agreed to participate—Meriel had ignored them, believing them to be teasing remarks made by a friend. Nothing more. And he really wanted—no, needed—for her to see him as a man, not just as someone with whom she enjoyed spending time.

He swam to the shore, climbed out of the water, and lay down on the grass to dry off. When he had offered to teach Meriel how to ride, he had thought to accomplish many things. First, the woman needed to learn how to maintain a good seat on a horse. If anything, so she could make it back home without killing herself. But he also knew his time with Meriel was nearing an end, and he wanted to assure himself of at least one more opportunity to spend time alone with her. Mostly, however, he fully intended to end all pretenses about his feelings not only for her, but regarding her desire to capture Craig's heart; a man who clearly did not want or deserve it.

The problem was that if he did manage to do all that . . . then what? *Nothing*, he told himself once again. He wanted nothing from her; it was simply unnerving for such a pretty woman to be so immune to him.

Hamish grimaced as he reached for his clothes. There was no time to retrieve a clean leine. He could rinse the one he had, but it would not be dry before he was to meet with Meriel. With a sigh, he began to put the dirty garments on, comforted by the knowledge that she would not admonish him—not out loud and not inwardly. That was one of the reasons he loved her.

Hamish paused in mid-motion. It was one thing to care for Meriel, but love?

He had begun to enjoy her company the moment they started to become friends. As their friendship had grown, so had his feelings and admiration. And as far as attraction, he had *always* been drawn to beautiful women. But love? How in hell did you know if you were in it or not?

Groaning with frustration, Hamish reached down and gathered his sword, then began the hike up the hill to the castle. By now he should have known exactly what love was and how it felt to be in it. When barely old enough to be called a man, he had been so completely entranced by a woman, he thought his adoration could never dissipate. Over the years, he recognized that attraction—even when most mesmerizing—was not the same as love. Something more was required, especially if marriage was ever to be considered.

Hamish had thought he could love Wyenda because he understood her, and for a while had been incredibly attracted to her. But once again, he had discovered something was missing. With Meriel, he was not acting like the lovesick fool he had been in his youth. And yet he eagerly looked forward to each meeting. He wanted to be around her. She made him feel alive, not just physically but emotionally, and each time they parted he longed for the next time they would meet. Wasn't that love? And if so, what did that mean?

The moment Conor returned, Craig was going to demand that she leave with him and go back home. Did he intend to convince her to stay? What would she think if he asked her to marry him? *Mo creach!* How would Craig react?

Walking through the gatehouse, Hamish realized that last question was one he could answer. Simply put, he was no longer concerned with his friend's feelings. If Craig did love Meriel, he was a fool for not saying so and acting on it, and Hamish was not inclined to honor a fool.

Meriel had had her chance to win Craig's heart. Now it was his turn to try to win hers.

"Are you ready?" Hamish asked with a lopsided, mischievous grin that caused Meriel to laugh as she took the offered reins.

His thick auburn hair, which he normally allowed to hang loose around his shoulders, was pulled back into a ponytail, so that when he smiled, she suspected she was getting a glimpse of what Hamish had looked like as a boy. "I thought I was, but now, holding Merry's reins, I am not sure. But if you help me up—"

Hamish stopped her. "Let's not attempt to do any riding until we are out of the castle. Do you think you can walk Merry?"

Meriel glanced up at the towering horse and swallowed. "If I have to," she answered.

Hamish was surprised to see her trepidation at just walking the horse—a small, docile animal in comparison to most Highland mounts. He was about to ask about it when he saw a heavy door swing open. Hamish pointed his chin toward the Lower Hall behind her and said, "I believe we are going to have a spy join us."

"Did you have any doubt?" Meriel asked. "The man cannot decide whether he likes me as a woman or as a sister, but either way he would feel compelled to monitor today's outing."

Hamish frowned but said nothing as he took both sets of reins and headed toward the gatehouse. Meriel, misinterpreting his reaction, asked, "Are all men so pigheaded? Or is it only you McTiernays?"

"You forget. I am not a true McTiernay."

Meriel followed, glad Hamish had offered to take Merry's reins and guide them through the maze of people and out of the castle walls to wherever they were headed. "That's right. You said there were many reasons for your being loyal to the McTiernays, but never mentioned them."

"None of them are interesting, I assure you," he said.

"I suspect they are, and more importantly, I'm half tempted to refuse to learn how to ride today if you don't tell me at least some of the more important ones."

Hamish glanced to his side and tried to give her a menacing stare. "I do not respond well to threats, Lady Meriel."

Meriel rolled her eyes and let go a big sigh in defeat. "I know. That's why I said I was only *half* tempted, but I would like to know why you left your clan and came to be with the McTiernays."

Hamish sighed. "I will if you promise not to ask me all the various little questions that are no doubt going to plague you with the knowledge."

Meriel bit her bottom lip. "Sounds even more intriguing."

Hamish could hear the promise of pursuit in her voice. If he refused, then she would ask him at every opportunity. He might as well explain now, at least in part. "As I told you before, I grew up in a small clan. My father was the laird."

When her mouth fell open in shock, he waved a finger to signal for her not to interrupt. With a grimace, she pressed her lips together, leaving him somewhat surprised that the gesture had actually worked. "We were a small but strong clan. My father had fought in several battles and believed that every man should know how to wield a weapon, especially his sons—"

"You have brothers?" Meriel blurted.

"*A* brother," Hamish corrected and continued. "Because of our ability to defend the little we had, we were able to protect our land as well as the wealth our clan had accumulated over the decades. Not much, mind you, compared to the McTiernays, but to our neighbors, we were prosperous. So much so that one of our more powerful neighbors approached my father with an offer of alliance. Not one like between the Schelldens and the McTiernays, but one forged with marriage, which, through offspring, would forever connect our clans together.

"Now my father was not a greedy man, but the other clan had a stone castle, while my father had only a small tower keep. Even more importantly, they were a much larger clan and could offer our men and women more options when it came to marriage. But even with all that, I doubt my father would have agreed if it had not been for me. You see, I had believed myself to be completely besotted by the other laird's daughter. So it was decided. I would marry his daughter and eventually become laird over both clans. Meanwhile, my father would share our wealth to help bolster the quality of life of everyone."

"So, did you marry?"

Hamish took a deep breath. "I did not. It soon became apparent that she preferred my younger brother, and he her. Seeing this, my father decided it would be wiser for them to marry."

Meriel whistled softly. "I can only imagine how I would feel if Raelynd had stolen the one I loved. I don't think I could be around her either. Especially if she took my right to lead as well."

"It was hard," Hamish acknowledged, shaking his head. "But in the end, I realized that I loved my brother very much and gave them both my blessing."

"But you did not become laird."

"Aye, and in the end, *that* is why I left and searched for a place my skills were needed and where I respected the leadership."

Meriel was teeming with questions. Hamish had kept his story focused on the situation that had led to his coming south, but had said nothing of his identity. She still did not know what clan into which he was born, or how he came to be part of the McTiernay elite guard. Furthermore, she suspected that asking him to answer those questions would be pointless. "Do you want to return?"

Hamish blinked, glad she did not push for more about his life and who he was. It was not a secret. Conor knew, as well as his brothers, including Craig. He had just been around for so long that they had forgotten he was not a true McTiernay. But Hamish had never forgotten. "Until recently, I never planned on going back. But now I could see myself returning someday, at least to visit." Stopping, he waved his arm at the wide expanse of fairly flat land. "And here, my lady, is where your first lesson shall begin."

Meriel looked around. It was a far more ideal spot to learn than where Craig had chosen. Tomorrow the grassy fields would be covered with drying laundry from the castle and village as the women gathered to keep each other company while they worked—that is, if the weather permitted. "Pretend I know nothing."

Hamish started laughing loudly. He could not help it. "Meriel, you *do* know nothing."

She attempted to give him an icy stare, but instead joined him in his mirth. "Fine. I know nothing. And that includes how to get on top of this monstrosity without someone shoving my behind up in a most humiliating manner."

Hamish grinned, once again reminded just how special a woman Meriel was. There were not very many in the world—male or female—who could laugh at themselves. "Before we get to that, let's discuss your fear of horses," he said, nodding toward her death grip on Merry's reins.

"I'm not afraid *of* horses. Only riding them."

Hamish was unconvinced. "Were you ever scared of the dark?"

"Of course. All children are."

"Not me," Hamish said with a shrug, "but my brother was. He was terrified until he was older. He knew it was irrational, and yet he refused to be in a room, even if he was asleep, unless he knew a candle was burning. One day, no one knows how, the candle caught the table on fire. Luckily, my brother awoke in time and doused it, but my father was still furious. Knowing that a burning candle was never going to be permitted again while he was sleeping, my brother and I sat down and talked. Soon after, he overcame his fears and it was like he had never been afraid of the dark."

"Hamish, whatever special words you used with your

brother to overcome his anxiety are not going to relieve me of mine when it comes to this large animal. His fears were irrational. Mine are not."

"Fears, irrational or not, are real to those who have them, and therefore powerful. But you can decide how much control they have over you. You reduce their power not by avoiding them but by identifying exactly what you are afraid of, and then, believe it or not, talking about it."

When Hamish first started to speak, Meriel had instinctively begun to withdraw, believing he too would tell her that all she had to do was face her fear—which was in her case a massive animal with enormous power. She was prepared to remind him that she *had* faced her fear, more than once, by traveling to and from her home, and it had changed nothing. But Hamish's suggestion was far from what she had expected. Did he really just want her to talk? "I'm not sure what you want me to say. Horses scare me. They always have."

The wind caught a piece of her hair and, unthinking, Hamish caught it and tucked it behind her ear. "When was the first time you rode a horse?"

"I never rode them. Until I was older, I always refused. Raelynd eventually goaded me into trying a few times, but until last year, when I first came here, I had never stayed on top of one for any length of time."

Hamish nodded, finally beginning to understand. "So you don't have a fear of riding at all. Horses, themselves, scare you. That explains why you didn't even really want to hold Merry's reins. Was there ever a horse you would get close to?"

Meriel cocked her head and said, "One. When I was little, Raelynd and I would sneak down to where they would train and break young colts. There was this spirited filly. I thought she was so pretty for she had white spots that looked like stars all around her head and ears. I would sneak down and feed her and she was always so sweet to me that I thought we had a special relationship. Then one day I went to watch them try to break her. Something went wrong and she went wild, stomping on the trainer until he was dead. I learned later that they found something under the saddle that had caused her reaction, but by then I had seen the truth. Horses, even nice ones, are powerful and have the ability to kill."

"You are right. And that is my first lesson."

"That horses can kill you?" Meriel asked incredulously.

"Aye. No one should ever do battle with a horse. These large animals know everything—your weak points as well as your strong ones. They sense fear and *that* is what makes *them* fearful in return, believing that they might have to defend themselves. When you are confident, they are. So lesson one for you is to build your confidence in Merry and her trust in you. Here," he said, handing her some carrots from the bag that hung from his saddle. "Feed Merry."

Meriel did so, and when Merry nudged her hand for more was immediately flooded with memories of doing the same thing as a child.

Next, Hamish had her walking Merry around the field, telling the horse what had happened to her as a child and asking the animal to promise never to hurt her. It felt silly, but Meriel also sensed the horse understood what she was saying. Afterward, she was surprised that standing beside Merry was no longer quite as intimidating.

"Next comes mounting the horse. Standing on the left side, turn the stirrup toward you. Now, holding the reins with your left hand and the saddle in your right, put your left foot into the stirrup, bounce a couple of times, and then swing your right leg over Merry's back."

On the third try, Meriel finally got enough spring to get her leg up and over. Hamish was about to mention that one should slowly sit down in the saddle, not slam into it, but kept silent when he saw the pure elation on her face. "Let me guess—this is the first time you have ever gotten on a horse by yourself."

"Aye," she said, beaming at him. "Can you believe it? I cannot! Teach me more, Hamish! I actually think I might be able to learn how to ride a horse!"

"Next is about balance. Let go." Her face went slack. They both knew she had demonstrated her lack of balance practically the whole trip from her home to the McTiernays. Holding on to nothing would lead to disaster.

Ignoring her growing doubt, Hamish began to lead Merry around. "Let go," he repeated. "Don't try to ride Merry, just feel her and move with her as she rocks you side to side. Look forward, not down, and when you feel like you might fall, hold on to her mane and right yourself again."

Meriel felt herself grabbing Merry's mane often, but as she became used to the sensation, she relaxed and realized that her being so tense was contributing enormously to her struggle to maintain her balance.

"Now, I've been leading Merry, but she is a trained horse and will respond to your commands. To make her move forward, squeeze her with your calves, keeping the reins loose. Remember to rock with her to keep your balance."

"What if I want her to stop?"

"Then use the reins. Don't yank them, merely apply pressure. Try it."

Nervous, Meriel swallowed, but when Hamish let go, she gave Merry a nudge and the horse moved forward. In the past, she had kicked Merry to get her to move, which had always worked, but abruptly. Now Merry began to walk and Meriel did not feel the need to grab on to something.

"Now, make her stop." Meriel gave a slight tug to the reins and Merry immediately responded. "Now, do it again," Hamish instructed as he went to mount his own horse to join her.

They circled the field several times. With her growing

ease at dealing with her horse, Hamish decided to see if Meriel would be comfortable with more. He never really believed they would get this far today, but then he had not realized that it was not inability but sheer fear keeping her from being able to ride.

They stopped and he jumped down to make sure that the girth on her saddle was still tight. "Now, riding at this pace will take too much time to get anywhere."

Meriel laughed in delight at her new skill. "I knew this was too easy. If we had traveled this slowly from Caireoch, I doubt I would have had an issue."

"Ha! We barely managed get beyond a trot, but I promise you that by the end of today's lesson, you *will* be able to keep pace with Craig as you ride home!"

Enjoying the gentle sparring as much as he did, Meriel stretched forward to pet Merry's mane and teased him back. "Aye, Master Hamish. I shall be a dutiful student and learn under your humbling tutelage."

Hamish felt himself warm with pride. Pure happiness was sparkling in Meriel's eyes, and it was because of him. He had made her smile. He had made her laugh, and in doing so he had never felt so much like a man. "Now, to move faster, all you have to do is squeeze your legs just a little more than you did for a walk."

Feeling much more confident, Meriel did as instructed, or at least thought she had. But at the last moment, Merry lurched forward. Alarm shot through Meriel as she realized that she had done something seriously wrong. Instinctively, she stiffened and pulled on Merry's mane as the horse bolted away toward the loch.

"Make her stop!" she screamed in terror, as if Hamish could magically order the horse to halt from what was rapidly becoming a distant spot. Soon the grass would thin and be interspersed with rocks. Meriel was about to throw herself off in a panic when she heard him shout, "The reins! Remember the reins!"

Immediately, Meriel yanked them as hard as she could. A second later, she was in the air. Her last thought before she hit the ground was that she should have jumped when she had the chance. Her back met the earth and the pain of the collision was at first startling but nothing compared to the terror of not being able to breathe.

The moment Hamish saw Merry rear up, launching Meriel into the air, sheer black fright had swept through him. Vaulting onto his mount's back, he urged the horse into a gallop. Her limp body sent a new wave of terror through him and Hamish bellowed, "No!" as he launched himself to her side.

Pulling her into his arms, her chest began to move again and he could see her visible fear turn into relief. He knew then what had happened. The fall had knocked the wind out of her. "Don't touch me," Meriel protested.

Hamish laid her back down and began to check her for broken bones. "Are you hurt anywhere?"

"I hurt everywhere, you *stràiceil amadan*. And I think you should know that I have decided to never listen to any man ever again."

Hearing her attempt at humor, Hamish's own heart began to beat again. He closed his eyes and gathered her tight in his arms. She was right. He was an arrogant simpleton. He was also an incredibly thankful man that she had not been seriously injured.

Opening his eyes, he looked down and saw her studying him. She was so beautiful, and for the moment she was all his. Suddenly, Hamish wanted her more than he had ever thought it possible to want any woman. Putting his free hand to her cheek, he held her face and then drew her startled lips to his, silently urging her to comply. Slowly, he moved his hand from her cheek to the back of her neck. Had skin ever felt so soft? So luxurious? Part of him knew he should end the gentle kiss, but he could not bring himself to do so while she did not resist.

Hamish continued to brush his mouth tenderly across hers, taking his time, determined not to scare her. He felt her shiver, but she still did not pull away. His fingertips soothed her back in the gentlest of touches, afraid that at any moment her small hands on his chest might shove him away. But they did not. Instead, their warmth burned through the material of his leine and into his skin.

What had begun as an urge to satisfy a secret longing was quickly growing into primal desire. Part of Hamish longed to ravage her mouth and taste what he knew would be unforgettable sweetness. But he knew if he did that, there would be no stopping him.

When at last his lips released hers, Meriel's chest heaved with the effort it took to breathe. While she had not intended to kiss Hamish, when his lips locked with hers, instinct and curiosity had compelled her to let him continue. Her last conversation with Craig had given her pause to wonder whether the intense passion and need she felt with him resulted from their close friendship and therefore could be experienced with any close friend. But if such desire could be found with someone other than Craig, Meriel knew almost instantly that it would not be with Hamish.

The embrace had been sweet, enjoyable, and prior to kissing Craig, she might have believed it to be one of the better kisses she had ever received. But it did not make her heart pound or her pulse race even half as much as the small peck on the cheek she had given Craig earlier that day.

"Marry me," Hamish whispered, stroking her cheek.

Startled, Meriel shook her head and stammered, "W-w-what did you say?"

"I asked you to marry me. After that kiss, you cannot

deny we are compatible physically, and I think the past few weeks have proved that we could be really happy together."

Meriel wiggled to get enough room to sit upright. "Hamish, I don't know what to say."

"Say that you could love me, for I believe I have fallen in love with you."

Meriel shifted so that there was now slightly more distance between them. "Hamish, I already do love you in many ways. You are one of the best men I have ever known. I love your heart, your outlook on life, your fierce loyalty, your ability to see the true person within, without judgment. And while we are and will always be good friends, we would never make each other happy if we married."

Hearing those words, Hamish leaned back and took a deep breath. Exhaling, he removed his ponytail and raked a hand through his auburn hair. "I really misjudged things, didn't I? I seem to be doing that a lot lately."

Meriel reached forward and cupped his face in her hands. "Don't say that," she said emphatically before dropping her hands to her lap. "You and I would perhaps get along too well. And while some couples need calm and serenity to make a marriage work, it would doom any relationship you and I were in. We may seem like carefree and agreeable people, you and I, but to be happy, we need to be with someone who ignites a flaming passion within us. You, even more so."

"I could argue with you, but it would not change anything. You love Craig and that fool does not deserve you."

Meriel smiled and shook her head. "No, he does not. But you do deserve much, much more than me. Someday you are going to fall in love, and when it happens you will understand why I cannot make you truly happy. She will make your heart leap and at the same time frustrate you to the point of insanity. She will push you, excite you, and in all ways be your equal. Wait for her."

Hamish pushed himself onto his feet with a grunt. "I did wait, my lady. Problem is, the woman you describe just turned down my offer of marriage."

Meriel rolled her eyes. "When you find the *real* woman of your dreams, I want an apology, followed by a long speech on how right I am."

Hamish offered his hand and pulled her to her feet. "Then I am quite fortunate, for the possibility of most men finding the woman of their dreams is so remote, it borders on impossible."

"Four McTiernays can prove you wrong."

"Ah, but I am not a McTiernay—" Hamish did not finish his thought, for it had completely slipped his mind. It had been replaced with one that he should have known was coming.

Hamish watched as Craig slid off his horse. His friend's face was filled with rage and all of it was pouring onto him. Stepping away from Meriel, Hamish raised his hand, but before he could utter a single word, Craig's fist met his jaw, sending him spiraling to the ground in a way that few had ever dared to try—and until now, no one had ever succeeded.

Chapter 9

Time had been moving slowly since the moment Craig watched Meriel and Hamish leave the castle. But it had come to a complete stop when Meriel's horse had thrown her into the air. And it was his fault.

Craig had almost decided to stay behind, keeping his promise to see to his own personal comfort before Meriel's. But he could not do it. Although Meriel had never said so aloud, he knew just how afraid of horses she truly was. As a result, he found himself watching them, forced to keep a significant distance away to remain unseen, waiting for the doomed lesson to fail.

But it had not failed.

Hamish had done the impossible and Meriel, who could barely touch a horse when standing, had walked with one, fed it, and then rode on its back without any assistance. Craig had told himself to leave now that he knew she was not going to be maimed or injured, but he could not tear his eyes away from the scene. Part of him was pleased that she was finally learning the basics of riding, but whatever happiness he felt was drowning in resentment that it was Hamish who had helped her conquer her fear.

For the first time, the fires of true jealousy burned within Craig.

Hamish flirted. He charmed. He dallied. And he successfully lured women to his side time after time. He had done so ever since Craig had known him. And to think that Meriel would be indifferent to his wiles had been foolish. Teaching someone how to ride was far from a typical romantic interlude, but in Meriel's case it was the perfect way—if successful—to woo her. And seeing Meriel easily guide the horse around the field, Hamish was definitely succeeding. The man had already secured her friendship. But if things continued, Craig wondered if their own bond would be enough to keep her from falling in love with his friend. And so he had begun to pray for something—anything—to end the happy moment.

Then it happened. Meriel was tossed high into the air and Craig knew the fall would be painful, and possibly even cause serious injury. And while it was ridiculous to think that he had caused the accident, deep down he believed himself to be partially at fault.

He watched her hit the ground and go limp. Craig's heart stopped. Then she moved her hand to her throat and he realized she was having trouble breathing. Grabbing his horse, he fought back the icy terror ricocheting through his veins. If something happened to her, his life would be empty, meaningless. Then Hamish gathered her in his arms and the twisting pain in his stomach changed from panic to fury.

Craig knew even before it happened that Hamish was going to kiss her. The abundance of emotion—fear, relief, and desire—made it inevitable. But when their lips touched and Meriel did not offer resistance, Craig's heart turned to stone and the sweat on his body chilled. He brought his horse to a walk and let the rage consume him.

* * *

Seething, Craig slid off his horse even before it came to
a complete stop and glared at Hamish, refusing to even
spare a single glance at Meriel. He didn't dare. Craig considered himself the calmest of his brothers, saving his anger
for the battlefield, but he could not remember ever feeling
so much rage at someone he knew personally. And on some
level, knowing Meriel was also the target of his anger and
afraid of losing all control, he kept his attention totally focused on the man who had turned his life into a daily hell.

If Hamish had said anything, muttered an excuse, or
pleaded for understanding as he approached him, Craig was
unaware. By the time his fist met Hamish's chin, all the
pent-up emotion that had been gathering as he watched
them exploded.

What little anger he had dispelled by driving Hamish to
the ground was quickly replaced the moment Meriel rushed
to Hamish's side and examined the man's cheek. As if
Hamish could be hurt by one simple crack to the jaw. The
man was slightly shorter than him, but his girth was sub-
stantial; he was broader than Craig and all his brothers—
including their eldest, Conor. Craig had the advantage of
speed, but Hamish was made of granite, and while Meriel
might be unaware, both men knew Hamish had gone down
because he had *decided* to fall.

Based on the pain radiating through Craig's hand, he
should have been receiving Meriel's ministrations, not
Hamish. He was about to say as much when she pivoted to
glare at him. "What possessed you to do that?"

For an instant Craig's eyes shut, and when he opened
them again all expression had been removed. Only the heavily etched lines around his eyes and mouth being a little

deeper than usual gave any indication to just how turbulent his emotions were. "You know why."

His voice, a soft menace, sent a shiver through her, but then, as if rallying to Craig's battle cry, she rose to her feet, her hazel eyes sparkling with indignation, and said, "Do I? Was it because Hamish was able to teach me how to ride when you could not? Perhaps it was because I fell off? Or was it that he was the one who made sure that I was not injured?" She took a step forward, either unaware or uncaring just how blazingly furious he was. "It could be that he kissed me. But if it was because I kissed him back—then I should be the one on the ground."

Craig's face hardened. He felt empty, angry, and cold. "It is time you left, Meriel."

Hamish, hearing the dangerous softness in Craig's voice, coupled with his ominous expression, silently agreed that it would be better if she departed. Sitting up just enough to lean on an elbow, he said, "Meriel, maybe you should ride Merry back to the castle while I take care of this."

Meriel whirled to face Hamish. She could feel herself losing what little composure she had left as adrenaline pumped through her, causing her to tremble violently. She struggled for composure, but soon realized that his condescending words had been meant not for her, but for Craig. Lying on the ground, Hamish had propped himself on his side with his legs casually extended, crossed at the ankles. The man was purposefully appearing unconcerned just to further infuriate Craig.

Meriel leveled a wintry smile on Hamish and then an even colder one on Craig. If the two of them wanted to play games and provoke each other, she wanted none of it. "*You* return with Merry. I need to walk and will go back to the castle when *I* decide I am ready," she said, somewhat mollified to see Hamish wince at the scathing tone of her voice.

Meriel pivoted and began to march away from the two men, praying she would be out of sight by the time she broke into tears.

A strained silence followed as Hamish and Craig stared at each other. Only when Meriel was out of earshot did Craig take in a slow, deep breath. "Get up," he ordered.

Hamish grunted. "I have absolutely no intention of doing anything so foolish. Especially as I am fairly certain I would end up down here again. And I suspect in a lot more pain."

Clenching and unclenching his right hand, Craig's mouth tightened. Unless he planned to roll around on the ground, he knew he would not get another opportunity to deck Hamish, but he was mollified that Hamish recognized just how dangerous it would be for him to rise. "How dare you kiss Meriel!" Craig finally spat out.

"How dare *I*?" Hamish returned, his own bridled anger coming out in his voice. "How dare *you* for spurning the only decent, let alone beautiful woman who would ever put up with your nonsense. I should get up and knock you down just for hurting Meriel as much as you have."

"If that is true, then that is between her and me. Not you."

"You mean *was* between you and her. You have a problem, because I am no longer a bystander but an interested suitor."

Hamish's sardonic expression sent Craig's temper soaring once again. "I will not let Meriel be added to your list of conquests," Craig promised.

"Nor would I," Hamish agreed, "but I also will no longer stand by and let you toy with her emotions. You cannot barge in on our time together, acting as if you have been wronged, when it is you that has no intention of ever offering her any kind of commitment."

Appalled silence filled the air for several long seconds

as Craig studied Hamish's expression and could find only honesty. "You cannot be earnest," he said roughly, already knowing the response.

Hamish scoffed. "What did you expect? That since you didn't want Meriel, no one else would? Or were you dumb enough to believe that men would fear pursuing her if you remained her friend?"

The truth hit Craig full force. "Of course not."

Hamish waved his hand and sat up, but still did not rise. Resting his arms on his knees, he said, "Lie to yourself then, but it no longer matters. Meriel now knows that she wants to be loved and is worthy of being loved. If you haven't already, you will lose her."

The muscle in the side of Craig's cheek flexed, accentuating his clenched jaw. "Not to you," he snarled, no longer sure if he could or would ever call Hamish a friend again. "I will not let her get anywhere near you. You would only hurt her."

Hamish shook his head. "What scares you more—that you know I wouldn't? Or that she just might choose me?" Shrugging his shoulders, he leaned back on his hands and recrossed his ankles. "But again, it doesn't matter. She knows there will be other men. I've proven that your friendship with her is not the only one she could ever have with a man."

"You know nothing of our bond. If you did, you would know that our friendship is not something either of us will ever abandon."

"You are family, so your friendship will endure, but eventually she will not need it. She has tasted passion and has learned independence. Someday she will desire someone else and will want to rely on him. And you will have no say."

Craig's anger was evolving into terror. "She loves me," he said, rebutting Hamish's prediction.

"But you don't love her," Hamish accused. "Or maybe I should have said, you don't love her enough."

Craig stared at Hamish in fulminating silence, knowing there was no point arguing. The truthful words felt like stones pummeling his body. Wishing Hamish would get to his feet so he could deck him again, Craig just glared at him. But Hamish refused to move, and Craig knew that the damn man would remain on the ground until he left. Pivoting, Craig grabbed the reins to his horse and went to get Merry.

"She's not going to talk to you."

Craig ignored him. Meriel *would* talk to him. He would give her no choice. He was not sure what he intended to say, but he just knew he had to convince her to stay away from Hamish.

As if able to read Craig's mind, Hamish shook his head and said, "You are about to be either very smart for once or unbelievably stupid. And I don't think even you know just which one you are going to choose."

Clutching Merry's reins in his left hand, Craig mounted his own horse and headed in the direction Meriel had gone. As he passed Hamish, he paused and said, "I know just which one you hope I choose. But know this. Meriel will never be yours."

Completely unfazed, Hamish stared back, his eyes level and unwavering. "This is the last time I shall ever step aside regarding Meriel. I shall become serious in my pursuit. As long as she is free, I will seek to claim her heart as my own."

Half in anticipation, half in dread, Craig left to find Meriel.

Craig followed Meriel's trail, thinking she had returned to McTiernay Castle despite her threat not to, for her footprints led in that direction. Located high over a ravine, the castle's immediate surroundings were rocky, uneven, and hazardous for even the most experienced of riders, limiting traversable paths in and out of the stronghold to two. The larger, more well-used path bent around the curtain wall and headed north, into the village and the majority of the nearby farms. The second veered south toward the training fields, forest, and the loch. But where the ground became grassy, the use of the path was less critical, and Meriel had opted to stray off it, either unaware or uncaring that it was easy to see where she had gone.

Craig approached the loch and searched the area where she and Hamish had picnicked, but only when he looked farther down the shoreline—closer to the forest's edge—did he see her sitting on the ground. He frowned. It looked grassy, but the pebbles on the shore had to be uncomfortable. Sliding off his horse, he tethered his and Meriel's mounts, freed the blanket under her saddle, and took a deep breath before coming close enough to get her attention.

He stopped two feet away, and he had no doubt that she could see him and knew he was there. When she ignored him, he stretched out the blanket on a grassy spot next to her. "Here, sit on this."

For a moment, he believed Meriel was going to continue to ignore him. Then she spoke. "Leave me in peace. I do not wish to see or talk to you."

Craig grimaced. That was not how he had hoped to begin this conversation, but he should have expected it. Crossing his arms, he said, "Wasn't it you who criticized me only this morning for refusing to talk, even when it was so blatantly obvious that we needed to?"

Meriel twisted her neck to look directly at him, keeping the rest of her body perfectly still. Nothing moved, only wisps of her hair caught by a sudden warm breeze. It was strangely chilling. "I also wanted us to be candid with one another."

"I'm ready to be honest," he replied, unable to hide the tension he felt.

Meriel narrowed her eyes and then suddenly rolled them in disgust. She returned her gaze to the water, continuing to ignore the McTiernay plaid he had laid down for her. "You still believe *you* have the right to be angry, when it is clearly mine."

"*You're cross?* With me?" Craig interjected, furrowing his brows in surprise. "About what? That I caught you and Hamish embracing where anyone in the world could have chanced upon you? Or was it that I punched him as he deserved for daring to treat you like . . . like . . ." At his unspoken insult her gaze shifted back to him. Her green-and-gold eyes flashed with suppressed anger, warning him to be careful what he uttered next. Part of him wanted to heed the silent counsel, but he believed she needed to hear what he had to say. "Like another one of his many conquests, not like Rae Schellden's daughter!" he finished defensively. "You and I both know your father would have given Hamish far more than a simple tap on the chin."

Meriel jumped to her feet and faced him, her back ramrod straight. How dare Craig spin this around on her! The man was impossible. "I am *furious*, not cross," she began, ignoring the accurate charge about her father's reaction. In her mind, Craig had given up any right to be outraged in her father's stead. "You did not *chance* upon me. You were spying, just like you have been doing since you arrived here. Watching me wherever I go just in case someone else has the nerve to appreciate what he finds."

Craig's normally bright eyes darkened to angry blue-black thunderclouds. "You knew I was out there. Everything you did was so that I *would* watch you. So if I *spied* something you now wish I had not, you have no one to blame but yourself."

Meriel snorted and crossed her arms. "Oh, I knew you were out there. So did Hamish and probably half the castle staff. But as far as my *wanting* you to be there? Why would I? You and I talked this morning, and we parted accepting what we are to each other. This afternoon was about me and my desires—not you. Remember? You and I are *nothing but friends*. First by your choice, and now by mine."

Craig's voice was cold when he finally spoke. "I am your friend. A good friend who happens to know Hamish extremely well. I have every right to strike him for kissing you. I'm still debating whether or not I should do more."

"Did you see me struggle?" Meriel challenged, spreading her arms out. "It was a *kiss*! No doubt you have seen much more on those fields without giving it a single thought."

A tense silence filled the space between them. The crease between his dark brows grew deeper and the lines that bracketed his mouth tightened. Raking a hand through his hair, Craig finally exploded. "You were kissing *Hamish*! You know him. And more importantly, *he* knew better than to misuse one of Laird Schellden's daughters."

"He was not *misusing* me. Is it truly beyond your ability to comprehend that someone might be sincerely interested in me?"

"We are not talking about *someone*; we are talking about Hamish. He may be loyal to Conor, but to women? The man enjoys them and then forgets their names—often on the same night."

Meriel waited until Craig was looking at her directly before she countered his argument. "Hamish asked me to marry him."

Craig scoffed. "And you believed him to be serious?"
"I did."

The cold gravity in her tone caught him by surprise and

several thoughts hit him at once, none of them good. Ice spread throughout his veins as he recalled Hamish's demeanor as he lay there on the grass, refusing to get up and engage him. The man had been infuriatingly relaxed. He had been his typical good-natured self, but with a touch of solemnity, which had made his pledge to pursue Meriel sound uncomfortably sincere. Craig had already decided to move back his and Meriel's departure time, but now he was fighting the impulse to throw her over his shoulder and set out tonight. The only thing preventing him from doing so was that she was here, at the loch, by herself. Unless . . . she had not refused Hamish's offer of marriage and had just asked for time to think about it.

Craig's heart stopped for a second and then started again, slamming uncomfortably in his chest as fear swept through him. "You'd better have refused him," he said in a raw, harsh voice.

Meriel could see the mixture of pain and panic etched in Craig's face, but it provided no salve for her own aching heart. "*This* time."

Her tone was hard, exact, and terrifyingly distant. Craig could feel part of him slipping away, and somehow he knew that when it was gone, he would not be able to get it back. In an instinctive urge to do something—*anything*—Craig grabbed Meriel's shoulders and pulled her into his arms so that she collided with his chest. When she opened her mouth to protest, he took advantage and smothered her words, moving his lips forcefully against hers.

As soon as he tasted her, his body reacted and he plunged inside her mouth again and again, drinking in her essence, needing to replace the pieces of his soul that were being ripped away. Realizing Meriel was no longer resisting, he moved his hands to frame her face, changing the kiss from one type of intensity to another. Slowly, deeply, his tongue penetrated her mouth in an effort to use his own desire to ignite hers. He could not get enough of her and never would.

Fully aroused, he lifted his head, expecting to see similar passion swimming in her eyes. But what looked back at him was not heat, or even tenderness, just cold detachment. He knew she felt something for him, but that she could push it aside and deny its existence, shook his core.

Meriel stepped back, out of his embrace. "You were right. Desire by itself is not satisfying. Good-bye, Craig," she said simply, and then stepped around him and began to walk away. There had been no bitterness, no ulterior motive.

Craig blinked. He stumbled back a step and started breathing heavily, unsure of what was really happening. All he wanted to do was protect her and safeguard their friendship. And yet, with her every step, she was not just walking away, but away from him.

Unease like he had never known began to swell in his chest, choking him. He fought to get it under control. Of all the emotions, panic was the deadliest, for it removed the ability to think, act, and be rational. He took a deep breath and closed his eyes. Images of his past and his future began to swim before him: A year ago, Meriel sensing the truth about his feelings on the unpleasant prospect of becoming a laird. Of her curled up in a chair and laughing with him about some secret opinion they shared about something or someone. Of Meriel dancing, smiling, her long hair swaying in a way that drew the attention of every man present. Of her rocking a baby in her arms, growing large with another child and reaching out to clasp the father's hand lovingly in her own. A barely audible sound tore at his throat.

That hand did not belong to him.

Panic no longer described the terror shooting through him as the truth of his future fully revealed itself. From the moment he and Meriel had spoken on that fateful ride a year ago, she had become the most important person in his life. However, instead of embracing the depth of his feelings, he had called her his friend, all for the foolish belief that it would keep him from becoming weak, exposed, and defenseless. But he was already all those things.

Meriel knew him like no other person ever had or ever would. He did not have to explain, or justify, or even pretend with her. With others, even close friends and family, he always had to repress a piece of himself, keep it hidden away, but with Meriel he was free to be himself. She was his soul mate. She might cause him to be acutely vulnerable, but she also made him an infinitely stronger, better man. For only when he was with her, could he find true inner peace.

Craig sprang off the large stone and rushed to catch up with her. "Meriel!"

Meriel stopped and turned around just in time to be pulled once again into his arms. Her body was instantly stiff and unyielding, but a moment later he felt her tremble, which gave him renewed hope. Unable to stop himself, he brushed his lips lightly, persuasively against hers, letting her feel the endless need and love inside him.

Meriel tried to suppress her feelings. It had taken everything she had to deny her body from reacting and keep her soul from getting swept away with his last kiss. But this was too much for her to fight. His lips were so soft, so beautiful, so tender, her eyes filled with tears and her heart clenched in her chest. Kissing him felt right. She could feel the urgent need in him, but this time there was more than just physical need in his embrace. He loved her.

Overwhelmed and unable to rationalize what was happening, she clutched his arms, unwilling to discover that she might be wrong; that he only desired her and nothing more. So when he broke off their kiss, she nearly burst into tears when he forced her to look at him.

Then Craig cupped her cheek, his touch so tender she could barely breathe.

"I love you."

Meriel held her breath. Three simple words. He had said them quietly and without elaboration, but as she stared into his deep blue eyes, she knew Craig had spoken directly from his heart. She had found the man that was supposed to be hers, and he loved her in return. "I love you too."

Craig exhaled slowly, raggedly, completely overcome with emotion. He had not lost her. Just the opposite. She was his. Their unique bond now unbreakable.

"*Is tú mo shonuachar*," he exclaimed, announcing his claim to her as his love and perfect mate. A smile broadened across his face and his blue eyes danced as they twinkled mischievously before he swung her around.

Meriel giggled, unable to help herself. "Put me down, you lunatic!"

He did as commanded, knowing she was his and that he would receive many similar loving endearments for the rest of his life. That knowledge sent another wave of elation through him.

He placed a quick kiss on her nose and then began to nuzzle her forehead, breathing in her scent. "I believe I have loved you since I first saw you force poor Merry to ride next to me when we rode from Caireoch a year ago," he teased, the only way he was able to handle the joy of his emotions.

Slowly, he began to press soft kisses down the left side of her cheek, his long eyelashes fluttering along her sensitive skin until they reached the responsive spot below her ear. "I guess those days of having to ride close by and help you are over," he whispered in her ear.

"Well, my bruised backside is telling me that I am not exactly a horsewoman yet," she replied huskily, refusing to let him know the havoc his warm breath was wreaking on her stomach.

He cupped her face in his calloused hands and whispered hoarsely, "Good, because there are many things I still want to teach you." Then, realizing how close he was to losing control, he swatted her behind playfully and turned to retrieve the blanket still on the ground.

Meriel pretended to be outraged, but the grin on her face gave it away. "I do seem to take instruction better from Hamish. Maybe I should—"

Before she could finish her sentence, Craig came back and crushed his mouth on hers with animal-like possessive fury. His tongue plundered with unleashed need and possession. Meriel put her arms around his neck and returned his kiss with sweet fervor. He had meant for her to feel and know that she was his, that she was completely claimed. But inside she was laughing with sheer joy.

Chapter 10

Craig placed a hand on the back of her neck and unhesitatingly drew her to him with the intention of tasting all of the passion she had to give. Meriel offered no resistance. Her heart was pounding. The desire she had worked so hard to conceal for the past several weeks heated her blood, demanding this time to know satisfaction.

This kiss was not like the other ones they had shared. Those had only hinted at the passion and need Craig was now conveying with his lips, which were igniting something primitive, something utterly feminine deep inside her. She wanted more and intended to lose all inhibition and show him just what he was doing to her, when his lips left hers. Meriel wanted to speak, to plead for his return, but all ability to think went away as his mouth moved delicately down her neck, tracing the sensitive vein that pulsated rapidly with the rhythm of her heart.

Craig nuzzled and lightly sucked the side of her nape, savoring Meriel's quiet gasps. Her head was buried in his chest and she clung to him tightly. A great shudder of need wracked through her and it created a raging hunger of his own. His mouth returned to hers and her lips parted, welcoming the sensual entry of his tongue. He could feel her hand slide around his nape, her fingers curling into the short, crisp hair at the back of his head. His desire was taking over, and he knew that soon all rational thought would be gone.

She was perfection, and he intended for their first time to be passionate and memorable. Knowing he was reaching the last of his defenses, Craig reluctantly pulled himself away from Meriel and rested his forehead against hers.

He had been totally naïve. He had believed his attraction to Meriel powerful and strong, but controllable—even if just barely. He had not been prepared for what it would be like when he became emotionally unguarded in the throes of desire. Even now, the need to taste her once again was almost crippling. If he did not somehow muster the will to step away and keep from touching her, it would be too late. If they shared even one more kiss, he would not be able to stop himself from possessing her as every instinct in his body told him he must.

When Craig withdrew his lips, Meriel was able to take a much-needed breath. She did not need to ask why he was pulling away from her this time. She knew. She might not have had personal experience with making love, but she was not ignorant of what took place between a man and a woman. And if the past few minutes was only a hint of the passion that would be shared between them, she was amazed at Craig's powers of self-control. She certainly had not felt any inclination to stop.

Allowing him to pull back slightly, she was about to let him free himself completely from their embrace when she looked into his eyes. They were an intense, piercing blue, and filled with a primitive hunger. The knowledge made her realize that while Craig had incredible self-control, he was barely restraining his baser, primal desires.

Meriel had been waiting far too long to delay any longer. She cared not about the setting or the time of day. What she wanted was him. Kissing her, touching her, and making her his in every way.

Reaching up, she splayed her fingers over his broad chest, drinking in his strength. She could feel his muscles twitch as her hand came into contact with his leine; the energy between them was palpable. She bent down to feather kisses in the V-shaped space where his shirt had become untied. Then, withdrawing just enough to look at him, her hazel eyes, open and luminous, locked with his in a powerful hold.

Craig held his breath. He had been touched before by women, had their fingers caress his skin, and enjoyed the pleasure it had brought. But not like this. *Never* like this. It was as if Meriel's fingertips were heated, making every fiber within him sizzle with awareness of the growing suppression of intense desire. Every impulse he had striven to suppress had now claimed his entire awareness. Meriel was more than he had ever imagined in a woman. More than he had ever wanted. She was his. And she wanted him.

He no longer possessed the will to resist.

Inspired by her open invitation, Craig discarded his noble thoughts and moved his hand to her neck, immersing his fingers in her soft hair. He breathed in her scent and then retook her mouth, cherishing the feel of her, relishing her reaction to his touch.

Captivated by the pliancy of her lips, he soon lost himself in their softness, his senses stirred by her passionate response. He wanted more. He needed more, and he knew she would not protest.

Meriel's arms stole around him as he pulled her tighter to his torso. His lips moved hungrily against hers, reaching down to the very depth of her soul, paralyzing her with their intensity. Despite the thickness of her gown, she could feel the throbbing mass of his erection. The intimate contact of his arousal only renewed her desire. Lacing her fingers through his dark hair, she met his driving tongue, thrust for thrust, taking and giving back in turn.

This time she would not let him prematurely end their embrace.

Needing to touch him, she traced the patterns of the thick veins in his arms and kneaded his well-defined muscles before letting her hands slide under his shirt. There they flattened on the warmth of his sculpted torso, exploring the softness of his chest hair. His wide firmness, the overall potency of his physique, enthralled her. His gasp when she ran her hands around to stroke the corded muscles of his back freed her mouth from his kiss. Before he could recapture her lips, she leaned in and kissed his chest.

Knowing she was the reason behind the quick, hard beating of Craig's heart created a desperation in Meriel that was quite outside of her experience. A deep, primal need grew within her, making her want to discover more. Without thought, she found the hem of his shirt and swiftly pulled it over his head, exposing his upper body to the afternoon sunlight.

Craig closed his eyes, straining against the urge to throw her to the ground and plunge deep inside her. With her every touch, his arousal surged higher so that now it spiked insistently in fevered pulsations. Unable to bear it a moment longer, he pulled her closer, sliding a thigh between her legs. She cried out and pressed back against him instinctively. She wrapped her arms around his neck and began to tremble with waves of desire.

"I need to see you, Meriel." His voice was hoarse and thick, scarcely louder than a growl. He pushed all of the reasons he should not be doing this out of his mind. With a groan, he kissed her again, crushing her to him as if he could take her into himself.

He began to undress her slowly, worshipfully, completely entranced by the softness of her skin. A deep groan of satisfaction escaped his throat as he slid her gown and chemise off her shoulders and down her arms. Then, with one arm wrapped around her waist, he lifted her slightly and let the garment fall to the ground, pooling around his feet.

Craig's jaw tightened and his gaze swept over her, taking her in from head to toe in one swift, heated glance. Then he kissed her again with all the love and ardor in his soul.

His arms encircled her waist and pulled her as close to him as possible, and he deepened the kiss, crushing her soft breasts against his chest. With a guttural groan, he acted on instinct and lifted her into the cradle of his arms, carrying her to the outstretched blanket.

Laying her down, Craig kissed her passionately, drugging her senses so that he could pull away and quickly remove the rest of his clothes. He moved to lie down beside her and everything went still as their eyes met. She reached out to touch him and he pulled her hand to his lips, kissing the soft flesh of her palm slowly and deliberately.

Meriel closed her eyes, a moan escaping her as he moved his lips to the inside of her wrist, kissing her again with a gentleness that bordered on reverent. Then his hands began to explore, lightly tracing a path over her sensitive skin. Her heart was pounding. Desire surged through her, driven, hot and heady and compelling. The hot, sweet throbbing in her lower region was no longer a simmering fire but a blazing inferno. Her breasts swelled and she arched her back, reeling from the sensations he was creating. He seemed to know exactly how to touch her, where to touch her. Meriel never wanted him to stop, and yet her body was craving more, but she knew not for what.

Craig took a sharp breath the moment Meriel arched her body against his so that she was completely against his length. Her nipples had contracted until they were needy little nubs pressing urgently against his chest. Once again the world around them was lost. There was only her and him, and his need to know, touch, and taste her in every way.

His mouth came down hungrily on hers and he kissed her long and hard. The last of the pent-up worry and tension that had been growing for weeks left his body. Meriel felt so right. He knew without a doubt that God had made her for him and that no one else would ever satisfy him again.

He began to slip his hands up and down her arms, lightly caressing the sides of her breasts. They freely roamed her body, cherishing every detail while saving certain places for later. Finally, able to withstand his need no longer, his fingers began to outline the tips of her breasts, bringing their already tight pink buds to hard crested peaks. Her breathing became erratic and Meriel again arched her back, struggling to get him to obey her nonverbal command.

Easing back to give himself more room, Craig sucked in his breath at the sight of the sunlight gleaming on her ivory breasts. They were firm and ripe, sending a shudder of excitement through him.

Craig looked up to see Meriel staring at him with so much trust and love, he nearly choked. Her eyes begged him to touch her. Complying with her need and his own desire, he cupped one breast, filling his palm with its softness. One of them moaned, he knew not who, as he used his thumb to tease the rosy tip already firm under his touch. It was not enough and he bent down to give her a swift, passionate kiss.

Meriel tilted her head back and sank her fingers into Craig's hair, groaning with pleasure as she felt his lips slide downward. Everywhere his mouth made contact, her skin tingled with arousal. He trailed kisses along the column of her neck and when he reached the base of her throat, his tongue began to swirl.

Running her hands lightly over Craig's taut back, she knew Craig was straining against his own needs. His muscles twitched underneath her touch. She basked in his strength as her breathing became more ragged. His lips trailed lower. Desire now pulsed in her every vein, a wanting so intense her body wept with it, dewing her most secret place. His tongue paused to draw circles on her shoulder. His mouth was soft and wet and firm and the feel of it over her skin was making her dizzy.

Craig could no longer define what he was feeling. He only knew that the sensations coursing through him were savage and primitive. She was innocent and deserved to be treated with care, slowly introduced to the world of love-making. And maybe if she had been less responsive, less compliant and not so damn soft and sensual, he could have slowed down. But it was everything he could do not to take her right then. Only his desire to make sure she experienced pleasure in his arms provided him the will to keep his own needs temporarily restrained.

"Just let me touch you, love. I need to taste you," he whispered, and then he lowered his mouth to her breast to fully encompass a pink bud.

Meriel sucked in her breath. At first, Craig did no more than gently hold the bloom between his lips, flicking his tongue over the sensitive flesh. She was unprepared for the sensations that coursed through her, caused by something so simple. Her pulse raced as he began to trace circles around her rigid flesh. Her body throbbed and, unable to stop herself, she began to squirm beneath him. And still he continued his blissful torture.

His lips began to gently tug the sensitive nipple and his teeth rasped across the very tip. She arched her head back, her mouth open, trying to draw enough breath. Again and again, he stroked the hardened peak. His tongue was velvet agony.

Instinctively, Meriel pushed herself more fully into his mouth, causing him to lose restraint. Capturing the throbbing nipple fully in his mouth, Craig began to suckle while his hand continued to caress her other breast. The added stimulus was too much, and Meriel began to writhe beneath him, twisting and moaning, her hands clinging to his shoulders. Her breathing became erratic, she needed him so badly.

For just a second, Craig raised his head. She let go a gentle mewling protest and a satisfied grin spread across his face. Then he switched to the other side, repeating his sensual assault. While he possessively cupped and stroked her swollen breast, he worshipped the other with his mouth. Sucking until the nipple was a hard nub, he could feel her growing ever more excited beneath him as her hips ground against his length.

Craig drank in her growing tension. She continued to writhe and run her hands through his unruly hair, all in an attempt to pull him even him closer. He reveled in the strained arch of her back, innocently placing a demanding pressure of her hips against his groin. The sensations she was creating were near unendurable.

His mouth let go of her nipple as he moaned uncontrollably, his pleasure in feeling her so close to him almost too much to bear. Both breasts were swollen. He had branded her, claiming her as his own. "You are so beautiful, you take my breath away," he said and then once again captured her mouth in a long, searing kiss that only made them both desperate for more.

Craig felt a tremor inside her heated thighs. "More . . . ," she begged. Hearing her soft plea, Craig had never felt more alive or more a man. A sense of certainty he could not put into words overcame him. And the need to have her became paramount. Obliging her will and his, Craig stroked the valley between her breasts before moving to caress the curve of her silken belly, and then lower to the swell of her hips. For several seconds, he explored the smooth, velvet softness of her thighs. Then his fingers moved up, hovering just below her soft mound.

His lips found hers again in a kiss that held nothing back. He waited until she responded with equal passion and made the next move. As badly as he wanted her, he had no idea how he would stop, but he also knew he was not going to push her into anything. "Tell me what you want, love."

Meriel's body answered for her as her mouth became ravenous. With a small, hungry, deep moan, she arched into the warm palm of his hand, her body demanding relief. *"Buìochas!"* she cried out, thanking God. Her whole body felt alive.

Blood pounded in her veins, her knees trembled. She began to shake and cried out when he finally touched her. It was so gentle she could not believe the pleasure streaking through her. His name thundered in her head. She was about to say nothing could ever compare, but soon the pressure of his palm was not enough and she began to rock against his hand. Then, slowly, he parted her.

Craig was overwhelmed by the moist heat waiting for him. With one finger, he circled the opening of her body, lingering, caressing as a honey flood dampened his hand. Eyes closed, her body twisting, she began to moan with erotic pleasure. With his other hand, he stroked her face. She was so hot, and tight, and wet. Craig fought not to rush into his need to stroke and touch all of her, but he could hold out no longer.

Plunging one finger into her liquid warmth, Meriel arched her back once again. The sensations he was creating within her were almost unbearable, and yet her body only craved more. She wanted more of him inside her and lifted her hips against his hand. But instead he eased the one finger out of her snug passage, using her own moisture to lubricate her small, swelling button of desire. He repeated the action slowly and deliberately, easing his finger into her and then teasing the small nubbin of female flesh. Then he did it again. And again.

Meriel heard herself shout at Craig as she pressed herself against him, seeking release from the tension suffusing her body. She only half understood what he was doing to her. Part of her wanted him to ease her suffering and yet another part wanted him to continue, regardless if it caused her to go mad.

Then, as if he knew she could handle no more, Craig lowered his mouth to her breast, teasing her nipple once more as he introduced another finger into her. Meriel felt herself liquefy as his mouth suckled and his expert fingers began to widen her slick, hot channel, stretching her gently.

Then they delved deep into her heat, probing her with exquisite care, finding all the secret, hidden places and making them tingle with need. Meriel could feel herself spiraling out of control with excitement. Craig seemed to know exactly where to touch her—how lightly, how slowly, and how deeply.

He stroked and caressed until she was twisting uncontrollably in his arms. She cried out at the feelings sweeping through her, tumultuous, turbulent, wild, and untamed, as he dove deeper. She clung to him as she felt herself reaching another peak, straining and convulsing. Her mind blocked out everything except Craig. All she knew was that she wanted to be even closer to him.

Craig's need for her had become excruciating and he could no longer deny himself release. His hands shook as he put them on her thighs and urged them to part, positioning his hips above hers.

When he looked down at her face, his eyes were dark and

deep. Her breath quickened and her breasts began to heave with expectation. He prayed the fervor he knew was reflected in his gaze would not scare her.

He put his hands on both sides of her face and bent toward her mouth. He gave her a gentle kiss. Probing gently, he dampened himself in the moisture between her legs, praying he could control his need for just a little longer. Her hands gripped his shoulders very tightly and he knew the anticipation was threatening to overwhelm her. Her trembling limbs clung to him, but Craig could also see that Meriel wanted this just as much as he. She was holding on to him, looking at him with such trust. He knew then that she would never let him go. He would never again be alone.

Craig cupped her face in his hands and whispered hoarsely, "You belong to me . . . do you understand?"

Seeing her nod, he settled himself between her thighs and lifted her hips. As slowly as he could manage, he began to penetrate. She was slick with need, hot, and tight—he knew without a doubt she was made for him. He paused only when he felt the shield of her virginity.

Meriel held her breath, waiting for the terrible, tearing pain. He was big. At first she thought too big, but he was moving gradually, opening her, giving her body time to adjust to his size as he made a place in the very heart of her. Then he stopped. Moving neither in nor out. A moan of despair, of desire, escaped her throat. Her body felt as if it were half ice, half flame. She needed him to continue with what he started.

Burning with need, Craig cried out the moment Meriel began to move in desperate need. His hands steadied her hips, arresting her movement. And still she felt incredible—warm, tight—all liquid pressure. His restraint was slipping and he could feel himself coming apart. Clenching his jaw, he locked his gaze on hers and then ripped past her thin barrier of protection, driving forward to the core of her body, making her his for all eternity.

Hearing her shocked cry of pain, Craig's body went rigid. But when she reacted on instinct and tried to pull back, he refused to let her, keeping himself buried deep within her tight passage. He trapped her face between his hands. "It's all right, love," he groaned, savoring the feel of possession. "The pain is over now, I promise." And to help bring her back to a state of arousal, his tongue plunged into her mouth, hungry in its quest to mate with her.

Pulling out slightly, he wanted to give her time to adjust, but the throbbing of his arousal was agonizing. He couldn't stop. He drove into her swiftly, filling her completely with one long, powerful stroke. Her eyes widened, but this time there was no pain reflected in the green-and-gold liquid pools. Craig took her mouth again and began to move.

Meriel was astonished at how her body could go from such anguish to such ecstasy. The sensations were mind numbing, all consuming. He was hot, huge, and rock solid, and stretched her very limit as he buried himself in her as deeply as he could. But he felt right. It was as if her body had been made for him. She met his thrust, urging him to move faster.

Craig grasped her hips, refusing to let her bring him prematurely to climax. His jaw locked and his teeth clenched as she clung to him. She was still incredibly tight, and each time he entered her it was like going through the gates of heaven. She felt so good, surrounding him completely, and he drove deeper into her melting core. Her eyes closed, her back arched against him, moans escaping her beautiful lips, begging him for something she could not name.

He dug deep to hold on and not spontaneously combust from their delirious friction, allowing his tightly reined desire to uncoil slightly as he urged deeper, farther. His pace increased and she matched him, raising her hips to his every thrust. And still it was not enough.

At the sight of her writhing, crying out in demand for more, the full force of his own hunger broke over him. Her hips were pressing so eagerly against his own, he could no longer restrain the intensity of this thrusts. And with a groan, he crushed her lips beneath his. He drove into her again and again, with a fevered urgency that left him reeling, breathless, unlike anything he had ever experienced.

Waves of ecstasy throbbed through Meriel as her body, of its own accord, followed the tempo of his. Her desire for him was startling. Every nerve had been awakened by wild erotic sensations. Their mating had become primal, completely unrestrained. She opened her mouth to cry out, and again he devoured her lips in a desperate claiming to which she submitted willingly, eagerly. Suddenly, every nerve in her body sprung to life. All she could do was cling to him helplessly, letting the pure and explosive sensations consume her mind and soul as she shattered into a million glowing stars.

A second later, Craig groaned, *"Mo shonuachar!"* and then thrust deep inside her shaking body. Holding himself there, he found his own release.

Craig lay half on, half off of Meriel, breathless, exhausted, and utterly shaken.

He could feel his chest rise and fall with each labored breath and wondered how she could stand the pounding sound his beating heart was making against his ribs. After several minutes, he wrapped his arms around her and smiled as only a satiated man could.

Meriel, replete, with the throb of his last thrusts still echoing within her, twined one of her hands through his. She had seen his grin unfold and knew that he was congratulating himself. Any other time, she might have been tempted to give him a poke in the side and remind him that she too had played a major role in his achievement. But as they lay locked together, his free hand stroking her hair, his mouth brushing her temple . . . Meriel could only sigh.

They remained that way for some time; neither wanted to move or speak. The love they shared before had been deep and profound, as two persons bonded together in absolute friendship and acceptance. But now it was something even more. A spiritual connection created from physical pleasure. Their souls had met and combined.

Meriel curled to one side and snuggled her backside close, giving Craig a view of her vulnerable nape and her glorious hair. He picked up a tawny lock and caressed it gently, marveling at the rich, warm shade of brown. She was the most beautiful, most desirable woman he had ever seen in his life. And she always would be.

Pulling her into his arms, loving how easily their bodies merged from two into one, he whispered, "Imagine a lifetime of this. . . ." He leaned forward and pressed soft kisses down the left side of her neck. "And this . . . ," he murmured as he moved to the other side. "And this . . ." Then he kissed her slowly, lingeringly, and with a deep, tender possessiveness.

Meriel returned his embrace and then, smiling mischievously, she let her fingers trail down his side. When he jumped, she laughed aloud. "Sure you want a lifetime of me, Craig McTiernay?"

Craig shot what he hoped was a punitive glare at her but knew instantly that he had failed. He hated to be tickled, and unfortunately the Lord had made his whole body extremely sensitive to the activity. Something Meriel took delight in.

He reached out and grabbed her before she could escape,

securing her on top of him with his arms. Immediately, she started to kiss him, playing with his bottom lip in an obvious ploy to distract him. He had planned to roll over and return the favor, but instead gave in to the sudden strong impulse to simply lie back and enjoy the unfamiliar excitement of surrender.

When their mouths eventually parted he gently brought his hand to her face, moving a wayward strand of hair from her forehead. Then, with just the tips of his fingers, he tenderly traced her face, savoring every hollow, every curve only he had the privilege to touch. "Meriel, will you marry me tomorrow?"

Caught up in the sensations Craig was creating, Meriel breathed a "Yes" before realizing the whole of what he had asked. "I mean, no. What do you mean, *tomorrow*?" She pushed on his chest in an effort to sit up, but Craig kept his arms locked in place. "What about my father? Your brothers?"

Craig, never more content than he felt at that moment, shrugged his shoulders and replied with all sincerity, "At this very moment, they hold little importance to me."

Meriel crossed her fingers on his chest, giving her a place to rest her chin. "I don't know," she purred mischievously. "I probably should take some time and think. It's not often a girl gets *two* marriage proposals in the same day. I need to make sure that I say yes to the right man."

Craig growled and rolled over so that she was pinned beneath him. He knew she was teasing him, but the reminder that he might have lost her today sent a frisson of fear through him. He feared he might have just become insufferably possessive. "You are mine, and the sooner we marry, the better it will be for everyone."

Raising a fine, arched brow, Meriel gave him another shove, this time successfully freeing herself as he shifted to his side. "You mean the better it will be for Hamish."

Reaching over, she caught the edge of her chemise and shook it out before sliding it over her head.

Craig propped himself up on his elbow and crossed his legs at the ankles. "Not just him," he replied, enjoying seeing her blush each time her eyes snuck a peak at him. "Too many of my brother's soldiers salivate when you are near."

"You are being ridiculous. None of them ever said anything to indicate they had even a little bit of interest in me," she said, shaking off the grass from her bliaut before putting it on.

They better not have, Craig swore to himself. But it did not change the fact that every time she was about, lustful eyes followed her across the courtyard. More than once had he had to remind someone in one way or another just who she was. "Well, they do take an interest," Craig said emphatically, "and will until we are married."

Meriel snatched his tartan from the ground and tossed it at him, hinting for him to get dressed. "Stop pretending to be jealous. I know very well that it is one of the emotions you most refuse to indulge in."

He watched her for a moment as she laced the sides of her gown, then he rose and folded the tartan around his waist, securing it with a belt. Meriel was right. He did hate the idea of jealousy. It was irrational and therefore uncontrollable, but now that he was being honest with himself, he knew that he had been consumed with it since his arrival. But that was something Meriel never needed to know.

Craig yanked on his leine and scooped up the blanket. After fetching the horses, he replaced the plaid cushion under the saddle and turned back around. He watched as she rebraided her hair, doing a surprisingly good job without a brush or any help. He was half tempted to tell her about all the grass tangled in the weave but decided against the idea.

She might force him to pick out each and every blade, and he had no intention of doing any such thing.

When she was done, he asked tenuously, "Don't you want to marry me?"

"Of course!" came her quick reply. It also held an unmistakable note of enthusiasm, calming any anxieties that might have been growing in him. "Just *not* tomorrow."

Craig stretched his arm out to hand her Merry's reins and watched with secret joy as she hesitated before taking them. Damn Hamish for actually succeeding in teaching her how to ride, but she still had much to learn. And this time, *he* would be the one to tutor her.

Taking her hand in his, they stroked Merry's mane and neck. "Just rub her like you are doing and talk to her. And we don't have to ride. We can just walk for a while until you are ready to try again."

Meriel dropped the reins and put her arms around his neck, pulling him close so that she could bury her face in his throat. Stunned, Craig just held her, not understanding the cause of her reaction or what to do. When she finally stepped back, he saw evidence of tears, but the warmth of her smile put him back at ease. "I think I just fell in love with you all over again."

Craig crinkled his brow in confusion, and it just endeared him even more to Meriel. She knew he had no idea of the gift he had just given her. In the past, he would have made her "face her fear" of horses. The man was stubborn, but once he recognized there was a better way, he did not let his pride interfere.

Once beyond the loch and the forest that hugged the shoreline, Meriel no longer felt quite as constrained. The open fields and wide expanse gave her the courage to try to ride again. Only when she threw her leg over and felt Merry jerk, did she remember the animal had actually thrown her quite painfully to the ground. But as soon as Meriel settled into the saddle, the gentle animal tossed her mane in welcome. Meriel urged the horse forward, careful to give the signal to walk and nothing more.

Craig watched patiently as Meriel mounted the mare, helping only when and how she instructed. If anything were to go wrong, he was not going to be blamed. But nothing did. Meriel was riding. He was tempted to pull her into a deep kiss, but restrained himself and instead brought their conversation back to a topic even two days ago he never would have dreamed of discussing. "Why the delay? Wasn't your eagerness to marry your whole purpose in torturing me these past few weeks?"

Meriel shot him a penetrating look. What she really wanted to do was punch him in the arm, but her lack of riding skill prevented her. *Something*, she promised herself, *I must soon rectify*. She loved Craig, but she also had no doubt that several times during their marriage she would be inclined to let him know just how irritating he could be. And evil glares—like the one she was sending him now—just did not quite achieve that objective. It mattered little that her strength would barely make an impact against his bulk. Her intention was not to damage or cause pain, but to get his attention. From what she had learned so far by observing her sister and her husband, nothing short of a log colliding with a man's head could make him see how idiotic he was being.

"As I have told you numerous times, my efforts—if there were any—had *nothing* to do with marriage. I just wanted you to admit your feelings for me and not lie to yourself or force me to go along with your absurd idea about love."

Craig gave her an exaggerated wink. "Now you are the one who is not telling the truth. You wanted me to be jealous. Admit it."

Meriel sat up straighter and looked straight ahead. "You may be somewhat correct, but only because I—"

"You wanted marriage," he finished for her with a smug smile.

"Not to you!" she blurted out.

The shock of her exclamation caught Craig by surprise. He reached out to stop her horse, suddenly very serious. "What do you mean, *not to me*?" he challenged.

Their eyes met. Craig's mouth was tight and grim as he stared. Meriel met his glare with one of her own. "What woman would ever want to marry a man who *refused to admit* that he even desired her?"

Craig drew his lips in thoughtfully and let go of Merry's reins, but he did not break his gaze. "But you knew I desired you. *Mo creach*, you knew I loved you even before I did!"

"Aye, but it didn't count until *you* admitted it." Meriel gave her mount a nudge with her legs and the animal began to walk away.

Craig rolled his eyes. For a brief while, he had thought that with love came a better understanding of women. *If anything*, he murmured to himself, *you become even more impossible to understand.* Suddenly he felt more sympathy toward his eldest brother. No wonder Conor fought all the time with Laurel. "So you do want to marry me."

"I already said that I did."

"Just not tomorrow."

"Aye. Sometime in the next few weeks. It takes time to organize a big wedding, and I expect many will want to see you in front of the altar."

Craig raked a hand through his hair. Staying away from her bed tonight was going to be hard enough, but *a few weeks*? Now that he had experienced heaven, there was no possible way he was going to last that long. And as far as a big wedding? He wanted none of it. "Give me one good reason—one that will convince *me*—why we cannot marry tomorrow."

Meriel issued him a sideways grin. "Otherwise you will hoist me over your shoulder and marry me anyway?"

Craig snorted. "Aye. I just might."

"And just who will you plop me down in front of to preside over the ceremony?" Her eyes glowed with pure enjoyment as comprehension dawned on his face. Father Lanaghly had left with Conan before his arrival and neither had returned, nor was it known *when* they would return. Only sometime before winter.

He was just digesting this unavoidable fact when she continued. "I'll give you three *more* reasons. My father, my sister, and her husband, known to you as your brother Crevan. All three of them would be highly incensed if they were not involved, let alone present at the wedding. And as we would see them every day at Caireoch Castle, they could make life pretty miserable for you."

On this she also had a point, but it reminded him that he had other options as well. "I will agree to delay our union *for a week*," he growled. "As soon as we get back, I will send a herald to Lindores Abbey. I have no doubt that Father Lanaghly will return immediately."

Meriel could not help but laugh out loud at his frustration at not being able to dictate things to his liking. Truth was, she was not sure she could wait much longer either. She had only said *several weeks* for amusement, knowing how it would rile him. "Let's get married at Caireoch. I want to be home, in front of my family and yours, when I say my vows."

"As long as it is at sunset."

Meriel nodded. It was one McTiernay tradition she had no intention of breaking.

"And small," he added. He was already irritated at the

heckles he knew he was going to get. Even if they were deserved.

"I too want it to be small, as long as one certain person is there to witness it."

"Father Lanaghly? He'll be there. I can guarantee you that when my message reaches him, he will waste no time in returning," Craig said, misunderstanding.

With a mischievous twinkle in her eye, Meriel shook her head. "Not Father Lanaghly. Conan. I want your brother to be there."

Craig's brows pulled together in a bewildered frown. "Why him, of all people?"

"I have my reasons," said Meriel simply. *Revenge may not be a mature feeling, but every once in awhile it can be satisfying*, she thought to herself.

Craig stopped his horse and indicated for her to stop as well. He rubbed the back of his neck, watching two riders approach them. He grinned triumphantly, pointing at the two figures. "Guess who just arrived?"

Meriel swiveled in the saddle and shaded her eyes to see who was coming. A second later she understood just why Craig was grinning like a little boy who got the biggest present. Conor McTiernay and Father Lanaghly had returned.

They stopped their horses and both men grinned at the couple. *"Ciamar a tha sibh?"*

"I am fine," answered Craig to the typical question of introduction, perturbed by their overly happy dispositions. Their horses were still burdened with saddlebags, indicating they had not yet made it to the castle, but their expressions were of men who knew a secret.

"And how are you, Lady Meriel?" Father Lanaghly asked.

"I am also well," Meriel replied. She too was suspicious. The father had always been a nice and gracious man, but she could never recall him being so *cheerful* before.

Craig pointed at the saddlebags with his chin. "I assume you have not been to see your wife yet."

Conor stroked the dense stubble on his chin. "Ah, no. She does not even know I am here yet. The father and I were just about to part so that I could come down here to the loch and wash off when we saw, um, you two."

Craig narrowed his gaze once again. It was as if his brother *knew* what he and Meriel had just been discussing. And yet the two of them were just riding. Not even closely. There was nothing about Meriel or himself that would indicate that their relationship had grown beyond friendship. "How is it that Father Lanaghly is with you?"

"I left the Lowlands soon after I arrived. There is no word about Clyde, but neither was one expected. You'll be glad to know you have another nephew. A very loud nephew, by the way. Colin's son is only a few months of age but can drown out all present if he is not happy. I quickly wished Colin and Makenna well and made my way back up north. I decided that I might want to make sure that Conan . . . um . . . was behaving."

It was now Meriel's turn to be confused. "Did Laurel send you there as well?" she asked, not realizing until it was too late that she was voicing her thoughts aloud.

Conor chuckled. "Uh, no. She had no idea, but I'll remind her of the dangers I faced if I returned too early, if she decides to lecture me."

"I think this particular lecture is one you are going to enjoy," Father Lanaghly added, wiping his nose, unable to hide his mirth.

Craig knew his sister-in-law had been involved in the scheme to bring him to McTiernay Castle. Conor had practically said so when he asked him to come and take over in his absence. But now it was evident that his brother knew exactly *why* Craig had been summoned. And by staying away, Conor had tacitly supported the whole plot. Though the outcome had benefited Craig, he just hated being manipulated, and his eldest brother needed to be reminded of that fact.

"Father Lanaghly, would you be so kind as to escort Meriel back to the castle? She is learning to ride, but does not feel more comfortable going faster than a walk. Meanwhile, I think I might join my brother. I have something to discuss with him."

Father Lanaghly nodded and Conor beamed. "I expect you do."

Meriel rode silently for several minutes, trying to decide how or even if she should ask the father why he was so happy. But before she could, he saved her the trouble. "You and Craig will want to marry soon, I expect."

Meriel's eyes popped open wide. "Aye. We were just deciding to have it at my home—Caireoch. But we both still want you to perform the ceremony." Father Lanaghly's smile broadened. "But . . . but . . . how did you know?"

Father Lanaghly eyed the grass embedded in her braid. He knew of only a couple of ways that could happen. He doubted she had been rolling with the children down the hills, so that left one likely option. "Oh, I have my ways."

Chapter 11

Thump! Thump!

Meriel tried to ignore the pounding sound outside Caireoch Castle as she bent over the chest, praying the thread she wanted to give one of the weavers was inside. If it was not there, she had no idea where it could be. Her room was a nightmare. Before she had left for McTiernay Castle, she knew where every scrap of yarn, material, and thread was buried. Then Raelynd had ransacked her room under some pretense that she was organizing it. Meriel had yet to decide just how she was going to return the "favor," but making a mess of Raelynd's bedchamber did not seem very imaginative, nor would it create the same level of frustration.

Meriel reached the bottom of the chest, but the thread remained lost. "*Go n-ithe an cat thú is go n-ithe an diabhal an cat,*" she muttered to herself, wishing her sister could overhear her. Meriel was not prone to cursing, but Raelynd liked cats, and sending one to the devil felt a little cathartic.

Meriel found the orderly state of her room to be highly annoying, but she was most peeved with her sister for not living up to her promise to look after the weavers and the seamstresses. After a week of dealing with friends and

family and guests, today was the first time she had had
a chance to truly sit down and meet with the women who
kept the castle and villagers clothed and warm. What she
had learned was that her sister had done an abysmal job, and
that was being kind. Meriel understood that Raelynd had
been sick during much of her absence, but not one weaver
had been given a single shred of instruction! And yet her
sister had found the time to come into her room and ruin
everything by putting it all up and out of sight. But for the
people who made the blankets, the tapestries, most of the
basic needs of the castle and village . . . nothing. Raelynd
had never involved herself with such matters before, so she
decided it was easiest not to interfere. As a result, the weaving and sewing staff had just continued with the last direction
Meriel had given. Fortunately, that was to make blankets for
the winter.

Thump! Thump! Thump!

Meriel pushed to her knees and rose to her feet to go to
the open window. She looked down, and from what she
could see, the wrecked cart that had earlier created quite the
stir in the bailey when it had collided into several barrels of
fresh ale, remained broken despite all the banging. She
glanced up into the cloudless sky. The afternoon sun was
beginning its downward path, but there were still a few
hours of light left in the day. The cool weather had been
unusually beautiful for late fall, growing cold only at night.

Thump! Thump!

With a scowl, she reached over to close the window,
hating that she had to choose between a stifling room and a
headache. Just as she clicked the shutter into place, she
found herself being whisked into the air. "Craig, wherever
did you come from?"

"My mother, originally." She swatted his shoulder.
Thump! Thump! Craig arched a brow at the muted but still
irritating sound. "It's no wonder you did not hear me come

in. But no matter now," he said, heading toward the open door of her room.

Meriel leaned over and began to nibble playfully at his neck. "Such a surprise to see you so early. I feared it would be long after dark before you could return."

As commander of Schellden's army as well as her father's elite guard, Craig's responsibilities were many. Their army was still depleted after losing many in the costly war with the English. Until they had replenished most of their numbers, his days would be long and draining. "Aye, I probably should still be out there, but you and I have had plans for this particular day since our wedding night."

As Craig descended down the stairwell, Meriel realized he intended to step outside with her still in his arms. She began to squirm. "Wait, just what are you doing?"

A bemused smile took over his lips. "I believe I am carrying you."

"I mean it, Craig! Answer my question . . . and . . . is your shirt wet?" she asked as her mind took a sudden turn, realizing that he was more than just damp with sweat.

"Aye. I jumped in the river before coming to get you. The state of my leine would have rendered the effort of washing my body useless, so I left it on. Lucky for you to be married to such an intelligent Highlander."

She had married a madman, she decided. It was practically winter, and though the weather had yet to become bitter and cold, it was cool enough for one to become quite chilly if wet—which she was quickly becoming as he held her in his arms. Meriel was about to say as much when she noticed that Craig was not carrying her to somewhere inside the bailey. He was headed to the gatehouse.

Meriel started to struggle in earnest. "Craig! Just what is going on?"

When he answered her with nothing more than a satisfied grin, she gave up and settled down in his arms. Only then did he offer her an explanation. "I'm taking you to our home. A week ago, your father watched us marry and then afterward proceeded to act as if it had not even happened."

Meriel bit her bottom lip, remembering. Her father had been far from surprised by the news that she and Craig were in love and had decided to marry. Moreover, he had been pleased knowing that both his daughters were marrying good men that not only came from an allied clan, but were ones he respected and already considered family. But his happiness vanished the moment Craig mentioned that he intended to take Meriel and move out of the castle and into his cottage. Rae Schellden might not have minded gaining a son, but he was not amenable to losing a daughter, and he made his feelings known on the matter. With the wedding in potential jeopardy of being postponed, Craig agreed to spend one week at Caireoch. As of that morning, their first week of marriage had passed.

"Rae needs to recognize that you are my wife first and his daughter second."

Meriel doubted her father would ever accept ranking second in anything, but she could not argue with Craig about the principle. "You speak as if living at Caireoch has been awful."

Craig twitched his lips. Residing in her old bedroom had sounded quite horrific at first, but it had been surprisingly comfortable. The room took practically the whole floor, so space was abundant. Still, he and Meriel were married, and he wanted them to live and sleep in their home. Mostly, he wanted privacy—something he was sure they would not have if things remained as they were. "How I feel about Caireoch is beside the point. The last of my family left this morning, and it is time for you and me to act like husband and wife."

"We have been—and quite often—if my memory is accurate," she teased.

"You know what I mean," he growled as he entered the village.

Meriel swallowed. They were becoming quite the spectacle, and Craig was either enjoying being the center of attention or oblivious to the stares. "Put me down," she hissed.

"I fully intend to carry my bride to our home and put her down after we cross the threshold."

"People are staring."

"Aye, I do believe they are."

Meriel inhaled sharply. "Put me down, Craig. Everyone knows we are married and have been for several days. So I do not think there is any need for you to follow tradition and hide my 'enthusiasm' by carrying me into our home."

Craig shrugged. "Maybe I need to hide mine."

Meriel gave a quick nod and a wave to two of the women weavers she had just spent hours with that afternoon. If she survived the humiliation, she was going to be a widow by her own hands. Then, seeing smoke rise from one of the cottages, she asked, "What about food? I did not think we would be coming to your cottage—"

"Our cottage."

"*Our* cottage tonight. What are we going to eat?"

Craig shrugged his shoulders dismissively and looked down at her. "When we get hungry, I'll run up to the kitchens and get us something."

He was smiling, and not just any one of the grins he typically wore. It was the same one Raelynd had been wearing practically since the moment of their arrival. "You look almost as smug as my sister. You realize that she actually believes *she* is the reason why we are married."

"Aye, Raelynd is a little self-satisfied, but after the past few nights of enjoying you in my bed, I can forgive her for being so infuriatingly right."

Meriel opened and then closed her mouth. She could try reminding him that it was *she* who suggested the type of kiss that sparked the realization of their attraction. And that it was *she* who mustered the nerve to leave and that it was *she* who did all the planning and made the effort that successfully outsmarted one of the Highlands' craftiest strategists. But she knew it would do no good. If Craig was going to give anyone credit for their coming together, he would give it to himself, for what he termed his "heroic" patience the afternoon he finally admitted he loved her.

"You say that now," Meriel warned. "But after a year or two of Raelynd taking all the credit for our happiness, I expect my being in your bed is not going to seem quite the worthwhile prize it currently does."

Craig pulled her slightly closer. He would have argued with her, for he had no doubt whatsoever that even after a few decades, nothing would compare with holding her as they fell asleep in each others' arms. But there was no time. They had arrived at their destination. Kicking the cottage door open, he carried her inside and slowly lowered her to her feet before closing his mouth over hers, searing her lips.

When she finally eased away, she turned around, instantly glad that he could not see her pained expression. The three-room cottage was large compared to most in the village, and despite his grumblings that he had no need of the space, it had been given to Craig because of his position. One entered into a long main room. A large window next to the front door allowed light to shine down on the large table and its accompanying four chairs. In the middle was the kitchen area, with a hearth large enough to warm the entire cottage as well as cook family-size meals. In the back of the room, farthest from the entrance, was a sitting area consisting of a large, thick rug and two padded chairs similar to the ones in the McTiernay and Caireoch Great Halls, just not of the same quality.

On the left wall were two doors. The closet was wide open and led to a small space that had probably been intended for a bedroom, but was being used by Craig to house an array of items, mostly associated with weapons and horses. And while she and Craig were not exactly two people who cared about tidiness and organization, it suddenly dawned on her that there was one significant difference in the kind of mess they created—his mess included dirt.

Meriel took it all in, examining every corner, every piece of furniture, shelf, and storage nook. Nothing was left uncovered or free for use. It was not that she had expected the place to be clean; however, she had assumed Craig would have picked up a little before bringing his bride home. But, if anything, the cottage was even more chaotic than she remembered. The only things that belonged to her were the few bags she had taken to the McTiernays. Seeing them stacked in a far corner of the spare room made her feel like a visitor, not a mistress.

Craig undid his leather belt, simultaneously freeing not only his sword but his tartan. Tossing the large metal weapon onto the kitchen table with a resounding thump, he let the kilt fall to the floor, not caring what potential muck it might have landed on. Grabbing the string on the back of his calf, he yanked the tie to loosen thc leather so he could slip his shoe off. After freeing his other foot, he grasped her wrist and walked through the kitchen to the back sitting area.

As she followed him, Meriel was able to quickly spy the second room, which she already knew to be the main bedroom. As expected, it was both very large and very messy, but thankfully the bed was the one place where Craig had not piled anything.

Craig stopped beside a chair and brushed off the two leather straps coiled on the seat, letting them fall to the floor. Meriel moved to occupy the second chair but was stopped by his hand on her wrist, still secure in Craig's grasp. He gave it a soft tug and when she got close enough, he picked her up and placed her comfortably across his legs. "I thought we could at last resume our nightly chats, talk about our day, plans for the morrow, or whatever we wanted."

Meriel leaned over and placed a soft kiss on his lips. "I don't remember ever doing so from your lap before."

"I clearly recall you telling me how you were reluctant to resume old habits. I am just trying to be obliging," Craig responded with feigned innocence.

Meriel chuckled and kicked off her own shoes. She decided to ignore the disorder surrounding her and focus on the positives of finally being completely alone with her husband. "So how are your men? And Callum? Is he faring well?" she asked before she took his earlobe between her teeth.

Craig sucked in his breath and closed his eyes. "Um, Callum, he is doing well," he lied. He had selected the young man to be his second-in-command, knowing he was new to leadership of any kind. But leaving an inexperienced second-in-command in charge for such a long period had caused some issues. Still, the man was honest, fair, extremely smart, and had a gift for instructing men. His ability to plan did not come as naturally as it did to Craig, but he was learning fast.

Meriel swirled her tongue in his ear. "Tell me more."

She was daring him to talk during her sensual assault and Craig knew he had to rise to the challenge, otherwise Meriel would realize the power she had over him. "Callum needs only confidence and experience. I . . . umm . . . I mean he unfortunately had neither when I left." Losing the battle, Craig changed tactics, pulling her back so that he could kiss her neck. "Though I think . . . the lessons he encountered he . . . will not have to relearn. Still, it might not be a . . . good idea for me to leave for an extended period for a while."

Meriel stretched her neck, giving him better access. "That sounds nice," she moaned.

"Aye, nice," he repeated.

Meriel tried to sit back and stroke his cheek. "I mean it. While I hope we will go and visit your other brothers someday, I'm glad to be home."

Craig pulled down the collar of her gown to give him access to her shoulder. "They can come here from now on."

"Now, that would not be fair. Besides, I want to meet Makenna. The way you describe her and your brother Colin, I cannot imagine the two together."

Craig traced her bottom lip with his thumb, still finding it hard to believe just how happy he was. "It is hard to imagine. And yet, they are a lot like Conor and Laurel. After seeing them together, you have no doubt they are with the one person in the world who can make them happy."

Meriel rested her head on his shoulder and smiled. Craig, the most outgoing and loquacious of all the McTiernays, was at his most romantic when he talked about his feelings using surrogates.

Craig kicked the bridle he had just tossed on the rug and a saddle sitting in the middle of the floor to give his feet some room to stretch out. "Even for me, this place is too cluttered. But you are mostly to blame for it being this bad."

"Me?" Meriel inquired as she played with the opening of his leine.

Craig pulled her closer, enjoying the feel of her head resting on his shoulder and her fingers running through the hair on his chest. His hand moved to cup her breast and once there, drew around her nipple. "Aye," he finally answered. "When you left me all alone, I did not seem to be in the mood to do much of anything, including tidying up the place."

Meriel slid her hand farther inside his shirt, enjoying the feel of his muscles moving. She would never get enough of touching him. "I heard you yelled a lot."

"I might have raised my voice a little. But I am sure it was warranted."

Meriel sat up and they locked gazes. There were touches of humor around his mouth and already the beginning of wrinkles near his eyes. His face held a wealth of inherent strength, but now a vulnerability lay there too. This man truly loved her and needed her.

Wrapping her arms around his neck, she urged his mouth down to hers. "You can clean up your things later."

"Why not now?" he teased.

She hardly needed to answer, for she could feel the evidence of his distraction hard against her thigh, and it only added to her own growing need. "Because," she whispered, tracing the strong line of his jaw with two fingers as she rocked her hips against him once, then twice, smiling as it produced a moan, "I fully intend to remind you of why marriage is oh, so good a thing."

Needing no further encouragement, Craig rose from the chair in one quick movement and gathered her into his arms. In a few quick steps, they were in the bedroom.

Placing her bare toes on the floor, his hands began to unfasten her gown, and in one swift motion it fell to the floor, leaving only her chemise. The candlelight cast a warm glow over her, and once again he was awestruck that she was really his. "You're beautiful."

She loved the way he stared at her, the passion and desire flaming in the depths of his eyes. "And you're absolutely smitten with me."

The love in her eyes was bright and clear, and he knew it would last him his whole life. "I'm beyond smitten," he said, yanking her close. "I'm bewitched, and I pray never to be cured."

His fingers curled around her ribcage and his thumbs began to massage her nipples into hard peaks through the fabric. Needing to see and touch her soft skin, he eased the sleeves down her shoulders and let the undergarment pool about her waist. Lovingly his gaze swept over her face before finding the last bow securing her chemise and with one tug broke it free.

Meriel looked up at him, feeling no awkwardness for her lack of clothing. She had nothing to hide from this man. Craig quickly threw off his leine and he stepped back, allowing her eyes to caress his body with their loving gaze. Her desire was evident when she glanced over his straining manhood.

Tipping her chin up with his fingertips, Craig kissed her with a hungry urgency, and Meriel felt herself respond with a kind of abandon that came from being totally in love. His mouth was hot and ravenous and she let herself sink into it, into his body, into his warmth.

She wanted him. God, she wanted him. She wanted him naked and inside her. But tonight she also wanted something else. Meriel pulled back just far enough to give him a push that needed no encouragement. Craig fell backward onto the bed, bringing her with him. But when his arms came around her, strong and purposeful, Meriel resisted, shaking her head. "Tonight it's my turn."

Craig looked at her in confusion for a moment, but he lost the thought once she bent her head to give him a lingering soft kiss on the mouth, then on his half-closed eyelids, beneath his ear, followed by his hard jawline. Little by little, she trailed a path downward, down his neck to his chest. Her mouth moved to his flat nipple and he gasped at the sharp pleasure as it surged all the way through him. Needing to taste her, kiss her, press her down fully upon him, he reached for her, but again she resisted.

Taking both of his hands in hers, Meriel put them deliberately at his sides. On their wedding night, Craig had introduced her to just how sensual and powerful his tongue could be. Ever since, she had been consumed with the thought of tasting him. And tonight she was determined to discover if her mouth could bring as much sweet torture to him as his did to her.

Craig took in her air of command and decided to let her have her way and to enjoy her ministrations, for the moment. Her movements were slow and chaste as she touched him reverently, tracing his curves and hollows. Taking her time, she slid her hand up and down his chest again and again, each time going a little lower. Daring to sweep even lower, she allowed her fingertips to travel a new path along the taut ridges of his abdomen, emboldened when his muscles contracted reflexively at her touch. She marveled at feeling the shape of him change with her persistent stroking and was inspired to place her mouth where her hands had been.

Leaning down, she touched his now tense nipple with the tip of her tongue. Craig sucked a breath slowly through his teeth, and she felt his manhood stir against her leg. She felt wanton, intentionally seducing him this way, but she also felt powerful. Her whole body ached to feel him need her like she had needed him.

Placing her hand low across his hard stomach, he buried one hand in her hair while the other rested in the middle of her back. Emboldened, she slipped her other hand between his legs and began to move up and down, caressing the bare flesh of his thighs until he shuddered in response.

As her hands reached for their target, Craig stilled her fingers in his grasp, bringing them up to his mouth for a soft kiss on her knuckles. "You don't have to," he said quietly.

Her hazel eyes caught his blue ones burning with passion, and her tongue swept across the taut outlines of his abdomen. "But I want to," she murmured and freed her hand so that her palm could slide down his chest, across his belly, until it reached his heavy, fully aroused manhood thrusting outward, ready for her touch.

Gently, she cupped his flesh in her palm before curling

her fingers around him. Craig groaned in agony, but she knew it came from such intense pleasure it bordered on pain. Lightly, her hands began to caress him, then with growing purpose. He seemed massive, filling her fingers. She felt a pulsating ripple go through him and her own insides quivered in return.

The moment Craig felt Meriel's fingers close around him, he thought his heart might stop. His muscles tensed and he arched his head on the pillow, rolling his eyes closed, his every sense heightened. All misgivings had vanished and his only remaining thought was that he must have more. Helplessly, he thrust himself forward, deeper into her palm, needing to increase the delicious pressure.

Meriel watched him for a prolonged moment, and then dropped her gaze to her hands. All doubt left and she began to dip her head.

The moment Craig realized what she intended, his body went rigid as another wave of need thundered through him. "No, don't touch me like that," he choked. "I won't be able . . ." He trailed off, stumbling over the words as she traced the bones of his hips.

His hands were clasped into fists at his sides. Opening them, he tried to pull her down to him, but again she resisted. "Shhh. But I want to do this for you," she told him quietly. "The way you do for me."

Fear was consuming him, fear and an almost intolerable desire. He clamped his eyes shut and clutched the coverlet in a fierce grip, half fearing and half anticipating the first touch of her lips. He had given her his heart and his body, but if he let her touch him, know him this way, she would have all the power. He would be at her mercy. The heavy weight of his manhood throbbed with anticipation and he could not make himself force her to stop.

The soft brush of her hair against his skin was followed by the moist heat of her breath. She withdrew her hands and for long moments Craig thought he would go mad with anticipation. Then he felt it, the searing heat of her tongue, licking him from root to tip.

Meriel allowed instinct to guide her. Pressing her hand flat against his groin, she held him steady as she followed the path of the prominent vein. When she reached the top, she opened her mouth wide.

A gargled moan erupted from somewhere deep within him and Craig's last thought before she took him into her mouth was that he would die from the pleasure if she continued and die from the lack of it if she did not. When the edge of her teeth skimmed lightly over the most vulnerable place on his body, he nearly exploded. He tipped his head back, exposing the taut cords of his strong neck and shouted, "*Mo creach!* You're killing me."

Meriel smiled, for she distinctly recalled saying the same thing to him when he had taken her into his mouth. This was without doubt the most intimate act she had ever performed, focused solely on his pleasure. Being joined with him, having him inside her body, was beautiful and even overwhelming. But this—this was just as potent.

Eyes closed and lips parted, Craig knew only sensual agony as the tip of Meriel's tongue circled him. He was torn between grabbing her and pinning her beneath him and simply lying back and enjoying the unfamiliar excitement of surrender. She was using every weapon in her arsenal to assault his senses. Her lips, her tongue, her teeth, sucking and licking. He emitted another tortured moan.

His jaw clenched tight and Craig knew he was about to lose control. He cried out, "No more. I'm going to—" and abruptly pulled her away.

Unable to play the role of gentle tutor, he pushed her legs apart so that she straddled him. His face contorted with barely suppressed agony. "I need you," he whispered, and without waiting, he brought her down so that she impaled herself on him.

Meriel gasped, filled with a sudden, wild abandon as the hot, shocking sensation of him filling her so deeply rippled throughout her body. Instinctively, she rocked against him, pulling him deeper into her. Vaguely she was aware of Craig reaching out for her, pressing his face between her breasts. The added stimulus caused her to loll her head back so that her hair hung down across her buttocks. She moaned as he took one of her nipples and matched her rhythm with the sweet tug of his mouth. Meriel arched her back more and rode him, feeling him tighten each time he pushed into her.

Clasping her neck with one hand, Craig pulled her face up to meet his and began to kiss her aggressively. He dipped his tongue deep into her mouth, relishing her ecstatic moans as their bodies rubbed together. They were both on the cusp of climax, but he was not yet ready to let either of them come. Breaking off the kiss, he lifted his head and sucked in air.

"Craig," she whimpered, continuing to rock against him. She was driving him insane. His hand on the small of her back tightened and pulled her even closer. He was of no mind to allow her conquest to continue any longer.

Before she could move a muscle, he raised himself, and with a tortured moan he deftly rolled her beneath him and plunged deep. He kissed her once more as he sank exultantly into the snug, tight channel.

She cried out as her body contracted around him, meeting each of his powerful thrusts with one of her own. The air around them turned into steam. Craig could feel Meriel's nails digging into his back. She was mindless with passion, writhing with it, needing him, ready.

Wrapping her legs around him, he spread her wide and pressed his face into the curve of her neck as Meriel clutched him to her, taking him deep within her. Then suddenly she gasped. Her hands curled into fists as her muscles clenched and unclenched in small spasms that made her entire body tremble.

Her soft cries of sensual fulfillment continued to be the most incredibly exciting sounds Craig had ever heard. A second later he surrendered to the hot whirlwind that would tear him apart and put him back together once more, a whole man.

Craig collapsed beside her, lying limp, awash with wave after wave of tantalizing tingles. He would never, ever get enough of her.

She curled into the curve of his body and they remained that way for some time, neither wanting to move or speak. Just enjoying the sensation of being so close.

"I love you, Craig," she finally whispered.

"And I love you, my perfect angel."

Meriel sighed. "I like that." She giggled. "Means I'll never have to change. I'm already perfect."

Craig nuzzled her neck. "That you are. I don't want you to change. I married the woman I want. I don't need anything more."

Meriel twisted around so that she could face him. Looking into his blue eyes, dark with passion, she said, "And I don't want you to change either, Craig. I love you for who you are. Don't ever doubt that."

"I won't," he whispered and kissed the tip of her nose. "Nothing would ever keep me from loving you."

Slowly he leaned forward to press soft kisses down the left side of her neck, and once again Meriel could feel the stirrings of his desire. "Aren't you hungry?" she asked hoarsely, as his mouth began to fondle her nipple.

"Aye, I'm famished," he replied, moving to her other breast.

Meriel swatted his back. "I meant for food."

"I knew that," he teased, continuing his assault.

Meriel knew that if he did not stop soon she would

willingly fall victim to his caresses. "If you and I continue at this pace, I will soon be like Raelynd."

Craig reluctantly stopped and pulled her once again into his side. "I am happy for my brother. They have wanted to conceive for some time, but I am also glad that it will not be us. Surely, God knows better than to give us a child."

Meriel tried to turn around, but he would not let her. "You cannot be serious."

Craig nuzzled her hair with his chin. "Children are the messiest of all creatures. Look around. Can you imagine an infant in this place?"

Meriel smiled, realizing that he was teasing her. "No, I honestly cannot."

"Besides, I want you all to myself."

"And this time should be for Raelynd. She has been trying for so long. It would not be fair to steal any of her attention. Have you seen the way she basks in Crevan's constant attention?"

Craig squeezed her close. "I'll smother you with attention if that is what you desire."

"I just desire you."

Craig closed his eyes, thankful. He had not thought about her becoming pregnant, but now that he had, the idea terrified him. Her mother had had terrible difficulties carrying a child to term, and it appeared after trying for a year that Raelynd would also be troubled. Meriel was her identical twin and it followed that she too would not have an easy time. Her mother had lost so many children, and he did not want to see such sadness in Meriel's eyes.

Aye, he wanted a family, but he wanted her more.

Craig cracked open the door of their cottage and peeped inside. Taking a deep breath, he said a silent prayer, reminding God who his wife was and how he could use an extra dose of patience. After three days of living together, he should have known what he would see on the other side of the door, and yet tonight, coming home, he had hopes otherwise.

Craig knew he was looking more and more haggard. Every leine he owned was caked with mud and sweat, so much so that his men were beginning to tease him for not having any clean clothes. Craig was beginning to wonder just when Meriel intended to do the wash, when this morning one of his married soldiers had slapped him on the back and said not to worry. That it was about three days after he wed before he could depend on the wash to be done and a good meal to be waiting for him. And based on the pile of clothes still on the floor and the lack of cooking aromas from the kitchen, Craig could only conclude Meriel needed more than the standard three days.

Pushing the door harder in an effort to budge whatever was in his way, he heard something tumble onto the floor. "Oh, hold on! You're home early! I need to move a few things before you come in!" Meriel called out.

Craig's mouth twitched. *She was surprised to see him?* If anything, he was running late. He waited as she began to shove aside whatever was blocking the door, but through the small opening that he had nudged open, he could see that his home had not improved. Just the opposite; it had become significantly worse. He was trying to be patient, but the place was beyond ridiculous!

Every day Meriel was bringing more and more of her things from the castle. Did it really escape her that there was simply no room for all of her things? Practically everything he owned was covered with some frilly item or something that most certainly did not belong to him. He did not mind clutter. He was comfortable with untidy rooms, but this was pure chaos and close to unlivable.

Meriel opened the door. She was smiling and her hazel eyes were dancing with delight. "Come in! I'm sorry you had to wait." She stretched her neck to see behind him and realized that the afternoon sun was completely gone and it was not dusk, but dark outside.

"Why are you bringing that in here?" she asked as he stepped inside, still carrying his targe. Normally he left the shield outside, propped up against the side of the wall.

Craig pulled her in close for a welcome-home kiss. "I need to do some work on it and don't have time during the day. Thought I would do it tonight while we talk."

"Oh, well, I had no idea how late it was. I must have lost track of time," she said brightly.

Craig nuzzled her hair. "By the looks of things in here, I assume we are going to be eating at the castle again."

Meriel beamed a bright smile at him. "You, oh handsome one, are correct. Just give me a few more minutes to finish something and I will be ready."

Craig watched as she went to sit down by a large pile of what appeared to be a variety of half-sewn items. Whatever she was doing, he was positive it was going to take significantly longer than a few minutes for the surrounding area to be transformed into something that approximated order. "You realize that we cannot keep doing this."

"Doing what?"

"Going to your father and asking to join him for dinner."

Meriel waved her hand dismissively before ripping two pieces apart. "He enjoys our company and I know my sister does not mind. She said so today when I joined her for the noon meal. There," she said, separating the two pieces and putting them onto two different stacks.

She rose to her feet and circled her arms around his waist. "Now we can go get you something to eat."

Craig could not help but return her smile and kissed the tip of her nose. "And just what has made you so happy this evening?"

Meriel pulled out of his embrace and, with her arms

stretched out, turned in a tight circle. "Can you not tell? All my stuff is *finally* here! At last I can begin organizing things so that I can find them. It seems forever since I have been able to do so."

Craig took in a deep breath, closed his eyes, and smiled in relief. It was comforting to hear that nothing more was coming into their overly crowded home, but it was even more reassuring to hear Meriel use the word *organize*. So getting things to where they should be was going to take four, maybe five days, rather than the standard three. It did not matter, now that he knew very soon his home and marriage would start resembling his expectations. "Just make sure there is still room for me."

Meriel put her hands on her hips and gave him a wicked smile. "I thought the bedroom was yours," she said with a wink.

Craig growled, suddenly hungry for other things, and tossed his targe onto the table, where it landed on a large pile of material, knocking half of it over. He was reaching out for her when she screamed and shoved his hand away, diving for the items that had just fallen. Placing them back on the table, she grunted and attempted to pick up his shield. "Find somewhere else to put that thing," she said, her tone laced with warning.

"And where would that be?" he belted out. "There *is* nowhere to put *any* of my things. I thought we would *share* the cottage, but right now this place looks like a woman's retreat! I've been patient, but a man would go mad living like this."

"*Your* things already took up every possible place I could put mine. I was lucky to get my clothes, let alone sewing materials, in here at all. *And*," Meriel continued, grinding the word out between her teeth, "I know far more about sharing a room, since I actually did so with my sister for the majority of my life!"

Craig lifted his shield before she toppled over in her efforts to pick it up. In doing so, he again accidentally knocked several items back onto the floor. He ignored them, just as he ignored the fact that several of the items that fell belonged to him. "You only *think* you know how to share space," he huffed. With his free hand, he made a wide gesture, pointing around the cottage. "That *room* you shared was twice the size of this entire place!"

Craig pivoted and headed toward the door.

"Where are you going?" she shouted at him.

He grabbed the handle and yanked it open. "To get something to eat," he growled, and exited.

He got no more than three steps when she joined him, practically running to keep up with his long, angry strides. "You are not leaving me behind," she told him, her tone defiant. "I'm hungry too."

Craig glanced sideways and sighed. The weather had finally turned chilly, and in her haste she had forgotten a covering. Tucking her hands underneath her arms, she was doing her best to keep up with him. Slowing down, he pulled her into his side to help block the wind and warm her. "I hate arguing."

"Me too." She spoke in a tremulous whisper. "We never used to fight. Why do we do so now?"

Craig chuckled softly. "You and I find it hard to make even small adjustments to our daily routines, so the idea of changing our lives, even if it is for each other, is rather difficult for both of us. But we will manage. We have one of the largest cottages in the village, and I am certain we can find room for our belongings. We only need to move things around a bit more."

Meriel, her face partially buried in his chest, nodded her head in agreement. "I'm sorry the place looks like I took over. I just did not want to move your things, in case you had them organized in a certain way."

Craig laughed out loud at the concept. "No. I have no method to where I put my stuff. I have a suggestion. Why don't you rearrange the front room? I do not really use it much, so it can be primarily yours if we can equally share the rest of the cottage."

"Really?" asked Meriel as she lifted her head and looked up at him as if he had just won her the moon.

"Aye." Craig felt a surge of pride, his mood suddenly buoyant. "I need to go with your father to visit some of the outlying farms. I thought about waiting for another week or two, but I think I'll suggest leaving in the morning. This will give you several days to organize things just how you want them without having to worry about me getting in the way. All I ask is that we find a place to put *my* things."

Meriel was radiating happiness at the suggestion. "I will. And I really don't mind having your things around."

"Even my targe?"

"Even your targe—of course, that is, as long as it isn't ruining the items that I love."

Craig rolled his eyes as they approached the Great Hall doors. He suspected this would not be the last fight they would have about his and her items, but he was glad the worst one was finally over.

Chapter 12

Craig tossed the reins of his very tired horse to the stable master and waved him good-bye. He had successfully avoided his brother, made sure Callum understood that he would address his concerns in the morning, and told Rae Schellden, quite bluntly, that he was interfering with his marriage. Craig refused to allow anything more to distract him, for he had already been gone much longer than he had intended.

He and Rae had saved their meeting with Schellden's most notorious farmer for last. Farlon lived on the northern edge of Schellden lands and had been in a continuous feud with one of the McHenry farmers on the other side of the border. For years, they had pinched each other's cattle, both men claiming they were only doing so in retaliation. Then last year, Farlon's son Tevus got McHenry's daughter pregnant.

The two married and the families called a truce, but Ian McHenry was alleging that Farlon had resumed his thievery despite their pact. It turned out McHenry was half correct. His cattle were being stolen, but not by Farlon—by Tevus. The young man had just turned seventeen and claimed he had no other way to support his family.

In the end, Craig had reluctantly agreed to Farlon's suggestion that Craig take Tevus back with him so that the young man could begin training as a soldier. What Craig had not counted on was that the new husband and father would not leave his young family behind. So with Rae's blessing, Tevus, his wife, and his baby, all made the slow and painfully loud way back to Caireoch. Before the trip, Craig was not sure about the prospect of children. Now, he was positive. He absolutely did not want them.

Craig sauntered through the gatehouse, trying to keep his stride normal and unhurried, but it was difficult. Practically since the moment he left home, he had had visions of his return. He would open the door and find Meriel eagerly waiting for him. The aroma of the dinner she had made would fill his senses and the house would be completely in order. But before he could praise her efforts, she would run and jump into his arms. He would crush her to him and they would stumble against the door . . . or the wall. Once, he had even dreamed they crashed into the table—which, of course, was clean. Meriel would tear at his clothing and he would just as impatiently remove her gown. Their kiss would resume and soon afterward he would make it unquestionably clear he had missed her as much as she had him. And to ensure they could both realize his fantasy, he had sent word ahead to let Meriel know that he would be home that afternoon.

Craig approached the front door of the cottage and shouted out a hello to one of the men passing by. Then with a loud *thwack* he dropped his shield against the outside wall. With all the noise he had just made, he had no doubt that Meriel had heard his arrival and was waiting impatiently for him to enter. But when he opened the door, Craig knew instantly that no one was inside.

"Meriel!" he barked despite knowing he would get no reply.

He stepped inside, and with his heel he shoved the door shut so that he could fume in private. Not only was there no meal waiting for him, it did not look as though one would be prepared in the kitchen anytime soon. Every single thing he owned was heaped into large, seemingly unstable piles around and on everything a woman needed for cooking. Where did Meriel think she was going to prepare their meals?

Craig unhooked his sword and tossed it onto the table, not realizing that it was the one place that had been cleared of items. He followed it with his saddlebag, which he promptly turned upside down and emptied. In doing so, he did notice the large mound of dirty clothes that he had specifically told her about before he left, infuriatingly untouched. Just what was he going to wear?

He was about to march over and pick the pile up and carry it to the castle himself when the door opened. Meriel staggered inside, visibly exhausted and huffing loudly. She was carrying a tartan pulled up at the four corners that was both heavy and awkward. "Since you won't help me, you could at least move all your things off the table *I just cleaned*!" Meriel wheezed.

She had hoped to make it back before Craig returned, but upon seeing his shield outside the door, she knew that he had arrived before she had a chance to set up dinner and surprise him. While he was gone, she had made enormous strides in making their small home livable, and had been eager to show him all that she had accomplished. What she had not planned on was snapping at him within the first thirty seconds of welcoming him home. But her arms were screaming in pain from carrying their dinner, and the first thing she saw as she walked in the door was all his stuff cluttering the table that she had made certain was completely clean when she left. It had taken more than a day to examine and find a home for each of the items in the massive collection there, and Meriel had no intention of ever going through the painful process again.

Craig's nostrils flared and his blue eyes had gone dark. Raising his arm, he laid it on the table and then, keeping his gaze firmly on her, he swiped the table clean, broadsword and all. With a look just as menacing, Meriel stared back, unflinching at the clatter and the noise his action created. Her guilt about snapping instantly vanished along with her apology. With a final heave, she dropped the heavy mass onto the table.

Breaking her gaze, Meriel began to spread out the dinner and tried to regain her calm. She had collected a significant amount of meat, bread, cheese, and many other things for a feast. But just as she was leaving, she remembered all their eating utensils were buried somewhere in the kitchen-now-storage area of their home. So she had made sure the cook included plates and cups and a jug of ale. It had all been heavy at first, but by the time she reached their home, her arms and fingers were in agony.

Yanking out a chair, Craig plopped down, grabbed some bread and pulled off a chunk, making clear his continued displeasure. The warm dough tasted good and the meat looked delicious, but neither did anything to calm his anger. Another castle meal was *not* what he had intended to come home to after being gone a week.

Meriel took a deep breath. She had a choice. Ignore the last few minutes or engage in a fight. Craig had certainly given her enough reasons to be mad at him, but it was just not how she wanted to spend her first evening with her husband since he had been gone. And since whomever he was mad at could not possibly be her—she decided to start all over. Leaning over his lap, she placed a soft, long kiss on his lips. "I missed you."

Craig puckered his lips barely enough to give her a peck,

and then grumbled, "Not enough to be home so that you could greet me."

Meriel pulled back. Again, anger singed the corners of her control. "I wanted to be here when you arrived. I had hoped to have all this," she said, waving at the food, "laid out and ready for you, thinking that you might be hungry."

Craig said nothing. He had been hungry. Hungry for her, and she had not been there.

Receiving no response, let alone gratitude, Meriel was caring less and less whether or not they had a fight immediately upon his return. She put her hands on her hips. "Well, don't tell me you do not like it. It is the best the cook had!"

"Let's just say it was far from what I expected." The low tone of his voice was inflamed and belligerent.

Meriel took a deep breath and fought one last time to keep control. *He is tired. He had a long trip and he is not intentionally trying to sound critical*, she told herself. Any minute, Craig would calm down, look around, and recognize the progress she had made during the week of his absence. He would say something complimentary and then she too would unwind. "Well, you must be glad to be home," she said, pleased she had been able to keep her tone somewhat cheerful, hiding her true emotions.

Craig selected a piece of meat and popped it in his mouth. Between chews, he said, "I was until I walked in here and saw all my things stacked in piles where tonight's dinner should have been." He pointed at the stuffed kitchen and then to the mound next to him. "As well as my dirty clothes *exactly where they were* when I left."

Meriel's face paled with growing fury. She had done her best not to escalate things, but if Craig wanted a fight, then he would have one. "I knew you to be many things, but I did not believe you to be selfish," she said coldly. "Look around your home. You can move without tripping. You can sit. And you can eat a meal, even if it *wasn't what you expected.*" Her eyes were now ablaze with smoldering ire. "I have foolishly worked late every night just to get everything ready for *you*, so that *you* would be happy. Little did I realize that some dirty clothes and a crowded kitchen would make it all meaningless!"

She pivoted and walked to the bedroom, closing the door with a resounding *thud*. Leaning back against the wall, Meriel could feel her tears begin to flow. Craig was never going to be happy being married to her.

She should have listened to him from the beginning.

She should have left him alone and never conspired to get him to follow her to the McTiernays'.

But mostly, she should never have let her sister trick her into kissing him.

Craig sat in the sitting area of the cottage and stared at the flames licking the stone walls of the fireplace. After Meriel had walked out of the front room and into their bedchamber, he considered what she had said. He even privately recognized that she had made significant strides in organizing the cottage. The small front room still looked to be a muddled mess of material, but it did look better. Maybe he should have acknowledged her efforts, but how hard was it to fulfill the two requests he had made—for her to make his dinner and clean his clothes? Both were completely ignored. The woman had *made* Hamish clothes in less time! She had prepared a picnic for Hamish that even from a distance had looked mouthwatering. At this rate, neither of Craig's requests would ever be fulfilled! Aye, he was mad. He had a right to be.

Deciding that his anger was not going to ebb without some sleep, Craig got to his feet and opened the bedroom door. He was relieved to find Meriel curled on her side facing away from him, huddled under the coverlet, asleep. He did not want to have another fight.

Tugging off his leine and freeing himself from the rest of his clothes, he slipped under the covers.

The weight of him getting into bed woke Meriel. "What are you doing?" she asked in surprise, her voice thick with sleep.

"This is my bed and you are my wife. We are going to sleep together in the same bed every night until we are dead—mad or not," he growled, rolling away from her.

Meriel yawned and said in a husky whisper, "Oh. All right." Her tone was soft and completely accepting. Minutes later he could hear her deep breaths and knew that she was once again asleep. He soon joined her.

Seeking warmth, Meriel moved closer to the heat source in the bed. Finding it, she snuggled tight against Craig's side, unaware in her unconscious state that she was doing so.

Craig instinctively reached out and pulled her to him, moaning as her lushly curved derriere pressed against his thighs. She shifted again and the erotic sensation of her skin rubbing against him brought him fully awake. He inhaled, smiled, and then frowned. Remembering how angry they had been at each other when they went to bed that night, he had not expected her to be completely undressed under the covers.

Carefully his hand slid down her arm, touching her smooth, warm skin. He marveled at her perfection—the softness of her body, her smell. She took his breath away. Even when annoyed, he could not get enough of her. Now that he was calmer, he recognized that much of his anger had stemmed from disappointment at her not being at home to greet him.

Propping his body up on his elbow, he studied his

sleeping wife and at once felt a sharp pang of desire. He had been gone too long, and he ached to see the fiery passion kindle in her beautiful green-gold eyes. He inhaled her womanly scent and moaned softly. Her mere presence had him fully aroused.

Cupping her buttocks, he pulled her up against his hardness; the result was an odd mixture of relief and anguish at the teasing torture. He edged aside the coverlet to expose the curve of her shoulders and nuzzled his face in her soft wavy hair. Moving the heavy tresses aside, he feathered kisses over the arch of her neck as his hand began a slow exploration, reacquainting himself with her body. God help him, he could not stop touching her, kissing her.

He buried his face against her throat with a soft groan of desire. His only thought was his overpowering need to make love to his wife in every way. Turning onto his side, Craig eased Meriel onto her back and covered her body with his own. Slowly he drew his thumb across her bottom lip before gently tugging it with his teeth. Without any hesitation, Meriel lifted her face. Craig kissed her, exploring her mouth like it was their first time. As her lips parted under the pressure, he retraced the path of his thumb with his tongue, glorying in the knowledge that his touch could make her react to him, even in her sleep.

She wrapped her arms around his back as his kisses became more demanding. Pulling her tightly to him, he pressed his hips firmly against hers, letting his unmistakable need for her be known. Meriel gasped, becoming fully conscious as his tongue caressed every corner of her mouth, kissing her with an urgency built up over a week of separation.

Craig edged to his side so that he could tenderly draw his fingertips down between her breasts and over the small curve of her stomach. Meriel shivered. Her whole body was responding to his sensual assault, but she needed to know he was no longer angry with her. Likewise, Craig had to understand that while she too might have seemed mad, she had only been hurt. That she had missed him terribly. That every night she had dreamed and longed for him. "Craig, I—"

Craig put a finger on her lips, stilling what she had been about to say before placing a soft kiss where his finger had been. "No," he said, his voice a whisper of rough velvet. "There's no need to talk. Not now."

His hands were caressing her entire body, disabling Meriel's ability to speak. She could only feel. His touch seared her skin and she wanted more. Slowly she slid her fingertips from around his back to his chest and then down until her fingers cradled his warm, hard, soft flesh.

Craig sucked in his breath. Lightly, her hands began again to touch him, then with growing purpose. Incredibly, his manhood thickened even more. Helplessly, he thrust himself against her palm, attempting to increase the delicious pressure. His one thought was that he must have more.

Grasping both her hands in his, he lifted them above her head and said, "I need you. I've never needed you as much as I do now."

Tracing the contours of her neck with his kisses, he stroked Meriel from breast to thigh, reveling in the incredible softness of her skin. He reacquainted himself with every inch of her body, refusing to let her bring down her hands and touch him in return.

"Look at me," he instructed, and with his fingers stroked her breasts, teasing her nipples.

Meriel jerked. Her body ached for his touch. She arched her back, thrusting her breasts upward, begging him to take her into his mouth. Craig obliged. He sucked on her nipple, nibbled, bit, and felt her quiver against his mouth. Relishing the sounds of pleasure and pain he elicited from her, his mouth continued to devour her, his tongue lapping the rough structure of one peak and then the other.

Craig was so hard he hurt, but he wanted to take his time and do some of the things he had fantasized about while he was away. He edged his knee upward and lodged it between her thighs. Then he pressed his hips closer, letting her feel the long, hard length of his erection.

"Please," Meriel groaned, as he splayed his fingers over her belly. She knew what was to come.

Craig responded by lightly moving his hand down over her soft stomach straight to the heart of her fire. He cupped her gently and eased one finger into her damp heat. Meriel heard herself cry out and tried to reach for him, but he held her hands firmly above her head. She squeezed her eyes closed. It was blissful agony not to be able to show him how much she was burning for him.

Craig was barely holding on to his control. He could not wait to lose himself in her again, but seeing her writhe and beg for his touch made him desire to do more. He wanted to touch her in ways he knew would pleasure her, and seek out the special little spots where she was extra sensitive. Her pleasure in every way heightened his own.

He eased his finger back out of the snug passage and used her own moisture to lubricate her small, swelling button of desire. He repeated the action slowly and deliberately, easing his finger into her and then teasing the small nubbin of female flesh. He did it again and again until Meriel threw back her head and cried out.

Smiling to himself, Craig started to kiss a path down her breastbone to her navel, tasting her with his warm tongue. Again, he slipped his finger into her, then added another. Her hips bucked, and he knew she was ready. Bending down, he took her in his mouth, his tongue hot and rough and insistent. He feasted on her, plundering the sweet interior she so willingly offered.

Meriel could not control her body. She writhed. She twisted. She shook. She buried her fingers in his hair, raking his scalp with her nails. Her whole being was on fire, delighting in the heat. Craig cupped her hips, lifting her tighter against his mouth. She shuddered again and again as he tasted the heart of her, refusing to let her climax fade despite her cries and weak struggles.

Meriel knew she could not take anymore. If Craig did not enter her soon, she would die. "Make love to me, Craig. *Please.*"

Craig raised himself up and leaned his head to hers. He nuzzled her ear with his nose and lapped its lobe with his tongue. "Whatever brings you pleasure," he breathed. Then he straddled her, shifting his hips onto hers, pinning them to the bed. Meriel gasped at the touch of his heated body. She had forgotten just how large her husband was, then was lost in sheer pleasure as he started to tease her opening.

Meriel moaned his name and wrapped her legs around him, pulling him to her with an urgency that matched his own. Waiting no longer, Craig lifted her hips and plunged between her thighs with one powerful surge. She was more than ready for him as he buried himself in the warm softness of her. When he was safely inside, he drove deep, seeking release and reassurance and the comfort of knowing she wanted him as much as he wanted her.

They strained together, their breath coming in short gasps. Instinct drove Meriel to meet each thrust, riding him with a wild abandon only he could create in her. A powerful force began building within her, becoming more fervent, more intense with each silken stroke. When Meriel parted her lips to cry out her pleasure, Craig instantly clamped his mouth tightly over hers, swallowing the soft sounds of her passion. A second later he joined her, surrendering to his own erotic release.

A hoarse exclamation of triumph and pleasure escaped

Craig's lips and he sagged against her. He lay there for some time as they both caught their breath.

Eyes closed, Meriel rolled onto her side and stretched, before curling into the curve of his body. A smile pulled on her lips. She felt decadent. Devine. Craig lowered his arm and slipped it around her, settling her head more comfortably on his shoulder. He felt good. Better than good. He felt magnificent. Conquering and all-powerful.

Long minutes passed. Meriel's fingers stroked Craig's chest. She loved the feel of his crisp hair, his smooth, hot skin, his wonderful scent.

Craig stroked her arm. "I did miss you," he said softly. "More than I thought possible. I think most of my anger came from my disappointment at your not being here when I came in."

Meriel digested the admission and felt somewhat mollified now that she understood what had made him so emotionally explosive. It had not been from her lack of effort—but the lack of her presence. "I will try to be here next time."

Absentmindedly, Craig moved his hand to her hair, enjoying the sensation of pulling his fingers through its softness. "All week I had visions of you eager for my arrival, cooking me dinner, and my whisking you away from the hearth and back to our bed the moment I came in."

Meriel giggled at the image. "And I ruined all your plans." She looked up at him. "Is my cooking dinner really that important to you?"

Craig shrugged his shoulders. "I just think it would be nice," he said, keeping private his real thoughts about Hamish and the meal she had cooked *him*. Meriel would tease him about being jealous and he would not be able to deny it, as it was the truth. He was jealous, but he was also curious. He saw what Meriel would do for a friend and was keen to see what effort she would put out for him.

Meriel resettled her head in the crook of his shoulder. "What if I try to cook dinner tomorrow night?"

Craig hesitated. "No eating at the castle?"

Meriel smiled. "No castle, no father, no sister . . . just you and me, and whatever I can make for us to eat," she answered.

Craig growled his pleasure at the idea, rolled over, and proceeded to make slow, sweet love to her again.

"Meriel?" The hesitancy in Craig's voice was undisguised. Part of him was annoyed with himself for again being shocked at the state of his home, while the other part kept vacillating between concerned and mystified.

Like yesterday, he had approached their cottage and made enough noise to ensure Meriel realized he had come home. And like before, he opened the door, eager to see both a dinner on the table and her beside it, radiating beauty and joy at his arrival. And once again, he found neither.

However, there were some differences.

His pile of dirty clothes was no longer visible, but he suspected that was because all of his belongings that had been stuffed into the kitchen were now on the floor covering them up. Unfortunately, they also consumed most of the table, three of the four chairs, a good portion of the floor, and from what he could see at the front door, at least one of the two chairs in the back. But what truly caught his eye was the kitchen area. Though empty, it no longer looked unused. It appeared as if a huge fight had taken place inside and Meriel had lost.

"Meriel?" he called out again, and a second later she emerged from the bedroom, proudly carrying a large black cooking pot. She flashed him a large, satisfied smile that reminded him of when one of his younger, inexperienced soldiers won a difficult training match against an elder. But, physically, Meriel did not look the victor.

Her hair remained partially styled, or at least partially braided, but the other part was unruly, with pieces of food embedded in it. If Craig had to guess, he would say that her face had become quite sticky with sweat more than once and that she had used her hand or sleeve or something with flour on it to swipe her brow and slick her hair back. The rest of her appearance was not an improvement, but it did match the state of the cooking area. It looked as if all the things needed to make a meal had exploded in his home. He blew at a feather drifting down in front of him and had a sick feeling that Meriel had also attempted to clean a bird.

Meriel sashayed past him and with a loud *thunk* placed the heavy pot on the dinner table. "Welcome home, husband," she said in a silky voice, reaching up on her toes to give him a kiss.

Although not really inspired, Craig returned her peck, secretly glad she did not try to initiate something more before leaving to go back into the kitchen area. He swallowed. "Ummm. What were you doing in the bedroom with the cooking pot?" he asked.

"Oh, I needed more to room to cut up the meat and the potatoes, so I decided to do it in there," Meriel answered as she started to search a pile of items crammed into a large wooden tub.

"On our bed?"

Meriel laughed. "Sometimes you men have the craziest notions," she answered, standing back up, waving a bowl and a spoon in the air. "Now you can eat! I cannot wait for you to try it!"

Craig inhaled deeply and peered inside the pot. The smell was far from appetizing. He sank down onto the chair again, perplexed. Meriel was obviously very proud and considered what he was about to dine on a considerable accomplishment. He sat down and watched her scoop out a large serving of what he assumed was supposed to be stew. Then she pulled out a chair with several fragments of unused material on it and sat down.

Craig was shocked that Meriel had no problem sitting on items that a couple of weeks ago he could not lay a shield on. He began to search for some bread to quickly put in his mouth lest he say something that might start another fight. "Where's the bread?"

Meriel's mouth twisted as her expression became one of guilt and frustration. "There isn't any," she admitted. "Or at least none you could eat."

Craig inhaled deeply again and told himself that he had eaten plenty of meals without bread. Another would not hurt. Purposefully delaying taking a bite of the stew, he looked for something to drink. "Is there any ale?" he asked, hoping his chipper voice did not sound as insincere as it did to his own ears.

Meriel wrinkled her nose and wiped it as if she smelled something unpleasant, and again shook her head. "I did not have time to go get any, but I did get some water. It's right there," she said, pointing to a pitcher on his left.

Craig picked it up and saw something floating on the surface. It was a feather. He was not surprised. If anything, he was more amazed that only one had made its way inside. He took his unused spoon and got it out. "Did you pluck a bird in here today?"

Meriel's face lit up with pure joy as if he had just paid her the greatest of compliments. "I did! Can you believe it? I tried doing most of it outside, but when it started to rain this afternoon, I had to finish the rest in here."

Meriel scooted his bowl of stew closer to him. "Aren't you going to try it?"

"I . . . I was waiting for you."

Meriel shook her head and sat back. "I don't want any, or at least not right now. My stomach has been unhappy with me most of the day. Besides, I'm so tired after doing everything to get dinner ready for you in time, I'm no longer hungry. But don't let that stop you."

Craig knew he could delay no longer, dipped the spoon into the stew, and took a bite. As he feared, he could not even swallow one mouthful and had to spit it back into the bowl.

Meriel immediately reacted. "Why did you do that?" she exclaimed.

Craig shoved the bowl away from him. "How could I not? I don't even know what that is, but I do know that it isn't edible. The potatoes haven't been cooked and"—he paused to sniff—"well, no sane man would eat *anything* that smelled like that!" he said in defense.

Meriel threw her hands up in the air and waved them about. "It's amazing you can smell the stew at all, given your own body odor! There is a river between the training fields and this cottage. Next time use it."

"I'm not the one who would give grown men night terrors right now, with food in my hair and blood and feathers all over my clothes. And I *might* have bathed before I came home if I had even one clean leine to put on! I'm guessing that I won't have any clean clothes to wear tomorrow either!" he yelled back, his anger in full bloom.

Hot, furious tears burned in Meriel's eyes. "You expect me to cook, clean, wash, and bathe, when you will not even help me at all!"

"I don't ask you to help me train the men, secure the borders, and protect the castle," Craig protested, uncaring as to the level of stress he was causing his wife. His patience was exhausted. "I have a lot to do, Meriel. You are the one who is home and has the time. Not me."

Meriel blinked back her tears, incredulous that Craig actually had the nerve to say—albeit indirectly—that he was busier than she was. He might as well have just come out and said that all things to do with the cottage were her responsibility simply because she was a woman! How did a simple promise to love him and live with him translate into being his servant? She knew that other wives did the cooking and cleaning, but they also did not work outside the home. Those who did usually had older children to help, and as a *family* they addressed everyone's needs. Well, right now their family consisted of her and him. And he did not have the sole right to the title of "busy."

"It must have escaped your notice, but my day is just as hard and demanding, Craig," Meriel said through tight lips. "Being married to you did not absolve me of my prior clan duties. I am still responsible for directing and assigning all the sewing and weaving that is needed to support not just Caireoch, but this clan. Winter is coming, and daily I have to go to the castle and answer questions, give directions, and even sit down and help. Right now there is more to do than people to do it. And yet I *still* came home and made *you* dinner."

Her ending snarl was like a slap in the face. Craig leaned in so that she would have no trouble seeing just how blazingly furious he was. He pointed to the nearly full bowl. "That was many things. But it was definitely *not dinner.*"

Meriel was flabbergasted that he was so furious that she had failed at her attempt to prepare a meal. "I did what the cook told me to do! At least I thought I did. How was I to know? I've never *cooked* before!"

Craig went still. "What do you mean, you've *never* cooked before? I distinctly remember you and Hamish sharing what looked to be an extremely tasty meal that *you* prepared."

Meriel looked bewildered until she finally recalled to just what Craig was referring. "You cannot possibly believe I had anything to do with what we ate that night."

"You promised that you would do the cooking!"

"I did not promise. I said something about the idea being interesting, knowing what would happen—disaster. But you *know* I have never spent any time in the kitchens. Not to mention that there was no possibility of Fiona letting me anywhere near her haven in a cooking capacity, and I don't blame her."

Craig shook his head. His face was a dull shade of red. "I saw you that afternoon—in the kitchens with Fiona— preparing the meal you and Hamish enjoyed. And what you and he shared was not this dark mystery that even a dog would refuse."

Meriel felt her temper start to flare again at the insult. "Of *course* you did. I needed you to *think* I was cooking for him."

An appalling silence filled the air for several long seconds. Through an extraordinary act of will, Craig managed to quash his rage and regain his self-control. Meriel *had* manipulated him. She knew it was one of the few things he abhorred, and that she had intentionally done so to him was not to be born.

He rose to his feet. To avoid her, he pivoted and marched around the table the long way, which was also the most cluttered pathway to exit the cottage. By the time he reached the door, he had tripped and nearly fallen twice. "I cannot and will not live like this, Meriel."

He slammed the door shut, leaving her to stare at nothing but empty space. *Well, neither can I*, Meriel said to herself. Craig might have had expectations as to what married life would be like, but so had she. And in her mind, so far *she* was the only one doing the compromising, trying to make things work.

Meriel grabbed a blanket and opened the door, knowing her father and her sister would welcome her home with open arms if she went to them. But there would be consequences to such an action. It would change her father's relationship with Craig. Crevan would be caught between defending his brother and dealing with his wife, for Meriel had no doubt that Raelynd would be on her side, even if Meriel was in the wrong. She and Craig would eventually get past their anger, but it did not necessarily follow that her family would as well.

Meriel stopped and turned around. She could not do it. She could not potentially hurt her marriage, her sister's, or even risk the clan losing a much-needed commander, over a fight. This was the life she chose and she refused to run away from it. She would stay, and when Craig returned it was going to be her turn to say a few things about how she could and could not live.

Turning around to face the evidence of her afternoon from hell, Meriel went and dumped the contents of the bowl back into the pot and began cleaning the mess of feathers and flour. When she was done, she carried the pot outside the village and dumped its contents. She then headed to the river, deciding she would rather freeze by bathing in the chilly currents than carry water back and warm it for a bath. After freeing her hair from the grime of her cooking attempts, Meriel donned her chemise, but she was unwilling to wear the filthy gown. Wrapped in a blanket, she snuck back to the cottage, glad it was dark so she had avoided the few people who were moving about the village.

Craig took both ends of his sopping wet leine and began to twist it in an effort to wring as much water from it as possible. He did not believe that just swimming while wearing the garment would render it clean—but it had to help some, if only with the stench. And while he did feel better physically, the absence of filth had not improved his mood even slightly.

Pulling the damp shirt over his head, he began to walk

along the river's shoreline, kicking rocks periodically in a futile effort to relieve some of his frustration. A shiver went through him, which only fueled his anger. He hated being wet and cold. Somehow the combination always seemed to make his skin overly sensitive. That he was swimming at this time of year, and at night, he blamed on Meriel. If she had just done what all wives did for their husbands, he would be home, warm and comfortable!

Shoving his freezing hands underneath his arms, Craig veered away from the shoreline and began heading back. He had meant it when he said that he could not continue to live as they had been. Something had to change.

He arrived at the door and took a deep breath before entering. Nudging it open, he could see that clutter was still everywhere, but the cooking area had been cleaned and all the evidence of the dinner and its preparation had been removed. Craig walked over to the pile of dirty clothes and grabbed a dry leine. He sniffed it and decided that it was better than being cold.

Changing shirts was a quiet activity, but he had made as much noise as possible, so she had to know he had returned. When Meriel did not appear, he let go a frustrated sigh and began to make his way to the back of the cottage. He was unsure what he was going to say once he found Meriel, and half hoped that she would start the conversation. He only knew that he was *not* going to start with an apology, nor was he going to gather her in his arms and tell her how appreciative he was of her cleaning efforts—despite how very much he was.

Craig peeked into the bedroom but could see nothing. Picking up the one lit candle, which had burned down to nearly nothing, Craig brought it into the bedchamber and lifted it high. Meriel was not there. She was not anywhere in the cottage. It had not occurred to him that she would flee back to her room in the castle, but she had. Pivoting, he put the candle back and marched angrily out the door. Had she not heard him last night? Had she not understood? They were married, and he did not care how angry either one or both of them were, they were going to sleep together every night and in the same bed! If she did not understand his meaning before, she certainly would once he was done.

Craig knew his facial expression reflected at least some of the anger he felt as he passed through the gatehouse. Normally the guards would have waved or shouted out an acknowledgment. But not tonight. As soon as both men saw Craig, they decided to pretend they had not. And he was thankful. Turning sharply to the right, he headed to the tower stairwell that led to the room she had shared with her sister, assuming he'd find her there.

When he entered the empty and clearly unused room, Craig felt his anger rise even higher. He immediately stormed back down the stairs and toward the Great Hall, fully expecting to find Meriel commiserating with her sister, blaming him for every fierce word they had shared. But again, he found no one inside. Turning around, he went back to the keep and spoke to the guard on duty, only to learn that his brother, Raelynd, and the laird had all retired for the night some time ago. Nothing of Meriel.

For the first time since leaving the cottage, an emotion other than anger was consuming him. With both hands, Craig roughly raked his fingers along his scalp in an effort to help him think. If she was not in the cottage or at the castle, where would Meriel be? Though not something she had ever done before, it was possible she was out looking for him. Or maybe she decided that she needed to go for a walk and think as well.

Craig looked up at the night sky, which was getting increasingly dark. When he had left, the moon had just passed its apex. Now it was nearly gone. Walking at night was always somewhat dangerous, but soon it would be very much so. As he envisioned the dangers Meriel could face, fear swept through him. He increased the speed of his gait and headed back to the cottage to grab a torch and a blanket.

Upon entering, he knew immediately that Meriel had returned. The candle was out, but the hearth had been stoked and was now brighter than it had been. Though he could not see her directly, the firelight created a shadow of her form, curled up in one of the chairs. He closed the door, but the ghostly figure flickering on the wall did not move. Craig walked over to Meriel and confirmed that she had fallen asleep.

He stared at his wife for several minutes, love for her filling every pore of his being. They were having problems, aye, but all problems had solutions. One just needed to look hard enough to find them.

Smoothing back her hair, Craig could see dried tear tracks on her cheeks and he could feel his chest tighten. He had not been alone in his distress, but his thoughts for the past couple of hours had been focused solely on himself. Not her. He had not realized how busy she still was supporting her father and the castle. And though it was a complete failure, she *had* tried cooking dinner. Most girls grew up with their mothers teaching them how to be wives. Meriel's mother died when she was young. Maybe he simply needed to be a little more patient as she learned how to take care of a home and husband.

Sliding his arm underneath her, he carefully picked Meriel up and sat her on his lap, letting her head rest against his shoulder. He softly combed his fingers through her hair and smiled as he felt the damp tresses. He had been a fool to think she had run back home to the castle. His comments about her appearance must have inspired her to take a bath, just as her remarks about his body odor had driven him to the river for a quick dip.

Craig kissed her temple. A small moan escaped Meriel as she nestled closer to him. The small gesture helped release the remaining tension in his body. She needed him. He needed her. They had each other, and as long as they did, everything else could be resolved in time.

Meriel stirred. Her brows furrowed into a deep scowl, as if she were having a bad dream. Stroking her cheek, he whispered that all was fine. That he was there now and would not let anything happen to her.

At the sound of his voice, Meriel began to shift from her dream world to reality. She was sitting on Craig's lap—a place she did not want to be, though she could not recall why. As her last thoughts and his departing insults began to crystallize, she remembered exactly what he had said. And while she had wanted Craig to come home, she did not intend to let him smother her with kisses and lovemaking to gain her goodwill. *She* would not be complying with all of *his* suggestions. This time, he was going to have to exert some effort into making this marriage work as well.

Pushing against his chest, Meriel attempted to get up, but Craig's arms tightened, keeping her in place. The fact that he not only could, but would force her to his will, made her feel nauseated for the umpteenth time that day. She thought about trying again to put some distance between them, but knowing the effort would be pointless, she sagged against his chest and began to cry. Tears slowly found their way down her cheeks using previously defined paths, and once again Mcriel found herself getting mad that she was weeping when she had every right to be angry.

"Shhh, there, love," Craig whispered against her ear. "Don't worry about the food."

Meriel blinked. Her throat swelled up and she thought

she might choke. *Did Craig actually think she was crying about her inability to cook dinner?* The man had lost his mind if he thought that she cared about her skills, or lack of them, in the kitchen. "I'm not crying about the food," she sniveled, angry again that her voice sounded meek and pathetic and nothing like the tone of her inner dialogue.

"Then what is it that has you so upset?"

Meriel hesitated. Part of her thought that if Craig had to ask, then what was the point of telling him? But she was not crying for one reason alone. Her days were filled with unceasing work. There was no time for her to enjoy any of her pastimes and she felt like everybody was clamoring to get a piece of her. She was doing her best, but it still did not seem to be good enough. "You'll tell me that I am being ridiculous."

"I promise I will not."

Meriel yawned. "I don't know how to explain it. Mostly, I'm tired all the time. It takes me forever to find energy in the morning and all of it is wasted on carrying water from the well. The other women have seen me struggle, and I know they are sympathetic, but they are busy with their own lives. By the time I am done getting ready for the day, all I want to do is lie down, and yet I have no time, for the weavers are waiting for me to get down to the castle."

Craig nodded against her head. "Water seems like a simple chore, but it can be demanding. You merely need to build up endurance. It will come with time. You will see."

"Mm-hmmm," Meriel answered, barely tracking what he was saying.

"And we've been eating at the castle for this long. I am sure your father will not mind feeding us a little longer until you learn how to cook."

"Father likes us to eat with him," she said slowly, her voice fading as her exhaustion once again sent her back into a deep sleep.

"I think I have found the solution to your problem," Craig said with a hopeful heart. "You just need to slow down, and that starts with ending your work at the castle. You don't have to do that anymore. That should help. Now, doesn't that make you happy?"

All he heard was a deep breath followed by a slow exhale. Craig smiled and lifted her in his arms and carried her to their bed. Tonight he would just hold her.

Chapter 13

As he approached the door to his home, Craig took a deep breath and opened the door. His heart sang as he inhaled the smell of bread and meats and ale on the table before him. Next to the scrumptious food was his wife, looking beautiful and serene. So overjoyed at the sight, he almost went back outside and started shouting words of praise to the Lord because, finally, his prayers had been answered.

He carefully put down his things where they would not cause any harm and then placed a warm, loving kiss upon Meriel's soft lips before sitting down on the empty chair next to her. Just by the smell, Craig knew the food had come from the castle, but as he reached over and began to pile food on his plate, he realized he no longer cared. Finally they were in sync. He had tried to speak with her in the morning about the solution to her problems with allocating her time, but she had refused to awaken before he left. Now he wondered if he even needed to. "So I assume you were right," he said with smile, "and your father has no issues helping us with dinner while you learn how to cook."

Meriel was pulling a small piece of meat off a leg of lamb when Craig's assumptions about their dinner hit her full force. Once again, Craig was telling her that he was not satisfied, that *more* change was warranted, and that none of that change was coming from him.

Last night as she sat waiting for Craig to come home, she went over every conversation they had had since they were married. How she had missed his prejudiced definition of "wife," Meriel was not quite sure, but she had. While she would agree that most of the soldiers' wives did assume certain house-related responsibilities, it was only because it made sense for their circumstances. Never had it occurred to her that women cooked *just* because they were female. She doubted many of the women would respond very well to learning that their domestic responsibilities were assigned *solely* on the basis of their sex.

"Aye, Father is very accommodating, though he would like us to eat there every once in awhile as *we* learn how to cook."

Craig caught the emphasized "we" but truly did not understand what she meant. "I think we can arrange that," he said cautiously.

Meriel wrinkled her nose at the meat, suddenly not hungry. "Which part? The eating at the castle or you learning how to cook?"

Craig started choking on a half-swallowed piece of fowl. He had *not* misheard. "I'm not learning how to cook," he clarified.

"And why not?" she challenged.

"Because I'm a . . . a . . ." Meriel stared him directly in the eye, daring him to say "man." "Because I am too damn busy!" he shouted.

"I am just as busy with my work supporting this clan."

"Then tell your father and your sister that you quit," he ordered, a little more forcefully than intended.

"I have no intention of quitting. So if I must learn new

skills to make this marriage work, then *so must you*. I am not your servant."

"No, you are my *wife*," he growled ominously.

Craig could once again feel anger starting to edge its way into the conversation, and he fought to keep it pushed down. For once, they were not going to have a huge fight before they went to bed. Still, Meriel's accusation that he thought her a servant simply because he wanted her to learn how to cook and support their household like every other woman did, riled him enormously. He was not being ridiculous! Compared to other husbands he knew and had overheard talking, he expected very little!

"Aye, I am your wife. I also happen to be a *working* wife who is responsible for more than taking care of a single household."

"Other women choose not to work until their young can help their mothers at home," Craig responded through gritted teeth.

Meriel took a deep breath and prayed for calm. "You and I seem to have fallen into some kind of communication trap. I think because we seem to know each other so well, we thought we knew everything. So, let me be clear, Craig. I respect women who raise children and take care of their homes. I always have, and after the past few weeks, even more so. But I have always supported this clan, and I will continue to do so until I am no longer able. It is who I am, and you knew this before we married."

Craig fought to keep his voice as calm as possible. "I assumed you would realize that you would have to refocus on the needs of your husband, placing them above those of your father and the clan."

"Just because I have not catered to your needs as you imagined I would, does not mean that you are not the most important person in my life." Meriel rose to her feet and took a step closer to him. Bending down, she gave him a small kiss on the cheek. "Enjoy your dinner. I'm exhausted. I think I will lie down for a bit, if you do not mind."

Craig sat there dumbfounded as Meriel sauntered from the table through the kitchen area to their bedroom, leaving him alone to eat. How were they ever going to resolve all their problems if Meriel kept refusing to implement his solutions?

"*Mo creach*," he muttered under his breath. He was out of ideas.

Thankfully, there was one person nearby who might be able to help him. His brother. For if anyone would understand his quandary it would be Crevan. Being married to the fiercely independent Raelynd, the man must have encountered this type of situation before. Probably daily, knowing his sister-in-law.

Craig got up and quietly left the cottage. Aye, if anyone had the answer to getting Schellden women to understand their roles as Highland wives, it would be his brother.

Craig found himself feeling overwhelmingly jealous. Of his brother, of all people. Which made it all the worse. Never had he been jealous of his twin. And to his knowledge Crevan had never been jealous of him either. They had been best friends all their lives, taking advantage of and leaning on each other when it came to their different personalities and ways of thinking. But jealous? And yet, Craig found himself overcome with it.

"Never?" he repeated, still finding it hard to believe that Crevan did not fight with his wife. How? The woman was only slightly less obstinate than Meriel, and Crevan lacked Craig's good-natured disposition. If anything, the two should have been explosive.

Craig stood up and began to pace. "Meriel and I fight all the time," he confessed reluctantly.

"Of course you do." Crevan shrugged his shoulders and stretched out his legs. The posture practically announced that all was well within his world and it made Craig only more agitated. "All couples f-fight their f-first year. You did not think you w-would be the exception?"

Aye. I did, Craig admitted, but only to himself. "How did you get to escape this torture?"

Crevan laughed heartily. "Escape? Raelynd and I f-fought practically daily about everything. Even in that month before w-we married, w-w-we got so angry at each other that now that I look back, it is amazing that I sit here right now, happy as I am. But don't misunderstand. I said w-we did not f-fight, not that w-w-we don't argue. Difference is that w-we try to re-f-frain f-from yelling—though Raelynd has a hard time w-with that on certain subjects—and, umm, w-w-well, as much as you w-won't like to hear it, neither of us goes to bed angry or leaves in the middle of a . . . uh, discussion."

If those condemning words had come from anyone else, Craig might have been tempted to take physical steps to ensure they would never be uttered again. But Crevan was unique. Only he and Meriel could correct him without fear of retaliation. Still, usually such censure would have at least pricked Craig's pride, raising his ire. Tonight, he just felt helpless because he knew his brother was correct, but at the same time, he still had no clear path away from his troubles.

"Before we got married, Meriel and I were so in tune we did not need to talk. We each seemed to understand what the other needed. And while it is still like that on most things . . . when it comes to living together . . . well, simply put, she is *most* aggravating."

Crevan reached back and intertwined his fingers

behind his head and stared at his brother thoughtfully. "I'm sorry you are not f-finding the marital bliss that I have discovered."

"Oh, I find it," Craig corrected. "Every night. My problem is that I lose it again by morning. Meriel just refuses to accept her role! She is my wife. I want to help her, but she won't listen to anything I suggest!"

Crevan raised a single brow into a high, incredulous arch. "Maybe . . . she doesn't like w-what you have to say."

Craig shot him an evil look, well-practiced after years of being so close. "I doubt you would be saying that if it was Raelynd who knew not the first thing about cooking or cleaning."

. The bubble of laughter Crevan had been suppressing erupted. "Raelynd has not the f-f-first idea about cooking. She might know a little about cleaning after last year and what Laurel and Aileen did to her, but I suspect if she really had to do any of the w-work herself, the results w-would be f-f-far f-from pleasant."

Craig narrowed his gaze and waved his hand around, his gesture referring to the castle at large. "You expect me to believe that? Your false words bring me no comfort."

"Every w-word I say is true."

"And you don't care that Raelynd cannot cook?"

Crevan turned his head slightly at the odd question. "W-what w-would it change if she did? Her having the skill holds no purpose in either of our lives."

Craig grimaced. "Meriel and I don't live at the castle—"

"By choice. O-o-one that Rae is still not happy about, by the w-way."

"Newly married couples need freedom." *And privacy*, Craig added to himself.

Crevan pulled himself upright and then leaned forward, placing his elbows on his knees. "I understand. Believe me on that o-one, I truly do. It took a w-while to establish some boundaries w-with Rae, but he now respects our privacy as he does yours, by the w-way. Otherw-wise, you w-would be seeing him every night at your doorstep. He may not like that you have elected to live in the village, but he respects your and Meriel's right to make such a decision."

"When is it going to get better?" Craig rubbed his face vigorously. "I think Meriel entered our marriage truly believing that she would be able to do exactly as she had been, just in a different location!"

"And w-what is Meriel asking of *you* that is so onerous?"

Craig sank into his chair. "I don't know. Patience until she learns how to cook? Honestly, I'm not too sure she ever plans on learning how to put together even a simple meal. Meriel would be happy to keep on abusing her position as the laird's daughter."

"It's hardly abuse, and you know that Rae, her sister, and I have no qualms w-w-with her raiding our kitchens. W-we don't understand w-why you don't just eat here."

Craig scoffed. "You're right. If she isn't willing to try to learn how to cook for me . . . I mean for us . . . we should eat here. It would be simpler."

Crevan, still leaning forward, tapped the tips of his index fingers together. "So she expects things to remain exactly as they w-were be-f-fore you married, and you expect her to do nothing but change."

Change. Craig cringed at the word. How many times had he and Meriel promised that they would not change each other? "Is it so unreasonable for a man to expect his wife to *act* like a normal, typical spouse? I'm only asking for a clean shirt and some decent food!"

Crevan shook his head, knowing that Craig was lost in his thoughts. His brother was listening, but not hearing. "If you w-w-wanted typical, you married the wrong w-woman. Meriel w-will never make you happy."

Craig's head snapped up and true anger flashed in his bright blue eyes. Crevan continued, now that he had his brother's attention. "Our w-wives are not traditional w-w-women. Never have been and they never w-will be and *that* is w-why w-we love them so.

"Look at Conor and Laurel. Look at *any* of our married brothers. All of us have chosen strong, smart, and often infuriatingly independent w-women. W-which also means we have stubborn, crafty, and w-w-willful w-wives. And because they are all of these things, they w-want—and even demand—more than most w-wives do of their husbands.

"Raelynd insists on having significant input into all decisions w-when it comes to the castle and the clan. It is something her f-father and I are constantly trying to balance as neither of us always trusts her judgment. But—and don't tell her I told you this—a f-f-few of those times, w-we have regretted it miserably that w-we did not. F-for you and Meriel, it sounds like autonomy is your curse. And how you deal w-w-with that is up to you and her, but let me add one last thought f-for my w-wife's sake. And f-f-for my sanity."

Craig sat back in the chair, his anger ebbing but not completely gone. He heard all that his brother was saying, but it changed nothing.

"Aye, the castle is w-well run," Crevan continued. "Raelynd is exceptional at organizing and overseeing, though sometimes she can be a little too demanding. Most of our 'discussions' are on that point, by the w-way. But Caireoch," Crevan said, mimicking Craig's gesture, "is a huge responsibility.

"How many times have you heard that our neighbors enjoy the w-warmth and hospitality of our homes? That our clansmen are not as belligerent as many Highlanders you and I have met? W-why do you think the games come here more often than some-w-where else? You've been to other clans, other castles. Too often they are in a state of chaos. 'Twas the w-way of McTiernay Castle before Laurel came. You remember. But it is not, nor has it ever been, that w-way here. And Raelynd w-would not be as successful as she has been at keeping this castle running if she did not have the support of her sister. Raelynd needs Meriel more than ever, especially now that she is w-with child."

Craig took a deep breath and slowly exhaled. He had come to his brother for comfort and advice and he was finding just the opposite. "I understand your not-so-subtle hint, brother, but precisely how is Meriel supposed to take care of her own home when she is exhausted after working here? I can learn to accept eating dinner here every night, and you know that I feel quite comfortable in a cluttered room, but how am I supposed to live in a place where I am not allowed even to put my shield down in fear of getting flayed for destroying something flimsy and, arguably, unimportant?"

Crevan sat back and with a nod of his head acknowledged his brother's predicament. "My knowledge of Meriel is that she is incredibly stubborn. She w-will do w-w-whatever she desires. Maybe you just need to encourage her to think of your home as a place f-f-for others beyond herself. Something to take pride in."

Craig had not thought of that. Meriel had inherited quite a strong dose of the Schellden pride, and no one was more tenacious once she had an idea in her head. "What if we should invite the family over?"

Crevan stretched out his legs again, a grin growing on his face. "Raelynd *has* been complaining that she doesn't get to spend much time w-with her sister since you moved out."

Craig rose to his feet and slapped his brother on the shoulder, thanking him. He returned home, much relieved to find Meriel exactly where he left her, asleep on their bed, unmoved, in the same position.

Huh, he muttered to himself. She really must have been exhausted. Deciding he needed to think more than sleep, he settled himself on the chair and got comfortable. It was not until the end of their conversation that his brother truly helped with an idea to solve his current situation, but Crevan had brought many things into focus.

The idea of change had been the most surprising. Craig had not realized it, but he had expected many things to change, and yet had done little of it himself. But it was time he did some compromising. First, he would give up the idea of coming home to a warm dinner. An easy sacrifice. Harder was accepting that he would have to continue to share Meriel with her clan duties—at least until Raelynd had her baby. But he would. Those two changes on his part should help enormously. But the last remained in Meriel's control. The state of their cottage.

Craig glanced at the bedroom and decided not to wake her up and talk about it now, despite his yearning to do just that. In the morning, she would be rested and in good spirits. *Aye*, he said to himself as he rested his head against the back of the chair, closing his eyes, *tomorrow we can talk*.

Meriel woke up and stretched her limbs, wiggling her toes. She felt good. She did not know how long it would last, but at least for the moment, she felt wonderful. Nothing had awakened her in the middle of the night. Craig had not aroused her prematurely when he got ready in the morning to head out. If only all days could begin thus.

Slipping out of bed, she grabbed a robe and stopped short when she saw Craig's large form looking most uncomfortable asleep on one of the hearth chairs. "Craig, why are you sleeping out here?"

"Wh-what?" His head sprang up, the pattern of the woven material he had been using as a pillow imprinted on his face. Meriel pressed the back of her hand to her lips to hide her mirth.

"What are you doing?" she asked, leaning against the door frame. "Did you sleep out here?"

Craig rubbed his face and stretched his arms up into the air. "I guess I did. Didn't mean to." He twisted his neck to one side and then the other. "I must have fallen asleep thinking about things."

Meriel gave a slight shove to the door frame and stood erect. "What things?" she asked hesitantly, and walked toward the chair next to him.

She needed to be sitting down if he was going to tell her once again that she needed to give up her responsibilities at the castle. How was she going to refuse? Because she would, despite the injury it might cause her marriage. She had thought about it as long as she was able before sleep took over. And her last thought was about all her duties and responsibilities. She might have become Craig McTiernay's wife, but she was still Laird Rae Schellden's daughter. Craig would simply have to accept that. And if he could not . . . A shiver went through her, for she still could not accept what that would mean.

"Me, mostly," Craig answered. "We've never talked about the times I spent in battle."

"I wanted to. You refused."

"I still do. No one should live through that hell. I won't live it twice by retelling it, and I will *not* have you experience it even a little. But during those times, at night, the men would talk. And the ones who did the talking were usually the married men. They would describe in detail what was waiting for them at home. Warmth, a loving wife, a family to greet them. And *every* story included a mouthwatering meal—probably because all we ever ate was what we could find and catch. Too often by the time we got our share it was cold. So the stories, the images, gave all of us something to look forward to. A reason to fight and live and never give up. And for those of us who were not married, they gave us dreams for our future."

"But you never wanted to get married."

Craig reached out and clasped her hand softly in his, stroking her palm with his thumb. "I just did not want to *admit* that I wanted to get married." He smiled at her and she smiled back. "So I think that is what has been behind my expectations and disappointments."

Meriel held her breath. When he did not continue, she said, her tone melancholy, "I am sorry I cannot be what you want."

Craig gave her hand a quick, firm squeeze. "You misunderstand. I truly did not realize I was demanding that you change into what I envisioned to be a normal wife. You have always been different from other women. That is why I was so immediately drawn to you. I had just forgotten that, until Crevan reminded me."

Meriel swallowed and her heart stopped. She did not want their problems to be known to anyone. "You went and saw your brother."

"Aye. He made me realize that while I've been patient, I have not been open to change. He told me that I have been wrong to try to change you, and perhaps need to be doing more of it myself. Like accepting his offer of eating at the castle with your family."

She tugged his hand. "Our family."

He smiled. "Aye, our family. *And* that you have an important role in supporting Raelynd with the castle responsibilities. My wife does not stay at home during the day. For now, she works as I do, and that requires adjustment, not only from you but from me as well."

More than mollified, Meriel suddenly wished that Craig

had visited his brother weeks ago. "It sounds like we both need to accept that things are not going to be exactly as we thought they would be."

"After talking with Crevan, I would like to invite him to our home. He and Raelynd as well as your father."

"Here? Why not meet at the castle?"

Craig shook his head. He needed the invitation to be from her to their home. "I think your father needs to see us here, happy and content. Crevan said that he would have been over here already but is waiting for an invitation. I could invite him over tonight."

Meriel snatched her hand from his grasp and sat up straight. "Don't you dare! He would order me home the first instant he saw this place, and probably behead you!"

Craig hid the enormous smile that he was feeling. Ahh, Meriel's pride when properly pricked was indeed the solution. "He knows we both are messy."

"It is not the *mess* that I care about," she huffed.

Craig leaned over and gave her a quick kiss on the lips. "I must go to work. How about a compromise? I will let you choose when to issue the invitations as long as you promise me that you will. And that it will be sometime soon."

Meriel bit her bottom lip. He added that last part just because he knew she would easily have agreed otherwise. "Fine," she said with a long sigh. "I will invite them."

Meriel took a step back and surveyed her home with pride. It had taken two weeks for her to keep her word, but early that morning, right after Craig left, she had forced herself to rise and go to the castle. While there, she met with her sister and for the first time listened attentively to every detail and description Raelynd offered about her pregnancy. When Meriel extended an invitation for her, Crevan, and their father to join them for dinner, Raelynd eagerly responded that they would. She had wanted to visit for some time, but Crevan had been overly concerned about her traveling anywhere without him.

Leaving her sister, Meriel went to the kitchens and asked them to prepare a special meal and deliver it later that day. She then went home and completed work on the cottage. By the time the food arrived, her home was not clean by Raelynd's standards, but in Meriel's mind it was close to spotless.

Peace filled her as she surveyed the small feast arranged on the table. It had been prepared by castle staff, but Craig did not seem to mind anymore that she herself was not doing the cooking. At long last, the fights were in the past. Once again, conversation was the focal point of their nights. They would enjoy the fare one of them retrieved from the castle, and then settle in the back room to talk about their day and their plans for the next. When one of them would eventually propose that they retire, the other eagerly complied.

Only twice had they opted to go to the castle to eat and visit; something Raelynd had pointed out during their most recent visit, and Meriel did pause to consider it. She loved her family very much. And part of her wanted to see them often, even daily, but even more she treasured time with her husband. She felt like their marriage had only recently begun, and she was reluctant to join the world when she had the option of spending time alone with Craig.

But tonight was different. Tonight she had news to share. The reason for her early morning trip to the castle was twofold. One had been to see her sister, but the other had been to meet with the same woman who would oversee the birthing of Raelynd's babe. And when the midwife confirmed the reason behind her lethargy and inability to keep down a meal, Meriel knew exactly how she wanted to share the news.

An abrupt knock on the door startled Meriel out of her reverie and she rushed to open the door. A cold gust of winter wind blew in and Crevan quickly ushered his wife inside. "I'm *fine*, Crevan," Raelynd admonished as she began to remove the layers of clothing.

Crevan pulled Meriel into a bear hug and then set her back down to help his wife. "You are in all w-ways f-fine, love, but you are also cold."

Rae Schellden stepped through the entrance and gave Meriel a huge smile. "So finally the father has been invited to his daughter's home." Meriel ran into Rae's arms, returning his long hug. "You see me almost daily, Papa."

He kissed the top of her head. "'Tis not the same, and you know it."

He looked overhead and glanced around. "It looks as I imagined it would with you and Craig as its owners—full."

"Papa," Meriel said again with a slight warning in her voice. It was one he knew well, having heard it all his life whenever he mentioned the state of her room.

"Aye, daughter, I agree. No lecture tonight. You have invited us here this evening and by the looks of all the food, it is to be quite a feast. Are we celebrating something other than our ability to maneuver in your and Craig's home?"

"Papa!" Meriel tried for a reproving tone, but her joy prevented it.

Rae slapped his hands together and rubbed them vigorously. "Where is that son-in-law of mine, anyway?"

Meriel peered out the window. The sun was now down, and these days Craig was always home by dark. "Something must have detained him. But he will be here soon," she promised.

Crevan pulled out a chair for Rae and then one for himself. Sitting down, he slouched to a comfortable position before stealing a piece of cheese and plopping it into his mouth. "So I'm guessing Craig has no idea that w-w-we are here."

Meriel licked her lips and gave herself a hug as she continued to stare out the window. "No, I only decided this morning. I wanted everything to be a surprise." Then, hearing Crevan's low chuckle, she turned to look him directly in the eye. "Do you know why he is late?"

At her sister's question, Raelynd moved from the warmth of the fire to join her husband and gave him a pointed stare. Crevan threw up his hands in the air. "I know nothing. Only that one of the men in the stable mentioned that my brother w-was not in a mood to be trifled w-with, but that w-w-was hours ago. I'm sure w-whatever w-was bothering him then has been dealt w-with and has passed."

"Do you know what it was?"

"I truly do not. But I did hear some rumors that two of the w-w-weavers have become ill, requiring the Highland's most skilled artist w-with a needle to humble herself by making blankets." Meriel rolled her eyes and settled into the chair closest to the window, tacitly allowing him to change the topic.

An hour later the conversation continued merrily, but they were all famished. Since she had no idea when Craig would arrive, Meriel announced they should go ahead and eat. But she hoped he would arrive soon. Not just because of their guests and her news, but now she was worried. The weather had turned markedly colder that day and the wind outside had grown bitter. Meriel knew that Crevan was also concerned, but there was little either of them could do about the situation.

"I did not tell you earlier today," Raelynd said, trying unsuccessfully to hide her enthusiasm, "but we finally have made some decisions about the baby."

Meriel swallowed. *Finally?* Her sister was only three months pregnant, but she was talking as if she were about to give birth. Meriel wondered if in a few weeks she too would be talking similar nonsense. "What decisions?"

"We finally agreed to where we are going to place our daughter's bed."

Crevan lifted Raelynd's wrist to his mouth for a kiss. "You mean our son's, love," he said softly.

Meanwhile, Meriel's hand went to her throat. "Not our old room?"

Raelynd immediately waved her hand dismissively. "Of course not. Those rooms are way too far removed from the rest of the keep. Crevan is going to partition the sitting room next to ours. Now if only we could agree to a name! You must help me."

Raelynd practically radiated with happiness. Regarding her own situation, Meriel was not sure what made her happier—that she was going to have a baby or that she finally knew why she had been so tired and sick. Her mind was still reeling with the knowledge that she was indeed pregnant. The concept of motherhood was still beyond her grasp.

Her sister, on the other hand, seemed so ready, so mentally prepared for becoming a mother. All the aspects that excited Raelynd, terrified Meriel. Her one comfort was that she would have her sister to lean on for advice.

An hour later, Meriel was glad the subject had finally changed from the baby to one that concerned only Rae and Crevan and did not require her to participate. Dinner over, Raelynd threw a small piece of bread at Meriel, hitting her squarely on the cheek. She grinned when Meriel's head snapped around to give her a menacing stare. "Stop looking out the window. It is you who is keeping Craig from coming home. All wives have the power to bring our husbands home, and you are not using yours."

Crevan crossed his arms and gave his wife a solid stare. "And pray tell, how does this power w-w-work?"

Raelynd stuck her chin up in the air and replied, "You must trick fate into thinking that you are no longer interested in your husband's whereabouts. *That* is when he will appear."

Crevan threw his head back and growled. "Do you hear your daughter, Rae? She thinks she commands f-f-fate!"

Meriel thought Raelynd ridiculous, but Crevan's mocking made her rally to her sister's side. Plus, it did not hurt to try. Determined not to look out the window even one more time, she turned around and was scrambling to find some question to ask her father to get her mind off Craig's absence when he burst in the door, carrying several bridles.

"What the hell?!" he blurted, seeing a roomful of his in-laws staring at him.

Meriel knew instantly that the passage of time had not caused Craig's bad mood to dissipate at all. His left arm and part of his face were caked with mud, and the portion of his face she could discern looked incredibly tired. She jumped up out of her chair and went to his side, giving him an apologetic smile. "I chose the wrong day to surprise you with keeping my promise, didn't I?" she asked in a faint voice. "I did not know."

Craig closed his eyes and cursed silently to himself. "Aye, it was not the best." He sighed, attempting to find the best way to ask his brother and Meriel's family to leave so that they could reschedule for another night. Any other day, he would have pushed aside his weariness and enjoyed their company, especially as it was the fulfillment of a promise Meriel had made to him. But not tonight. Not after the day he had had. "We were breaking in that new wild horse—"

"The one you found on the ridge last week?" Rae Schell-den asked.

Craig nodded and raked his hands through his hair. Both he and Rae hoped the animal would not prove to be too much for them. The black beast was a monster, and if he could be broken he would be an excellent war horse that could carry any size Highlander for long distances without tiring. "But so far, the beast is winning. But I have not given up," Craig muttered, tossing the muddy bridles haphazardly into the front room.

They landed with a soft *thud* on one of the various piles stashed in the room.

Seeing where they landed and the mud splattered everywhere, Meriel reacted violently. "What did you *do*!" she shrieked, running into the room.

He followed her to see what she was so upset about. From what he could see, it was only another set of materials that had no purpose. "It's just a little mud, Meriel. You can wash it off," he drawled unapologetically.

Meriel seethed inside. She had always known that Craig did not truly understand her work, but she at least thought he respected her. Meriel picked up the fragile black linen cloth that was on the top of the pile and had received the brunt of the grimy onslaught. Uncaring that her family was a few feet away and could see and hear everything, she pulled it out for Craig to see. Stitched on the black surface was a detailed outline of a woman lovingly carrying her newborn babe. "*This*," she hissed, "was to be a present for my sister. And no, Craig, *it cannot just be washed. It is ruined.*"

He reached down and grabbed the bridles. Each of Meriel's words had been uttered coldly through gritted teeth, and the shards of bitter anger struck deep. Guilt washed over him when he realized that he had been deservedly admonished. But it was the wounded pride that spoke for him. "What do you expect?" he growled. "I arrive to a houseful of guests, when all I wanted was to come home, clean up where it was warm, and after grabbing something to eat, get some sleep."

Meriel's eyes glinted and she could feel her lungs squeeze so tight that it was difficult to breathe. "*You* were the one who suggested having everyone come here."

"Aye, I did. But was it too much to ask that you send word that you wanted to have it *tonight*? Or even *ask* whether today was a good day?"

All at once Meriel was desperately weary. Her head hurt, her legs trembled, and she knew she was in danger of falling to the floor. "I wanted it to be a surprise."

"Guess what! I'm surprised!" he yelled as his angry gaze swung over her to the group who were rising to their feet in the other room. Then, in a much calmer voice, he said, "What a wretched day. I'm going to ask our guests to lea—"

"I'm pregnant."

The cottage went silent. The murmurings between Crevan, Raelynd, and her father as they bundled up to leave, immediately ceased.

Craig just stared at her. "No, you can't be," he muttered softly, though he was screaming the words in his head. The dread in his voice was unmistakable.

Meriel swallowed. She had anticipated the look of pure joy on Craig's face at the prospect of becoming a father, not this reaction. She was a fool. A month ago he had told her his position on having a family. He did not want one. But they had both better get ready, for in a few short months they were going to have a child. "I met with the midwife this morning. I am going to have a baby next summer."

Craig stood there, stunned, unable to digest the news. He did not want it to be true. It could not be true. But he knew it was, and it felt as if he had been given Meriel's death sentence.

Raelynd bustled around her frozen-stiff brother-in-law to give Meriel what hug she could while trapped under several blankets. "Congratulations! I cannot believe it! My sister and I are going to have children at the same time. I'm so excited. And don't worry about him," she said, using her thumb to point over her shoulder at Craig. "He is just in a state of shock that he is about to become a father. He's tired, and I think he wanted to keep you to himself a little while longer. But trust me, in a couple of months he will start to feel like another layer of skin, he will smother you so much."

Crevan came up and put his hand on his wife's shoulder and gave her a loving squeeze. Raelynd beamed at him. "I would not have it any other way."

Rae then gathered Meriel into his arms, tears forming in his eyes. "My babies are having babies. If only your mother were here to witness this. She would be so happy." Then in a whisper he added, "Do not worry about Craig, sweetheart. He's happy. He's just scared."

Before Meriel could ask him about what, Rae let go, told Craig to take care of his daughter, and followed Crevan and Raelynd out the door, leaving Meriel and Craig to fight alone. But neither had any fight left.

"I cannot believe it is true," Craig said gently, putting his hand on her shoulder in a possessive gesture.

Meriel shrugged him off; she did not want to be touched by him. "What do you expect after making love to me practically every night?"

Craig pivoted to keep her in his sight as she maneuvered around him to get back into the main room. When she headed to the chairs, he followed her, stopping her before she could sit down. "I *thought* that since your mother and your sister could not get pregnant easily, neither would you."

"Well, you were wrong. This truly has been a wretched day for you, hasn't it? First work, then an unwanted surprise party, and worst of all, you find out your wife is pregnant with your child."

The despair in her voice was so acute that it caused him physical pain. He gathered her in his arms. "Learning that you are going to have my child is the best part of my day. Not the worst."

Meriel gave him a slight, unsuccessful shove. "I know you don't want a family. You told me so a month ago, but it was probably too late even then," she murmured against him, her voice cracking. "I guess you were wrong about that too. God doesn't know better than to give us a child."

Craig frowned but did not say a word. Instead, he knelt down and slipped off her shoes, glad Meriel did not protest. Then he gently removed her gown, lifted her up, and settled her into the chair, nestling a blanket around her. Once he was satisfied that she was comfortable, he went to the table and picked up the pitcher of water, thankful that it was full. He then poured it into an empty pot and hung it inside the hearth. Venturing back to the table, he selected several pieces of meat, placing them between two pieces of bread. Once he finished eating the makeshift sandwich, he downed some ale and went back to the fire where he removed the pot and set it down next to her chair. Meriel was curious but was too tired to ask what he was doing or why.

Craig went and fetched what looked to be a scrap piece of bluish material and said, "Can I use this? Get it wet?"

Meriel shrugged in resignation, too tired to argue and tell him that the soft silk cloth was imported and she had planned to use it in a wall-hanging someday. Dipping it in the warm water, Craig began to wipe her cheek clean of the mud that had transferred to her when he held her close. Then he quickly removed his shirt and washed the mud off his face and arms. He took the pot and disappeared outside into the cold. A handful of seconds later, he darted back into the cottage, his head wet from dumping the remaining water over it in an effort to remove the last of the mud.

Rubbing his hands briskly in his wet hair, Craig shivered, walked to the back of the cottage, and said, "Brrrr. Winter will be here soon." Meriel was watching him with large gold-and-green eyes filled with the despair she felt inside, but if he noticed, he did not say anything. Instead, Craig picked her up and sat down, cuddling her in his lap. "I need you to warm me up."

Meriel felt her heart breaking. He was being so kind, so *nurturing*, but deep down she knew Craig wished her to be anything other than pregnant with his child. And while she would have preferred waiting to start a family, now that she knew his baby was growing inside her, she wanted it more than anything. That he did not feel the same made her feel incredibly alone.

"Meriel, I want the baby." The words were soft and heart-felt, but she could still hear the fear in his voice.

She shook her head, not wanting him to lie to her.

"I do. I want us to have a family. Very much. Nothing could make me prouder than to have a son with my jovial disposition and your stubborn streak, or a daughter who drives her mother crazy because she loves horses and cares nothing for the artistry of a needle." He took a deep breath. "But to have a child means you have to carry it. And your family's history when it comes to pregnancy terrifies me. I cannot lose you. I will not. I am not like your father. I do not have the strength to continue living without you."

Meriel sat with her cheek against his warm chest, listening to the racing beat of his heart. "I'm healthy. I am strong. Nothing is going to happen to me."

Craig nodded and hugged her tightly to him, unable to speak. Nothing would happen to Meriel. He would not let it. After several minutes, when he found his voice once again, he said, "I guess this explains why you have been so cranky lately."

Meriel pinched his side. "Aye, it explains *me*. Now, if we just had a reason that could explain your irritable disposition."

"What are you talking about? I'm always cheerful."

"You certainly were not tonight."

"*That* was an exception." He paused. "I am sorry for ruining your party. It looked like it was going well before I spoiled it." Meriel shrugged, suggesting that she had not enjoyed the event as much as everyone else had. "What happened?"

"Nothing, really. It is only that Raelynd is so *happy*. She actually enjoys being pregnant, while I find it miserable being sick and tired all the time. She's already planning names for her child and is in the process of setting up a room and everything. We cannot even find ample space for our things. Where am I going to put a baby?"

"Shhh," Craig murmured, unhappy that she was still distressed. "We will adjust."

"How? We have both been so insistent on remaining 'ourselves,' we don't know how to be any other way. The past couple of months have proved that."

"And the last two weeks have shown that when we want to, we can make things work."

"It's not only that. *Raelynd* is the one who should be a mother. Not me. I know nothing about babies, let alone raising a child."

Craig closed his eyes. "You will be a terrific mother, and trust me, several times in the course of our child's life will he or she be thankful that you, and not their aunt, are their mother. Think about it," he said, very serious. "Who would you want to teach you life's harsh lessons—you or your sister?"

Meriel giggled. "Lyndee *can* be a little demanding sometimes."

"*All* the time," Craig corrected. "I'm not sure how Crevan deals with it."

"Simple. He's just like her."

It was Craig's turn to chuckle. "You are right. But even if you were not, I would want only you to mother my child. There are things you will give our son or daughter that no other person could. All the qualities I love about you. Your gift of beauty and your quiet—well, *usually* quiet—resolve, your untold stubbornness; all of these I cannot wait to see grow in abundance in our child."

Meriel sighed deeply, finally content, at least for the moment. Craig let go the breath he had been holding. Everything he said was true. He wanted their child. He thought Meriel would be an incredible mother and would bestow all her wonderful gifts on their babe as it grew into an adult. But that did not allay his fears.

Meriel had just fallen asleep when a loud banging on their door woke her. "What . . . who is that?" she asked.

Craig lifted her and put her back in the chair to go find out. Refusing to wait, Meriel rose and wrapped the blanket around her and followed him. He grimaced and was about to tell her to stay back, away from the cold, especially as she was in her chemise, but there was a stubborn glint in her eye and the last thing he wanted was a debate about who was going to answer the knock.

Yanking the heavy wooden door open, he recognized one of the castle guards. "I've brought news," the guard said gravely. "Your sister, my lady, has fallen ill. And your brother, Commander, has asked for you to come at once."

Craig's expression went blank and he nodded. He closed the door and leaned against it. His greatest fear wrenched his insides. Meriel had already rushed back to their room to put on a clean gown. A minute later, he felt a shirt being tossed over his shoulder. Mechanically, he put it on and then went to make sure Meriel would be warm enough for the short journey.

They arrived at the castle and went straight to the keep but had only started ascending the first few steps when they met Rae, who was coming down. His face was grave and unshed tears brimmed in his eyes.

"The baby did not survive," he said simply.

Craig had served either for Rae or with him for years. They had seen atrocities of battle. Witnessed close friends die in painful, god-awful ways. Horrors that should never be spoken of, they had experienced together. But never had Craig seen Rae look so despondent. Craig wanted to scream at the injustice, knowing his brother felt even worse. And deep down, the fear he felt for Meriel had just grown exponentially.

"Crevan, upstairs?" Craig choked.

"Aye," Rae answered, but when Meriel went to follow her husband, he touched her arm and shook his head. "It's best if Raelynd doesn't see you right now. Wait until she asks for you."

Meriel stood immobile as she digested all that she had been told. Her sister, so happy, so thrilled at the knowledge that she was soon to become a mother, had just lost her baby. It was unfair, wrong, and cruel. And deep down, Meriel knew she was to blame. Her legs went weak, and the world went dark.

Craig caught her before she fell. "I need to get Meriel

home," he said brokenly. "Tell my brother that I will return once I know that she is all right."

Craig pivoted and felt all his emotions start to boil within him. Never had he felt more helpless. The people he loved most in this world were hurting, and he knew this time there was no solution that could make things better.

Soon he might be joining them in their despair.

Chapter 14

The faint light from the dying fire in the hearth revealed Meriel's dispirited, shuttered expression, igniting an emotion other than desire to stir in Craig. Fear. They had received the shocking news of Raelynd's and Crevan's loss almost two weeks ago. Meriel refused to go to the castle, saw no one except him, and barely responded to his attempts at conversation. He was losing her bit by bit, and he had no idea what to do.

After Raelynd lost her baby, Meriel had been consumed with cleaning their cottage. Her need to work, to keep busy, he understood, but then it went beyond removing the clutter. Every corner had been cleaned. Every item was put away; and if there was not room for it, it was disposed of. For two days, Craig had tried everything he could think of to get her to slow down. He cajoled, commanded, even pleaded, but all attempts to sway her from the task seemed to create only more anxiety within her. Eventually he stopped trying to interfere and returned home several times a day to force her to rest and take some nourishment.

On the fourth day, he had come home to check on her and found her sitting on the vacant floor near the hearth, staring at her hands. The place was so organized it felt empty. Nothing was in view. Not one thing was on the floor or in a pile. Nothing was out of place. Craig felt like he had entered Raelynd's home, not his, and it was then that he realized what Meriel had been doing. Maybe not intentionally, but being barred from her sister's bedside, it was the only way Meriel had to show her sorrow.

Meriel looked up at him. Her large green and gold-flecked eyes were bordered with tears. "There is nothing more I can do."

Her voice had sounded so small and weak, he was not positive that she had even spoken. He knelt down and took her fingers into his and kissed them. He then gathered her in his arms and placed her in one of their chairs. And with few exceptions, that had been where she remained for the next week.

Craig glanced at the dying fire. "Are you cold?"

Meriel looked as empty as the room she sat in and gave him a noncommittal shrug of the shoulders. He tossed another two logs on the fire and the warmth from the hearth began to creep into the chilly room. "I have some time," he lied. "We could go to the castle."

Meriel gave a slight shake of her head.

"You need to see Raelynd."

Meriel's gaze finally locked onto his. "But she does not need to see me."

Craig sighed, wishing Rae had not performed a vanishing act right after telling them the news about Raelynd and her baby. Since then, Crevan had handled all that he could at the castle, but he refused to leave his wife's side for very long. With Rae gone and Crevan constrained, the majority of the clan responsibilities had fallen to Craig. At first he embraced the extra work, as he needed something to focus on besides his fear for his wife and the sorrow of his brother and sister-in-law. But Meriel's grief had become personal. For some reason he could not fathom, she believed herself to be partly responsible for the tragic loss of her sister's baby. And he was not sure anything short of seeing Raelynd, speaking with her, and hearing from *her*, would convince Meriel otherwise.

Craig went to the table, grabbed a leather pouch he typically used for carrying water, and began pouring its contents into a bowl. He laughed, but no joy was in the sound. "I thought you might like some soup. I asked the girl in the kitchen to find a way for me to carry it back here, and this is what she came up with."

Meriel curled up into a tighter ball and pulled the blanket Craig had laid on her that morning even tighter around her. "I don't want any."

Craig's face clouded with uneasiness. She had been eating so little that her face had become gaunt. Initially he had been angered, thinking that she might have been intentionally trying to starve their baby, out of guilt, and hinted as much. Instantly her lifeless demeanor had vanished as Meriel had become nearly violent with anger. "I love my baby!" she screamed so loud her voice cracked. And in the next several minutes, she had made it clear that for him to suggest anything contrary to that was heartless and untrue.

But his anger had quickly morphed into concern, then alarm, and now he was truly frightened. "Meriel, please eat. If not for you, then for our baby."

"I will, just later."

A glazed look of despair spread over his face and he squatted down in front of her. "Look at me, Meriel. You do not eat. Just as you do not sleep. You do not talk to me. You only sit. Please tell me what to do."

Meriel stretched out her thin hand and caressed his cheek. "I am fine. The baby is fine. I eat when I am hungry and I do sleep when I am tired. I sit because I have nothing else to do."

"What about the castle and all the sewing stuff that is so important?"

Meriel reclaimed her hand and pulled it back within her huddled form. "If the weavers have questions, they know where I am."

Craig sighed and leaned his forehead against her arm. "What happened is not your fault. It's awful. It's horrible, and it is in every way unfair, even more so because you were both with child at the same time. But that is *my* child in your womb. I want him to be strong and healthy. I need him to know his aunt, and her lunacy for order, but he will be raised by his mother. I need her back. Return to me, Meriel. Please."

Hot tears began to stream down Meriel's face. "I don't know how. I do not think I can. I so need Raelynd's help, but how can I ask for it now? She hates me, and I have given her the ultimate reason why she should." Meriel stifled a sob. "I promise that I will get better. I only need some more time."

Craig smoothed the hair from her face. Time. This was not the first she had asked for it. But he was more convinced than ever that time was not the solution. She and Raelynd must find a way to be close once again.

Craig left the keep after learning from the housemaid that Raelynd was asleep and that she had no idea where Crevan had gone. Exiting into the bailey, he looked up and studied the dark form pacing atop the closer of the castle's two large drum towers. Recognizing the shadow as belonging to his brother, Craig headed to the tower stairwell and began to climb.

Crevan glanced at the emerging figure. When he recognized Craig, he returned his focus to the few stars visible in the partially cloudy night sky.

"Stargazing," Craig said simply, knowing that was what his brother did when he needed to think.

"Aye."

"Been here awhile?"

"Not long enough to form any answers."

Craig inhaled. The answer was short but well understood. While he had been worried about Meriel, his brother had been just as concerned about his wife. "Has Rae returned yet?"

"No."

Craig leaned back against one of the battlements and crossed his arms. "Where did he go anyway? And why?"

Crevan looked at his brother. "W-where? I have no idea, nor do I know w-when he w-w-will return. But I do know he left to grieve. He mentioned to me once, quite some time ago, that he pre-f-ferred to mourn in solitude."

"I can't imagine the memories this has raised."

Crevan returned his eyes to the heavens. "I hope you never w-will," he murmured softly, his voice filled with sadness and loss. "Did you know right here, on top of this tower is w-where Raelynd and I f-first met? She didn't know who I w-was. But I knew her. Even at sixteen, she w-was so f-feisty. So f-full of life." He looked back at Craig. "I'm scared, brother. More than I ever have been, because I do not know what to do."

Craig nodded. "That I do understand."

Crevan pursed his lips and then yanked up the door to the stairwell. "Let's talk," he said glumly and began to descend.

They entered the Great Hall and saw a servant laying down fresh rushes in the empty spaces where the old ones had been crushed. Seeing Crevan's gesture of dismissal, he left, leaving them alone. Crevan went behind the screens and returned carrying two mugs and a pitcher of ale. The men made their way to the other end of the Hall, where the main hearth was always kept burning during the winter months. Crevan placed the items on the table next to the chairs closest to the fire. Spying a log one of the servants had brought in but not yet added to the fire, he tossed it in and then joined Craig, pouring them both a drink.

"You tell me your troubles. I'll tell you mine," Crevan said before swallowing the mug's entire contents in one gulp.

It was an old expression they had shared since they were young boys. Both of them had been prone to mischief, though never of the same kind, and oftentimes they had found themselves in trouble concurrently. The bond forged from those moments, sharing and sympathizing with each other's woes, was what enabled them to seek out and trust each other's counsel. And tonight, more than ever, Craig needed his brother's advice.

"I am afraid for Meriel. She eats just enough to remain alive. She barely engages in conversation. And after sitting all day in a chair, she cannot sleep at night. I'm losing her, Crevan. She is getting weaker and I am terrified what will happen if something happens to our child. . . . And based on her mother's history and what happened to Raelynd, I am terrified that something might. When that happens, Meriel will truly lose the will to live. I cannot lose her. But I already know that I am."

Crevan heard his brother choke back a sob. He had cried privately so many times this past week, he did not think he had tears left to shed. But he understood his brother's fear. "Raelynd no longer will leave our bedchamber. A few days ago, she finally rose and ventured out of the room, telling no one she was doing so. But she had not gone far before she overheard three or four of the servants talking about what had happened. After hearing their comments, she locked herself back in our room and opened the door for me only when I promised I would not force her to leave."

This captured Craig's attention. "W-what did they say?" he asked, his voice ominous with a promise of retribution.

Crevan poured himself another drink. "Remarks like God needed another angel. That everything w-would be just f-fine again soon. At least she could try again. It was only her f-f-first loss. Another baby w-would make her f-forget this one."

Craig relaxed, for the remarks his brother just listed sounded rather well-meaning and far from horrible. Some of them he thought should have been a little comforting.

Crevan lifted his mug and swallowed some of the contents. "I cannot remember all the ones Raelynd rattled off, but those are the ones that made even me angry. Deep down, Raelynd and I both know that no one was trying to be hurtful, but w-w-when she told me w-what they said, I w-wanted to gather everyone together and yell at them until they understood—God does *not* need another angel. He has plenty. And if we ever do try again, another child would *never* replace the one w-we lost."

Craig downed the rest of his ale. He had not thought of those comments in that way. Seeing it through his brother's eyes, he realized such remarks did more to pacify people like himself, who could see his brother was hurting immensely and felt helpless. The words did not actually provide comfort, despite the good intentions of those who spoke them.

Crevan leaned forward and put his elbows on his knees as he spun the mug between his hands. "What those women said was bad enough, but it is the midwife that I had better never see again."

"What happened?" Craig asked, knowing that what happened was really irrelevant when it created that much animosity in Crevan. The woman was going nowhere near Meriel. If Craig had to beg, bribe, even kidnap her, the McTiernay midwife, Hagatha, was going to be there at the birth of his child. Even if the old, crusty woman had to live with them for a month.

"She did nothing *wrong* exactly, but . . . well . . . I don't know. Maybe she has seen death too many times to care anymore. Raelynd had just lost our baby and the midwife was the first person to know. What my wife needed most was a sympathetic face. Someone to say she was sorry and that she was there for her. That it was not her fault. *Anything*. But she merely stood up, washed her hands, and told her there was nothing she could do. That was it. Told me to let her rest and then left."

Craig was at a loss for words. He was in many ways afraid to say anything, lest his good intentions be misinterpreted. But he had to agree that the midwife should have been more sensitive. Perhaps Crevan was right, and after seeing loss too many times she could not be. But if that was true, should she be a midwife to expectant mothers? Did he want her around Meriel in case things went horribly wrong for them as well? Craig knew the answer to that. Absolutely not.

"God, Craig, what am I going to do?"

Craig sat transfixed. He had no idea to what his brother was referring, but he knew that it did not matter. He had no answers.

Crevan got up and began to pace. "Raelynd knows our baby is gone, but she swears she can feel it kick."

"I did not realize she ever could."

Crevan took a deep breath. "I don't think she could. She just imagined it so much and was so eager for us to have this child. How do I tell her she doesn't feel something she insists she does?"

Craig tilted his head and twitched his mouth in understanding. "I don't think you should. As you said, Raelynd knows the truth. If she needs to feel the baby for a while longer, then let her. You and I have known men who have lost a limb in battle and for years can still feel it itching."

Crevan returned to his chair, slumping down so he could rest his head on its high back. "I think I have monopolized the conversation long enough. You came for a reason."

"One that I now know you cannot help me with, just as I cannot solve yours. Meriel blames herself for your and Raelynd's loss, and I cannot convince her otherwise. I think the only one who can is her sister, but I can see now that getting them together is not possible."

Crevan's brows came together sharply. "Raelynd needs her sister as well, though she keeps refusing to let me send for her."

"Aye, Meriel refuses to come until asked."

Crevan shifted in his chair, his expression clearly perplexed. "But you said she blames herself."

Craig nodded. "Aye, and in a way I also feel at least partially responsible. I'm the one that compelled Meriel to organize a party, and I am the one that barged in angry that night and started arguing, creating so much stress that—"

Crevan held up his hand. "Raelynd was beyond excited and happy when we left, knowing she and Meriel were both pregnant. I can promise you there was no stress. And if anyone is to blame, it is me. She had been cramping all week, and I wanted her to stay in bed, but she refused. I should have made her, and if I had not yielded to her pleas to go . . . So tell Meriel that whatever danger Raelynd was in, *I* knew about it, and it was *I* who did not protect her as I should have."

"Let me guess—Raelynd feels that she should have listened to you."

"Aye, but she does *not* condemn Meriel for what happened. She is only angry and hurt that her sister has not once come to comfort her."

"And for that, you should blame me," came a booming voice from behind.

Both men turned around and saw a large, imposing man walking toward them. Rae Schellden had returned and he had overheard at least the last part of their conversation.

"Go get your wives and bring them back here. If they are asleep, wake them. If they refuse, carry them. But from what I just heard, tomorrow is not soon enough for you four to hear what I have to say."

Crevan and Craig glanced at each other before they both downed the rest of their ale. There was nothing to be said. The father figure in their lives had given them an order, and while both men were not typically inclined to follow such dictates, this time was different. They were desperate for solutions . . . answers . . . anything, and Rae Schellden had given them hope that there might actually be some.

Rae watched as Crevan deposited his furious wife in the hearth chair next to her sister and then grabbed the remaining seat beside her. Like Meriel, all she had on were her night clothes and a robe, and her hair was pulled back in a long, unkempt braid. Both women looked haggard and their husbands fatigued. Some of it was caused by the exertion of getting the women here, and some by their resistance. But Rae knew that he was also a major reason behind their current states.

He began to stroke his snow-white beard thoughtfully. "I . . . I'm sorry." The simple expression gained him the attention of all four people, for it was something they hardly ever heard—Laird Rae Schellden apologize. "I made several recent errors when it came to my family, starting with leaving when and how I did. I should have been here to help, and instead I reacted on instinct."

He paused, but no questions came. It did not matter. He knew what those questions should be, and it was past time his daughters knew the full truth. Rae cleared his throat, looked directly at Meriel, then Raelynd, and continued. "Unlike what you may have believed, and I will admit to encouraging that belief, your mother and I had no problem conceiving children. However, with one exception," he said, pointing at his daughters, "she would always lose our child before it could be safely born."

Rae paused and straightened his back, locking his fingers behind him. It was an unconscious maneuver to distance himself emotionally from the past, but the pain of each loss was etched into his face. "After awhile, I heard people say that your mother and I would get used to it, or that it was not the same as losing a child that had been born and lived," he began, his gruff voice singed with resentment. "Maybe. Maybe not. But I do know that the loss of a child is not something one ever learns to endure. And each loss was painful, and remembered—regardless if your mother and I ever actually held the baby in our arms."

Craig pulled Meriel close to him. "You are a miracle," he whispered.

"All children are," Rae said, the anger gone, "but aye. Meriel and Raelynd were our miracles, and we would never have been blessed with them if it had not been for your mother's willingness to keep trying when so many kept telling us that we should give up. That God obviously did not want us to have children." Turning, he knelt down in front of Raelynd, gathered her small hands into his, and looked her in the eye. "Listen to *your* heart, Raelynd, not to others, even if they are trying to be kind. As long as you are healthy, and you and Crevan desire to try again, then do so. But just as important, if you both decide that you do not want to pursue having a family—for whatever reason—that is your right as well. People, friends, even we loved ones, want to help, but we are not the ones who have to live with your decisions."

He stood up and went to stand in front of the fire, his back straight and hands once again locked behind him. "During those bad times, your mother and I needed time to grieve. At first, we each preferred to be alone to mourn. Only then would we come together and lean on each other for comfort. That was how we handled sorrow. So that night, when I learned of the loss of my first grandchild, I left. I did not think. I knew the clan was in good hands, and I went to mourn as I have always done."

Rae swallowed and again stroked his beard. Both his daughters were staring, wide-eyed, digesting what he was telling them. He licked his lips and then pointed first to Crevan and then to Raelynd. "*You are not to blame*," he said slowly, clearly, and without any doubt. "No one knows why one mother loses a child and another does not. You could have remained in bed every day and still lost your baby. But then you would be blaming yourself for lack of exercise. Believe me, I know this to be true. Your mother and I had to fight the inclination to blame ourselves, each other, the cooks, or something else."

He turned and pointed to Meriel. "Just as you are not to blame. Aye, you and Craig were having a rather heated discussion that night, but when we left, Raelynd was chattering happily about how your children would play together." Rae saw how the image he spoke of hit Raelynd hard, and knew such comments would hurt her from time to time. But he also knew that she could not insulate herself from them, nor could he avoid all such topics in an attempt to protect the feelings of his daughter. For they were unavoidable. But it was Meriel he worried about. Even now, she kept her body facing away from her sister, as if being in her presence was somehow wrong.

"I should never have told you to stay away from Raelynd, Meriel. I thought I was doing right, but *I was wrong.*"

Those three words were even more powerful than his first two. Meriel had never heard him say them before, and for the first time she glanced over her shoulder at her sister.

Raelynd stared across the small space, her cheeks wet with tears. "That's why you did not come? Why you stayed away? Because Papa told you to?"

Meriel blinked and several more tears joined the ones that had been flowing only seconds before. "At first, but I also knew I would be the last person you wanted to see because . . ."

Raelynd's chest began to rise and fall rapidly, but finally she finished her sister's sentence. "Because you still carry your child."

Meriel nodded. "You never asked for me and I knew that was why."

Raelynd could feel Crevan's strong hands on her shoulders, giving her the support she needed. She wanted to deny what her sister said, but knew it was, in part, true. "I . . . I still do not want to see a pregnant woman, but . . . I have desperately needed my sister. I so wanted you to bang down the doors and force your way in, telling me that I had to love you. That you wouldn't let me stop. That you would always be there for me. That I was not alone."

Meriel gave a soft cry and both women went into each other's arms.

Rae watched in silence for several minutes as the two most precious people in the world to him reconciled. The relief on their husbands' faces was immense. Only when his daughters sat back down, this time holding each other's hands in a tight grip that promised never to be broken, did he continue.

"Raelynd, some days will be harder than others. Tragedy cannot be locked in a cage, and in the most unexpected ways and times something is going to trigger a memory, a hope, a thought that will result in sadness. When that happens, do not become silent and hide it from others—and that includes your husband. If you need time alone, take it, but let one or all of us know so we can help, if only by staying away and not trying to pressure you.

"And during those times, Meriel, do not feel at fault. You and Craig have been given a precious gift, and neither of you should ever feel guilty for wanting and loving your child. With each and every loss your mother and I mourned, there was always at least one pregnant woman around. But I can say with an honest heart, we never once begrudged her her happiness.

"It's hard to put into words, but I remember your mother once saying that it was hardest for her when an expectant mother rubbed her own stomach. She would cry on my shoulder and say over and over again that it should be us. That she did nothing wrong. That it should be her patting her stomach, whispering to her babe while her other children played around her. And I thank God every day that she was able to do that at least once, with you two."

Raelynd nodded, understanding in a way that only a person who had experienced a similar tragedy could. Turning to look at Meriel, she said, "I am truly happy that you are going to have a baby. I need you in my life, and I *want* to be an aunt." She sniffled and leaned her head back onto Crevan, who had quietly picked her up and placed her on his lap after seeing Craig do the same with her sister. "Of course, it may mean that Crevan will have to let me cry on his shoulder some."

She lifted her face to look into her husband's adoring eyes, which said without words that he would always be there.

No longer plagued with guilt, Meriel's face finally expressed all the terror she felt at becoming a mother. "Oh, Raelynd, I am so scared. I cannot even take care of Craig and me. How can I possibly raise a child?"

Rae coughed loudly into his hand, regaining both couples' attention. "I have an idea about that very subject. And this time, you and Craig are going to listen."

Epilogue

Craig quickly made a dash across the room to intercept his infant son's rapid venture into his mother's things. "I ask you, brother, do you see how fast he is now? Did I exaggerate?" Craig asked with unbridled delight.

Crevan leaned against the stone wall and tilted his head in partial agreement. Shaun McTiernay had crawled across the room with undeniable speed, but what was truly amazing was the baby's skill in maneuvering through the maze of items cluttering the large space. Craig picked up the wiggling, active boy, and took him back across the room so that he could watch him once again scurry over to his toys. Hearing no accolades from Crevan, Craig's pride prompted a challenge. "There is no way your son will crawl faster than mine by the time he is ten months of age."

Crevan's jaw twitched and he shifted his gaze over to his wife, rocking their baby, who had turned two months the day before. Aye, his son was small. All babies were, but Crevan prided himself on having an accurate memory, and he could have sworn that little Shaun at the same age had been practically as tiny. "Aye, I w-w-will agree, because at ten months, Abhain w-will be w-walking."

Craig stretched his neck to gander at his latest nephew. "Would you like to stake a wager on that claim? How about the father of the faster son gets to name the next child of the loser?" he suggested, knowing Abhain had been far from Crevan's first choice when he and Raelynd had been discussing names.

Abhain had not even been on the list for consideration. But the week before his son's birth, news came that Raelynd's cousin had named their son Crevan. If anyone had told him three years ago that Cyric—a man he once considered weak and immature—would become one of his closest friends and allies outside of his brothers, Crevan might have considered ending their lives just to spare them from their own idiocy. So when Raelynd suggested that they return the gesture, Crevan had almost capitulated. But in the end, he finally agreed to name their son after Cyric's father and Rae's brother, Abhain, a gesture he knew had touched his father-in-law profoundly.

Crevan broke out into a gambling grin. "I do believe you and I have a w-w-wager—"

"Over my dead body!" cried Meriel before he could finish.

"Not over yours, Meriel, over *theirs*," Raelynd chimed in. "And I get to choose the method of their death. As of this moment, only I retain the right to name any of my children."

"I have no say at all?" Crevan quipped.

Raelynd shot him a scathing look. "I shall let you contribute, but based on the lunacy you were about to agree to, you, my love, have relinquished all decision-making rights when it comes to naming our future children!"

Meriel looked at Craig, who was on the floor helping his son stack wooden blocks, which he had made and sanded down before Shaun could even hold his head up on his own. When Craig finally shot her one of his most charming grins, she said, "Don't look so smug, for I fully intend to follow my sister's lead. I cannot believe you would think that I would let *your brother* name our next child!"

Craig tried unsuccessfully to look mortified at the idea. "But, love, Crevan would never have had the opportunity!" Seeing he was not convincing his wife, he shifted his attention to his son. Lying on his back on the floor, Craig lifted Shaun up in his arms, his face one of complete joy at hearing his son laugh. "Your uncle Crevan had no chance at naming your brother or sisters, did he, little man? You and I both know that you are the fastest Highlander ever. Who needs to walk when you can zoom around like you do on your knees?"

Crevan grunted and rolled his eyes, resuming his relaxed position. "If he is f-faster, it's only because he grew up in an obstacle course. I just pray Shaun does not inherit your or Meriel's propensity for collecting things."

Craig and Meriel looked at each other and then surveyed the large tower room. Upon her father's insistence, they had moved back into the castle and into her old bedchamber. The move had been swift and surprisingly easy—the exact opposite of her transition to the cottage.

In this familiar setting, she could "organize" things and put them exactly where they belonged, which, after years of sharing the space with her sister, took no more than half the room. This left Craig plenty of space for his things, especially as they did not have to contend with unnecessary items such as pots and pans for a kitchen. Even more room was available when they realized only one bed was needed, enabling them to create a four-chair sitting area for visitors.

Craig had initially agreed to stay at Caireoch only temporarily. After the fright Meriel had given him, he had welcomed having others around to help monitor his wife during her pregnancy. But he soon admitted living at the castle was not the negative experience he had assumed it would be. After the second time an incident occurred in which his immediate availability had been an asset, any sense he was mooching off his father-in-law and brother vanished. Over the course of the next year and a half, countless issues came up—large and small—and the ability for Rae, Crevan, and Craig to quickly meet in private had been a considerable advantage.

Craig knew he was never going to return to the cottage, and gave it to Callum, his second-in-command. For a while, it had caused some consternation among some of the more senior soldiers because the cottage was one of the largest homes and Callum was without a wife and family. But that home was also a symbol of leadership, and with the heavy burden of helping to train and lead one of the Highlands' largest armies, the young man earned the privilege every day.

They heard two soft knocks on the door before it was slowly nudged open. "Can we join you?" Laurel asked as she and her youngest daughter came into the room.

Meriel immediately rose and waved her over to where she and Raelynd were sitting. "We have been expecting you for some time! You arrived ages ago."

Laurel began to make her way to the group of chairs when Shaun darted in her direction, only to stop and block her way. He raised his plump arms, and she stooped down and picked up the cherub-cheeked infant, rolling her eyes at the petulant look of his father, who was still lying on the floor.

Laurel stepped over Craig and carried the boy to where the women were sitting and sat down. "Is it acceptable for Bonny to be in here?"

"Oh, of course. Brenna and Braeden came up right after you arrived. I would have come for you myself if I had known it would take so long."

Laurel bounced little Shaun on her knee and cooed, "That was all your uncle Conor's fault. He has to have the last word on everything. If it wasn't for me reminding him that he is not the ruler of the Highlands, Scotland, or, more specifically, his wife, he would be a terror. Aye, he would," she said in a playful, singsong manner to the sunny child. "Braeden told me he was banned from coming back."

Meriel bit her bottom lip. "Not banned. I just said that he could not return unless he was willing to leave his wooden sword in the hall."

"Ahh," Laurel replied, still focused on Shaun. "That explains it. Now that he is ten, he truly believes he is old enough to begin training! Worse, his father encourages him." Shaun began to wiggle. "He is truly going to be a heartbreaker, Meriel. I do believe he will have the McTiernay dark hair color and build, but I think Shaun will end up with your hazel eyes."

Meriel sighed and nodded in agreement as she picked up her son, who had decided that if he was going to be in someone's arms, they had better be his mother's. "I think so. They've been blue, but his eyes do seem to be changing into a deeper shade."

Laurel waved her seven-year-old daughter over to her side. "What do you think of little Shaun, Bonny?" she asked, seriously interested in the answer. Her youngest daughter had always been around older children and it was not very often she had to spend time with those younger than herself, let alone infants.

Bonny tilted her head to study the squirming boy, causing her amber-colored hair to cascade all around her. Even at the age of seven, it was clear that Bonny was going to surpass even her mother in beauty with her unusual coloring and deceptively fragile features. Succumbing to Shaun's growing insistence, Meriel put him back down. Bonny continued with her observations.

Laurel waited patiently, knowing the answer to her question would come. Most would have believed from Bonny's silence that she was ignoring her mother's request, but Laurel knew that her daughter gave every direct question true consideration. She also knew that if Bonny was this analytical at age seven, she would be near frightening at twenty. But that was some time away.

"I think Shaun is most likely the same as most babies. They make a lot of noise and they smell strange. I agree they are cute, but mostly I think they take way too much work. You were very smart, Mama, not to have any more."

Raelynd threw her head back and laughed. "You, little Bonny, have not changed at all!"

Laurel hugged her daughter close. "Not a bit. And I love my little girl just the way she is. Don't ever change, sweetheart."

Several shouts outside got the attention of everyone in the room. A second later, Crevan and Craig could hear their names being shouted. They quickly said their good-byes, kissed their wives and then their sons, and left. Bonny immediately went across the room, crawled onto the padded shelf serving as a seat, and opened the window a little wider so that she could hear.

"Get away from that window, Bonny," Laurel admonished. "You are becoming as bad as Brenna about listening to other people's conversations."

"I am not," Bonny hotly denied while ignoring her mother's instruction. "I only wanted to hear what Uncle Crevan was asking Papa about Hamish."

Meriel asked softly, "Have you heard from him?"

Laurel shook her head no. "He left right after he got word from his brother, but that was not all that long ago, especially if one factors in the winter weather. He will send word when he is ready."

Meriel nodded. "I think it was good he went home. He had things to resolve," she said without going into further detail.

Suddenly, the door swung wide open and two silver-glinted eyes surveyed the room. Spying her younger sister in the activity of eavesdropping, Brenna dashed to Bonny's side so that for a second, only a mass of pale gold curls could be seen. "What is going on?" she asked.

Laurel opened her mouth and closed it, shaking her head. "Aren't you going to say hello to your aunts?"

Brenna partially turned around. "But I did! I came to see them first before I did anything!" she protested, and then again asked Bonny to fill her in on what was taking place in the courtyard below.

Bonny shrugged. "Nothing of interest. First they talked about Wyenda, then Hamish, and now it's boring stuff about training soldiers and something about food."

Meriel arched her brow. "Wyenda?" she asked, clearly curious why the woman would be a topic of conversation between her father and the McTiernay brothers. Unless . . . "She and Hamish did not marry before he left, did they?" It would be something that Craig might have kept from her, knowing how she felt about Wyenda's and Hamish's relationship.

Brenna, overhearing the question, answered for her mother. "Wyenda married sweet Gil. Mama is not happy about it, but Papa got really mad one night and made her promise not to talk anymore on the subject."

Raelynd's brow puckered. She had never met Wyenda, but got a detailed description of the shallow woman from her sister. She did, however, know Gilroy. "Wasn't he the tall, sweet guard who always called you his McTiernay angel?"

Brenna once again nodded and came to stand by Rae-lynd. "Aye. He saw Mama on top of the Star Tower one night in the snow. She thinks it sweet how he remembers, but Papa does not. Something about her almost dying that night."

"That's enough, Brenna. I can speak for myself," Laurel lightly chided, knowing that reining in her daughter was like trying to harness the wind. "Poor Gil. I guess he thought Wyenda was an angel as well. Though after seeing them after several months of marriage, things might not turn out as I feared they would. Gilroy certainly adores her. He even built her a huge cottage on the far side of the village. And though I find it hard to believe I am saying this . . . they seem happy."

Meriel narrowed her gaze. "I would love to hear Aileen's version of this supposed love story."

Laurel wrinkled her nose in a frustrated grimace. Aileen was her best friend and the wife of Finn, Conor's com-mander of the elite guard. "It is too bad she had to remain behind and help Conan while Conor and I are visiting you and our newest nephews. Because I'm sure Finn has not shackled Aileen with annoying restraints on her ability to offer opinions."

"Oh, I am sorry she could not come. It was grand fun when she came last time. But where is our favorite forth-right personality? Isn't Maegan with you?"

"Hardly," Brenna scoffed, once again participating in the adult conversation as if she belonged. Sometimes it could be annoying, but Meriel and Raelynd had both learned long ago that they learned far more when she did. "*Nothing* can convince Maegan to leave when there is a chance Clyde is coming home."

Raelynd stood up and began to walk with Abhain, who was no longer satisfied with the limited rocking movement from a chair. "Crevan's youngest brother? He is coming home? Meriel and I have never met him, as he did his training in the Lowlands with his brother instead of here. When?"

Laurel raised her hand, palm out. "We do not know he is coming. Do we, Brenna?"

Brenna exhaled and shook her head, understanding she was to say no more. Bonny, however, had missed the cue and added, "I think Maegan is right. Uncle Clyde will come home to see Uncle Conan get married."

Brenna lit up, believing she had just regained permission to offer her opinion, since Bonny had. "*Everyone* is going to want to see Uncle Conan get married." Brenna then jumped over a pile of materials and threads. "Bonny, watch this!" she hollered and then made a running leap onto a stretched-out piece of material, sliding across the floor.

"Brenna Gillian!" Laurel hollered as she jumped to her feet, finally having had enough of her oldest daughter's behavior.

Meriel waved her back down. "I told Brenna it was fine when she came to visit me earlier."

"That child." Laurel sighed, falling back into her chair. "She is still young, but even so, the more I look at her the less I see my sweet baby girl and the more I see the woman she will become."

Raelynd shook her head, refusing to let Laurel get them off topic. "Talk, Laurel. Tell us all you know about Conan. And begin with answering the question: *Is it true?* Is Conan—the most aggravating, the rudest of all Highlanders when it comes to women—getting married?"

Laurel shook her head and pursed her lips. "I promised Conor to let him break the news."

Meriel glanced down at her son, who was still fascinated

with his wooden blocks, and leaned forward. "You kept your promise. Bonny was the one who made it known. So answer the question," she pressed. "Is there really an intelligent woman out there who would even *agree* to marry Conan?"

Laurel took a deep breath and exhaled, staring at nothing as her mind drifted back to the last several months. "Aye. There may be."

Blinking, Laurel looked up to see two very dubious expressions. She laughed out loud. Oh, how she loved her family. Especially the women the McTiernay men chose to marry. "How can you think it so unbelievable? Not so long ago, many thought it just as improbable—maybe more so—that the two most stalwart, marriage-opposing people in the Highlands, could admit they were in love and find happiness in matrimony."

"Not fair," Meriel murmured, knowing her sister-in-law had a point.

Laurel chuckled. "Wait until you meet her. All I will say is that with Mhàiri, Conan just might have found someone who is not only beautiful but can surpass him in the areas in which he prides himself most—knowledge and wit."

Raelynd looked at Meriel. Meriel stared back for several seconds. They rolled their eyes simultaneously. *Surpassed?* they thought but did not say aloud.

Regardless, Conan vowing to love and cherish a woman was something they were going to have to see to believe.

Please turn the page for an exciting sneak peek of
Michele Sinclair's
next historical romance,

A WOMAN MADE FOR SIN,

coming soon from Zebra Books!

Prologue

Buckfast Abbey, May 1816

He had tasted death. Rolled it around on his tongue and licked its dry, cracked lips. He had drunk from death's dark soul and then done the impossible. He had survived.

Fate's plans for him had not included an untimely and disgraceful demise, but something profoundly more meaningful. Revenge. Its sweet flavor would mix with death's, and he would know satisfaction at last.

He turned the final corner down the dank stairwell and entered the oval space filled with the scent of old vellum. Only this room prevented the long days from becoming a living nightmare of pain and torture. In this small area lived the past. Written on countless aged scrolls were the lives of once-powerful leaders, who, like he, had seen their lofty attempts at fulfilling fate's decree hampered by lesser men. But death had determined those men unworthy to walk these lands of promised power. *They* were the ones who deserved his sentence of physical damnation, not he.

Time, the monks said. Time to heal his wounds. Time to reflect on past indiscretions and do penance. He, of course, complied and joined their devotions. And his reward was this room of solace, quiet, and promise. Fate had drawn him here. The answer to his future lay somewhere in these cool stone walls along with a promise that not all was lost. That all he aspired to be and have was still within his grasp.

He moved over to remove a small marker in one of the numerous carved openings used for storage. Placing it on the small wooden desk, he turned, pulled out the next scroll, and uncurled the sheets of vellum. Carefully, he secured the ends with heavy rocks. He sat down slowly to avoid any more pain than necessary, and began to read aloud.

> *"I, your servant, am unable to show you, noble lady, anything worthy in my deeds, and I do not know how I can be acceptable to you. . . ."*

The words of the manuscript filled him, flowing over him like a balm on his raw wounds. He had been wrong. It was not a king's secrets he was searching for, but a queen's. He continued on.

Hours passed, and though no natural light could shine into the small enclave, he knew it was dark outside. The single candle that had been lighting the room was nearly gone. The monks would be searching for him, telling him it was time for another devotion, solemn ceremony, or some mysterious rite in dedication to God.

A debate began to play out in his head as he continued to read. He knew he should return. Tomorrow would come and the scrolls would still be here. But fate was with him tonight. If he chose to leave, it would surely forsake him, leaving him scarred, ruined, and powerless for his remaining days. Here beneath his fingertips was the answer for which he had been searching. He could not abandon fate's gift. It might not come again.

He flipped to the final page and read the end.

Nothing was revealed. No secrets. No messages. And yet he knew his destiny was intertwined with this woman's story.

How this ancient manuscript had made its way into the abbey's dark walls was a mystery. He could spend years trying to find out whose hands had held this scroll, only to find out the hard-gained knowledge was meaningless. So why had fate placed such words in his grasp? Why was his soul so affected by this woman's inexplicable victory?

He knew if he did not find the answer, fate would forsake him once again. It had little time for fools. It certainly did not deliver enemies and resurrect kingdoms to unworthy men.

"Hallo?" called a voice whose accent spoke of a life lived in a variety of places. "Son? Are you down there? You have missed the divine reading, and supper is nearly finished. Are you well?"

He sighed deeply and returned, "Yes, Father, I am coming. I am afraid in my studies I lost track of time."

Crunching footsteps echoed against the walls. An old man dressed in black robes appeared. "What is it that had your attention for so long today? What did the Lord bring to you?"

He stifled another sigh and brought his hood farther up to shade the majority of his face, though he knew the old monk had seen the monstrosity that lay underneath the brown folds. The man had found him washed up from the sea and had brought him to the abbey to tend his wounds.

He should have died. And though the monk might believe it was his God that had revived his nearly dead carcass, he knew better. It had been fate. Something the old man would never understand.

A withered hand poked out from the arm of the black cape and glided down the vellum outstretched on the table. "You are reading the *Encomium Emmae Reginae*. It is very old, written many years ago by a monk of St. Omer in praise of his Queen Emma. Few take interest in that which occurred so far in the past. So little history was captured then. It is difficult to tell the truth from fiction." The aged monk paused to cough violently into his hand. His remaining days were few. Consumption was taking him, slowly and painfully.

"My apologies, Father. The staleness of the room makes it hard to breathe," he said, and then waited patiently for the monk to continue, for the man was one of the few in the abbey who had studied any writings that were not directly related to scripture.

"This accounting, while biased, is believed to be true, unlike others."

His heart momentarily stopped. "Are there other stories of the queen? I mean, here at the abbey?" he asked the old monk, hoping his tone reflected his eagerness rather than the apprehension he felt. For he was close. He knew he was.

The monk rolled his eyes upward and began to nod his head. "There is supposedly one other text written about the queen at that time. There was once another person interested in the monarch, and I will tell you what I told them: The accounting is highly questionable and cannot be considered reliable. Its value is in understanding how stories were embellished back then. . . ."

The old monk stretched his head back and surveyed the dusty scrolls stacked in various-sized cubicles within the walls. After a minute, he stretched out his arm until the tips of his gnarled fingers touched a single scroll nestled in a group.

As he watched the monk slip the document out of its resting place, he realized it would have taken many more months at his present pace before he had read the item. The monk gave it to him and he laid it out, anchoring the corners. Bending over, he read the simple legend. The handwriting was jagged and the scattered drops of ink indicated it had been quickly scribed. But it was legible.

His heart began pounding with renewed hope. He heard the old man's opinion of the story, that it was an allegory and not one of truth.

But he knew differently.

Fate had not deserted him.

Fate had been with him all along, as it was with all great men.

"You said only one other had seen this, Father. Please, tell me. Who was it?"

Chapter 1

London, late July 1816

"Millie, do not shake your head at me! I absolutely insist that you come! Of the three of us, you know the streets by the Thames the best. And Jennelle, do not think because you are sitting behind me I am unaware that you are at this very moment rolling your eyes," Aimee added as she glanced back, affirming her guess. "Millie fled through those alleys on foot in the middle of the night just a few months ago."

Millie felt her jaw tense and tried again to make her best friend see reason. "*Charles*, Aimee. *Charles* was with me. It was *your* brother who knew where to go and managed to save me from—"

"And since then you have gone with him a dozen times or more when he has needed to visit one of his ships," Aimee interrupted. She knelt down and clutched her oldest friend's fingers in her own. "I not only want but need your help, Millie. But know that your refusal to do so will not sway me from going. Tonight is my last chance, and I *am* going. Even if I have to go by myself."

Aimee's voice was soft but emphatic. It was completely

out of character for the tall, willowy blonde, who was typically very sweet and gentle. But today, her bright green eyes snapped with a compelling urgency that conveyed her threat was not an empty one.

Jennelle was about to offer a word of caution when Aimee cut her off. "It is a *brilliant* plan. Millie, tell her," Aimee said to the most adventurous of their group.

Nicknamed the Daring Three when they were just children, the three girls were best friends and nearly inseparable. Even Millie's recent marriage to Aimee's elder brother had not split them up. Aimee was positive that if she could just get Millie to agree with her plan, the ever-so-logical Jennelle would follow. She would be compelled to, from sheer friendship.

Millie, now sorry that she ever mentioned her husband's strange mystery, laid a hand on her agitated friend's arm. "It is a bold plan, Aimee, but I am unsure why you would want to get involved. I think Charlie has his own ideas about routing out the thief. Should we not just wait . . . ?"

"My brother may be your husband, Millie. And you may find him intriguing and his tediousness an adventure, but since you became Lady Chaselton, I must finally tell you the truth. You have turned into quite a bore!" Aimee rose to her feet and began pacing. "Four months ago it would have been *you* planning this night raid, and it would have been Jennelle and I holding *you* back."

Millie opened and closed her mouth, unable to deny her friend's accusation. "I expect you are correct, Aimee. I have tempered my inclinations a bit, but you must understand that as Lady Chaselton I cannot continue to act as I once did. Charlie would kill me if he found out," Millie said, tucking an escaped dark lock of hair behind her ear. Never had she managed to keep the thick wavy mass under control for long.

"That is a crock, Mildred, and you know it. Charles would be upset, but he has caught you in many a more provocative situation, and he still fell in love with you *despite* your ways. I am asking you for one small favor, one small adventure, and suddenly you turn prim and proper. It is unfair, I tell you! After all the crazy exploits Jennelle and I have joined you on."

Jennelle's dark red eyebrows popped up at the mention of her name. "It is not a small favor, Aimee. Dressing up like men, leaving in the middle of the night to stow aboard Charles's ship to catch a thief, is *not* a small favor." Despite her red hair and flashing blue eyes that hinted of her Irish ancestry, of the three of them, Jennelle was the one who was most able to remain calm and cool in even the most dire situation. As the years came and went, Millie and Aimee wondered what, if anything, could break that cool composure, and secretly hoped to be around if it ever did.

Aimee walked over and sat across from her two friends, deciding honesty was the only way she would get them to understand and agree. "Please, please do this. Reece has been in town for nearly a month and has refused to see me. No matter what I do, he avoids my company. Can you imagine, Millie, what it would be like if Charles suddenly no longer wanted to see you or speak to you?"

Millie bit her bottom lip; she could not imagine the pain Aimee just described, but the mere thought of not being able to talk with Charlie, even when they disagreed, was horrifying. Aimee had been in love with Reece Hamilton, Charles's best friend, since she first saw him when she was six years old. Almost nine years Aimee's senior, Reece had been amused by her infatuation, but it was not until last Christmas that their relationship changed—significantly.

During the war, Reece's and Charles's visits home were infrequent. Consequently, it was customary for Reece to pay Lady Chaselton and her daughter a visit when he was in town. He would relay any news of the war and the well-being of her son, just as it was expected that Charles would visit Reece's family. Last December, it had been three years since Reece had seen Aimee. It must have made a difference, because this time he kissed her. And according to Aimee, the kiss had been no ordinary one. She was now certain that Reece was the only man for her and that her destiny was tied to his.

Millie sighed. "Tell me your plan. All of it. And, Jennelle, pay attention for problems, for I believe we are going on an adventure tonight."

Jennelle rolled her eyes but knew all was lost. Millie had acquiesced. But what did she expect? For marriage to change her petite, excitement-seeking friend? For Aimee to suddenly stop seizing every opportunity to convince the one man she had ever pined for to love her? Jennelle held her breath and then exhaled long and soft, realizing she was the only sane one of the bunch. And a sane person really *should* be tagging along on this crazy escapade.

"I'm unsure as to the intelligence of this idea, Aimee, but tell it to us once again."

Aimee felt alive and excited all over. The rented hack hit a large cobblestone and her fingers fluttered to Millie's for support. "I cannot believe I am finally going to see him again, Millie. It has been so long. If I have to endure another Season of pretentious old men, or worse, loquacious, overly eager *young* men and their tittering marriage-focused mothers, I really shall perish. You have no idea how fortunate you are, Jennelle, that your father is not compelled to see you advantageously married. And, Millie, you are the luckiest of us all to have convinced Charles he was in love with you and to ask for your hand. If only Reece would do the same."

Millie took a deep breath and blew a wayward strand of her dark hair off her eye. If they were caught, it was highly doubtful that she would be able to convince Charlie of anything again. She glanced out the window. They were just about to cross into Shadwell at Thames, the main entrance to the London Docks. "I want your promise, Aimee, that *if* we stumble across the thief you will not make a single move until all three of us are sure that he is Reece. Charlie is still not positive this latest event is a simple prank."

"But you said the thief was only taking odd objects and the items were different each time. Some were of value, but most seemed to be only of interest to Charles. Besides us three, Mother, and Reece, who else would know what my brother really values?"

Millie twitched her lips, uncomfortable that Aimee refused to consider any other possibilities. "I *said* that it was the randomness that made Charlie question if it really was a thief, or Reece playing a practical joke."

"Ah, but you also said *only* Reece would be interested in the items taken. So, it *has* to be him. And when I catch Reece playing another prank on Charles, he will have no choice but to speak to me. All I need is five minutes. Five minutes and I will know whether what happened between us at Christmas was real or *a passing moment of passion*," Aimee countered, contemptuously gritting out the last few words that had haunted her for months.

Millie again glanced out the window and tried to dismiss the ill feeling pressing on her chest. "I hope so, Aimee. I really hope so. Now, when the carriage stops, refrain from speaking unless absolutely necessary. Use the hand signals we discussed and stick to the shadows. I went with Charles to visit the *Zephyr* a couple of days ago just after it arrived. They had a lot of cargo and less than a hundred ships were anchored in port. With so few needing slips, there is a good chance Charles's ship is still moored." Millie began praying but stopped when she realized her prayers were in conflict. She did not know whether she wished for the *Zephyr* to be inaccessible from the shore, thereby ending this insane quest, or for Aimee to be happy.

The carriage rolled to a dead stop. Once more, they agreed to the plan and then proceeded out of the hack. Moving toward one of the large warehouses, each watched out for the other while remaining as much as possible in the shadows. Only a sliver of the moon peeked through amassing rain clouds to light the narrow alleys. It was difficult to see, but dressed in male attire and the dark cloaks Aimee had pilfered from some of the younger footmen, it would be just as difficult for a passerby to see them.

Aimee fought the instinct to pinch her nose. She had heard about the strong odors around the docks, but nothing could have prepared her for the overpowering aromas coming from the buildings they were skirting. One smelled of tobacco, another of wine. There were the unmistakable scents of fish and brandy, and many more. On their own they could be pleasant, but together the stench overwhelmed the senses.

Millie stopped short, and Aimee and Jennelle very quickly saw why. Dock laborers, sack-makers, watermen, and the various London poor who made a living by the riverside were swarming the alleys and the docks where the ships were moored. "This has to be the craziest, most insane thing we have ever done," Millie hissed, ignoring her own rule of complete silence. "I cannot believe that I actually let you talk me into it."

"I didn't *talk* you into it," Aimee scoffed. "I threatened you into coming with me. And I would have made good on my threat too—*that's* why you are here. Besides, I thought you did this before."

"I was with your brother, Aimee, and that makes all the difference. In case you have not noticed, this harbor is quite large and the docks that support all the ships are huge. Charlie knows this area, not I," Millie argued. "Scrambling around here in the dark, praying to God that we are not caught, is not what I call a well-thought-out plan. Aimee, I really think we should return."

Jennelle was about to voice her wholehearted agreement with Millie's assessment of their precarious position when Aimee piped, "Look, isn't that Charles's ship, the *Zephyr*?"

Millie followed the tip of Aimee's finger and grimaced. Several hundred feet away, rocking against the dock, was one of five ships her husband and Reece owned in a small but very profitable shipping company. While her husband preferred to remain in England to oversee the accounts and assist with cargo decisions, Reece elected to remain at sea primarily aboard the *Sea Emerald*, a unique ship he had built to move light cargo with exceptional speed.

"Millie, look! The ship is still at the dock! And there is hardly anyone near it! This is destiny. My plan just has to work. To sneak aboard and pinch something would be too easy for Reece to resist."

Jennelle glanced back and forth from Millie's wan, uneasy expression to Aimee's expectant and determined one. "She is going to do this, with or without us, Millie," she whispered.

"I know, I know. I also know that we could stop her if we really wanted to."

"True, but she would never forgive us, and you and I both know she would only try again with a plan even more dangerous. And next time she will not ask for our input, help, or even let us know."

"Jennelle, sometimes your logic leads to the most dreadful conclusions," Millie grunted. She turned to Aimee and pointed to a newly emptied wagon. "I'm going to move toward the *Zephyr*. When I give the signal, follow my lead. And watch out for the dock laborers. There seem to be several out tonight."

Jennelle trailed Millie as they advanced around the wagon and slowly crept up to the *Zephyr*. A minute later, they verified the entry was clear and began to tread softly up the wooden planks. Aimee followed, stepping past an unconscious man posted as a guard. Charles was right. The men were asleep, allowing any thief easy entry. She slipped by the sprawled figure and located the hiding spot Millie and Jennelle were crouching behind. Quietly, she hunkered down with them and waited for what she knew her friends hoped never would come.

But it did.

Jennelle pointed to a dark, lone figure. At first Aimee thought he might be a sailor, but his movements were not purposeful as he moved in and out of view, skulking about the ship. Then he began peering into boxes and containers that had not yet been stowed below. She elbowed Millie and pointed. Millie nodded to indicate that she and Jennelle were also witnessing the unusual movement in the shadows.

The figure neared. Whoever he was, he was hunched over as if trying to mask his height. Regrettably, Aimee knew right away that the man was not Reece playing a prank on her brother. Reece was much bigger than the creeping thief, and unlike the dark unruly strands she was spying, Reece's hair was the color of sand kissed by the sun. More than that, he was incredibly tall, which was why Aimee had been drawn to him as a child. She had inherited the unusual height of her mother and had loved being near anyone that made her feel petite and beautiful rather than tall and awkward. Now, at one and twenty, she possessed a slender figure, pale gold tresses, and large green eyes every Society matron wished her unwed daughter possessed. And yet, around most men, Aimee retained the uncomfortable feeling that she just did not quite belong.

"That's definitely not Reece. As soon as he is gone and

it is safe, we need to leave," Jennelle whispered. Aimee nodded, saddened to know her plan, which had been going so well up until now, was not going to work.

They waited almost half an hour after the movement in the shadows had ceased before attempting to vacate their niche. "Come on," Millie murmured, indicating the direction to disembark.

Millie led the way, slowly creeping alongside the same containers the thief had hid behind in an effort not to capture any attention. Jennelle followed carefully, tracing her friend's footsteps and quiet manner. Aimee was about to follow and exit their secluded hole when she spied movement across the ship.

The moonlight briefly caught a bright blue-and-gold scarf before it was hidden again behind a cloak in the shadows. Aimee recognized that scarf. It was the one she had given Reece at Christmas. Later she had overheard him telling her mother that he never wore such items and would give it to one of his men. That man weaving his way around the deck might not be Reece, but he definitely worked aboard his ship.

Aimee bit her bottom lip and quickly developed a new plan. She wished she had the opportunity to discuss it with her friends, but she would tell them tomorrow afternoon if it worked. Right now, she was not going to waste any opportunity to confront the man she loved.

And with that last thought, she did the unthinkable and got herself captured.

Millie stopped suddenly, aware that something was amiss. She spun around and grabbed Jennelle's shoulders. "Where is Aimee?"

Jennelle's wide blue eyes grew large at the alarm registered on her friend's face. "Bloody hell," she replied, using one of Millie's standard phrases. "I don't know. She was right behind me."

Millie whipped past her. "Come on, we have to find her. Some men were still on the ship, just on the other side. I thought we could sneak out without their noticing."

Jennelle heard the worry laced in Millie's low voice and it frightened her. Millie *never* was flustered in tight situations. She was courageous and *always* had a plan. "What are we to do?"

"Stay here, Jennelle, and hide. If anyone—and I mean *anyone*—comes near you, scream as loud as you can. I'll whistle twice, just like we used to as kids, when I return."

Jennelle nodded, dumbstruck when Millie pulled out a small pistol and checked it to make sure it was ready to fire. She adjusted the hood of her cloak, and two seconds later she was gone. Jennelle watched in awe as the petite figure moved silently with such speed, darting in and out of view as she moved around the ship. For twenty minutes, Jennelle waited, wondering what could have happened to their friend.

Two low-pitched whistles came from nowhere and then Millie appeared, lines of fury and panic etched in her face. "She's gone, Jennelle. They took her in a small boat and she is now far offshore, headed for some ship anchored in the bay."

"But you said there are a hundred ships out there!"

Millie's large lavender eyes had grown dark with fear. "I am to blame. I should never have let her come."

Jennelle shook her head vehemently and swallowed. "No, Millie, she was coming anyway. You and I both knew it, and deep in our hearts *that* is why we came."

Millie shook her head. "I led her straight into danger. I was the one who decided to leave. I went first instead of watching out for you both. I was unprepared, and if *anything* happens to her I will never forgive myself, Jennelle. Never."

Jennelle took a deep breath and forced calm logic into her voice. "What are we going to do?"

"The only person who can help now with the speed and the resources needed to find Aimee is Charles." Tears began to fall down Millie's cheeks. "Good God, Jennelle! What am I going to do? He will never forgive me for putting his sister in danger. How can he?"

Books by Bestselling Author
Fern Michaels